Preface

The journey of the Kindred One.

I'm kneeling in front of you, in this world turned to ashes,
The kindred souls I've seen, the light in my eyelashes,
turn fiery orange with the hope to rise up from my grave.
The day I'll face my truth, with the strength of my youth, I must be
brave.

The sword I handle reeks of the Undead Settlement,
with a bonfire as my way home, I will achieve enlightenment.
To the everlasting Lords of Cinder, this is my wish...
"To end my people's suffering, and for my life's retirement."

As I walk up into The Kiln of the First Flame,
a knight made of dark intentions came,
waiting for me to see my death,
and lunged right at me before I made a breath.

I stabbed my sword unto his chest,
the sound of his bones cracking was the best.
He dropped dead when I kindled the First Flame,
putting his name under great shame.

The undead were sent to heaven,
with good intentions that are worth to be mentioned.
I looked up to the gray-orange sky saying,
"I did a good job." and the colors of his aura went flying.

Written by; Eric Matthew Grefalde

We return to the house as the day is drawn a new, and this melee is started a new. This city is wide awake as the day has dawned, yet it will stay blissfully unaware of what has transpired. Our hero if he can be called that wasn't even sure this is where he needs to be when he started this venture. The benign nature that has been a blight to this noticeable soil, though it wasn't easy to just see all the monsters.

Most cities would have a reason why they needed to hide these facts. This even as it has no real sense of itself or nature, it just is the abomination that can be ascribed to the essence. That is it as the concept and meaning are foreign, and those words can't truly find the expression. To all those in this immaturity, as this is said to all that is difficult to comprehend. Even with this ignorance, there are those that come together, with those slight difference that have to be appreciated.

Within that house, as those, we speak of slumber, though the elders aren't yet fully sure. In truth can any that are trying to secure its health, say what is the truth about this occasion. This would be good if those doing good hadn't attracted the most ruthless of all killers. It would also be easy to see that which uses words as his lament, as even he is the worst. Things are now placed to change things greatly, can this be as to the fact of the nightmare of vampire kind?

His faculties were aroused as he began to sense the truth, this event that was arranged to give the impression to be tailor established just for him. After all that had been acknowledged to be a truth, can one of the old ones have literally arisen?

There are many narratives of what they do, there was a wonder how true any of these stories without a doubt were. Even as most will confirm that the earliest form of language was given to us from them. If a being was so as they say, evil, why would they gift the world such a gift?

He was always amazed at the untruths he had discovered, and he had the curiosity that they believed it would go unchallenged. Then again they constantly tell us that what we do is of a diabolical nature. If they were sure about this, is it possible all they would have us know is a lie? Is that which is truly evil of a relative individuality to that certain person, and not a personification to the individualism?

When you are in the assurance of this, you have to ask why this city of all those around?

Why could it not be New York with all of its diversity, or Los Angels as they appeared to notice nothing at all? A number of cities I could name is beyond this one if he is real, why did God forsake this city?

As he laid there in the midday sun that blazed, rising to break his train of thought. All that had proceeded him came back to him, and the quintessence all wasn't that open. Even at his advanced state of years, even he was clueless at the goings on of all of this. His indication to the nature of all his time made it exactly difficult to go too far back. Can it all be lost in these centuries of time, he knew what that meant, he would always know what that meant.

The factor that if it did come back to him to reality, it would crowd in and this depression would take him over. So he finished what was in his glass, as he had to whisper, as another man came into the room. "Is it ready for me now William?"

The man that stood without a single lock of hair replied, "Yes my Lord."

His short stout form now got up, as he didn't enjoy wearing clothes before he stepped out of the day. So he allowed his robe to hit the floor as he walked past the narrow form of William. Though just as you can barely see him, his lifeless form would betray him to being far younger. He now said as he was always concerned for his employees, "Now whatever you do, don't take that long to lay down yourself William."

As they cleared the room the first real beams of light came in, tracing out the patterns of opulence within this abode. This heat of the day was just a forbore of what was to come, as all that was new saw this and woke fully. How could so many be so fooled by so few, those facts were now being told to all that needed to know.

Could all that happened beforehand just be the forewarning of what is to befall this fair city?

Or was this just like most the accounting of that like a risk board, and all is set to a predetermined number of events?

Likely would not happen, but whom could unquestionably tell.

Just another day in another city that had no understanding of the depravity that lurked down below. What would they care of these fairy tales, as they could shape much, though most certainly didn't amount to anything?

On the other hand, you have to ask, or did they?

How can such dark matters fall on so few, or even the one? When so many depend on the outcome of it all, would they lift that finger to help these scatterings? There is much to think upon, as to this fate that can't be seen. Just how will this all end?

Chapter One

The start of a new week.

<u>Day Eight</u>

This will have its problems, as it is a new start to the period. With no knowledge of anything new that may be happening, we just started as if this was just as much the same. Now for the kickoff as it is extraordinarily advantageous, to begin with, the most obvious, as I am sure you have questions.

When it comes to the differences of those kinds of the individual species. There is a multitude that could be communicated, as to what is in a title yet that which is most common about the self. An excellent example with this would be that of Naomi as she is, for most know them for the hunters they are. It is as for the basic sense to them, as if you tried to lose their desire to hunt you, you would be hard pressed to escape her lineage.

Some examples are far more invariably out in the open, just like that of Kitty's friends, as they're generally named Kooks. More over as you meet one they imply to be few short of a full deck. This is caused by the noticeable insight they so cherish, as with all that is seen has them wondering what is real, and what is not. Yet it is this same said effect that leaves them with a certain clarity so that in a sensitivity they have a truer knowledge than most.

You can understand as it leaves a race like mine in the dust, as we had a foreknowledge of our learned state. I think you could have called us the most book example at one time, though how things change. These same said books taught us the disrespect toward all others, and with that, we left to the simplest demand we could. Which has left us following whatever whim comes along, and has made most this distressing barbaric outlaw to those that would guide us? It is no wonder that when anything is disturbed, they will always look to my race first, as we signify mostly malcontents.

Now as to what is normal, even as we are we attend the weakest race first. This couldn't be in this reasoning, as there is an example of why I have gone this way. As to that is Tony's race, not that they haven't a way to power, just they aren't known to use strength to receive it. So as you have read in my last edition I am within a precarious state, as I have one lying right next to me. Yes, his remarkable daughter is now to lay with me, not as much by hers or my choice, but through circumstance.

As to the state of their race, there is much to tell, though it is best you know why I started to like this. From her highly inquisitive state of being as the lady, she surely is, with the want to fathom all things. Maybe it is as best as they can be known, with the finding out of the truth and the whole truth. Within their titles are also a knowledge of them being the beautiful people, or vampires, tantamount. Not that this is all acquainted toward them, as the crumbliness branched has hit many in one way or another.

You can in a way also get knocked down by the same reputed stick. To use this as good or bad, but to tell you the truth there is no real interweave state. As to who would be closest to the center, I can tell you the two families that aren't close would be Tony's and Paul's, though I may ascertain Cheryl was a better example. Well and to be totally honest here, Tony never received his full lot, though not a judge of male flesh. I will swear Paul did better in this category, if his manly features weren't so apparent, it would be easy to mistake him for a woman.

From what I can see the two examples, Cheryl did receive the lot advanced. I can't be sure as to this as I only knew the early example of her, in a drunken state. So it is with the obvious oppression that I feel this, which is doubtlessly wrong of me referring to her womanly state. As I have no real knowledge of anything, even to that of the two sisters, as I only saw them after the fact.

Elizabeth is highly unusual with her own kind, as they're more astute with the base averages. They aren't known for being as inquisitive as she is, as knowledge does give the impression to escape their attentions. I can say from the two prescriptions Tony has given me, she has changed for the greater. He spoke that her hair had been chopped out to a great shortness, and you could never tell that now. Then you have in essence that he called her hair red, I can't ascertain if this was from ignorance, as to the quintessence that auburn does have red in it.

Oh, he also did a scribe to how pale her skin was, as it is an absolute peach color now. Though that isn't exactly true as to she resembles a bronze effect, with just a reasonable amount of yellow. I think the actual term is bronzing of the skin, though I would say that was a person that had been out in the sun a lot. Like I will readmit to you, I can't be sure as to I had no foreknowledge. All he was able to describe was over time, nothing was said from the start, and much you maybe just learning.

With all, I could surmise with her as she is now, that the complete mixture of features did sit well together. Just to explain one as we undressed were her breasts, as they were so insurmountable round in their perfection. I had to wonder and be amazed that most women had to desire this shape to their own. Now to be truthful she hadn't that athletic body most women loved. Though her angular placings of the same curves also seemed to be well placed.

This fact could now be surmised without the understanding of the latent music in the last volume. At least in the back of our minds now.

To be truthful I had to hope this was a vision Kitty had seen, as too laden those so young down with this. There is a lot to be misunderstood about her kinds demeanor, except that everything has a why and recompense. It is always decidedly hard to ascertain the reasons, as to understand the perversions that could await such an act. As to the honest intention as to the vision, I now lay next to, with such unequivocal perfection. The truth is breaking my resolve that has existed with me an extremely long time now.

As to what Naomi has used as a title, I could be in a way aligned with the same said capes. They are those of the rudest endeavors toward those that are the youngest among us. The truth that is behind this life which we like to call hard, is their aspiration toward the younger of this race. Not only would I ever bring this into our children's lives, because it was my lot to break that same said idea. Plus any source or application that would be suggested any were higher quality than another.

Now you can understand why what I have done is so hard, with the dealings of the most recent news. We are now contrived to do which is loathsome to me, as I have made a small level of contact. With that knowledge comes the certainty that we have those that could be called darlings within this house. I have already covered as to the beauty of some, not that they would ever approach just women.

Kitty would be hard pressed to cause this adventure, as to what she has said, Mr. Sharpie would make many new smiles. The fact is that with her exceedingly animated nature, as to the generalities of how she speaks. Then you have that so petite body of hers, which if I heard right she has no qualms about advertise everything.

Naomi is different in her attitude, as a spider that would enjoy you to enter her web. Though with a pride that suggests to show off herself, like those men of old that would dare you to remove the pebble from her should. This gives you ample version of her well-defined curves and ample breasts. Then you have the fact of her species need for finer clothes, that amplify this because of their need. These garments give her outline of being nude, she is finally covered as it were. The light is well seen why many would froth over her.

Knowing they have been around just a while, many would know not to take advantage of them. It is uncanny as you can see the likeness of the two sisters, and yet have also as many differences. The younger Pepper just edging out the two of them in height, a petite as they are. I'm astonished to what would genuinely be their hair colors, though I have to admit the youngster's blonde implies more natural. Then you have Cibilia's that has to be dyed, no one's hair is that red.

Oh, I just remember this tale, of a young man and his strange hair color. Now I can't say his hair was red, but all wanted what he had, so his hair ended up being his own demise. Yet, yes there was one reference that his hair was the color of a fire, so maybe that is what happened to her. As similar as they are, as also as diverse as they appear to also be. It is emphatical to see the fury within the older of the two, which in hind sight does resemble her hair.

Then you have the lesser of the two, and she implies to show. Well, affection towards everyone and anyone. Having a favor toward any real gender I have to be guarded upon, as I truly have no idea here. Though there are many that have preferences toward both. Which if I had to make a choice, I may lean that direction.

Then you have my new daughter as she has an affinity toward the affections she so wants. In the cast of the die with her friend does show her to have some real love toward her best friend. You could easily look at this if you didn't know her like I did, and say she had a preference toward the fairer sex. This is a fact of her wanting to be loved, and not the virtue of a decision for that. With this fleeting thought, I had to shake it off, as even within her she has this certain perfection.

With that, I can't say that of her best friend, as it hasn't been an easy thing to get to know her. Then you have her most definite perfection, this I also can't ascertain from her before hand. Cheryl does create the impression to have the natural nature of all Native Americans, though far lighter complected. What I have seen of her race is unknown, though as a whole I have confirmed much. As all have this noble countenance that places them above all, even those that have a certain plainly look.

Of all the ladies in this house, Pepper and she were setting the standard for their length of hair. Mary maybe the most disposed to this aspect of the elderly, as because of her want and affection. I have to be clad for now, as she has her own new child to take care of, though for a short while. But as to all these gorgeous ladies in this abode, none genuinely holds a candle to Liz. As to many would ascribe to just like anyone, and the lot is truly that sensual.

Yet she has this certain enigmatic level just above, that if it was her choice she could claim that certain ten. In her own humility, she would never allow her aspiration to say any such remark. Then you have the notion if anyone implied to use that remark to describe her would most assuredly receive a scolding. Now you have to understand that this perfection lounges next to me, it was easy to see her luxurious curves, as her back was so overly exposed.

These lines that were utter perfection were aligned with the sheets that covered her. She had no blankets as I had to steal them to cover my private area, as I knew she would be embarrassed by my exposure. The sheets hadn't covered her back, as it was easy to ascertain where the crease was to her buttocks was. Though the same said sheets didn't adhere to her curves perfectly, it did allow the example to be well seen.

With these same beautiful tresses laid out as to her movement, though not so matted as humans would be. This spoke to the fundamentals that she already seemed to have a level of comfort with me. Her most likely angelic way would venture to cover herself more completely when she woke. I would not try to disclaim this until she had her own favor to admit it. In all my existence I have to say I have only seen another like creature as her.

It was uncanny how close they looked, as to their style, and well auburn hair. I can't claim to ever see her sleep, as when we were together we had more on our minds than slumber. You have to understand that I have not slept well for ages now, so even as I did slumber, it was just a slight venture. It was to my enlightenment that I ventured with her, and she taught me the none existence that the elders lead. To be truthful it was absolutely easy to remember her, not for the sensuality we had, but for the severe lessons, I try to teach the kids.

This has over time cause me the foreknowledge to be extremely restrained around all children, not just my own. They have to understand as even I am, it is decidedly easy to cross this line in your own prowess and power. But in my light, I would never cross this impose that I have placed on myself, no matter how difficult it may imply. I could spin an entire tale on just what had happened there, though I do believe it would be a dogged repose. I can tell you I truly don't want to relive that narrative to be truthful.

It was a certainly easy thing to imagine things now, within her stature, that would cripple this budding relationship. There is this fact as to how uncovered she was, that I could just lean over and get my desire. No, I could never impose myself on any of our children. I couldn't envision I know thinking like how I thought Tony, her father was.

Unexpectedly I realized I had to make the lot, as I was looking at the ceiling as a count to the boards. As I saw the slightest move of her entire body, even as what I understood was now exposed. Not that I wanted it, as much as for now I wanted to protect her virtue. Though how could a man that wanted her virtue to do such a thing. Then came a moment of exaltation as her breasts did move, as she seemed to just blow out with a force. She was awake as my own virtue was for her.

My next thought was to get out of bed as to not arouse her, though waking it did convey the impression of impossibility. I carefully unwound myself from the covers, though making sure I was still covered. Then I barely leaned to unlatch my bedroll, to see if my blue shirt I had ascertained was not too wrinkled. I had made my mind up to just use my own old leathers this day, then the meeting came to the forefront. No, I could do what I had desired, though may be, later on, I without a doubt hated all the prompt and circumstance.

He decided to make an attempted to rise without

any warning to Liz. I did get one leg free without much happening, it was the other so close to hers I had to concern oneself. As even I tried so desperately to remove it, the vestige seemed to touch her more wholly. This caused her to realize something was here with her, with a start she shot up in our bed. Without real repose as to what had happened, Liz drew up to full as she drew back. I had seen I had to do something to settle her horror at this moment, then realized a gentle touch may be warranted.

I had to smile at her even as the hour was too soon, and whispered, "Hello there sleepy head."

I swear this is true, even as uncovered as she was, she truly asked this. "Are you going to wear that awful shirt?"

I had to shake my head with an even bigger smile, "We have a meeting today, and I did aspire to wear it until I remembered that."

She took it close to her as she remarked, "This shirt has small spots on it. Most likely your typical blood, guts and gory stuff."

Well, I can tell you I had no idea about all of that, though it did engender me to her as all I could do was smile. "Most likely. Why?"

I swear she had this extremely disapproving look upon her face, as she instructed me. "I can see that you're a man, have you any idea how hard it is to get out of that material."

I had to honestly reply as I had never truly tried, "If it gets too bad, I usually just get a new shirt."

I also had to figure she had no idea how we were sitting there, as our private areas were covered. Little of anything else was, as all were exposed to the freedom of the room, well and the air.

"Well, that can't ever do again if we are to sleep together, I mean as we have to save on all things. I am right?"

I had little chance to reply, "Yes, w..."

She cut me off in near exasperation with, "Now! Then! This can't be the first step anymore! Just to go out and buy a new shirt when you need to be obliged. We have to get these washed after an engagement. We'll have to see in the way as to what they have as washers." Then she just shot up and moved to the closet as she spoke, "Let's just see what we have for now. What do we have?"

I had to think of the beautiful sight I had seen, and had half expected to not warn her. I had also thought that maybe Pepper had increased my allotment of shirts. I mean she had been in here extra long except for the lingering Mary. So I made to move to see for myself when Liz came around with a copper shirt. She shook it in front of her as she asked, "What size are you?"

I just gave her what I knew, "About an eighteen neck, if it fits I wear it otherwise."

She gave me a look as she spoke with a virtual

disdain, "Wow! I can't believe this resembles like your exact size, and the color fits you best. Here try this on as I look some more." I think most men would be appraised to just look, this was not my way as I now had to clear my throat. I did also place on the copper shirt too, as, after a second or two, I was forced to clear my voice again. She came out with her hands on her hips as she simply asked, "What?!"

I had to point at her private area, as to bring her condition to the forefront. Maybe that wasn't the best of ideas as for when she noticed she seemed to curl up and venture back into the closet. I then did my best to give her the sheet she was wearing, then retreated to our bed. As soon as I was covered back up, she seemed to gingerly move back to the bed.

I then had to point out the obvious. "Liz, you do realize that I have seen many a woman's body?"

She was staring at the ceiling as she had to confess, "I have seen a few male bodies in my life as well."

"I don't see where the problem is then?"

"In my full garb, it has truly been a long time since my body has been seen."

"Oh, I see. Well, I truly didn't mean to embarrass you."

"I wasn't embarrassed."

I had to smile as I had to ask, "Then why did you cover up like you did?"

She had to give a slight giggle, "I without a doubt don't know, I mean you saw me in my full glory last night, and didn't run."

"Why would I run?"

She just laid for a moment or two before answering, "I don't know that either, it just gives the impression of being the appropriate thing to say. I mean they all, the sisters I meant. That."

"Liz you have to know this, which for some reason you haven't ascertained. You do know that you're gorgeous right?"

"Thank you,"

Then she hit her head as I had to ascertain why she did this, "Why did you do that? I mean the hit to the forehead."

"Thank you!" She acclaimed as she went into, "Who says that, I mean honestly."

"I don't understand?"

"Another compliment would have been better."

I had to shake my head as I had to say, "Not if it isn't truthful, I mean false platitudes are the worst."

"I have to agree with you there." Then she seemed to take a slight look at me, I know because I was fully looking at her. Then she admitted, "Yeah. I can assure you nothing I would have said would have been a platitude. Just in-case no one has ever told you this John, you are an uncommonly striking man."

I had to chuckle at that as I jokingly say, "Now we roll around and have sexual favors with each other."

She laughed with me for a moment, then she seemed to get profoundly solemn. After just a few she then had to say. "Would that be so bad?"

Okay. This was definitely unexpected as I replied. "What?"

"Oh," Was what she said next, and after we laid there for another moment or two. She requested, "Would sex with me be that bad?"

I had to reply to her honestly, "No and yes. No, because I can see us having a wondrous time, as I do to you which you may have never imagined. No is within a terminology of sex, I genuinely don't want to have sex with you. In all my existence I have found it far better to make love with a woman. Sex is such a messy act, if this is going to happen there has to be a reason behind it. So we can have sex, but only if you allow me to in reality make love to you."

I don't think any one could fully comprehend what I meant, even though I had to hope she knew. She then after another moment or two asked, "Will it hurt like my first experience?"

Again came the truth, "I can't venture to say, though if it does I promised to stop on your word. I have said to all the girls, I have no scheme to take away your virtue."

She got up on her elbows, as she looked at me. Then she threw off her sheets, which I then retrieved and placed it over her. I came close to her as I took this as a yes, and whispered after our first kiss. "Allow me to show you the way, as making love is truly an art form."

As I now made several kisses that deepened, with the align of our tongues. I did caress her tender part on her behind, which caused her to insinuate to wiggle out of it. I had to ask, "Is this making you uncomfortable?"

She replied, "Yes. But I'm sure this is what I want, so please continue."

I will tell you more next chapter, but I do warn you. When it comes to the delights between a man and a woman, I do not this freely share. I will share what I must to just advent what she that is in question tells me I must relate. Though she has had to also help me, as I surely shared far too much. Then again I will only share this one more time, not within this book as it was. The understanding that our sex life was free, and without remorse. Not that I can say that the first bonding action did its work, though the careful implementation of many more times to make it assured.

Chapter Two

When things are worse and no one knows.

Day two standing before a burnt out bar.

We are now on a scene with several individuals, as the black SUV's pull up with their blue flashing lights. Many police and fire trucks with ambulances with the suspicion of hurt or dead. Many are working diligently to put out the fire, and also keep it from spreading. No one notices the strange hearse that pulls up, as it may suggest, though three of the clergy vacate the vehicle.

Father Michael

I had no idea that they would call me this easily, but I knew enough to come when the bishop called. Even he wasn't here on his own volition, as a suspected spot had been destroyed. In both of their slumber they met the member, he had not understood there was a burgeon of the investigation. In fact, he had never truly been a fan of the

Jesuits, so he hadn't been that kind to this ridiculous gentleman. What he had told them had to be just a cause of a wild imagination, that certain sort of evil could not possibly exist.

He had also transferred a lot of information on their drive, and he had always been taught evil was just that. All this evil is evil for and unjust demeanor, yet they can be brought a just reward if they're left on their own. Then you have the whole thing that didn't sound the Catholic, with all his drivel about with all that is good, then there has to be evil. Weren't we in the business of bringing the lord to the unwashed masses, he had to wonder if what he had heard was the truth.

Not that which this individual had to say, he had to be some kind of kook. What he had thought was what sister Mary Elizabeth had said about being choked off by the church. He had no way to explain that it was more of the bishop, even though he did suspect the call came from higher ups. His lineage had been to become the next bishop, but when it came to him he wasn't sure he was ready. Not for the post, but the lack of knowledge when he came to this city.

As they now checked cameras he also explained how he had placed cameras on every avenue. They had moved to the first one, and they had nothing as it had not even been set off by the explosion. The next one had a few shadows, with about four pictures, though real notice was on certain vehicles. Now we never made it to camera number four, as what we saw on the third one to counterbalance. As he saw a painted figure as his only words, the great Harlequin, why is she here?

My concern isn't for what he said honestly, but on

what I saw there. I spoke nothing of my concerns as I saw her, and the picture wasn't that clear. I had never seen her out of the usual habit she wore, but the way she seemed to stand. Then came on the eighth picture, and she had looked straight at the camera. No other picture had ever made it cleared to him, that if these things were as evil as he said. Then how could anyone truly join them, let alone a Carmelite nun? Was that honestly a picture of her in the flesh, and out of her coverings.

He had to be overly tired as his mind had to be going, as he seemed to just not eliminated. Then when it came to getting back into the car he had to ask, more for his own peace of mind. Could he look at that eighth picture once again, and as he turned it encompassed and compassed. His mind wasn't playing tricks on him, I mean it did so look like her, but she could not have been that bare-breasted harlot. No Carmelite Nun would ever go without their habit, let alone in such a disgraceful way.

They let out the bishop first as he told the good sir he would have to make a report to his eminence. Now they drove back to his church as he seemed to question about the picture Father Michael had requested. He explained it away as he had to be mistaken, as that picture could not be whom he thought it was. That seemed to settle everything until they reached the front of his house.

To which the man then said, "You do realize they can transform anyone into what they are."

Father Michael had to surmise, "What do you mean sir?"

His reply was to certain aspect haunting, "They can transform the best among us into their vileness, with men nor women not exempt."

I then had to ask, "Surely you aren't suggesting that they could even do this to the Pope?"

He simply chuckled, "By Heavens no. What I'm saying is that they have been known to turn deacons, head women of the auxiliary, and many comparable. I also have to watch all your body, not that it happens often. There has been the case, though it is rare, but an even holier person being turned. This is one of the assertions of the investigations, because of those that happened many years ago now."

"Are you talking as to the likes of priests and nuns? This does convey the impression though highly unlikely to me, but I have to know."

He seemed to look away, then he came back with a small piece of paper, so neatly folded. He placed it into my hands, he held my hand fast, as he told me. "This information can't be kept, so as soon as you are sure of it, please for my sake destroy it. If I'm found out, I will deny I ever gave it to you. Now good night my dear friend, which I hope I can call you that."

With that, he then rolled up his window and just drove away. So then as I would, I placed the paper on the counter of my room. I would read it after four days because the night sleep would cause me to forget. It was only the advent of the cleaning lady, that would cause me to remember about it. I would read the script, that was in an older language, though not hard to read. At first, I would deny it changed everything, but in truth what was on there would rock my world.

One singular older Indian stood off waiting.

You could see his noble nature, with his hawk like nose. He stood for awhile waiting on his chief, then he could feel his presence. He turned to meet him as the noticeably tall Native American walked up, with a low voice he requested.

"What has happened LoneOwl?"

He then replied, "My chief it is as we have been told, as we picked up a certain scent of those that are dead. I sent him along to proceed my gathering, this is why I have lingered here so late. These old eyes did see much of the world of man, but more in short order is what the world of the dead was shown. It is most baffling as to what was done, I saw them come out of the building. The world of the dead did their work profoundly well, as I have seen them come out of that."

He now pointed to a burnt out building, and he had to ascertain what this meant. "LoneOwl? Are you telling me they destroyed that building? Or is there more? I know your ways."

He seemed to have a smile on his face, "Yes there is. I would have said they were up to their old tricks, if not for my vision. I know I could not be the host, so I had to stand and watch further. I can tell you that more did happen, though only this lone figure did see it. Well, he in point of fact heard it."

The Chief's impatience was getting the better of him as he said, "Out with it man. I'm not as all those that can't sleep, and my children need me this night."

"Excuse me my chief." He now gave him a slight nod as he went on, "My age doesn't allow me to remember the pains of fatherhood. Once all had been cleared up, and just a few were left, I saw movement. Whatever it didn't come out, but seemed to wait its time. Men poked around I believe putting out hot spots, they worked so hard. Then a man came in one car, he allowed all to leave, and he was about ready to leave."

He now pointed at a single car, "That is where he saw something." He moved his finger, "He went to investigate, in the darkness he could not see anything. I perceived an extraordinarily large hand come up, he pulled with a strength unknown. The poor man never had a chance, as he was obliterated. It wasn't easy to understand that the man was trying to scream, yet I was here alone and couldn't apply for any assistance. Now he was done with, and the figure than did throw the body over there."

He moved his hand one last time, "Now I saw the figure arise, I can't tell you what it was. I know it looked more like bone than a body, and that it did move off hurriedly. I dare say that even the speed of you daughter couldn't sustain. Then that is only a judgment upon what I saw, though if it is what I suspect I would dare say she would need help if she caught up to it. As we are of the forest, and we know of these dwelling of the evilest, I would have to say the figure was among those."

He now turned back to the chief, "I have caused this enlightenment to be caused, the first wasn't here to destroy this building. I do believe they were here to destroy that evilness, but they didn't succeed and he means vengeance."

The chief now blinked at him as he had to ask, "What concern does this have to do with us? We have never interfered in the leeches deaths unless it warrants the saving of our human's lives. Old man do you have a point in all this?"

He nodded, "I do. Though for now, I do believe it is best just to watch, not get involved. I have seen that we will get involved, and I would say wait till we can absolutely know. As you were told of all the criminals coming from all the locals. You even have to ask why, though I do not believe they're directly involved. With this, I have seen that they have a certain level of culpability, to the level I have no clue."

The chief was about ready to speak, as he now added, "Then you have three that wore collars."

"What?!"

Was all he could say as he now went on, "I moved here as I saw them inspected the front of that tree. They seemed excessively interest in the path of the youngsters. I had to wonder why there were three of them, I ascertained that only one knew there was something wrong. I had to be contemplative with the essential details that there they did pass because none other could explain that."

The chief now moved to look down at the front of the tree, as he exclaimed with disdain. "Oh lord cameras. They got a picture of all those walking dead?"

"The actual same my chief."

He bowed as the chief knew any evidence was bad, he never had dealings with the church. He had been told how bad they could be, so he knew this was even worse. He had always trusted his shaman, this seer was such a different thing than he knew. He understood that they truly didn't like one another, he also contemplated that he gave him a perfect breakout.

So he said virtually as if he was having a tooth pulled, "Fine! We'll set your darn watch, but this better not be a gross hunt. Gross is like hunting with a shotgun and only having solid slugs. You can say you saw the bird, but truthfully when you dig the shell out you have nothing left."

The older man known as LoneOwl then replied, "I hope so too my chief, not that I don't trust my visions. I would just hate for my first incorrect one to be this one. Shall we leave now, as I assess we won't be needed here anymore."

With this the chief wheeled and started to walk, then LoneOwl cleared his voice. He looked back as he saw him just looking at him, though he knew what he wanted already. Then you have the reason why he just walked away, the man honestly unnerved him. He then grudgingly said, "Do you need a ride back to the reservation?"

He nodded his head as they walked back to his truck in silence.

Detective Jimmy Hershel

I had no idea that there would be another possible case. I mean why would they call for all the paperwork about that for last night. Looking at it over this has to be a simple case of arson, I can see how it would be strange.

Then I had to reread a part of the report because I did find it hard to believe. Then I had to ask in decidedly low tone, "Why did a dive like that need so much kerosene?"

It wasn't that this was a common case, but in truth, it wasn't my department. I didn't want to be seen as treading on another's job, this was absolutely weird and I had to seek a link. Somewhere. Worse was if the Feds found out what he was doing, what has this to with anything that has to do with national security?

Back to the House

As you know we had just truly kissed for the first time, not the last thing we would do over the next three hours. I'm extremely slow and deliberate at what I do, as it all started, and I made sure I place a kiss everywhere on her face. Now most men would go to massaging her breasts, but I truly believe time is the game. So my first approach was to lightly kiss her neck, also with the barest touch of my tongue.

Liz had sex before, in truth this was the first time anyone cared to make love to her. Now I did move to her breasts as I was particularly careful to treat them with kisses and slight heavier touches of the tongue. I think when I moved just reasonably down, she expected me to go for the prize. I knew that the breasts need the touch of my hands, as I moved to her upper stomach. The first breast I did massage as I also allowed my teeth to drag across her flesh.

You could say with the slight moans she had never been treat with such exalted delight previously. I was a cad or a tease I would now go for what I desired, but I was not as I moved to her lower abdomen. Not that this was enough as I also massaged the other breast, and near the crown of her private area I gave a slight bite. It roughly seemed as if she would crawl out of my grasp, even as her body seemed to quake in the excitement of what was to come.

This is the place where I'm certainly drawn not to tell, I will tell you that over the days since this first time, all you have to do is use yours over active imagination. I can tell you that we all feel differently upon this, and I was, even as I showed her why we thought of blood bonding as incredibly intimate. She had no idea how our senses would work, as my teeth penetrated her skin. The pain would be the same for us as humans, though human would then feel a numbing sensation. Not us as our senses are far acuter, so the pain reasserts its effect as pure pleasure.

I wish I could explain better than this, as it is a sensitiveness beyond the amorous obscene. Which in hindsight is why many that have tried to explain, have done a piss poor job. I can tell you that she, Liz couldn't get enough, and as we are we could go perpetually, save for the want of vital fluid. I also have to confess as to the belief that we might have bonded, it became an assurance after this evening.

What I told you about why it is so bad, is the exact truth, as a breaking could kill one or both. I can tell you we had barely ended on term when we would start another. Not that either of us truly wanted to stop, it was more concern over the health of the other that we had intervals. Now we had just started another round when a simple knock came on our door. Do end this with slightly more, you have to understand that Liz was terribly reserved at first. Now she was having so much fun, she was giggling and pulling me into her, and I can say I was absolutely happy as well.

So when the first knock came we had barely heard it, then I do believe we placed it as that we were hearing things. Not that was ever a thing with our species, we could always hear rather well. Then came the second knock as it has now assured us what we heard was fact. I swear as soon as it sounded Liz rapidly pulled the sheets to her chest. Not that I was ever concerned what someone may see, so I did without a doubt nothing but observe Liz.

Well except for my normal tone voice, "Come on in."

Liz screamed, "NO!" She then smacked me with, "John! We have no clothes on! What if it was one of the kids?!"

From the other side of the door came Peppers voice, "Don't worry Liz. I may not have thought of opening the door, but my parents rose better kids."

I then had to ask, "Pepper why are you knocking on our door?"

There was a slight moment, then she said, "Oh yeah. Paul sent me up, he told me that a car just drove up the drive. It has a real quiet horn, so he thought you may not have heard it. Heck, he heard it, I heard nothing. But he told me to go so he could keep an eye on it, he does believe it is that William guy."

"Oh shoot," I said frantically, "I truly nearly forgot."

Liz then said, "That you Pepper."

I then added, "Pepper wake your sister, and knock on Naomi and Kitty's door."

I looked at her and Liz continued with, "Also I think Joe and Bert, of course, you can do Bert with Naomi. John, what does the dress have to be?"

I replied, "Dress?" I then said to Pepper in a louder voice, "Tell them to dress nicely also."

"Anything else John?" Even I could hear she wasn't that happy, so I said with I hoped somewhat comfortable tone, "No, thank you, Pepper."

We both could hear her moving off, but she never actually said another word. Liz came out of the bed with her sheet covering, and I had to smile at her. As she realized what I was doing she had to ask with a shy giggle, "What?"

I pointed at the bed as I had to mention, "After what we have been doing over the last few hours, do you genuinely think there isn't a part of you I haven't seen?"

She then looked down her makeshift dress as she had to admit, "I guess I legitimately don't have anything to hide from you."

I had to come close as I had to tell her something she may not have thought, "We are bonded for sure now, but in truth, you have the world to hide from me." I pulled her close and tightly so we could feel every aspect of our bodies. "Yes. You are in the Biblical sense known to me, but in truth Liz we don't know the aspiration or true desires of either. So you can't hide your body as I know it oh so well, but we still have so much to learn about each other."

I then pulled the sheet out between our naked bodies and threw it on the bed. She then leaned into me as I kissed her so deeply, then she drew barely away and spoke. "The meeting."

I released her as I move to our closet, she was right next to me started to pull things out. She then had to ask, "Should we all dress well?"

I had to smile, then something dawned me, I had not asked how Pepper knew it was William. It occurred to me his master would never show here without foreknowledge of who was in here. It was a no brainier that this was the set up before the meeting, so to myself I had to think for a few. The overriding problem was they were most definitely capes, and they were known for the worst. Not that I could truly ascertain their intentions, but the worse case scenario was too terrible to hold an opinion.

So with all this, I had to confess, "I don't know. So for now, I'll say yes."

Chapter Three

The calm meeting before the beginning of the storm.

Now I have to tell you it without a doubt took
longer than I had expected to get ready. I have a way of
getting dressed using my speed, where I can be done
within the blink of an eye. As soon as I had the things out
prepared to do my best, this is what came from Liz.

"You know how to do that right don't you?"

I had to ask my own question, "What?"

"The pants and the shirt can be set right, all you
have to do is just before fastening them up. Grab the sides
of the shirt, pull it back to make the stomach flat, then
finally do up your pants. The shirt may look all wrinkled
from the back, the front, however, is superior and taunt."

All I said back was, "Yes ma'am."

She continued as she ascertained the content of the closet, "It virtually is as if someone thought I was coming like they had a message or something before hand." She moved a few things around as she searched the closet, she pulled out a two piece dress. Then she moved to the dresser as she seemed to be noticeably happy at what she was doing. With this, she retrieved a pair of panties, a bra, some stockings, and what looked like a towel. I then went in and retrieved my boots, she seemed to be disgruntled about that. She then went in and said, "I know your boots would be more comfortable, but as this is a formal event I'm willing to bet these would work better." I grabbed them and was about to put them on when she quaked, "John?! Aren't you going to wear a pair of socks?"

I answered her plainly, "Socks take up room in my bedroll, so it is usually easier to go without them."

By this time she was already rummaging through my drawers, in a second she showed me a pair of dress socks. She then threw them at me saying, "Try these, they look far better with your outfit."

The time it took me to place on my socks and shoes, which Pepper again had done an excellent job. She had on her panties, bra, and stockings, which is when I found out what that towel was. I think the ladies call it a slip, but she also had out a pair of those old lace up shoes. I had to inquire after allowing a reasonable amount of information to flow, "Someone plausibly did know you were coming, and she doubtlessly told Pepper to get ready for you. I'm always a wonder when Kitty does something, then again it is the way of her species. I do have to ask, are you going to place on your shoes before your clothes?"

She smiled at me as she replied, "Yes. Normally I

would sit to get dressed, this being as important as it is suggestive of, wrinkles would be bad." Then she picked up my coat, she placed it over my shoulders as she kissed me on the nose. I mean literally on the nose, well we would do a lot more that were beyond a kiss on the nose. "I know you have to scoot to get to the William."

She then brushed it with her bare hands to make sure it was straight. It had three buttons I only did up one, she seemed to look at me again with a critical look. When I did up the lower button she seemed to be happy, though I wasn't so sure about the tie she handed me. I had to assert, "I think we can do without the tie."

She pleadingly asked, "Why?"

I had to explain, "Liz my kind has more to do with the utility of an outfit, not how good we look. I will ask you if I had to unexpectedly fight, would you like me better with gore over me?This black tends to show the viscera far better, that is why I usually wear brown. There is always a fact that leather can save your life, and it also has a more natural look. I do understand about dressing fine for this meeting, but some things are hard to change. As I have never truly worn a tie in far too many years."

She then crossed her arms and asked as if she were angry, "Anything else?"

I hadn't caught it at first, "Well yeah, the thickness. Buckskins are also great and do offer protection, but nothing does a well as good old fashion thick leather coat. So overall we have to wear that which protects and is utilitarian."

Now I caught it as she said flatly, "So. Overall. We

should be utilitarian. All for our protection? Am I correct in what you're telling me?"

I pulled her close as I softly spoke, "Not in everything. I do believe your kind are far better in whatever is the most beautiful. I will also tell you two thing, you could make burlap look sexy. Never would a sack of such cloth stay too long, as it would never be up to honor." I kissed her so deeply then, "I believe the finest cloth wouldn't be good enough for you, then again we must at least appear to be human."

She then giggled as she struck me and asked, "Whatever do you mean sir?"

There are certain things you should never discuss, but I felt I had to give her some truth. "I have a friend that is your kind, well many truly. With your realm there never has to be fighting, so she was never required to wear any kind of armor. In fact because of their, and now your condition. They can use their whiles to defend themselves, so they like to accentuate their bodies. This leads to wear the most flattering clothes as possible, that is their sense of defense." I had to look away as I had to add, "They're real proud of their bodies, to the point of wearing essentially nothing. I truly mean nothing as in nude, even though they know the outside world. Well."

"John tell me?"

"Liz because of their nature they're called the hedonist race, and try certainly hard to live up to that name."

"Oh okay." As soon as the words left her lips a realization came over her face. "OOHH!" With even more surprise on her face, as she seemed to nod her head as things would be disclosed. "You, a, ya, mean as in, a, and nothing to, then," she seemed to shutter, "O, ah. Oh, my! Ooh, my! I, a, I can do that, I. Can I?"

I knew they just treated it as just so much, as the norm for all interested. I had to qualify that with, "Yeah." I had to add as I realized this was me, and not Tony that should have told her. "I hope you don't get angry with me, I just sort of thought you needed to know. This, of course, was something Tony should have told you, and that also means with others outside this house."

She blinked at me as she simply spoke, "How could anyone do that? You were being truthful with me, and I think I would have been angry if you would have kept it from me." She then giggled as she waved her hand at the bed, which I had never even picked up once that she had made it. "Do you think I could think less of you, when and with what we just experienced."

I do have to say I may not be a quick witted as I think myself as I absolutely nearly shouted, "NO!"

Now I was ready to leave, but I also knew I had to explain that away. So I calmed my voice, "No, I mean. Sorry didn't mean to raise my voice, you won't have much to worry about though. Pepper is to a higher degree extremely affluent in the use of her wiles, in truth, there is no one here to cause her to take that next step. Tony in his ways will be a good teacher, he is so young and I can assure you he has no idea how to use his abilities. I have no quandaries he can teach the basics, in this it will take someone known in all the ways. I'm sure he isn't our man for that."

"Hmm, hedonist?" She just seemed to say, then inquired, "Well I do have another question then?"

"Okay shoot. I mean just ask."

She seemed nearly amused by what I said, "Since my type is like that would it pay to dress more sensual? Or as the matter may be, is it better to dress in a more sexual nature?"

I had to admit, "I literally don't know. I mean they do dress . . . or at least undress so sexually implies the way. Their approach does give the impression to be far more on the sensual side, and that speaks to dressing more sensually." She then looked at what she had, and I had to add, "You may want to get more input from Kitty and Naomi first though, as they may have something that can help you lock it in better."

She then said as I did the last little things and was going out the door. "Are you going to serve breakfast this morning, or are you going to allow Paul and Cheryl to do it?"

I had to ask, "What do you mean? Oh, breakfast!" I have no idea why I thought to add this, "Nope. You have to understand Liz, our world can be as cruel or kind as any other. Though with the way we are, you always have to be prepared for the worst. Now I'm not telling you something will happen today, but it is always best to assume it may. If we are forced to move to an ambush, you know more effectively what I'm talking as respects."

I had no idea if I was saying this correctly, "In a way I never want you to think darkly of any of us, in general of our world it maybe for the best. So as to breakfast, most likely as a way to amend what may, we don't primarily look it as breakfast. I know you haven't been here long enough to have a weapon of choice. Think of it maybe, that even the mildest of our lot have weapons of choice. So now think why?"

She had to ask, "Tony doesn't?"

I had to clue her in with, "His weapon of choice is a good pistol, though he won't admit it."

"Everyone then does?"

"Well no. Bert and Naomi don't have any, then when their claws come out they genuinely don't need weapons. Kitty and Andy also rely more on their obfuscate, but they have to have weapons to get their surprise. Now Cibilia, Mary, and Sammy rely upon hand weapons like me, and we appreciate handguns can add a level of equality."

I blew out as I can never tell how these words will go over, "Joe needs a cannon so he can have time, but given that time his works have terrible challenges to others of our kind. Now with Paul and Cheryl, they in effect don't like to fight close up, so they tend to be better with ranged weapons. Tony, Pepper, and now you tend toward the faster weapons, like pistols." Then it came to me, and I had to be happy about this. "Wow. Thank you so much, Liz. You caused me to look upon this far more completely."

"I'm glad I could help. Ah. Why?"

"Several reasons come to mind," I had to chuckle with my delight. "I think we're in our way coming together as a cohesive unit as you brought this to light for me. Then you have where our power lies, this knowledge will help place things together. With the quintessence that we can't truly give the type of training, they truly need. This is, of course, terrible, as the connection that has appeared now. We can in point of fact branch out in differing aspects, even as incomplete as it may be."

She seemed practically remorseful with a sigh and her next remark, "Yeah. Everyone except for me."

"Technically you aren't our newest member."

"Yeah. I know as a vampire Sammy is younger, though just at life he is far more experienced than I."

I knew what she meant, and I had to agree with her on a few. Then it came to me, "As soon as we get back, I think I'll talk with Mary." She looked at me with confused eyes, and I realized I hadn't said enough. "Well, Cibilia is best for training you the extra stuff. I do believe Mary and presumably, Cheryl could show you thing no man could possibly know. I have to meet with Naomi, and hopefully, we will be done with this William fast. Hmm. Well, I may ask Naomi if she would think all the girls should attend. With what we need I'm not sure about any of this, but I do think it is a good idea."

She now giggled at me as she commented, "Basically a how to be a lady101. I'm not sure it is that great of an idea, as most ladies are so different. I'm not saying it won't be helpful, we do tend to have our own thought processes."

I had to lift one eyebrow as I had to admit, "I don't know, maybe suggest it to Naomi. Then she can come up with a better way to handle it."

I now had to move to the door as I knew this had taken far too long. I then pointed and ascertained, "How long will you be?"

She replied, "Just a few minutes more."

I helped her out as best as I could, then we walked down the hall. We were met by Cibilia coming up looking for us, I could also see the other kids were doing what we were doing now. She then also told us she had forgotten something, and she was having to run to her room. I then told Liz to help her, and that she Mary and Cheryl had to get the kids ready. Each floor had five rooms save the forth which only had two, well take away storage and maybe more.

Each floor also had two restrooms except for the fourth floor. The first floor which had no bedrooms save one, so all the restrooms were, as a matter of fact, half baths. In all, I had not ascertained the second and third had two large rooms, and we had taken one of four. The prospect of having as I thought, possibility of two more, made for eight smaller rooms. Now the floors all had an extra room, every accouterment was truly placed on the first.

The first had a particularly large and particular significant dining room, as to the essence that we don't without a doubt need it. Well for the normal use I mean, the kitchen was also made with size in thought. With all the extras we need, that is well placed, with the extra refrigerators, it does give the impression of being smaller. The basement even though it doesn't have to be explained here, was a sectioned one. It was three-quarters underground, with three off areas for the use as a root cellar.

Knowing us even in passing we truly had no use for basements, save three of our races. Luckily we had none of them here, as that would be even harder to explain to certain of humankind. Our garage was made to fit four vehicles, with another six spaces to park, I have no idea why. Above the garages were also four small dwelling places, though by us, not truly in use. So understanding this, it is also easy to see I wasn't in the kitchen right away.

The patterns did fascinate me as I walked, I will say that maybe turning on my speed may have been better. I did get to the room after some time, and I had to look at what we had. Bert was profoundly dapper in an excessively dark blue suit, I came up and straightened his lapel. He wore one of those bola ties, I wish I had thought of that. I had to think Naomi had helped him, as he seemed to match far too well for a guy.

Naomi had on a dress, as of late all I had truly seen was her tight fitting battle garb. It was yellow with some kind of covering green flowers, this set her apart from everyone else. Though she pulled it off so well, I felt what I had said upstairs was a good choice. I now had to move to Cibilia, and I can tell you, she was rocking her usual red. I mean the dress went down to her ankles but was so open in the front, it was showing off her long boots.

You can't finish this out without a Kitty original, I mean a white tutu kind of dress. This thing was tight, but also eminently refined, accented with whitish pinkish tights. Whereas she always has on her two ponytails, tonight she had a single one trailing down her back. Now for the most potent of the lot, as Joe was dressed in all black. It was noticeably easy to see it was also all silk, with a jacket that went to the knees.

I had to wonder if he had a top hat, he would look the part of an undertaker of old. You doubtlessly don't know this, but this was the model look of his kind. The only part that wasn't black was his incredibly dark blue tie, which was also exceedingly okay with his outfit. Naomi, I have to add, as her hair was always in a long braid, she had it acknowledged. I had no idea her hair was so long, even with all the waves, I could easily see it was barely over her butt. Even as beautiful as Liz's hair was, I had to say that Naomi's surpassed hers by far.

This was it, so I decided to advise. "Joe you're in the center with Kitty, Cibilia you will be outside them to the left. I'll be to the right, Bert you'll be outside me, and of course Naomi outside Cibilia. Now let's move . . ."

I got cut off by Naomi, "John shouldn't we have Cheryl or Paul with us?"

I shook my head as I answered, "I thought of that, but as to many capes are, I had to just be a meet to the actual meeting place."

She nodded her head, then we moved out as we came down the driveway. It was easy to see that by now William was extremely impatient with us. I bet he would find it funny that it was unmistakably me that caused this delay. My kind, or as Cibilia was here I should say ours, are known as the most disruptive by nature. The one thing we are also usually acknowledged as the first to a gun fight, with blades. I know that may sound funny, but unlike me, most of my race prefer blades.

As we came particularly close he folded his arms and asked in their usual acid way. "I have been waiting here for an eon, did these fine your ladies cause in this."

Of course, I would never admit to any fault as I said, "That is extremely unkind of you as your kind always claims to be the most civilized."

It was easy to see that I had provoked something in him, but these types are world renowned at resisting their own anger. "I'm known for my patience, but all this time has tested my moderation."

I then had to add back as I also understood he may expect more from me. "We have no qualms about doing what needs to be done now, then again you called this meeting, not us."

"Yes. It is just like your kind to beat your chest, with an over ambitious bravado. Will we just allow all modesty leave our discussion, or shall we unambiguously expel the civilized demeanor?"

I came forward and simply said, "Take the first shot, I can guarantee you won't take another."

Kitty then screamed, "Desist!"

William then started, "Well this was never my idea, but even my master has his limits. He told me to set this up for him." He then handed me an envelope with a simple, "He provided everything in there, even directions, he is allowing you an hour from when I get back."

I took them from him as was what he wanted, I

then had to say. "It was fun sparring with you, maybe we can do it again."

Naomi then had to say, "John we don't want to start any fight we may not be able to handle."

Now I did something unusual for my kind, as I turned my back on him and made my way back to the house. I had to give additional information, "I had all your snipers found out, and have no worries they would have all proceeded you, William."

Naomi made sure everyone else walked backward, even with this knowledge, and a slight cough laugh. We walked back to the house, as she had to whisper ever so low. "Do you think it was wise showing your hand like that?"

All I could do before we reached the door, was give her such a big smile.

Chapter Four

There are many things before the storm.

Now with what I had done, I apprehended that there could have been a few that would be apprehensive. What I speculated wasn't as deep as was shown, with all the eyes of those not as ancient penetrating me. I had to give them what I doubtlessly felt about this situation.

I said so all could now hear, "What? I just showed him what I understood he thought of me."

Now with that I particularly received a belly laugh from Kitty, it was easy to see no one else appreciated my form of humor.

With that Naomi chastised me, "John he could have been his right-hand man! Is this how you want to start this event?!"

I had to figure everyone had heard that as Liz was

right there asking. "What happened?"

Cibilia then explained, "John just barely stayed one step from calling that William guy a punk. Man, was he angry too, I mean he nearly threw the instructions at John."

Tony then asserted, "Everyone in the kitchen now, we have to get this started."

With that, we walked into the same said room as Naomi interpreted, "Tony's right, he said the guy has given us an hour from when he gets back."

I can tell you I was moderately happy with myself as we all moved together. I had to do my usual moving a few of the younger guys, even as I had demonstrated, they still tended to take better than offered to the ladies. I then placed the packet on the table, it was remarkably simple as it had a map with drawn directions on it. Then there was a diagram of a building, and it showed us coming in from a certain direction.

I then freely associated it, "Suggests simple..."

I got cut off by Mary, "John you're..."

To which she got cut off from Naomi, "John why did you do it?"

I had to say, "Tony understands, I..."

To which he now cut me off with, "John I knew this had to be done, I have no idea why you antagonized that William."

"Well, I just..."

Mary said now with passive strength, "JOHN!"

"What Mary?"

"This may sound absolutely stupid, and I'm sure no one has thought of this. We honestly should have had him meet us here, I mean how much gas do you have in your cars?"

I had to put my hand on my head as I bent slightly to Naomi, as she shrugged her shoulders. With that, I then turned to her and ascertained the obvious, "How much gas do you have?"

She then acknowledged, "Enough to get us there and back, maybe moderately more. That won't do as we would have to at least make two trips with everyone."

I had no idea what to do when Cibilia came up with an observation. "Andy how much gas do you have in that beast?"

Andy then reciprocated, "About half a tank. You know though I don't have a license."

I had to smile as I had to inform him, "Don't worry Andy we have enough that can drive."

Naomi then inquired, "Yes. But John we can't drive evenly, as I'm sure Mary's car can barely hold four, let alone the six we require."

I then said, "Well you drive one and I will drive..." Then I had to think as I murmured, "Bert has to go with me and Mary with you. Hmm..."

She then inserted, "Well Mary has to keep Sammy with her, so I suggest Cibilia as a backup for you."

I then nodded my head as I added, "Joe is behind me."

Cheryl then asked, "Are you kidding me? Sorry Mary, but her car is so small he'll have to hang out the window."

Okay, I had to admit that he was genuinely tall, and I had not taken that into account. Naomi then suggested, "Listen to Mary and I can take the car, this means Sammy can sit behind her."

She then had to look at Pepper to Paul, as if she was trying to make up her mind. Tony then solved her conundrum with, "Well Cheryl and Paul have to go with Joe and me, I mean these guys are capes. Not that I want to throw them right to the wolves, but they are best to handle the beginning part. I figured Joe and I can attempt to explain things to them, even as unschooled in this as we are."

I had to look at Kitty and understood right then he was right, so I then turned to Bert. "Bert you'll have to come out the side door as Kitty will be next to me. Now no one else come out until Naomi and I are out, Bert and Mary follow us afterward. We just stand there as whoever chooses to do this, that will be either Paul or Cheryl."

With this Tony took up, "Cheryl as it is I hate to say, it'll doubtlessly be you, even though it also could be Paul. I have to tell the both of you what's up, and we'll need a list for her." I then pointed to Cibilia and Pepper as he added, "Blood and money are always first, everything else can come later."

I then quickly added, "Ammo too. I mean if this is to be done, we desperately need that."

He nodded his head as Naomi established, "Pepper you ride with me, that means you're behind me as Sammy will be behind Mary. John, I think Liz should be behind you, and Andy has to be close at hand for Kitty."

I had to ascertain, "Andy are you ready if she should dig in her nails?"

He nodded his head so Tony then interjected, "Okay I think we have it, just one more thing. Andy, how is your battery, I mean will the thing even start?"

I had to ask, "Is it that VW micro-bus?" He nodded his head, so I then explained, "Don't worry if we need to, we can push start it." I thought about it for a moment, then I had to inquire, "You think we should wait, or is it better to just get this started?"

Cibilia then had to investigate, "John I know you think of me as the best fighter." I nodded my head, "So why aren't I with Naomi?"

I was about ready to answer, but Tony beat me to the punch. "Cibilia you have to realize you're the figurehead to the house now, and with that, you need to be protected."

Now the way he had spoken that was outside the normal way he communicated. In fact, it was very nearly like he was being as sweet as he could be, to me uncommonly sickening. Kitty placed her hand on my arm and shook her head no, that brought me back to what happened the night prehensile. I supported the problem with Sammy, and I do remember Kitty with Andy. Then I had to think of the unusual pairing of Pepper with Paul, finally, I remembered throwing the blood bag at Cibilia.

I know my eye had to have become particularly wide as I realized it, she had Tony in her arms. Oh my, even at a year older, Cibilia had more internal strength than Tony had. Now I also could remember that Cheryl was in the arms of Joe, though that would have been a real close draw. Well maybe not so much, I forgot how close Joe was to his beast. So everything had to mesh up properly, and yeah even Liz and me. I mean her species were always close to their human kind, whereas there is no doubt my race is also close to our monster.

While I was in my thoughts he explained more, I can't legitimately tell you what he had disseminated. I had ascertained that it was better to go now, so I stood up as I had to look at them. "Get whatever is basic to you, then meet us at the cars." They all just looked at me, so I went on, "Listen we have to see a few things, I myself would prefer to give you personal time. We have to make sure as best as we can it isn't a trap. So, as I said. Now let's get a move on it, we're moving in ten, or less."

Now I moved out to the garage, as this dirty bus had sat here since I had then brought their vehicles home. I got in as both Kitty and Naomi watched, you could see how relieved Naomi was when it started right up. It was easy to see it did need work, as when it did start it blew extremely black smoke. Now I hadn't made Bert know what it meant when I had explained things to Andy.

Naomi was there as it was decidedly hard to talk over the engine, so she made sure he understood. While she did that Kitty and Andy moved to the back of the bus. Tony came back and made sure that Paul and Cheryl could hear them. I gave a slight turn to Liz as I then said as loud as I could, "Listen to them, you may never need it, but it can't hurt to know."

Naomi then came to me as she came close and said, "I'll do the search pattern, that thing is way too loud, everyone would know to hide." I had to nod my head, Then she added, "Okay. We're going now."

With that she jumped on the driver side, I realized what she was doing. Now she wheeled out of the driveway, and I place this bomb in gear and we pushed ahead. The directions were easy to follow as we had been this way on a few occasions. Then she stopped, I knew we were short of our target, so I also knew she wanted me to wait. So I put it in neutral and set the parking brake, then hung out just somewhat then waved her to move.

With her leaving I then directed all to keep an eye out, the time gave the impression interminable to me. I had to figure it was even worse for the kids, finally, Naomi came up from behind us. I placed a finger up to everyone as I got out, I then looked across at Mary and had to ask. "What did you see?"

She replied, "I think we're okay. I had everyone looking, and no one saw a thing. Especially Pepper."

I had to take a look at her, then I said, "Let's get this over with, Mary, Bert knows to get out with Naomi, you get out with me."

She nodded her head, so I then jumped into the bus and we drove onward. We all knew what we were doing, and I had to figure most also understood where it was in the vicinity of in the end. Naomi carefully drove up, as it was our way to never attract attention. I did have to wonder if this was the perfect car for that, as you can surmise it is exceptionally loud. I then drove so I could see Mary almost right next to me, then shut the darn thing off.

There was a small car that I knew as William's, behind it was an exceedingly large limo. The first two got out of the small car, I understood neither would be William. With that I then directed Bert to get out, I watched him move rather well, I was impressed. Then two more got out of his car, I had figured he would be in the limo. I did have to formulate how squished he would be if she had been in his small car.

Now Mary and I would get out, but you have to know about these three men and one woman. You could say that any movie that had the FBI in it, and these four with ear pieces and black suits. I think the general idea is founded, as we all now watched William get out of the limo. I had to hope as Cheryl got out of the car, that all that Mary had told me about her was right. They now walked toward each other, and it was easy to see who was the master here. It wasn't undoubtedly William.

Now you have to imagine this, as the two started talking, and I had to worry she was going to be overwhelmed. I swear the more they seemed to converse, the more he seemed to be sweating. If that were possible for a vampire, then you could very nearly see her playing him like a marionette. I had to look at Mary as she looked at me with the biggest smile and mouthed. 'I told she was a wiz at this.'

Finally, she came back and came close to us then revolved. I had to ask, "How did it go?"

She shrugged her shoulders and replied, "I think I got everything, though he said he has to talk to a Jeeves or something like that."

I had to ask, "Do you mean Giaus?"

"Yeah, that's it."

I had to look to see if Naomi had heard that, and she had as even I had to be surprised at this. Okay, let me explain. He isn't like a rock star in our world, but with his position, he is well known. You could say he without a doubt doesn't like to deal with small potatoes like us. Cheryl then had to ascertain, "John is he honestly that important?"

I had to suggest reasonably, "Not that important. I would say as important as the president is to the free world."

"What?!"

I saw William coming back as I had to point, and she went to her work. I had to take a step back as I said so Tony could hear, "Tony! Giaus is at the forefront of all this."

All Tony could say was, "Oh Shit."

Then Cheryl came back and said, "He wants to talk

to our elders John." I lifted my hand to William, then Cheryl added, "Not him John, that Giaus guy."

Well howdy. I knew this unquestionably was different for him, as I then said to her. "Help Kitty to depart." I then also said, "Tony I'm sure he doesn't know you're an elder, so stay here and take charge. Mary take Naomi's place so she can join us. Cibilia, Joe, and Bert join us, Sammy take Bert's place, then we move after he extricates himself. That may take a few guards as well, so be patient."

Naomi, as we came close, asked, "John he only asked for the elders?"

I had to agree, "Yeah. We need to do this as they're the authority within the house, otherwise, he'll never respect them."

Now Naomi and Kitty switched spots, as her spot was on my right. I then said so they could hear behind me, "Cibilia is central, Joe you're to the right, Bert to the other side. I glanced back as they started to get out, Tony line them up right here."

He saw where I pointed and started to do what I had said, I did have to be glad who we had. You may ask why, because both Cibilia and Naomi wore a tight skirt. Now Cibilia's was extremely short but as tight as it was it would not show anything. Then you have Kitty's and even as with hand flips, with her tights she had on you couldn't see anything. Now to the why, as this state is known for its wind, an excessively large breeze occur then.

It wasn't strong enough to cause Naomi or me to stagger, but Kitty was essentially overwhelmed. I had caught her just in time before she landed down on the ground. As I did this I could see that both Bert and Joe had to do the same with Cibilia. As they straightened up we could watch his guard get out, and they looked the part of the first four. Naomi helped out Kitty as Cibilia's sister Pepper and Cheryl came forward to help Cibilia.

Now was the time to see Giaus get out of the limo, and a pair of strange saddle shoes hit the ground. Then came the vision of a big hat, like it was made of fur or something. He took a few steps away as William closed the door for him, I had to check my eyes as the coat appeared to be fur also. Then he finally turned and we were all taken back, I mean was he literally wearing a purple polyester suit?

Now we all walked toward each other, and I will tell you all of us were looking at each other. I know we paced each other, though even as slowly as we did, we seemed to close far too quickly. We stood maybe two or three paces apart as I now had to ascertain. With one eyebrow raised, "Giaus I presume?"

Now I had not genuinely seen how Kitty was squirming, as we all saw as he answered back. "Is it to the fantastic John I'm speaking, Naomi I have heard of how great a huntress you have become. Ah, Kitty. It has been a decidedly long time."

She seemed to get even smaller as she said, "Hicky poo Blueness Weasel meuw...purrrrrr..."

Okay, that was like a cat meow, but different, and in a certain way added a purr. I could feel something as I had to look up, and there was Naomi beaming her eyes through her like me.

Chapter Five

Just when you think you know who the enemy is.

In a barren just south of the city

The haze lifts to reveal three men traveling with deliberate actions. These same actions if unknown to most, areas if they're looking for something. No one would care to understand if they had an inkling of the horror they hunt.

The older of the three then stands straight up sniffing the air, as if a dog chasing something on the wind. No word is spoken as another just makes a bare grunting noise, this transaction is enough to inform. Their prowess is easy to ascertain as all gave the impression to look in every niche. With this, they come together to appreciate the slight marks on the ground.

The original has the aspects of to use his fingers to trace these marks, with hand signs he then communicates with them. This allows the others to go off in different directions, and the old gave the appearance of following a trail. After just a few step he starts up another tired jog, within moments they're out of sight of the scene. This may have been the hundredth stop in their actions, they knew all too well the horror they hunted.

In all they had done, now for a couple of weeks, they did for the little one he took. They hated this land that was so flat, with barely a tree to hide their existence. This was far different as even they could hear the war-drums in their ever-present ears. When they crossed their brethren, they would sound the warning that has been with them so long.

This was considerably hard to understand, those local people would never understand their affinities. None of this mattered anymore after what happened, they had to get her back or find her dead. They had much in the way of a friend here, though Oklahoma and South Carolina tribes had not talked in a while. The next step was presumably the easiest, though no meeting was ever as easy until they absolutely met.

Back to a small part of the city

You have to understand about me, I had met her kind before and knew you should never be surprised with what they can and will do. Even as I had this understanding, I can't say that I realized where her entire life had taken her. This also means that as it was with my knowledge, I was doubtless the first to recover.

I put my hand out and said, "Hello Giaus. It is good to meet you."

He then had to ask, "It is a pleasure, John. Now may I ask why we have more than the three elders?"

This was an easy reply, "Well we are three that decided not to take a forwarding roll in the house. So I figured you would want to meet the leadership that has come to be in place."

He then looked at Kitty, I think he was about to say something, but I think his recognition stopped him. So he now turned to Naomi as he asked, "You are a huntress of renown, and you're okay with this?"

Naomi confessed, "Not at all at first, though John talked me into giving them a chance. They have proved their worth, so I have excepted this cause as well."

He had to smile as he related, "Ah. I see. John, you're trying the great experiment?"

This time it was me admitting, "I have explained all to them, and that if things get out of hand we may have to revert to the ancient ways. Though even with this, the most experienced of our lot wasn't chosen. They do well, as I have had to warn restraint as well."

He nodded his head as he said, "I have never been against the great experiment, though I have no reason to genuinely for it either. I will support this as far as it goes. Now can you introduce these few to me?"

I then acknowledged as I moved my hand to each, "This is Cibilia, she is of the same house as I'm and now the Princess of the house." Now she took his hand, and I expected some southern thing, not the curtsy she truly did. "This is Joe, and we may need your help with him later on, as he is a true mage and our house judge." He then placed up one eyebrow as they both shook hands with Joe ending in a bow, this made me think maybe Tony had a few words with them. "Finally we have Bert who is a child of Naomi's lineage, and the best to be the house sheriff."

With what Bert did told me that Tony had most definitely had a talk with them. Once all the greetings and bowing was done, then Giaus went to work. "I have no idea if Cibilia was the best choice, as even her name inspires the true nature of your kind. I can also see that there may have been a simple influence in the choice of the other two. I have to comment on their choices to the leadership. Now, why do you need my help for the younger as it were judge?"

This had been nothing I wanted to admit but had no real way around it. "Joe is considerably young as it were and at this time had been doing his best to learn rather rapidly. None of his kind can truly be experienced enough to understand in scholarly pressures. He needs an instructor."

Then he had to state the obvious, "You do understand I do not hire all these children, not that I don't respect what you have done here. There is truly only one man for this job, and even you have to comprehend this is no association for the youngsters."

Now it was my time to place some base truths, "Giaus you're trying to insult me? I know if you took the time to learn all of our names, you have also taken the time to learn what has been going on here. You also understand that I do work alone in most cases, and you haven't asked yourself why has John stayed?"

"I truly can't say that I have, though I did understand that two elders had come to this fair city. You also understand that there must be a reason why I'm here. It may take a considerable amount of time to fill me in, and I'm sorry I had to point out that you aren't a true elder Naomi."

I had to shake my head as I now filled him in, I also knew I couldn't tell him all as we would be trouble for so much. I finally finished, "Now you see why I'm committed to these children until this infection is clear of this city."

He had to shake his head as he had to ask, "Did you know any of this William?"

He came to his side and replied, "We had our beliefs, but no real acknowledgment. So we dare not till we could be truly sure, the other night as to what I saw. I had better acknowledgment then most my lord, I'm sorry, I should have at least mentioned it to you."

Giaus then turned to me and ascertained, "We need this fungus out of this city, can I count on yours and these children's help?"

I nodded my head as I also said, "That is why our demands are so high. We have had a few scuffles and it has cost us in gasoline, ammo, and sanguine fluid. I will also tell you that we will give our lives for each other, but none of us will give it for you."

He nodded as he also spoke toward William, "I want them to get all they need, even if we don't get her back, we are forced to deal with this problem."

William then complained, "But Lord!"

He waved his hand as he spoke, "I said granted, now do it as best as you can. That is my word. Do you understand me?"

He then turned away, but before he took one step Cibilia had to ask. "Giaus I'm sorry about this, but why the gaudy suit?"

He gave a slight turn as he answered, "It sets me apart from everyone else."

Then he returned to the car, William then spoke to us. "As he orders so it shall be done. Though we do have a problem at hand."

I knew what it was beforehand, "You don't have all we need right?"

"Yes. I have been known to work wonders, but even this would take some time. Will it be good to meet you at your house tomorrow, as I have no idea what it'll take to get all this."

I had to ask, "You know we can't do a thing without any of this, even these two cars aren't close enough to making it home." He nodded his head, "Then I guess we're forced to wait till the morrow, maybe sooner if you need."

William then nodded and added, "We'll have to use long-range fire to help suppress things, so I do believe we can get you the long range stuff later. Now don't worry I will be trying, I'm just putting less priority on those."

I had to think for an instant, so it was Naomi that took up the conversation. "We have to have control of the ground, so we attack from three sides. You'll have to place your weapons first, but on a map, you guys place where you're firing from so we can make a plan. This will allow us to set up our attack, that should be a good plan."

I then had to point at William, "One stray bullet hits one of our personages, and I will swear to come looking for you William."

He then remarked, "I do this for my Lord, just like you with your kids. So I swear I will not target anyone, even you Jonathan."

"You have a crew then, now go tell your lord."

That last part I said with all the disdain I could, though I'm sure they already understood my disrespect for the elders. We then started to back off to our cars, I then whispered, "They have no respect for what we have done, but let them know we mean business. All of you do as us elders are doing, we need to send a message."

I had no idea what Tony was doing, and I was eminently happy when I got back that everyone was already in the vehicles. As we backed up I could also see the collapse of their defense also. They melted away two by twos, with a fixed formula from the ages. I then said as I could see the front of the cars, "Get in like you got out, anything else will be seen as a reason for an altercation."

I got into our vehicles nearly last as they drove off, once Naomi and Bert were in, we were ready to leave. I pointed forward so they knew to just drive out, even though my comprehension told me Naomi already knew this. With this, we then made our way the short distance to our house. I knew what had to be done, as we all got out and moved in the back door.

Then I spoke loudly, "Everyone into the dining-room ASAP. We need to do some extra training. Naomi and I will start this, so everyone is ready to get dirty." I then looked at my watch, "You have twenty-three minutes to change. NOW MOVE!"

This caused a flurry of activity and voices, I knew they all understood this was important. So I didn't quell all the voices, plus it was easy to see the purpose they moved with full intent. We, Liz and I started to throw clothes back and forth, I advised her that lose clothes were better for now. I could have again placed on my speed, we were doing so well I didn't see the need. We were out of the room in less than ten minutes, it was easy to see that Liz barely was with me.

I then spoke to her, "Go hurry everyone up as best as you can, I think Naomi knows what we're going to do, but we do need to talk."

She nodded her head as I head to the dining-room, we precisely approximately met at the door. I then ascertained, "Did you send Bert to hurry the others up?"

Her reply was, "Yes. I take it you did the same with Liz?"

"Exactly, Now do you have a clue why I called this training exercise?"

"I figure basic calisthenics and possibly the same

with our fighting style. I also got all the bokken I could find."

I simply replied, "Good."

As the room started to fill up, with that both of us started to move things out of the way. Well I mean we and as we directed the kids to help because we had to get this started. As all were out of the way, we then came front and center.

I then announced, "You have to realize that Naomi and I prevail as experts at fighting in the vampire way. Naomi can you show the basic defensive position, then we'll show the attack. I will assure you that we demonstrate this because our races can pick things up quickly. Most of the human race have to be taught one thing at a time. Kitty, I know you don't need this, but I also know Andy does, so please just stick with us as we train. After this first part is done, then you and he can go off on your own."

Naomi then got into a certain on the verge of sitting position, I then picked up a bokken to help me. I then walked around as I had them do it one at a time, with that I used the bokken to straighten them up as a likely tool. After I was satisfied we started movements, too many it would have looked like simple Karate, it wasn't. Then we moved to the attack since I was better at this, Naomi now took my place. For two hours we moved back and forth if you had ever seen a dojo we looked like a well trained one.

With the end, I stood up and pronounced, "Kitty go ahead and take Andy off for his version of good training."

She then did as I said, so I then also added, "Tony take Joe, Cheryl, Pepper, Liz, and Paul with you. You will have to make two teams since we don't know where Joe is. I suggest making him a team leader, then you have the essential details that he'll be the after leader. So I suggest Cheryl and Paul on his team, that means Liz and Pepper will be on the fore team. You may want to assert extra training with everyone, I mean go through all the numbers. Do you know what we need?"

He then replied, "Yeah, I think so. Can I keep the weapons you lent us?"

I had to smile as I said, "Of course. Do you want my canon too?"

He shook his head as he had them all move off, that know only left six of us here. I then said, "Cibilia, Mary, and Sammy come here, I want Naomi and Bert to show you their fighting style."

So with that, they all did as I had told them, Naomi then had to say. "We aren't going to hold back like we usually do."

With this the two of them start to throw each other around, you could easily see how their fur seemed to rise as they got into it. I had been pointing out the reason why we legitimately didn't want to be next to them. Once they were done I moved to my car quickly and retrieved a long black bundle. Then we got the bokken, and each started to swing. I went around and showed them what they did wrong, and I also struck them if they held back.

I knew I had certainly created more than their

share of bruises. I did have a surprise as Sammy seemed to be better at countering my strikes. Once we had done this for another two hours, I had everyone come in to discern the facts of what just happened. Now we moved the seats back, and the last two had to tell me they couldn't find Andy or Kitty. I had to smile at this as I had to sit them all down, as they were finally done.

Now I took out the black bundle, and as I unwrapped it I explained. "Okay now. We don't have the tools I would love for all of you, but as we get in the thick of things we'll need hard-hitting weapons." Now I pulled out of the small bag my abomination, though I was sure they had no idea about this. As came into full view a sheathed Katana sword, and with that I allowed the flat gray blade to be seen.

Then as I allowed them to look at it closely I warned, "Don't let the blade cut you, wherever it does I can guarantee won't heal even with drinking blood."

Naomi came close and looked with an inquiry, "Oh wow. Is that what I think it is?"

I nodded my head as I said, "I just call it the vampire killer today, better than to know its real name." I then said to Naomi, "Would you like to do the honors as we definitely need the other elder here."

Naomi then excepted the challenge, "Kitty and Andy allow them to know where you are."

Liz essentially jumped out of her seat with a loud scream, and Mary said in a loud voice. "Oh, Shit!"

Liz had gotten poked by a needle that Kitty had

given to Andy. Kitty seemed to just appear in front of Mary, and I mean like nose to nose.

I put my hand out as I said, "Kitty will you please take your seat?" She did as I had asked so I went on, "Now what they can do isn't invisibility, but dang close enough. They have the ability to cause you not to see them, the term is technically called obfuscating. If you're good enough you can catch them, most have no idea what to look for in what can be seen. I had to figure that Kitty made it easy, though I do believe a butcher knife would have been too much."

Kitty then requested, "Boy Toy telling Blue Countless Angel me be sorry."

Andy then said, "I'm sorry Liz, Kitty told me to stick the one I ended up by real hard."

I then had to amend that with, "Like I said, thank god it wasn't a butcher knife. This was done to explain and help out the two of them with their abilities. You can see how potent this kind of surprise can be, now we haven't been able to do this all together. I do hope that the main teams have seen enough to realize how we can be together. I will tell you this, to be honest, usually, the capes hire our kind, Naomi and me, to be at each other's throat."

Naomi then explained, "That is why John had you watch us train, and we then watch you do the same. Bert and you three now know why we have to watch for each other, it can get messy. Tony?"

He got up and elucidate to, "We didn't train with them, but I had to show all of you why we do certain things. Now as you already know with what Joe has told me, normally Cheryl and Paul will get sniper rifles. This frees up Pepper and Liz to use assault rifles, we still have no idea what we'll get from this Giaus guy. John, do you want it from here?"

I nodded my head as I continued, "Tony's right, and because we have no idea, we'll split up our two most powerful teams. Naomi and I have no idea of our path even yet, we'll come from the sides though. This means that all of you will have to lay the best pattern as you can, did he explain combat shooting?"

I had to look at them as they all nodded, "Okay, now this can't necessarily kill, it's just to get as many targets as possible." I place one foot on a chair, then leaned on my leg. "Usually we try to kill as many as possible, this time our target is a person. None of us knows this person, yes, so I will not waste a life on whoever this is. You get into trouble, you back off as best as you can."

I then got up as I moved to Kitty and placed my hand on her shoulder. "Now as you think of this, that means Kitty and Andy will start in trouble. Like I said I will not lose one person, so don't mind me if I keep going toward Kitty. That means you lose a step, you have to at least try to catch up to her in the end."

Naomi then came in, "Me too. Now when we get there her and Andy will be securing her, so all of us have to also move forward. Tony and Joe as you get there make a circle around them as best as you can. Remember we don't want to lose anyone, you may ask if this can happen?"

I had to add this part, "It could and presumably will, even as we will try hard to save you." I then had to say with a contrite voice, "Is this whoever worth one of your lives, I would have to say no. So why can this be so important to us? We need things like gasoline, though we could just fight with knives. Know that every elder will try to keep you alive as best as we can, but one last thing. Look at the person next to you, and ask if you can protect them."

I made sure everyone has to be peering around as I finally pronounced. "Okay, the last few hours are all yours, party it up all you want."

Chapter Six

The real party before the dawn.

When it comes to things to do, there legitimately wasn't that much for kids. I mean we didn't even own a deck of cards, though just playing around and doing the grab butt thing was popular. Then I had seen that thing that had caused so many problems, and with that Kitty was right there with another tape. I came to that point right away, I also had to call out loudly with asseveration toward the possible.

"Does anyone have any kind of music we can listen too?!"

I knew the way we were bonded it undoubtedly couldn't happen again, well it can in a technical sense. Just I felt it wasn't appropriate to break the new bonds we had now. I did understand that this may have hurt Kitty's feelings, I'm sure all saw my resolved for it not to transpire again.

Cibilia then acknowledged, "I'll go get what Pepper and I brought with us."

With that, she was out of the room, and Naomi decided to inform me. "I have some old Motown tunes, I just thought these children may have been too young to enjoy them."

I had to nod my head in agreement as I confirmed, "I'm sure you're right there, but it would be enjoyable to hear some Smokie. And of course the many others."

She then asked, "You want me to go out and get something?"

I had to set her in place, "No. We can save that for a later date, maybe make a party of it also."

Cibilia then came into the room carrying a case of tapes, and Peppers was right there saying to all. "I think you will love this one right here."

Cibilia seemed to get frustrated right away, "Pepper not again."

I remembered the other night before the incident Pepper had picked the music. So I determined, "Cibilia it is your turn since Pepper chose the other night."

Pepper then complained, "Noo! She'll pick something unmistakably dark!"

I then supplemented, "It is okay Cibilia, though

maybe something we can dance too. I mean I wouldn't want to start a dance with a song no one can dance too."

She then looked carefully and then proclaimed, "Ah! God is in the rain, it is hard, but even Pepper loves to dance to this one."

I now looked at Liz and said, "I want to dance, but we may have to watch them so we can catch up with their style."

She then replied, "Sounds like a good title, but I'm sure you're right or at least follow as best as we can."

With that I watch the two of them seem to stretch, so I figured we had to do the same thing. Tony joined Cibilia as Paul did the same with Pepper, then this uncommonly melodic tone appeared to start. It had this particularly strange sort of vibration to it, and the term godlessness kept repeating. Though they did give the feeling to start to move their hands weirdly, then came this authentically hard beat.

With that they seemed to move their knees relatively without their hips, I had never moved like this before in my existence. They also moved their arms in turn, and Liz and I were trying desperately hard to follow along with the beat. I could see that both Paul and Tony were having the difficulties we were having. Then I looked over at Andy and Kitty, oh my Lord they were naturals at this.

I could also see Cheryl taking Joe out to the dance, and she literally started it out with an extreme motion. You could ask why I had to figure it should be the other way around, well because I had never seen anything like this beforehand. I couldn't believe how natural it seemed for the ladies, even Liz by now seemed to be picking it up as fast as anyone there. In seconds I decided to try and add a few of the dance steps I did know, and I had everyone now stepping and whirling. Don't get me wrong, I'm not sure I had been doing any good.

In fact, I even found a few 60's moves that seemed to work, as we were approximately moving as one. Now nothing unusual absolutely happened, but I want to relate this because of how quickly the entire room was dancing to this music. I can also say I did sort of like this music, though I would find out I like true heavy metal even better. Whereas Liz would find that she enjoyed what Pepper did even more.

This was not a division within the house, as I could even see Naomi had been truly getting into this stuff. I can also say in a long time I had not seen as many smiling faces. Cibilia and Pepper went around helping those that had difficulties. Soon we were all moving surprisingly similarly, Liz and I changed up enough to tell you we were always dancing. Not that I can say we were legitimately following what would be known as Industrial dance.

I can also tell you we were doing the best we could, with twists of the arms, and overhand turns. You also have to understand that if I had weapons this would be a legitimately good training song. I even had to show some of the moves I did to Liz and then showed the battle moves. This I think made here as happy as it seemed to me, as we even moved in tight with our moves. Many accepted what they saw, and with some depredation, they assumed to do what we did.

Then there came the most obvious song that had changed everything. Well that and the entrance of another, as Cibilia apologized making a move to change the song. As it became silent except for giggling from everywhere, a voice came out of the dark hallway.

"I honked my horn but no one answered, so we decided to come in any way." Then William came into the room, "It appears we didn't have as long as I thought we would have, so the event will be on tomorrow." He then directed the few he had with him to come in as he asked, "Where shall I place this?"

I then directed, "Kids get a few chairs out so they can place their packages down somewhere."

With that everyone seemed to converge with chairs, and both Naomi and Kitty joined me. They started to place down three boxes, as William explained. "We were about to get a few weapons for you with certain pistols. The only sniper rifle we could get was a sorry one I regret."

He then presented a Nordic 22 sniper rifle, to be honest as what it was, it wasn't bad. Just it genuinely wasn't that effective against our kind, so looking at it in that sense it wasn't great. Then he took out a tapering form of an English broadsword, when I saw it I was elated. Though as I swung it I did realize that I already had my weapon. I had to look at my three as I then handed it to Cibilia, though that would be a problem.

I then said clearly, "Tony go through the ammo, Cheryl and Paul go through all the blood. All negative goes into the freezer, now for the thing, we need most, the money."

William then handed me a master card as he now added, "I was able to place a hundred fifty dollars on here, Giaus has also told me to tell you this. We are attempting to straighten this out, as soon as we can, the rest of your money will be placed on there. Now he isn't shorting you on this, but apparently, we have reached our limit for new cards. He wants you to beg his forgiveness, and hopes that it is at least enough to start."

I then looked at Cheryl as she had set all this up, "What do you think Cheryl?"

She then came over in front of him and exclaimed, "You know this isn't the proper way to work things, but we can give you a break. So instead of charging you interest now, we'll give you twenty-four hours to straighten this out then we'll charge you the remainder of what was agreed."

He had to admit, "I know you're right, what will be your interest if we can't get this straightened out?"

She looked at me as I had to say, "William you know the proper percentage rate is fifty percent, and that is a given as well as you understand."

"I know, but this is so unusual for us, we have never had these problems before this time. Can't you give us a break?"

I was about ready to cut it in half, but Cibilia beat me to it. "I'll tell you what, if the House agrees to it, we can give you thirty percent as it is unusual." With that, she looked around the room, with everyone nodding she then directed Cheryl. "Cheryl finish this out, but everyone has said yes to thirty."

I watched as Tony went through the ammo boxes, and they seemed to have given into all our demands. I did have my own thing to do, as Cibilia had to give up the sword for her lighter blade. By this time I had them move outside and now had Mary swinging the blade. Tony then also brought out a long knife as William was leaving, I then handed it to Mary. She seemed to do far better than I had hoped, as I came close to Tony.

I asked, "He doesn't look that happy, I take it Cheryl did well for us again?"

He had to smile as he simply said, "Thirty percent with three vials of elder blood, can you believe it?"

"Wow," I had to proclaim. Then said to Sammy, "Sammy swing this I want to see how well you do."

Now came something great, as he squared up without my help. Then he seemed to just know how to use it, I had to have wide eyes as I saw this. Even within my surprise, I had to ascertain, "Sammy you are honestly good with that. I have to ask have you ever used one of those before in your life?"

He then told me the truth, "When I was young I thought of myself as a knight of old, so I joined a group that trained to fight with these kinds of weapons. I do have to admit I didn't think I would be this good with it, I mean it has been years ago."

I then had to tell him, "You remember me telling all of you how easily it is for us to pick things up especially from our past?" He nodded his head so I went on, "Well it is also the same for old knowledge that we thought we had lost, what we used to know implies to come to the forefront when we need it. As a human, you may have known, but in practice just barely been able to do that. As you are now it gives the impression to come as we can barely grasp things, though one thing, it is better to aim for the neck."

He smiled at me as he affirmed, "I can assure you I can do that as well."

I then said, "Okay girls you'll be on the inside, that means the closest to where Tony's crew will be. Sammy and I who have the big hitters will be on the outside, so we'll be the ones hanging here. Naomi and Bert will be out in front of us but also originated between us, so keep your space. Now let's go inside so we can see what we're up against in this situation."

As we walked in Tony had to ask, "John what about the girls, I mean Liz and Pepper, they'll be forced to be on the outside as well."

Naomi then came up with a map as she said, "Simple, as my guess is that he has the ladies toward you. This means you set them as Pepper toward Cibilia, they'll protect each other because they're sisters. Mary and Liz will want to protect all, but they're also pragmatic enough to know to come to each other's defense. That means that Cheryl behind Mary will stand her ground for Mary, and the only unsure thing is how Paul feels for Cibilia."

Tony looked noticeably surprised, "Wow, is that how you had set everything up in the end?"

Okay. I hadn't, but that sounded so great, so I had

to add one more thing. "Paul will defend her because from what I have seen he honestly likes Cibilia, not that he has any problem being with her sister. This will add to his wanting to defend her for Pepper's sake, and of course, Pepper will be right in front of him. Now let me see what we have?"

"Genius." was what he said.

Not genuinely, but it felt good. So as we looked at the map I had to also assert, "Tomorrow we break up between yours and my vehicle, we also need gas though. Cheryl and Paul will pump the gas, Tony you allow Pepper and Liz to pay for it, or maybe just one." Kitty came up then and I said, "How long do you need Kitty?"

Kitty then replied, "Twenty mikes sir!"

She in point of fact stood at attention as she said this, I nodded my head as I had to admit. "Sounds good to me, we'll presumably need the same Tony, then you need to move. What was his time frame, Naomi?"

Pepper then said as she read an actual letter, "This reads three hours from sunset, we may have to look into that."

Then she pulled out her phone so I went on as I looked at the map. "That means battle dress right after we wake up, no high heels as this looks like a field. Got that Cibilia and Pepper?"

"Hey, these aren't . . ."

Pepper cut her off with, "Sunset is at six thirty tomorrow, should I set my phone?"

I had to take a look at her phone as I had to admit, "I didn't know a phone could do that."

"Well old phones couldn't, these new smartphones are great. Now you can get on the internet anywhere, it's like having the information highway in your hand. Oh, and Cibilia shoes aren't literally high heeled shoes, they're more like wedges."

I had to ask, "Can she fall off them and make terrible sounds when she falls?"

"Well yeah."

In truth I knew she had only said this in defense of her sister, I think many siblings would do that. I turned to Cibilia as I said, "My order even stands for wedges, is that clear?"

She nodded her head as Mary had to ask, "That is for all of us then too, am I right?"

"Yes. I just directed it toward them because they appear to have a propensity to wear higher heels."

"John you're our teacher, you have to learn to include everyone. Not that you have ever shown favoritism, but directed to a single person and someone may think they can get away with something."

I now turned to her with a smile as I admitted, "I stand corrected, no one should be wearing higher than one-inch heels. If you can get lower the better, as we don't want anyone to give us away anytime sooner than needed. Is that clear?"

Naomi had to laugh as she asserted, "If that were me, John, I would have yelled, then corrected myself."

I had to laugh as well as I knew I would have normally done the same thing. I then added, "Okay, we have . . ."

As I looked at my watch Pepper interjected, "Forty-three minutes till sunrise."

Man, they were getting to know me so well as I had to continue, "We need to load magazines till then, so let's get after it."

With that, the boxes hit the floor, and weapons came out like they should have in the end. Tony also went after every extra magazine he could find. I then showed them an easy way to load the devices, and within moments we had a chain going. Cheryl and Paul also helped after they made sure everyone had a bag of blood. They did have to ask if the fresher blood was better. Tony told them the truth as all blood does the same.

It is also true that fresher blood does taste far better, so they decided to go with that. Tony seemed to be so good at this I had to ask as we decided in making him the leading teacher and that all curriculum would go through him. Most agreed with my assessment, with the usual back and forth about it. As usual, it was Liz that led all the pros and cons about it. She also had to point out he wasn't even close to being a true elder. I literally think that helped them out more over their decisions than anything else.

Once we got done with this we all move to our

rooms, it has been truly amazing how well we seemed to work together. Liz and I came into our room, it had been genuinely surprised how familiar we were with each other. What I mean is that she seemed to not have the same misgivings of undressing in front of me. Then as we laid next to one another it was so easy to talk about our days. When it came to close our eyes, I pulled her closer as I knew this is what she wanted.

You could ask if we did more, as I have said before, I honestly don't like to talk what a man and a woman do in private. So none of your business.

Don't allow John to fool you, he has a real gentle spirit on the verge of being like a big Teddy bear. I did have to prompt him as he was still afraid to go too far with me as my old profession. We did get into things, all the same as before, with a few new tricks he showed me. I will honor him and not get into all that, but I'm sure you can use your imagination.

Oh. One more thing he'll hate me telling you, he is a real gentleman in bed as well. I think that is why I learned to love him so much. One more thing, he has most of the tricks in the early stages, we are relatively equal in the tricks we have shown one another.

Chapter Seven

The fire can be worse than the squabble.

Day Nine

It was uncanny how they seemed to think of everything, not that I had any doubts. I had to allow things to go through my mind as I went through a literal list. Well, and how I unquestionably didn't want to disturb Liz, not that she could have been woken from her slumber. She was an extraordinarily surprising woman, as I had to ask once last night if she was okay with all of this. I did have to explain as it did come out at the most inappropriate times.

I loved her answer as it seemed so simple. It is true that when I joined as an acolyte I swore to do no harm. I do believe that as long as I don't start it I'm fine, though the commandment reads; thou shalt not kill. With recent studies it was found out the word kill was incorrectly used, the actual word was supposed to be murder. I also understand that murdering is killing, the wanting defense to keep from being killed though does not constitute murder.

Then you have the essential part that within what we do, as sisters is what I mean. Our lives are dedicated to the service and help of others, with this it doesn't directly amend that notion. In the long run, it does help us get to the goal we desire, so with the mark of our end position. I do believe that I'm helping out the greater of the whole. So within this, we could say by doing this one service not added to the whole. I'm in a sense helping out the whole as it can be said and possibly saving a certain level of humanity.

Okay, I have to ask you. How do you argue with that? Not that I absolutely and truly wanted to, and with certainty, it had answered my question. So here I had been now knowing that sunset was soon coming, going through what we had gained. Now I hadn't gone through the pistols we had, but just from the glimpse, I saw I had to figure there was one for all. I also had to go through all the blades we had now, and I could see everyone with one also.

I had to whisper in a low tone, "I think he thought of everything."

To this came from Liz, "What was it he thought of everything?"

I had to ask, "Oh I'm sorry. Did I wake you?"

"Not legitimately," she answered, then asked,

"You didn't answer my question?"

"Oh, that William. I'm doing a mental inventory of all he brought."

"Well, I would be lying here thinking how wonderful last night was. Did you think last night was great or was it so much ho-hum?"

I had to chuckle as I replied, "Babe I used going through the inventory, so as not to turn you over and have my way with you. I mean I would love to right now also, but I also know sunset is wonderfully close and we would surely go past our time limit."

She had to giggle as she had to admit, "I do know with your age you have had plenty of women, then you have basically understand that I know absolutely nothing. It can't be an easy thing to always have to be showing things, and I do worry that I will become boring to you."

I had to admit to her, "When you love someone like we do, nothing can ever be truly boring. So when..."

She now cut me off, "John did you just use the L word?"

"Yeah, I guess I did. Is it okay?"

She turned to me as she had to point out, "You do realize that we are bonded, and yeah these feeling could be love. I do have to ask you as you know far better than I do. Can we literally give these feelings to genuine emotions, with the possible later effects of this bond?"

Okay, maybe she was right there, as I had to

virtually wallow in this assessment. "I guess I would have to say yes to that, even as we are excessively emotional creatures. I will also have to say as to the knowledge of this, it is hard to break free of this even within our own understanding. So I also think we have to give into them, even as you asserted if I'm right."

I had never been that much of an emotional creature, but I can tell you that my chest was exceedingly heavy right then. I can't tell you that what had been going on was absolutely love, even as it felt like my heart would have been ripped out of my chest. "I do believe if we are to do this right we must proceed like this until we're sure this feeling will never fade."

Was what she had to say, I had to sit up as I think I also slumped tolerably as I said to her. "Yeah. That may be the best thing to do for now, though I'm not sure this will fade."

Now I can also tell you that I felt like going into a corner, and well, doing what a person in my condition would do right now. With this, I had to suck it up so no one could see my true emotions right then. She then added to that, "Good, plus our minds genuinely have to be on what we need to do today."

This caused me to look at my watch as I could see we had maybe ten minutes left. So I stood up and worked noticeably hard at getting ready extremely fast. I can tell you that when I put my mind to it I can get dressed surprisingly fast. Not that any human could positively keep track of me, and I was at the door within about a minute. To us though sixty seconds is an eternity, and yes I mean I was clothed that fast.

I now stood at the door as I had to say, "Hurry up and get ready, we need to move as soon as possible."

With that, I now moved through and made sure every door received a good knock. Then I made it down to the kitchen and I placed out all the blood we would need. Then I placed out all the extra knives and pistols, labeling them all so everyone had one. Well except for Naomi and Bert as they legitimately didn't need them. With that as all, I could think of was done, I sat down heavily as I sincerely didn't want to think.

I do believe that everyone thought I was all business, as I made sure everyone got what they needed when they came into the room. There did have the appearance of having a general soberness to everyone, as we made to get all out on the road. Then as we made for the cars I wasn't honestly concerned where anyone sat. At first we just did as we could, finally Tony pulled me aside as things seemed to be whirling around in my head.

He had to slap my back as he had to ask, "What is wrong? Your head positively doesn't convey the impression of being in the game."

I then told him, "Oh nothing."

Naomi then came over and asked us, "Are you guys going to come, or are the two of you placing this on hold."

Tony waved her over and she seemed to come, and he had to confess. "Somethings wrong Naomi. I mean John says there is nothing, but he isn't his usual take-charge person."

Naomi took one look at me, with that she then spoke to him. "Go make sure everything is fine, I can talk to him."

So as he ran off she asked, "What's up with you?"

I told her to like him, "I'm fine, honestly!"

"Undoubtedly?!" She asked, then in return she added, "I could see you weren't when I came out, but even you know we can't go into this if you aren't a hundred percent. If anyone truly knows this, there is no one like you."

I had to admit she was right, so I took a big intake and said. "I'm fine now. I just had been realizing how many we may not see tonight, and to be truthful it made me feel melancholy. With as long as I have been around I have never had a chance to reason through this until after they were dead."

Of course, I had lied, but I was the big bad enforcer, I had to get with the program. So I then shook off what had happened and I started to bark orders. I will also explain that my feelings truly didn't disappear, as we now moved with purpose. When you feel something so new to you it can cause you to be as it had been misplaced. The major problem when I get this way is that people tend to die, well be destroyed.

We already had a plan so we moved to the gas station, and as we parked. I could see that Liz was at the edge of the door, so I had to wonder as I asked. "Why are you just sitting there Liz?"

She looked at me as she replied, "I have to wait till

Pepper gets done, then I'm to exchange the card with her as I then pay for gas."

So I had to ask, "Why didn't Tony just have one of you pay for the gas? That is why I added the statement or one."

I think even Liz had thought about that, as all she did was shrug as she now moved out to her task. With this I watched closely, things did suggest the appearance to work out like clockwork, so I had no problem with that. I also watch Paul as he had been finishing up Naomi's vehicle, as I couldn't legitimately look at Cheryl at the rear of my car. Liz then got out so Cheryl could get into the back seat because this was a set event we had no real reason how we got out of our cars.

We finally came to a stop at the appointed place, and we had set to park separately for ease of protection. I had to look after Kitty as she took off, I made a note on my watch with the time. I had to wonder how many of these youngsters would not be coming back today. I also had to get what Tony's reason was for what I saw at the gas station.

So I inquired, "Tony as I said Liz and Pepper, or possibly just one. I have to ask why you went with two instead of my later suggestion of just one?" He looked at me as if he were in trouble so I added, "I just want to know, you aren't in trouble or anything. Plus everything seemed to go so much smoother than I thought also, so I see no damage."

He then did as I asked, "Well I had thought of the two choices, and after a reasonable amount of discussion with Pepper it genuinely made sense. I mean the cars were over full, with that sight the clerk may have gotten suspicious. Pepper had told me how they used to take trips all the time when she was younger. What struck me was that she thought they had never fooled the clerks. I had to think on that with things like spring break, those clerks doubtlessly never thought of it like that. You know sort of like a kid abusing their mommy or daddy's card."

Okay, that did amuse more or less as I had to say, "Well Tony I have to give it to you, that was rather smart, also to the point of genius yourself."

Naomi now hit him on the back as she agreed, "Well done you!"

I now had to turn to the girls as I said, "Liz you will be in the air until you see Mary, now she may need your help. Whatever you do don't cross her line, she may accidentally do what she honestly doesn't want to be doing in the end. Mary keep an eye out for her, you'll know things are about ready to start with seeing her. Cibilia and Pepper I would tell you the same, there is an unwritten word that I do believe you understand."

Naomi then came in with, "Sammy I know we have said this over and over, when Bert and I get into it, we can lose our own identity. What you and Mary can do to Pepper and Liz is terrible, the worst part is when we go at it things can truly get stretched. The reason why we say this is it is possible we could extinguish two of us if this happens. Not that neither John or I want to do this, that is why we tell you this."

Now I looked at Pepper as I had to assert, "Pepper we need to look at each other's clocks so we can do this right. I have just over five minutes before we leave."

Naomi then interjected, "We go in a straight line till we turn, when I turn in you'll have about twenty feet forward to walk. Bert and I will be out front, so Sammy you'll have to watch for me. Pepper and Liz you'll have to follow us at like twenty feet when you see us turn inwards this is your time to come and tell Tony. He already understands not to move for twenty minutes, we'll set out time as well waiting as we may be early."

Pepper and I had set our clocks as I wanted to say one last thing. "Bert and Cibilia get down immediately, you need to watch each other. When I and Sammy are set we'll give a slight wave, Bert will give that to you Cibilia. Now Mary Naomi knows to do this so just keep an eye out for her will you. When you see Pepper and Liz getting close Mary and Cibilia give a big wave just in case. Now, this is for Liz and Pepper, the rest of us will keep on the little waves."

I saw that I literally didn't have any time, so I stood up and said quietly. "This means to get up and be ready to move, now we have to get into place."

With this we did as I had said, that meant that I was in the lead. I had to walk also listening to the noise they were making, in truth we as vampires don't make much noise. I had to think we were right as they weren't making any use of our natural stealth. So I placed my hand down so Cibilia knew to stop here, and then Bert and I moved onward. We then moved out as things got flatter, I then pointed at the edge of the light.

He seemed to know what I meant, and as I got into place I gave my wave. I was particularly happy to see that he did exactly as I had hoped, as he now waved to Cibilia.

Now it was time for me to pull out my cannon, as I pulled my Desert Eagle. I made sure it was well loaded, even as I also knew I had one more particularly full magazine. I then reached back and unsecured the leather strap on my sword.

Then I decided to look at my watch to see where we were and realized my one mistake. With our enhanced eyes, I could see my watch, but it would have been so much better if I had at least glow in the dark numbers. To be truthful, as I had never worked with others, I had no use for one save to tell the time. Finally, I saw something, this caused me to look at Bert to ascertain things. Seconds later I could see his slight wave, and I stood up to see what had been going on around me.

I then directed him to move forward, and I had to hope he knew to be slow. I mean we legitimately couldn't trip this before Kitty was ready to start the action. Now came something I hadn't thought I would hear, especially with all the precautions we had taken. I heard someone say a four letter word, loudly I may add, though I couldn't recognize the voice. All heads seemed to turn to the sound, I knew this was bad, though I had no idea who could have in point of fact been there.

It never takes me long to react when we're in trouble, as my canon now went off in a good report. You may think it was by mistake by the way I said that I can assure you the vamps head that seemed to disintegrate unquestionably wasn't happy. Of course, this caused them to all look at me, with a sudden howl they had to know something was up beyond what was their norm. There would be no doubting it that Naomi allowed me to know she had been starting things as well.

I didn't wait to assess the situation as my weapon went off again, and now a few were coming toward me. Bert then seemed to jump a few with claws out, it was easy to hear that other weapons were now showing their reports. I now moved rapidly as I loosed what was left in my magazine, and they closed in on my position. I had to wonder if they were reacting to this, as a few went to where they had something staked out to the ground.

I know placed my pistol away rapidly and retrieved my blade off my back. I loved this because in the dark it absolutely appeared to smoke, now it didn't, but you can see how that would spook a few. Then I started to wade through them with a blade that never seemed to flash. As a matter of fact, in a lot of ways, it seemed to be devoid of anything, less it touched someone. Swiftly I could hear the report of what had to be semiautomatic fire.

I can tell you that caused me to smile, which also seemed to cause people to take a few steps back. Kitty and Andy were right on time with their excitement, and you could easily see the turn of things. Now I could see here near whatever was staked down, and there would be a few mounds lying there. It was easy to see that she had given a few extra smiles, as their heads were no longer there.

With this, because it was easy to see them I held my ground until I was sure Naomi and Bert had passed. I then had Mary and Cibilia wait behind as we now followed Bert and Naomi. We got to a point where we were sure they were completely on the run. I then barked orders for Mary and Sammy to help clean the area up, then return to us when Naomi told them. Cibilia and I know turned back toward the group, and we made our way so we could take care of ambushes.

Finally, I met up with Tony and had to ask, "Where is Kitty? I expected her to be with you."

He then replied, "There has to be something honestly wrong John, she ordered me off and to find you. I think it has to do with that mound staked down to the ground."

Now I also barked at him, "Send Pepper out with her sister Cibilia, find Giaus as soon as possible. I think we may need him, also make sure everyone else is secure. Then keep an eye out for the others as they come back in toward this finish. If you see Naomi tell her we need her as soon as possible also."

With this I used my full speed and was there in a blink, to be truthful I don't know if Liz had seen it. I had been standing next to her as I had to ask, "How long has Kitty been doing that?"

As I took off my coat she seemed to jump out of her skin, then she recovered. "Since Tony left looking for you. I think he knows what's going on, but he didn't say anything. What's she doing?"

I then handed her my coat with my weapons as I answered here. "Keeping her alive. We can cause some healing, but at this state, it'll take an eminently large infusion of real human blood here."

She did her best to carry my stuff as she asked, "Why? I mean if I understand our blood can heal humans, why not us?"

I came close to Andy as I had to ask first, "Is she alright?" I then turned to her as I answered, "Our blood causes their blood to work far better, and with the combination, we can heal humans yes. We still need the reaction of the blood, because we drank earlier we still have some of that reactivity in our own blood."

While I explained to her Andy reasoned, "Not long, though if I remember she has maybe another five minutes."

I came close as I had to ask her, "Is he right Kitty?"

She shook her head as Liz asked, "Why don't we just go and get that guy?" I started to roll up my shirt sleeves as she added, "Maybe we can just make a line of donors till he can get here."

I now sat next to Kitty as I had to tell her, "We don't know how old she is, if she is too old she could drink you dry. I'm having Naomi come in as fast as she can, but we're even going to have to be careful with her. As we just don't know." I then had to say in no uncertain terms, "You indubitably need to go and help Tony, Andy go as far out as you feel comfortable. Are you ready Kitty?"

With this she pried her mouth off her, I brought her close to me as I now allowed her to lock onto me.

Chapter Eight

When things are the final, we then confess our past.

Excerpt from

Twilight Voices

by William Allingham

Now, at the hour when ignorant mortals
Drowse in the shade of their whirling sphere,
Heaven and Hell from invisible portals
Breathing comfort and ghastly fear,
Voices I hear;
I hear strange voices, flitting, calling,
Wavering by on the dusky blast, –
"Come, let us go, for the night is falling;
Come, let us go, for the day is past!"

Her mouth in this basic hunk of sinew with no
actual flesh could be seen starting to putrefy. If it wasn't

for her aspiratory response, there would be no way to recognize she endured. I understood her to be female with a few perceptible apperceived within this same said filaments. With the also realization of Giaus's relatively mundane use of her or she, his resource had been truly nothing.

It was also effortless to perceive that our sanguine fluid would merely be maintaining her existence. Our intent was that she could hang on until the aforementioned person did arrive. I also understood there would be soon slight effects to the effect of her own sanity. Inside me as I had to wonder if there is such an important concern for her dispossession. That was within sight as I also had to place what relevance she seemed to have to him as well as us.

With this, I had to look at Liz and convey, "If I black out to make sure my arm comes out of her mouth. I also know you're proud of helping others, so listen to me carefully. Whatever you think of, or how noble you think you may be. Do not replace your arm as to mine, I mean no. Like I told you we have no way of knowing her age, I can assure you her pull is extremely strong, even as disposed as she is. What we do know is for some reason Giaus has an interest in her, and he reeks of being an ancient."

I had to move the little hair she had away from her face, as she had been drinking deeply. I could also ascertain that the little true vital fluid we did have would be doing its work. It would only be recognizable to our eyes, as modulus of flesh were now appearing. I could hear the sudden sound of excessively quiet foot-pads, this caused me to look in that direction. The darkness had been a jumble as my sight cleared, with the running approach of both Bert and Naomi.

My vision locked on to Naomi as she closed, "You may have to spell me soon, though you will have to watch unusually closely." I had to look at her as she had been still drawing in, "I can tell by her draw that she is old, to which is her real age, I can't tell you. So try to gauge her draw as you are that old, though she may be closer to your age I have surmised."

Kitty then interjected, "Noie. Wild Child will spell the great harlequin again, I neew me hab da little." She then got a little closer as she added, "She older, though stinky not be the oldest lessie, so to upedy in dar. Kinky isn't the truth, these be the days ta Kitty be inny and outy."

Okay, I understood she honestly didn't want Naomi for some reason to spell me. Then I think she meant that she was older, but not old enough for this one. I had to think that little part was to tell me Naomi thought she was tougher than she was. I also knew Kinky to them means strange things, though with that last part I was totally lost. I then directed Liz to come close, and she did as I directed her.

I then whispered to her, "Kitty has seen something bad if Naomi helps out this person, but if we continue on we will need blood. Make sure you are right there when Giaus shows up, we'll need blood desperately. Also, tell Andy to be ready to carry Kitty, she might not have the strength to walk."

She whispered back, "What about you?"

I assured her, "Oh I will be able to walk, though I may need guiding as I will have to concentrate solely on that."

It was now my turn to pry my arm out of her mouth and to allow Kitty to take over again. Now as old as we were we could doubtlessly do this several times, though I also have to admit blood loss is that which we no longer have. So as we set there I had to worry about another fight, then as I stood I heard a low rumble. That was surely not a good thing, so I turned to Naomi as I had to give the warning.

"Naomi we need to start to move, it may be easier to find us near the road. Let's pick her and well help her up and move as rapidly to the road as possible."

This now caused Andy to come in, of course with reasonable assistance from Liz. Mary was right there so I had her go ahead and help Andy with Kitty. Naomi and I then picked up the other body, which I'm happy to say started to feel as if it were gaining weight.

I then said to Liz, "Go to the road and keep an eye out for that limo driving up on us Liz."

We were getting close to the road as Liz seemed to just appear out of no where. I could see she had been carrying something in her arms, as I now saw the decidedly first big flash with a low rumble. Seconds later William was there as he helped us carry the lady now, and Andy had broken the ladies grip on her arm. Liz gave Kitty a bag as Andy now helped her walk to the cars, while we changed direction as William now directed.

Liz was on the spot with the remainders of the bags, as she seemed to literally inhale them. We made it to where Williams car was now parked, as he now broke into his trunk for more blood. I swear it was right then that the limo came speeding up, as it came screeching to a halt. I could see that Cibilia and Pepper had done their jobs exceedingly well, as they now bailed out of the limo. I could also see that Cibilia had a few excessively small vials, and she right away uncorked one and literally just poured it down her throat.

Giaus was essentially with us as fast as the girls were, I then told Naomi to make sure everyone was in the cars. Then as I had said that I had to wonder if I had been too late, as a stream came across the sky. As to all things, the fully blasted radius of sound now filled the air, to the point as it retreated was ever so quiet. With this I had to look directly at him in charge, this acknowledgment was clear as we all understood.

This caused us to do our jobs, as I barked orders for all not helping to return to the cars. With my enhanced hearing I could hear it getting close, so we did as we could. Naomi was cleared as it was just Mary and me now, we set her with a mess of blood and guts on his fastidious upholstery. He now did me justice as he gave me a bottle of blood, not that I could drink it as in a hurry as we were. Now we turned and I had to tell her we had to move at speed, so we did as we could.

It was also easy to see on our approach that there were others in our driver seats. They saw us and started to move, Mary was concerned about this.

I then explained, "We need this as to how close the storms are, just use your speed to get close to the cars. I'm sure Naomi has already instructed someone to give us a hand. Allow them to help us, but you also help yourself as soon as you can get a grip on something solid."

I was right there as I saw a brown hand, I then locked my thumb and used one final leap. Now my other hand that wasn't locked onto his hand, secured the part that held my side view mirror in place. These two now allowed me to leave the ground, as I made my way into my car head first. I did have to wonder who could be driving my car, except I had a much more pressing matter at hand.

So I looked over as from behind me came, "Oh good, I was worried she wasn't going to make it."

I looked at her as it was Liz and ascertained, "Did you see if Mary made it in time?"

She nodded her head, "Yeah, Naomi had her, then I saw Sammy reach out, and he just pulled her in with one pull."

That made me profoundly happy as I then said, "Good for Sammy, I think he is going to be a good additive to our family."

This is about the time I looked at who was driving, and at that emphatically particular time, the loudest crack of thunder hit us. I could easily see that Cibilia had been doing the best she could, then again she also seemed to be driving by the seat of her pants. So I then moved over so Bert could take the window, I then moved my foot to the gas so we could keep going. With that because of how small she was, we did the change over with her going over me.

Now it would have been extraordinarily easy, though I now had to say she undoubtedly loved those honestly high boots. I mean she seemed to have the time to change out of the tennis shoes she had been in for the battle. With this Bert indisputably had to help her get one of the boots passed my foot on the gas peddle. Once we finally made the full transfer I realized I could have taken my foot off the peddle. I mean we were positively driving into this squall that had been working up to our detriment.

Now as a way I tried to outrun this storm, even as I knew eminently well that would never happen. Liz had made her move to more of the middle of the back seat, and I could barely see her profoundly white knuckles. I knew I had been driving way to fast if we were humans, though we aren't, and only fire would matter in a crash. I did have to say loudly, "Hold we're going for it."

She then complained, "John can you please just slow down some?!" When she realized that Naomi was just barely maybe forty feet in front of us. She had to add to this, "Do all of you elder vampires drive like maniacs?!"

I then had to assure her, "No. What we are moderately wary of the oncoming storm, as you get older you will understand."

"John!" With that screech, Joe whom kept her from getting behind me whispered to her. I had to think he had read all about it, as finally, she came back with, "Oh I see. John, you could have told me that you know!"

With that a curtain of rain hit us, and I took my foot off the gas. As I then said without taking my eyes off the road, "Would you rather me drive safer, or try to explain to you while I tried to drive safely?"

She then confirmed, "Well drive safer, but it is

stressful not knowing."

With that, we came skidding around the final corner, as I had to say with a warning. "We aren't slowing down fast enough, everyone hold on as we may hit the back of the garage."

I knew I could do this, though it has been an extremely long time since I have had too. With this, we made the corner of the driveway and slid somewhat into the lawn. The rear-end now fishtailed tolerably, I worked hard at keeping control. Now came the time I had to apply the breaks, and I had to hope they did their job. I could now see everyone clearing to one side as there was no real stopping us now.

As we broke the plane of the doors you could hear the tires catching the dry pavement. I was terribly happy because even though we did hit the back of the garage it wasn't hard enough to harm my car. Now we had them all bail out of the car, and I immediately moved to the front of the car to assess the damage. I do believe that if my car was modern instead of made in 1969 there would have been far more damage.

Now with a whoosh, the wind came in brushing in the rain, as Naomi hurried them all into the house. I then joined her as I would be forcing people to move also, I think they were all afraid. I mean they all knew we had hurried for a reason, and we would tell them when we got into the house. As we got the extensively last through the back door, Liz had been standing right there with her arms crossed.

Then she had to ask, "Is it true that we're supposed to be afraid of the rain?"

I had to look at Joe and also ask him, "Joe what did you tell her?"

He came back with, "That as a race we tend to be scared of thunderstorms for some reason. I couldn't go any further than that because I just barely read the title; Why we are forced to avoid thunderstorms and all the reasons why."

I had to look at Liz as I had to correct what was told to her, "We aren't scared of thunderstorms, just the results that can happen, and why we created the impression to attract lightning. Now let us get away from any windows from the direction of the storm."

With that, they all did as I said, though I also think that Liz had been partially confused with what I pronounced. I was surprised that Liz and Mary were the last two through the door. I would find out later that they were talking about a certainty that if I had known would have made me nervous. My concern wasn't what they were talking about right at that time, so we just moved into the room. Pepper had moved to get a few towels, once Paul had seen this he did the same thing. He was eminently good at following her lead, though I truly hated that, I could see that he and she would be extremely good together.

Paul now asked as he had been finishing handing out towels, "John we all heard what Joe has said, is any of that literally true?"

I had to give him some correct feedback, "Not exactly as it were, though in a sense it would be wise for anyone to be wary of a thunderstorm."

Naomi interjected, "Paul everyone can conduct electricity, we just have other things to worry about also."

Paul had to shake his head as he scrutinized the possible aspects, "You have to be kidding right?"

Tony then implied the facts, "Think about it, if we are to get rid of ourselves the best way is through inhalation. Lightning doesn't always cause a fire, but if it does, with that much damage what would we be able to do. We would become crispy critters, and we would have to just sit there and watch our ends. I can assure you nothing I legitimately want to do, and as we think, I'm sure you would want to either."

I then had to chuckle as I thought of the next thing, "I know you would have loved to get dry clothes on, instead of coming to this dusty room. I can also tell you it is better to know where the storm is, then trying to put on a shirt or a skirt. So until we're sure it has passed we'll stay here, then everyone will go to their rooms. Make it fast though, as we have no idea what's lining up behind it."

"I don't get it." Liz questioned? Then added, "Why?"

I had to figure we had the time, "Well this will keep us close to the center of the house, not that you will get hit by lightning. If you know your human factors you know that is a rare event." With this, she started to point at all the windows within the room. I had not literally thought of this, save they were away from the storm. So as to make a good place for us I made a search from room to room. To my noticeably own dismay, I had been learning that there were no rooms free of windows.

After this full understanding came to me, I had to amend what I had said. "Okay, maybe this isn't the true center of the house. So I guess we can make a move around the house, just try to make an effort to stay away from windows. I do think every floor landing has at least two chairs that will be helpful. If you think you may need it bring chairs with you."

She then said, "If you're that worried why don't we all just move to the basement. We can all take kitchen chairs down, and then all sit around in a fairly small group like campfire girls."

I had to admit even though I understood that Liz had been being sarcastic, her thought process may have been better than any of ours. "Okay, Liz I can see what you're saying, though within that you may have had a good idea. Everyone grab a kitchen..." I realized something right then, "Well dining room chair as we now move to the dining room, we will be staying away from the windows. Then as we may, we will allow rooms to go get changed."

With this, as we were already close, it had been an easy thing to do. The two of us Naomi and I did make an assessment of the room and saw that there was a small area that was best. This would be no meeting so as they got to set all the youngsters started to talk amongst themselves. Now to be truthful they honestly stood little chance of being hurt by a lightning bolt. So it was highly easy to understand why they didn't truly listen to the storm.

Now as to all the elders, as even Naomi has had enough blood to worry about this. As we drink blood we use everything of it, except for all that iron. Over the years it causes us to in a way become vampire lightning rods. Also as we get older we lose the blood in our system, as we become easier to ignite. Again there are the essential details that it is rare, though far less rare then for the children. You can just imagine that every one of us just watched the ceiling as the storm passed.

It is strange how we change, as I was young I loved to listen to it. It always seemed to have a way to lull us to sleep, though we have no worries of that today because we no longer truly slept. I was taken out of my certain aspect of thought as I saw Cibilia shaking her head.

So I had to ask, "What?"

Her response was, "Wow all of you are genuinely out of it. I mean if you took half a second you would realize the storm is letting up now."

I then moved to the window as I had to look around, "Naomi and I will check it out and see if it is all clear. I do think you're right, so everyone place your chairs where they need to go. Cibilia I want you to run everyone through their drills when they get redressed. Bert after her you do the same with what Naomi usually teaches. Joe, I want you to teach them after that as much as you can get away within an hour. Now anything that has to do with blood use isn't what I mean, just basic history and stuff like that. Now, Andy, you will have a class on hiding, you're teaching, not hiding yourself. Any problems and everyone comes to Tony, and he will see if we need to come back and help any of you."

They were typical kids as they seemed to give a

communal moan. I did get a couple of yes and okays from a few. We had no time to ascertain who said what as the two of us now moved out for this exercise. It was already apparent that we had truly waited too long, as it was already far in the distance.

Naomi then asked, "Do you think it will be far enough for Bert to do his work?"

I placed my hand up and concluded, "I'm not sure, you may want to be sure before he appropriately starts. He does have an hour though."

She then said with surprise in her voice, "JOHN!"

It was weird right then as I had to inquire, "What Naomi?"

She placed both hands on my shoulders as she responded, "You looked like you were going to fall. Even though we know how tough you are, I think giving that lady your blood took it out of you. I'm willing to bet Kitty is even worse, I want both you and her to drink some blood before we go on with training."

I smiled as I had to admit, "She did give a hint to take scarcely, I hope she hasn't passed the line. Then you have the essential part that I had to use adequately enough of that sanguine fluid to do a few of my feats. It is also true we can never tell when we overextend ourselves. Yeah, we may need passably of that vital liquid."

"The two of you have also been pushing yourselves for nine days straight. It is no wonder that either or at least both of you haven't failed yet."

Even as I am, I knew there was a lot of truth in what she had been saying. I had to add, "Hey I'm not the only one here, I have seen what you have been doing too. You and Tony have pushed yourselves as hard as we have, then you have the essential part that both of you are so much younger."

"Just a moment I think they're looking for an answer," as I could even see them approaching the kitchen. She opened the door and spoke, "Okay, we have assessed it and it is fine. Make sure all the chairs are out of the way, then all of you get back to work. Paul could you be a dear and come here for a moment."

He immediately came and asked, "What's up Naomi, I came right away."

"Good boy Paul, now let me ask John this one question." She now turned to me with it, "With my thirty-seven years as a human, then twenty-eight year as the undead. Everyone I ever cared about hasn't made it to the death house as of yet. Lately, as I have moved through this life, I have had to ask myself if it is truly worth it. I can also tell you these kids have given me a new lease on this existence. My question if I'm right here, but you have existed as a vampire now over three hundred years. How have you literally done it?"

I was completely honest with her, "I won't tell you an untruth with that it was extremely easy because it wasn't. The day my master had taken me he ripped my life apart, I had a real human life. In a sense that maybe precisely how I was able to do it, as to what he did to me was eminently unjust. That is also why I'm so against allowing humans to come into this without foreknowledge of what we are. To be honest, as I did recently make a child, I couldn't, even as it had to be done, force Mary into this life."

I had to chuckle at that as I added, "I offered her complete death, which I had hoped she would take. Not because I truly want her dead, or as they are they wanted this also because those are the worst. Don't get me wrong as to my beliefs, I have always been a profoundly lonely person, and this was a source of certain relief. I in my time have made a few children, though I have failed to make a proper vampire. They have all sought out their own demise."

I had to look away as I was remembering, "I virtually gave up any hope of ever getting a fitting child. In the most recent I have to give to the fact of resolve, that this new purpose did give me light enough to categorically do it. I also know this is far from the old, with a certain level of new effort to the end. I have also tried to make a vampire my companion, as we do have to know there is a loss there as well."

I had to look at her with a somber expression, "With them, it was never the same, and many would prefer to use then take the real step. I think I have finally found a true daughter, and I truly hope she never finds out about the other ten. I used the same words with them all, and that is even why I think a word can be so cheap. Though the word is of the greatest nature, as it is the word of love."

With this she just seemed to continue to blink, I think that maybe I hit a cord. "So, um. Were you honestly alone all those years? Then you came here because you felt the pull. Paul, aah."

He wiped his nose as he said, "Yeah Naomi?"

"Make sure he and Kitty get enough blood and don't allow anyone disturb them at all. John, you genuinely have to share that with her."

I knew what she meant, though I also had no real secrets from her. It was just Naomi had no idea about Kitty, so I finished with one final remark. "She already knows."

Chapter Nine

The differences aren't as plain as you may think.

<u>**Near the downtown area**</u>

Near the downtown area, there are three figures, one is in all his ceremonial garb as he moves just out of sight of the public. They know the area well as they have been drawn her many a time, tonight he has made it profoundly different. The wise old man has seen something and knew he had to come to this area. The dusting of the smoke which is meant to cleanse all, then he sits with his legs crossed. They understood never to get involved, they were just here to protect the shaman.

He appears to fall asleep, though it is easy to ascertain that he was in a trance. This portion always amazed everyone as every kinda vermin seemed to come to him. Not your usual city vermin mind you, as he was now surrounded by every kind of the woods. He also seemed to have a name for all of them, and even like this, he spoke in a haunting tone.

"Ayv advanvtesgy itsula wili gydodi nihi gohi iga dinadanvtli Koga."

It was easy to hear his Cherokee, it wasn't so easy to understand what he said next even as they were of his tribe. It was common to see him talking to an animal of its own kind. Now all left save the crow, that figured since he called upon its name, the Koga. Then within seconds to it had also left, in truth as they all understood, it hadn't indisputably. The old man was exceedingly good at using animals, and through his now chat he had been seeing with his eye.

The Koga has always had the sharpest eye any time of the day, even at night when they usually did their best. Whatever it did now the old shaman seemed to emulate, they did want to move because they knew what would be going on from this point. Then as they sat there they could hear extraordinarily well that the world did have the earmarks of to blowing up the beginning. They had never heard such gunfire before, and it all seemed to start with a cannon shot.

He then seemed to come back to life, as he looked at them and with simple English, he spoke.

"We need to move now, but the approach is terrible. So we will have to move uncommonly if we can, you may want to call in Sarah."

With that, he pointed the direction they needed to go, and then erupted from them were simple whistles. Moments later they came upon a field, and they could all see what had been going on as some took a body off the field. He then started to place his hand out to show mounds of something, as a coyote just joined them.

One then spoke to it, "I think Wild Raven needs you to go out and take a look around these grounds. Be careful as they just ran off, and make sure you make a line right to us if you get in trouble Sarah."

With this, the coyote seemed to sneak off, and the one that spoke said as she disappeared, "They say evil begets evil, though..." He seemed to look hard, "I feel this evil may have been one-sided."

The other now spoke, "It is heavy as a large stone, I feel it to brother. I don't feel it the way the others went, can it be this was truly a one-sided event?"

The first then pointed at a close target as he ascertained, "You see that brother, is that not a wild mark of the beast. The Great Spirit has left them unfounded, that usually means they can never be happy. Let us move out and survey as much as possible, but also remember we can't lose sight of Wild Raven."

A third now showed up as he added, "We will, and even more, though time isn't on our side either. We must report to the council as soon as possible as our chief has said."

The absolute first had to look seriously as he pondered, "We must then do this extremely quickly, this will be with some kind of response. This has to succeed before the morning, as they could come back even to see what has happened."

With that comment, they all started to move

around to ascertain what there was at this distance. It was easy to see that they had done this before, as all paths became jagged and differed from each other.

Just as they started the third had to question, "Do they always hide themselves this well?"

The first knew this to be sarcasm so he remarked with the opposite answer. "This is because they are of the notion of the European bloodsuckers. They all think they know us, though they have never taken us by surprise. To our own this is to our advantage, this will cause us to lose few brothers."

The second now added what he thought, "Yes, though they do try my patience, why don't we just use this advantage? How can we genuinely do this as we are, or will we stay within our human flesh?"

With that comment they all were in agreement, then they all seemed to transform. The second and third went to the full wolf stage, though the first hovered somewhere in between human and wolf. Not because of some mistake he had made, but with the full knowledge that they were at their most powerful in this stage. Now where once humans did stand were moving beasts, with an unknown direction save to them.

The one also known as Wild Raven seemed to see something, so he outstretched his arms. With a darkening shadow a huge raven did now appear, then as the night was all around he seemed to disappear.

Two men trying to see what they can

They had heard about it for days, getting where it

did present a problem. This morning they had gotten word it would be here, it was easy to see this tip was the first legitimately good one they had. As they had to sneak this far after they left their car in a noticeably small wood. One seemed like he had done this so many times had hardly made a sound. The other thought he had been on many stakeouts, had troubles getting from point A to B.

They had stopped to genuinely count what they saw. It was hard to tell if these were truly whom the informants had told them about with a degree of accuracy. The numbers were right, the amount the highers-up had figured was over fifty. Even with all their movement, they had gotten a good count, not that they had the ability to take on sixty-five by themselves.

The main man on this mission would never be willing to take a partner. He had to look back as he saw how much he had been struggling. A normal agent would never have these problems, he had to figure he had to be a big wig making a name for himself. Not that he had ever heard of any big wig with the name of Madison. I mean isn't that a girl's name anyway?

He turned back around to allow him to catch up, though there had been no way he had been going to help him out of here if they got into a situation. Right then it happened, as he heard an extremely loud noise and a grouping of terrible cuss words. Well not that he hadn't used a few himself, like when he got this guy assigned to him. He knew he only had one call, as he now dove into the dirt. All this trouble for an obvious newbie.

As he hit the dirt though he had been terribly happy, as the blast was ever present in his ears. Now he had to carefully look above the weeds, and he saw what he never thought he would see. They were being attacked by those that were experts at killing them. He had to ponder the effect as they moved, then the one with the cannon seemed to disappear. He had to change around as he now saw another's claws dig deeply. Then barely beyond sight, was that a werewolf?

Oh my god! Where did those in the center come from, and are they? Yes, yes! Those subs have to be illegal contraband, look at the way they're lighting them up like Christmas. Now he had to get back down as he heard a bullet whistle through the air. With that, he saw that Madison trying to get up, as he made a fast low crawl to him. The only thing he could think of doing would be to knock his legs out from under him.

As he came around he had to look at him eminently closely so he could hear him profoundly well. "Snipers, but if you want to stand up again go right ahead."

He had to ask back with the same level of a whisper, "But why? I mean we literally need to see what's going on, this spoils everything."

He had to look at him as he had to question him, "Knowing that there were over fifty, ask yourself why they just sent us and not a platoon of marines?" Then he pointed to the small group of woods, as he added, "Crawl like I do, from there we can be undercover. Then we can use the bannock to see things."

With this, they both did the low crawl back, and by the time they pulled out the binoculars. The fight was somewhat over, he watched as they crossed his front. The man had no idea how many there were, it was easy to see that at least one had gotten hurt. With an efficiency he had only seen in the military, it was no wonder that he had to be amazed at who they worked for after all of this commotion. This time of night he had wished he had brought extra equipment.

It was never easy to see with normal binoculars, as he looked he had to figure a few of the mounds he saw were some of theirs. He wasn't about ready to make a note of how many there were, he was assured that the others outnumbered those few. Heck from all he saw of that small group he had to figure maybe a dozen. Though using the term may be over a dozen would get him laughed at in the end.

Out of one side of his vision, he had to take a good look, and now he pulled up Madison who had barely made it to him.

Madison had to whisper, "Are they all gone?"

He had to answer with a definite maybe, "I don't know. You see those wolves though?" He nodded his head, "They never show themselves until the area is clear. That is all I have to go on though, so if one of us takes a bullet to the head. Well, take what I said as wrong." With his comment, he ducts down with a sudden reaction, as he also added. "I think we have enough to return to the office, so just head into the trees."

As they now pulled out for the third street where the federal building was at, they were practically hit by a fast-moving limo. He had to wonder where they were in such a hurry too with such speed. He did have his own worries as they now speed to their offices. This was such an uncommon way to do things, with a level of secrecy he had never encountered before in the bureau.

Two men of the cloth now meet

The man from early now stood in an extraordinarily barren part of the city, surprisingly close to an extremely large mall. He had seen that Father Michael and the Bishop, could never remember those that were of no addition to his case. This was the usual way to meet these few as they never like to stay in one place. He in his own right was excessively important, though like the other is just the level of a bishop.

A wonderfully venerable man now got out of the long car, he then came over to him and dropped to one knee. The older then placed out his hand, and as were their way he pulled it closer as he kissed his ring.

With this, he practically spoke with disdain toward the other, "I hope you have a lot more than you did last time Father Horscio?"

He replied, "I do believe I may have to much evidence as to how long it has taken us to get here my Lord Francis."

"Show me what you have."

With this he then pulled out many files, it was easy to see he had been into many confidential files. He then started to point things out as the elder read, then when he got to a certain part Horscio spoke.

"Even as great as the information is, this essentially clenches that there is a real problem within this city."

Then he read that part with as much care as he could muster, what he read was the truth of it. He had to reread it again to make sure there was no mistake. Then he had to ask just for their own safety, "None of this has been generated has it?"

He nearly looked dejected as he had to quiz, "Have I ever faked anything before this date my Lord?"

He then took all that he had as he turned to him, "This looks noticeably promising. You will have to remain diligent as I deliver this to the general. This is enough to convict this city, you know how thorough he likes us to be. See if you can pull any of these loose ends up, we need a complete view."

He then bowed as he stepped back to his small car, it had been nothing then he had expected. The elder then got into his car as well, as his driver now drove off into the night. He had to stand there for a few, as he realized the magnitude of all this. There had not been an advance in his career since his early days, this now assured it. He had to wonder if there would be more, and the fascination of all of what he now knew.

There would always be some investigation somewhere, for so many years he had been on the edge. You have to figure that he had also been where he needed to be, then to seemingly follow a source to a city. There would never be a real name for that person, all we could ever tell was he seemed to absolutely, not like his particular own. He was the one to prove the name they did have for him was entirely wrong.

He had to figure no man wanted a name like that,

where would he have gotten a name like Clarence from anyway. It had been proven that he is in their society a nomad, and they look upon them as terrible. Well not that anyone would ever voice that to him, he is after all known for killing his own. This world is remarkably evil, and with the likes of this one, it made it even worse. Not that he ever believed in his kind before he came to work for them.

He had to reason as now he knew, what other things besides vampires were they hiding from this godforsaken world?

It is a fact that this world has been for a long time covered with Godlessness. He had experienced the reality of him for himself, with this knowledge he had to wonder why the masses were so ignorant. Then like so many reasons why he had became what he is, he went to where he was used to be in the end.

It was more of a way to cause him to believe as he whispered, "God is real, I know because I believe. God is real because he released me from my sin. God is real, the penance I will always do it for him. He watches me as he does all his beloved. His truths are in the book, they lied to cover up the truth. He gave the world his truths, though he also said they would make them sound like lies. His grace is all over those of disease, the destitute, even those that are gone have this."

He now took a deep breath and repeated, "God is real, I know because I believe. God is real Because he released me from my sin. God is real, the penance I will always do it for him. He watches me as he does all his beloved. His truths are in the book, they lied to cover up the truth. He gave the world his truths, though he also said they would make them sound like lies. His grace is all over those of disease, the destitute, even those that are gone have this."

With that, he finally got into his car, with just a few more thoughts. He then turned it over, and he was gone just like that.

Giaus and Williams short chat

He had no idea what he could speak out loud even as he knew he had to say something. "Lord, I have to ask, was this all seen in the plan?"

Giaus looked up as he replied, "How could anyone plan for something so terrible to happen to a friend?"

He shook his head as he added, "That isn't what I meant, you give the impression of knowing so much. What I meant was did you know that the Enforcer would be here?"

He was happy to hear this, though he was known for the level of truth he displayed. "No. I'm sorry to say, though I did know he had been in the area. I never did anything to positively see where he would be, then you have the fact I had been getting aggravated by these few."

The lady now seemed to look at him as William now ascertained, "Then you knew we were going to be stuck here if we hadn't found help."

"Yes, it was fortuitous that we saw him moving to that drinking establishment. Not to be critical here my dear, I had wished that you had been much more careful."

She now moved her hand as she still couldn't speak, so William spoke what he thought she may want to happen. "Lord how could she have known this city was so infected, then you have the fact of what John told you. You know I'm not one to jump on another's side, but it is simple for even me to see she had no chance."

He now looked upset, "I know that I just thought she could have run away. I'm angry about this as it is, not all the children, but those that would infect this city. I know for what it is worth about John, and in her position, Kitty is no leadership model. With all that the only other part he has is two children to help him out with all he intends. I can say I would be pulling you out my dear, I can't see John leaving, so this presents a certain problem for me."

William then acknowledged the thought, "You mean to leave dear Veronica here my Lord?"

Now it was he that shook his head as he announced, "I plan on making a hunt of it. I have to free up John for what his job is, I need someone that can handle this. I know that he is the best choice if he wasn't dogged with so many youngsters. This also presents a more difficult problem, as you saw he means to make them into an independent house. As you know I have never been for this, but I also have never stood in any of their ways."

Veronica now pressed his arm, even though her grip wasn't truly back as of yet. William, of course, stated the obvious, "I do believe you have a volunteer in Veronica my Lord."

He looked deeply into her eyes as he asked her,

"Charming Veronica, this isn't for you."

Then he seemed to look out the window, William then interjected, "Lord she's crying."

He looked at her again and asked, "Does owning a city mean so much to you my dear?"

She couldn't tell him exactly how much it just meant to unequivocally be away from him. So even though it had never been a good thing to lie to an elder, she did what she could. With a single nod, it spoke volumes to him, though also in fear of him categorically finding out anything.

Chapter Ten

We have company, the likes Unknown?

It always sees this world as it is, then again you can deepen your view and truly see. We use many words to describe it, and they also relate to the fact of it in general. You could say it would be absolutely too easy to wallow in our own insecure delusion. When you have lived so long it is hard to explain the infancy you enter our lives. This darkness can be so ever present, as the shadow takes over what is real. In our own depression we are released, and yet are we ever truly let go.

We are overdrawn into the steam of all, are we there as the recognition can't be seen. Ask yourself as you have seen within all this, as to what has been enticed into this. Would it be better to do the largest and allow the world to see? Then as we turned all to a point where it affected the entire world, but not seen?

This is a thought that is usually rejected by all the

young, and then the older have no where to unquestionably ascertain. Even the rare can't contrive this, as the rarest of all beings truly understand it. There are those that would think they know better, and in the light, you may have even heard of many of them. I do also know that it is a level that can't be truly understood outside that loop. I can't either tell you that I will fully understand it here, but if you look at what I'm about ready to write. Look for what could be secrets, terms of unknown nature, and the recognition of others.

Now you have how we ended at last with Paul, he had done his job well. Even as I was the one that sent him off, he was first to be all over Kitty to make sure she drank. You could even hear the overriding beat of an echoed tune, it seemed as ominous as ever. As I do believe we all went our separate ways to avoid a confrontation. I myself was caught in the library where I saw my daughter and she that also seemed as my daughter. None would allow anything to go forth till I drank, I relented because of how important the training was.

I found a book of our kinds rare writings, though nothing that was more important to Joe. It was uncommonly good to bring your abilities back up, and it had been an extremely long time since I read our script. I will also be honest here and not try to tell you I made it far, I said I could read it, I never said I was good at it. In fact, as I was on the second page I saw her, I looked at her standing in the hallway.

I then had to inquire, "Liz you looking for something?"

She turned to smile at me as she replied, "Yes John. Naomi sent me up to get you as I just got done."

It had not even dawned on me that no she wasn't among those that looked for me. She and Sammy needed so much training that even Tony would have never released them. I acknowledged this fact with a nod as I also said, "Well it looks like you found me."

I smiled back at her as I joined her, she then had to add as we walked downwards. "I don't think I haven't used many of these muscles in a long time, I may be sore tomorrow." I had to chuckle at that so she had to ask, "What is so funny?"

I field the question with a certain gentle humor, "You are. You still have no clue what you are, you do remember when I said one sip of blood and you're as good as new."

"Oh," She mused. Then ascertained with the same humor, "I guess that is kind of funny."

Now I had to go for why we were walking together, "Did Naomi tell you why she needed you to come and get me?"

"I don't know truly, just that Tony came in as he had been still working. He whispered to her, she turned to me and asked what I had been doing. I told her I was on my way to Tony to see what I needed to do next in all these things. She then said, 'No you're not, you go get John while I go get Kitty.' Then I came as fast as I could, though I had no idea where you were."

"Did she designate to be excited?"

"Not as much as if she hadn't found you," came

from down the hall as we both now looked that way. She relatively as quickly added, "Perfectly large limo pulling up in the driveway, I'm sure we have no time anymore."

With this I started to bark orders, I knew they weren't here to create trouble. It would be best to move things so nothing else would cause any trouble either. I told Tony to be on the edge of the room, but not in it. Naomi as she is, had to be in it as a full member of our kind. I then instructed Cibilia, Joe to be ready, and that Bert had to do his best beside Tony. Once we got to the living room Naomi had been explaining that no matter what Cibilia would come in first.

I could hear the door creaking as I also added, "Cibilia you will sit next to me, Joe you stand behind Naomi." I saw them moving in the hall as I felt one last thing had to be said, "If Giaus grants you permission to enter."

I want to place a reality here, in truth I could have cared less about any of these capes. I did know I had many untrained children, and we literally could do without many of them. Then you have another fact, which is precisely more of a hindsight. I think I have become rather attached to all of them. We had only indisputably given them one way in, though I had to doubt they would have taken any other way.

One man came in with a pistol drawn as I had to say in a loud voice, "How rude!"

The expression on his face was priceless as Giaus stepped in and said, "I said casual, don't you peons know what that means."

William then said from down the hall, "No weapons! No weapons! That could get you destroyed!"

Giaus placed his hands on his hips as he had to ask, "Was this guard instructed in Elysium or is he just ignorant?"

"Micheal you may think you're in the right dear man, but both of these men could pull you apart without looking. I would put that piece away."

I had to then ask, "Does he at least know how we can resist the pain, William?"

Giaus now turned to see me as he placed his hands out with the request. "May I have a seat?"

I placed my hand out to the chair in front of me as I spoke, "Sit wherever you would like too."

I was about ready to ask about the house leadership, when he said, "Where is that wonderful young man that screams the height of a tall building. Oh, and that delight that has the hair of fire, she legitimately becomes your kind, John."

He was still in a god awful suit, but it was easy to see he was busy with his own problems. I could see the recent marks to help that poor woman, I now had to let them all know. "Cibilia and Joe if you haven't clued in yet, that's Giaus would be inviting you into the room."

Of course, they came in with a modicum timidity, as Naomi had to get them to hurry themselves up. I knew he was allowed up to four guards, another came in with a line. What they did was place three chairs down, Giaus had to add as he knew explanation was in order. "My darling came with us, she insisted. She may make a terror of your furniture, so we deemed to use chairs. Though she still isn't healed enough, so we have two more so they can help her. Is this also okay of an additive?"

I was the senior of them all, and I knew he looked for me to answer. I did have to look at all six as I even took in Bert with this one. Well with me that would have truly been seven, no one knew what to say, so I went on with just a fraction. "I see that no one has a problem."

With that, another woman that looked like a doctor, came supporting another. William was behind all of them as he made sure she was sat well. By now you could see the long hair beginning to appear, and she was well formed in certain areas. I could see that Cibilia was about ready to say something, so as to her state I had to speak too.

"Yes, children. In her present state, she still wears no clothes, as even the simplest would cause damage. Treat her as if she were any other person, soon she will look the part extraordinarily much. We must always endure becoming whole, and that can be a sight that can show the death we are. Though this is normal for us, not the sight, just the action."

Giaus came in with, "Yes. The sight can always be extremely repulsive, but as John says it is normal. I forget how young your kids are John."

Mary then had to ask, "John what do you mean not the sight, just the action?"

Giaus then had to ask, "You allow them to call you

by your first name?"

Okay, I could have told him the truth here, but I also knew I had to hide that fact as well. "I met these kids they had no one, I saw a need and decided to always keep it formal. You also know me if you told me right, you also know I have always preferred my first name." I could see Mary getting ready to give Giaus the what for, so I added, "Tony explain why that might not be so wise."

Tony immediately moved Mary to the side as he explained, and of course, Giaus now spoke. "Ah, yes. I do remember that I have gone away from more than one name. It fills two roles, as I never have to tell anyone. Then you have the fact of having to come up with a new one all the time."

I had to chuckle as I had to ask, "With a name like Giaus you truly worry about the naming system?"

"What's wrong with Giaus?"

"Come on? Even if you use the newer spelling, you have to admit that screams Roman."

He had to smile as he conveyed, "I do like a good hearty name, and I see you have some knowledge of how old I am. I guess that is profoundly fair since I have the same knowledge about you. Then again you have never had to hide that fact."

I had to take a hard look at him now as I had to ascertain the reason why he was here. "So, have you came to debate the affinities of age, or is there another purpose for your visit?"

With this, he finally expressed the authenticity of this standpoint. "I needed to send you a message, I'm not sure how well you will hear her. As you know anyone could have carried it, but she wanted to talk to you people personally. She has to be looked after still, so it made sense to kill two birds with one stone. Mine will be short and sweet, oh and I think William has something to add."

I placed my hand out for him to continue, "As you know I never interfere with cities, no bodies knew about this. I will not have this at all, I want to know everything. I mean I want the whens, the whats, all the wheres. I also need these gentlemen gone, I can use so much for the first part. It would take a time to set up the second part, but I see a ready need here. I had a thought as you were already here, with so many helpers. It may be legitimately easier for you to do the second part."

He sighed as he said, "I know you have to do this to save your kids, but I told you all this so you would also help me out with all needed."

I then had to say in the absence of the actual statement, "Plus it is always friendly to ask first also?"

"Yes, yes. Plus it is always commendable to ask first too."

I had to look at William with a big smile as I had to ask, "Are you ready to deal with Cheryl again William?"

He had to look to where she was standing, then the figure had to whisper something. He then spoke incredibly sweetly to her, "Yes mea femina. She is the one I told you about, she could genuinely be et filia tua with her ability."

I had to turn my head as I had to add, "Cheryl smile. You have no idea, but William just paid you a huge compliment."

With this, even Giaus had to give a great belly laugh as he added, "I see the part about your knowledge of languages was correct. You see Cheryl the words he used were Latin. Mea femina means my lady, then the part with et filia tua kind of means your daughter. Now you see why John said it was a compliment. I think I will leave the rest of this to the kids John. Guards! We move!"

With that, he now got up, and the rest except for one guard left with him. William now spoke, "I dare not even try to negotiate with her again, but I will do what I need to do. Now to complete this settlement, Giaus has seen cleared the three you asked for with our agreement. He decided to add two to that, he understands for you because of what you are, you desire no frills. It was the amazement on how well your youngsters worked together. He would also like to add that if he had half that could do as well as you have with these few. Well, the world would be more celebrated to his presence."

I had to correct him on this as it wasn't absolutely precise, as he also had to add to this. "They have done astonishingly well also, though the ability isn't that great, it does come with their own desire. I also know you understand that William."

With that, the lady placed her hand out as she said, "William is trying to be amiable, he just unimpeachably has no clue."

I had to put my eyebrow up as he included, "She

asked me to try and be nicer to you, so for her sake yes I'm trying."

I nodded my head as I had never seen this side of these guys. "Then I thank you for all the instructors and the kids."

He then pulled up a bag as he went on, "Giaus had me place what I could on that card tonight, and to assure you there will be more on the morrow. Now for this, since you are so much a part of this city. Oh, I should say this was supposed to be Veronica's, as it will take her awhile she gave hers up for your house."

I had to look at her as I had to ascertain, "Veronica is your name?"

In as quiet as a voice as I could muster, she gave me a slight affirmative with her head as William when on talking. "As you know there has always been a network for ease of use. Recently they have uploaded everything online, and there are still a lot of bugs. We have some of the best tech people working on it so it'll be easy to see news as it may be."

Then he handed me a thing that looked like one of the notebooks, just this one had no paper. I had to inquire, "What am I to do with this?"

He looked at me, then to Kitty, Naomi was next, finally, he settled Cibilia. "I have no idea if you know how to use this young lady, but do any of the kids have any technical knowledge?"

She nodded her head as she said, "Yeah, Pepper is genuinely good with anything technical, but as I'm willing you mean aware. Hmm. I'm willing to bet Paul or Andy are our guys."

Paul then had to say, "Yeah, but I have no idea if this house has any hot spots, what you think Andy?"

Andy came forward as he asked, "May I?"

I gave him the thing right away, and he looked just a second. "Yeah, we have an old one. You'll have to update that absolutely fast, this laptop will get bogged down real fast. I mean these guys here were ancient, it isn't even high speed."

I looked at him as I now had to ask, "Is that something that can be done? I mean whatever he had been talking about in the end?"

He was quick to reply, "Well have to, but I do suggest you restrict usage to maybe just a few."

Veronica then added with a wisp, "Not the computer, he means the internet usage."

I realized we may have gone too long, so I started to do a few extra things. "Tony you take control of that and between you and Cibilia are to figure that out in the end. Paul get us at least two containers of blood fast, Liz I know you may have done something like this before in your career. Tony do you think Pepper is good enough to help Liz, Mary give Liz your blade."

Now because of what had been going on, I knew I couldn't be aggressive. My normal reaction would have been to do something, this was one of those situations which required tact. Tony then ascertained, "Pepper this could be gross, but it will seemingly cement us in with these guys. You think you can handle this?"

She nodded her head as he then continued, "Good. You and Liz are going to get behind the chair, Liz, Mary's knife is too big, but I'm sure Andy's will do."

With that as they moved I had to add, "William you may want to make sure they set right, listen to him for now girls."

He then came in with, "I know the two of you're new at this, but try to use that knife on the ribs. Pepper is it?" She nodded her head, "You'll need to use your fingers with the help of Liz, open the wound and slowly pour in the blood. I want to warn you as she can't take it all, so for the container, you may have to make three or four holes."

Liz now looked at me and it wasn't hard to understand what she had been thinking. So I spoke to her worries, "Yes it'll hurt, no there is no way around it. I would try to help myself, but as one of the house-elder and or leadership, it is best if we don't move. Liz a slice does nothing, you have to dig that knife deep."

With that, she did as I had asked her, and you could see the pain in Veronica's face. I also saw how well the two of them worked together, I had been pleasantly surprised. She then opened her mouth as for one of the elders, we could see that it had been doing its work well. I had to add one more thing before I could allow her to go on with her thought.

"Remember even if she looks okay, she needs this." I had said, with a certain pride I had to assess this entire situation. Then just as an extra, "See how we are, so barbaric insight with this heathen nature. How close we are to that where we started, yet we are and can be more than we are. Why not just do as our carnal desires tell us, step into the reality of what we are. Because we strive to be more as a whole, and this is why we say after all we are civilized."

Chapter Eleven

The truth comes out and caused me to suspect.

*There was this great poem about darkness, see if it sounds
familiar at the beginning:*

I had a dream, which wasn't a dream at all.
The sun has been extinguished.
The stars did dangle in eternal space.
Rayless, pathless, stuck on this icy earth.
Swung blindless and blackening on this moonless air.
Morn came and went, and came again, yet brought no day.

With men had forgotten their passion in dread.
In this their desolation, and all hearts were chilled.
Into a selfish call, as they prayed for the light.
As they sat in the frost around watchfires, on their thrones.
The places they crowned their kings were mere huts.
The habitations of all living as which they dwell.
Were as the beacons did burn, the cities did consume it.
Men became comfortable in their blazing homes.

To look upon more which were as to so normal,
Happy were those that did dwelt within the eye,
Of these volcano's, as their mountains did touch,
A fearful hope was all in this contained.

Forest were set to the flame, but hour by hour,
They slowly fell and faded away, and the trunk were
crackling,
All extinguished with such a crash, are they all black.

The brows of men by the despairing light,
Wore their unearthly aspect, as to by fits,
The flash did fall upon them, and some had to lay down,
In their fear they hid their eyes and wept, some did rest,
They clinched their fists upon their own chins and smiled.

They hurried to and fro,
With the knowledge to fill their funeral piers, they looked
up,
With mad disquietude of this dull sky,
The pall of a past world, and then again,
With curses cast down on them to return to the dust,
They gnashed their teeth and howled, with the wild shriek.

Then they were terrified and did flutter on the ground,
Like a flap of the flightless bird, the wildest brutes,
Came to them finally a calm, and cowards, where vipers
did crawl
They did twinned themselves among the multitude,
Hissing as if to bite, yet fangless, they were slain for food.

All wars for the moment were no more,
He did make a gluten of himself, as the meal was brought,
Much was the blood, with each he wasn't satisfied,
Gorging himself in the gloom, no love than did leave.

We had done all as to what needed to be done, and now we had to wait upon her. This is just a small part of something Lord Byron had written, they say he wasn't one of us, I do wonder. As you can see though it is written in a human state, I have to wonder if he knew more. Then again it wasn't as if we hadn't been lied to before, and that was my great fear with these few. We have a certain term for them all, though I will admit that it doesn't apply to all.

The term you may ask is capes, it refers to our kind so old they think the invention of the wheel was wonderful. In truth over time, it has changed to be related to those that act to a vampire like state. Like William, if you came across him anywhere you would know right away they were one. Though his kind has a problem truly moving away from being capes. Veronica's kind is usually known to also be like that, Cheryl and Paul had the line to be like her.

I have to say as there is much that will be said, I'm genuinely happy I was completely wrong about her. Now back to our story, as she is though the book may always be out on her. After one final moan, it was easy to see she was ready to talk.

She started with, "I know this may not be much of a surprise, but Giaus sent me here to take control of this city. As you may also know he would have me leave till this problem is taken care. He may leave you to your own devices, but if I'm to even in the future be the leader of this city, I can't do that. You also know that I'm not set up to do what needs to be done, so I have to do things as you expressly know well."

I had to interrupt her as to fully explain what she

meant, "Children that means as we were, so we are still. The capes have allowed their power to be known, we're on our own again as it was."

Liz then scolded me with, "John! Even I can hear what she is saying, but it is literally rude to interrupt when a lady would be speaking!"

Veronica smiled at her as she went on, "Yes, though he does have a right to do this. Giaus has promised me all his support, and as it is, he is already calling in people. Experts in their fields, with a set prowess in scouting and sniping. Now as you also understand anything like this takes time, so again you're left alone. I had to find a way to make this right, so we also placed other sources together. It may take a few days also, but we plan on getting all your kids need. Yes, John. That means that the capes are cracking open their bank books on this also."

William then added, "As you may have surmised we aren't the usual leaders of a city, and this is Veronica's first try. Giaus is as unsure of her as he is of all of you, he has seen what you have shown in this first trial. When they came to infiltrate those outsiders, like New York, Miami, and the such. He had a heck of a time taking care of it, we had to wonder where they would be coming from next time. No one suspected the decidedly middle of the country, even we are at a loss exactly why also."

Veronica then came back in with, "We're going to set up in the downtown area, this hasn't changed since that is where we always start. I have bought a few pieces of property, one is to be a nightclub sort of lounge. We also felt this is a noticeably good start for all of us, I don't mean just us as in William, Giaus, and me. I have made a back room where I can add things so I can help you with the kids. I also know you have no reason to trust me either, so we'll start slowly with just Paul and Cheryl."

William added, "Giaus decided that was a good idea, he has also told me that if you have to leave we can figure something out with another thought. He doesn't want to keep you from your normal job."

I had to interject, "He has no idea, though I do believe my job may be turning. I'm not saying that I'm a teacher as it may, but even I can feel a change in the air."

Naomi then spoke with such elegance in her voice, "We all came here with another in mind, yet the tide has been high all the way. I have been a huntress all my life, I do not want to give that up just yet. We of the elder cast have all felt the strangeness in the air since we got here, even Giaus can't deny this."

William then admitted, "Yes. He has. It is also so strange about how it has come about, with such disaster that it threatens to snuff it out in the end."

I had to be direct, "That's Bull!"

Liz jumped in with, "JOHN!"

But it was Kitty that now took the show, "Kitty see truth false meanie try to spin, he no hide from Great Harlequin, he knows better. Needer be as seen to the highest, deen ya eat those that cash, and yeah to the low." She got up as if to dance as she moved across the floor. "Dragon lady be here though not, she emerald and amber, sky of shadow. Noddy inny, see the Aszure that be, then that which are low, made high. Even Pretty Boy hab ta bein inner, and he long to see though as blind as those that see."

Now she came close to William, "Dirty is what you see, yet the truth nebber sees. Lights are bright as they burn, you see as the stake takes away. Tender is the bold bright light, it is darkness that comes to all. No one can be seen, is plain, as Honk honk. Vale removed to you then and you see, bright crimson flame come, but no baddy." She now moved to Veronica, "Amber lady see yet has no clue, and is as bright as all."

She now returned to her seat, "It be big dreams, we all see as nightmare, world be firmament again." Now she seemed to frame her face, as she did this batting of the eye thing. "Not all want, not all see, not all take, some will reject. Take a picture, it is worth a Billy ton de million in da speaky speaky."

Now she placed her hand out as she added, "Amber Lady be finished with what be said next, John not speak no more. He be Demon Lord Yes, but he also gentlemen. You speak now."

Veronica, as I did, suspected she meant for her to speak, "I'm sorry if I'm wrong. I have to add I will not take this city if you don't want me, but please give me a chance. I also have given you a gift, not as to this, but for saving my life. I dare say if I had spent one more day I do believe I had been going to comprehensively die. So in all, I have said you may not believe me, I'm censer in my affection in you few. No one has ever done anything so great before for me so great."

"John Kitty told you to shut up," came out of Liz's mouth. Then she added, "I also believe this is a time for

Cibilia to show her ability. Cibilia please take it away."

Cibilia then spoke, "Veronica I can say that we have no reason to trust you and that we were so short on things, we had to help for that alone. Now that you know the truth of that, we are also as new to this as you are. John taught us a great lesson here when he could have just said no, he gave us a chance and said yes. He may not understand that we have learnt that from him, and as he has done, so must we. I can't say it'll be a match made in Heaven, then again we are vampires."

Everyone got a chuckle out of that, "If you are all willing to accept us as this brood right in the middle of your fair city. We can do the same as we were here first, and John has also told us what Giaus can take from us. We don't want this, and if it happens then you'll have a lot of enemies you don't want. So here is my decree, so as John has done with us, we extend that same courtesy to you as well."

William then spoke, "That is all she is asking for, I can see that she has a friend in you."

Veronica then interjected, "William be quiet! I know what you're doing, I think this has to be said in honesty this once." He bowed to her, so she went on, "What he said was true, and I will honor you as best as I can for this. I would shake your hand, though that maybe a scant gross right now. I'm a lady of fine delights, this is far beyond me. I will be back, but right now I have to go and lay in a bath of . . . what do the older vampires call it sanguine fluid."

I swear everyone laughed with that one, well everyone except for me. I think she had been genuinely making fun of the way I talk, well and Liz says there had been no mistaking that jab. With this, as she got up, I moved also. I had Sammy pick her up with comfort, then as they moved out both Naomi and I gave guidance out to everyone. It isn't a normal thing, but in her condition, I do believe it was for the best.

This also gave Andy time to get with William, and they set up the laptop. Though all knew more had to be done, I can't tell you as I'm at a lose with that thing. Another thing was that the house had its complete power turned off for some reason. I had no idea how to know this, I mean we had lights, wasn't that enough. William explained that many places just disconnected one source. So in a sense, the lights were running off that, but it truly didn't have power. I absolutely didn't see the problem.

I undoubtedly think it was a way to get more money out of us, everyone else told me I was wrong.

There is a time that we were now entering, and in a way, it was a null time. I mean to say it was that is easy because nothing happened on the big picture. In truth, there was no real time where something wasn't going on truthfully. Many had seen the rescue of Veronica, many couldn't in all respects make out what truly proceeded. Even as it is you can see where things were going, as they drove off we had another visitor.

I have had to ask also if I can relate this story, she has allowed it. I have been restricted to the basics, as it was truly unusual. One was part of us, the other was not. The plain truth of it will come later, though as it is right now I have to stay situational. As you know Giaus is quite old, so even as he left his dead space remained. All the elders were the ones that realized that it lingered, even without proof.

I mean it is easy to say something doesn't feel right, but most won't listen unless they see. Let me tell you that the first step in a few had taken place, and a new queen would be born. Believe this, that it was Tony that had caught on what was up, though again to his credit, just conjecture.

So after they had been gone for a portion, Naomi and I on separate volition decided to check the original location. It was also understood we couldn't tell the kids, I'm not sure any of them could have handled this. There are things that are also easy to ascertain, and to our own ignorance, we missed all the signs.

Now as the normal side what we did find wasn't a good thing, as it literally took three of us to discover a gentleman. Well let me start as I saw that Pepper had been creeping up on something, and no I had no idea. I can tell you she had been doing an excellent job, though it was the blood that caused this. Naomi had also come into this light, from a completely different direction. I had decided that if she had found what I had been searching for I would allow them to reveal themselves.

Finally, she did as we had explained to her, as she grabbed hold of whatever it was. Then I heard the scream and the fist that came crashing against her. She had been off in her positioning, as I now wish her teeth had dug in deeper. You also have to understand that neither of us knew what she would be tracking. I came in with speed to see how I could help her, as Naomi did the exact same thing. After all, we both felt it, and in truth, we were far more concerned about Pepper's safety.

Now as you also know that Kitty can see certain things, though neither of us worried that she wasn't out here. Right about this time she had moved to Liz and Sammy, and she brought them close as she whispered. "Wild Child and Demon Lord about to make a tragedy, Bright Princess and Crimson Master may want to run to aid friendly. Seeping Death be there being ya don't hurry."

This was enough to get Liz to ask quickly, I think above all of us she had been having an easier time with Kitty. She replied in decidedly simple words after Liz inquired, "Where?!"

"Out Front."

Liz had been out front in a moment, Sammy knew she was profoundly understanding, so he followed. Just about now they were there to see me throw an eminently ragged man to the side. Pepper got pushed away toward Naomi, I had been right there as Liz placed herself in harm's way. Sammy now moved to help out Liz, though knowing as they did had to wonder if they could stop me.

So as he helped her out he yelled, "JOHN! JOHN! STOP!!!"

With the raggedy man and I replied, I just asked, "WHAT?!"

The other said, "Oh, Sammy, there you are. You know I have been looking all over for you."

Yeah, I had to think the same thing, I mean I had to have thrown him like ten to twenty feet. There he would be talking like I hadn't just knocked the heck out of him. Now I got this from Naomi, as she saw everything, she was wide-eyed. You also have to understand that Kitty calls me the Demon Lord for a reason. When I go full-on vampire they say I could scare the heck out of anyone.

She saw the full transformation, and when Liz had placed herself in between me and the raggedy man. She saw me go from full-on, to a calm teddy bear that fast. Anyone that knows elders of our kind also will tell you we can't go from hero to zero just like that. Liz, on the other hand, had a way to do this with me, and I can assure you she would ever be the one. Now you understand why Naomi was so wide-eyed with what she just witnessed.

I had to look past them as I also had to ask, "Do you two know this raggedy man?"

Liz looked behind her as she had to admit, "Johnny?"

Sammy came in with, "DUDE! Do you know how close you came to just being dead?!"

I had to say, "Naomi I think we came across another friend of Liz and Sammy's, though you may have to say bye to him you two."

He was human and there was no way we could take in a human. I had to wonder if he could figure any of this out though, but I wasn't going to press our luck. Then Liz had to ask, "John do you see that?"

I had to turn as I also had to request, "What? I don't see anything." I could also see the hunger in Pepper's eyes, so I added, "You too may want to get him out of here, and I also think maybe an extra source of that sanguine fluid. The kids might be over the limit, what do you think Naomi?"

She shook it off as she said two things, "Yeah. I mean yes. John, we honestly need to talk, and it is more important than any Shovelhead."

I had to look at her with that queer statement, as I also added, "Sammy get Pepper out of her."

About now Tony came trotting up, as he also had to ask two things. "Hey guys, I saw you out here. What's up? Plus what is with that guy that looks like death had been hovering over him?"

I had not even thought of using that ability, then again we don't use it as regularly as Liz and Tony's type do. So I used my eyes as they were the only tool for this, that is when I had been able to see it too. You see we can see degrees of life, the more life the more we can see. When you look upon one of us you see virtually nothing, as the human body gets close, well it begins to fade. Now I had been seeing what both Tony, Liz, and perhaps Pepper if the beast wasn't so close.

I had to pull Liz and Tony close as I had to whisper to them now. "Say goodbye, Liz. Tony Sammy knows this guy too, give them the time to say their goodbyes. Liz, I hate to tell you this, but this Johnny's life is fading, I can tell you he'll be dead within just a couple days."

She came right back with, "Can't we just turn him?"

I had to take a look as I also had to ask, "What do you think Tony?"

He replied, "I don't see enough left, he may have just hours."

Naomi had also joined us as she added, "It won't save his final demise, but we could ask someone to ghoul him. I mean I know most proper vampires don't like it, but it would give him maybe a year, possibly more if we caught it in time."

Man, I had to stare at her as if I were willing her to shut up, though it didn't stop there. Tony then had to add, "It could be done, but there are a few problems with that, first, both Sammy and Liz would have to agree with that knowledge. Then we would have to also get this Johnny to agree to it, with the problem that it was Pepper that found him."

I had to add, "Oh great! Put off today so they can suffer tomorrow, that's a real good idea."

"John!" Liz had to bitterly say, "This isn't up to you, and don't get angry just because what I said to you this morning. You have been on one all day because of that."

Okay, I wasn't about ready to get into that here, in fact, I genuinely wasn't going to bring up the subject. I had to stand straight up as I had to say, "You would love that if you had approximately brought the big powerful Demon Lord to his knees! I can't help how I feel and that you feel nothing at all!"

Yep, I said that. I can also say I was absolutely embarrassed after sounding off, and I wanted to go hide my head as well. There aren't many that could have done this to me, as I was there so was Mary and Kitty. They had to drag me off as I was about ready to just start yelling. Now Mary did have some control over me, but nothing like Liz has over me till this day. Kitty knew this, and it was her knowledge that had Mary and a few others dragging me off this in the end.

Chapter twelve

To the heart of the matter.

Now you know where my title came from, even as
it is this wasn't over as of yet. The situation of this Johnny
wasn't left up to me, it was brought before the whole
house. Kitty knew all of this and had Paul and Cheryl
passing out two bags of that vital fluid to all. We would
talk long and hard about what happened, yet not right now
as it was. Tony did his best to keep everyone back, as he
also had to take control, as I had been having nothing to
do with this.

I can also tell you I no ifs and or buts wasn't happy
at all, as they now brought this Johnny into the room. I
had to say with ablated tone, "That smell all of you
kiddies are now smelling is fresh human, to which I'm
unmistakably against this."

Liz placed her hand out as if she had been trying to
get me to shut up. "John this is not decided yet, will you

please give it a rest."

I put my hand out as I had to say, "Go right ahead, you know my vote. I can't abide ghouls in our house."

Naomi then came in with, "John we all know how your kind feels about them, but he is a friend of theirs."

I'll be truthful with you, what had happened was fresh on my mind, though that was also a concern. Cibilia then came in as she had to ask, "John am I the house Princess?"

I had to admit, "Yes, Cibilia you are?"

"You can criticize me after we get done, but can you allow what you have placed in order to work."

I had to nod to her as I had to admit, "That's why I did this, I'm sorry Cibilia. Go right ahead."

"Joe you know all the rules, you represent the general vampire populace. As the house head, I will represent the house, that means that Liz and Sammy can represent this person."

I had to add, "You mean human?!"

Liz stomped over as she came close, as she literally spit in my ear as she spoke. "He still doesn't know what we are, are you willing quintessentially to have him killed?"

"It would be far better for all of you."

She stood up as she had to essentially yell, "How

do you Know?!!!! Categorically can you tell me that?!"

To be truthful I couldn't, so I just answered, "Go right ahead."

Now you have to know I honestly detest ghouls, as they're trouble for us in a human shell. Oh, maybe this is a good time to explain a ghoul, as this had been going to happen. You see when we make a vampire you have to drink them to the point of death. With a human that hasn't been drained, their system can fight off what ours can do. So after they drink a portion of our blood they can become hooked like a junkie.

Now for the blood, it can also react with their blood, causing them to heal tissue. It isn't a given as they still can do all as a normal human, but I saw one that lived to a hundred twenty-five. He looked maybe in his fifties. The one downfall of these guys is that they're human and like humans can be tortured. This is another ending to many that believed in them, and they convey the impression to bring the worst.

So in a way it can save this Johnny, just after all this happens you now have a weak link in the house. Naomi did everything with the help of Tony. Cibilia and Joe did a wonderful job in their leadership roles. The only stinker in the bunch was the eldest of the group, and he wasn't happy even with himself. Tony had explained that he needed a minder, someone that would also be his protector. Those kids had no idea what that entailed, I had to leave.

What I mean is they sure as can choose Pepper as his minder, which called for her to get him a meal and a bottle. Mary helped her there as we had never allowed her to drive a car. I'm not sure an extra order of fries and a happy meal constitutes a meal. Then you have fundamentally they got him the cheapest bottle of what he called wine. I put my foot down when they were just going to allow him to sleep.

Though I did goad Pepper into it, as I reminded her that she was the house garment procurer. Also that even as her sister was the house princess, and how would it look if her ghoul was a bum. Johnny may not have been indubitably happy, as this caused a few to get scrub brushes to work the dirt out of their belongings. By now I had to go to my room, as I laid back with the chair against the wall when Liz came in a huff.

I wasn't paying attention, so how did I know? It may have been by how hard she slammed the door, then again I knew this had been coming also. She pointed her finger at me as she said with venom in her voice, "How dare you!"

Okay, what had I been going to say, I played it off as if I didn't know what she meant. "How dare I what?"

"You know I just said that this morning because I wasn't sure I knew how I truly felt."

I had to blink as I had to say, "I spoke honestly on how I felt, how am I supposed to feel after getting shot down so hard."

"I DIDN'T SHOOT YOU DOWN!"

"WHAT DO YOU CALL IT THEN!"

I mean that is the way I felt after all that, as she

went on with, "YOU TELL ME ABOUT THE BONDING PROCESS! THEN AFTER YOU SAY SOMETHING LIKE THAT YOU EXPECT ME NOT TO HAVE DOUBT?!"

"NO!" I had to think about this, "I MEAN I GUESS SO! I DON'T KNOW! ALL I DO KNOW IS I SHARED MY RAW FEELINGS WITH YOU! THEN YOU HAD TO SAY THAT!"

She now threw open the door to storm out, when she ran straight into Naomi. She pushed Liz to the chair and made her sit down, then she kicked my chair. I had to ask, "WHAT?!"

"Jonathan Williamson I will not have you have that tone with me! Get over here and join in what I'm doing."

She was profoundly direct with what she said to me, so I had to figure it was better not to antagonize her. So yeah I moved my chair to the other side of the table, then she started with a simple question. "Liz I don't have to ask this of John, in fact, I do believe the whole house knows how he feels. If you were being honest with yourself, without any of the knowledge you've acquired. How do you honestly feel about John?" She stopped her before she answered and added, "Before he pissed you off to no end?"

Now she had to give her interpretation of how she felt, "Confused admittedly. I mean when he spoke those words my heart jumped for joy, then came the confusion."

"Can you elaborate upon that?"

She turned to me as she confessed, "John what I feel for you is an extraordinarily intense feeling, is it, love? I can't say because I just don't know. You have to understand I was a sister just a few nights ago, I want to know so much about this. I mean everything, how to be a vampire, then you tell me about the sensuality. You know what that means, well I don't. I have to learn so much, what happens if I fall to my true emotions."

She turned to me as she had to inquire, "What if I had to do something that drove you wild, and we were together. Would that fact cause me not to be able to learn? I know how I feel but you have to understand, you have to be absolutely patient with me."

I now had to think as I had not thought of any of this, I had to say. "I do understand, though it may be different, I promise I understand. You have to also understand this also, I also have no idea. You have said you know I have been with many women, that is true, which I now hate. I can also tell you why I hate this, as for what I feel for you I have never felt before this particular time. You could say that this may be the second time I have ever felt love."

This was a time I had to go back to a place I had not been in a long time. Now you will hear this only once truly, so listen hard.

"It was long ago, and I wasn't what we are now. I had found a wonderful lady, we were incredibly happy in our meager life. She gave me two beautiful daughters, with the way the world had been when I had been barely able to keep food on the table. But we survived. Then came that fateful night, when a vampire had been looking to escape the authorities. Not human, our authorities. He saw a way if he could get on a boat, so he did the unthinkable and turned a family man into a vampire."

I had to look away as I had to go on, but even my eyes were getting wet. "I had no idea what I was. All I wanted was to escape and get home to my wife and kids."

Naomi came in with, "John you didn't?"

I had to shake my heads as I felt a tear pass down my cheek. Liz had to ask, "What did he do?"

Naomi then confessed, "When we are made we can't help the thirst, a human-like your Johnny would be an easy pick. John did the unthinkable, even as his mind told him it wasn't right."

I had to confess even more, "Yes. We usually can stop after that, but what can you do after a loving wife is a husk? I had two daughters, and I had just taken their mother away. I literally had no choice,"

I had to stop even as I could hear my own voice choking now. Naomi nodded her head as Liz had to say, "Wow. Though maybe suggestive of the wrong thing to say, you had to drink the blood of your own daughters."

Naomi then had to ask, "Were there no orphanages?"

I nodded my head as I had been finding it extremely hard to talk, "He . . . he had . . ."

"Oh, the vampire had tracked you down?" I had to nod my head again, "So indirectly caused the death of your wife, and directly caused the deaths of your daughters."

Liz seemed to transform as she had to say, "John. You have lived with that for all these years."

I had never heard such a beautiful sound, it in point of fact lightened my dark mood as I spoke. "I knew he had been looking for me, I also knew I couldn't allow him to get my two beautiful daughters. So as I held my baby I drank the youngest, I laid them to rest on the bed. If you hadn't seen the slight blood, you would have thought they were just sleeping. Then I lift up my oldest and took her to her new bed, we could never afford it. We had gone a few meal so she could have it, then I did what needed to be done."

I had to sit back as I had to confess one more thing, "She was so small. I understood our vampire strength after that, you see she looked as if she just slept. Except for her broken neck."

I had to take an appropriate deep sigh, as I know told them the truth. "I can't ever tell you I never had a women, human and vampire alike. I also can't tell you what I thought I had every time was love, but to my mind, after it was always easy to move on with that same love. The thoughts of them never crowd my mind like what I did you, my wife and daughters. Because of this, I have come to the point that I had never been in love with none."

I now had to look at Liz as I confessed, "Until I met you. The problem is like you I have no idea, so what is this I have professed? It was my real and true feelings at the time, and as what we are in all my years."

Naomi had to say, "Oh!"

Liz, of course, had to ask, "What?"

"Liz this world is not cordial, and many are always doing things to see what they can get. As you know what John is, though he has said over and over to forget it. John would be a prize under anyone's belt, so in his well, over three hundred years he had never been refused. John has no coping tools to this thing we would like to call vampire relationships."

With that, she had to turn to John as she had to say, "Listen John. I know this is all new to you, we could break the bond and see what happens. Even you know that would be plain stupid with what we are facing. I do have a proposal though since she is a fresh vampire as well as a new woman so to speak. I say the two of you tread noticeably softly and see where this goes. Is it a good thing, well you know it isn't. In truth, it is all we have till we are sure the city is free of these Shovelhead's."

She now turned to her and said, "I know what you mean, so does John, but you have to be kinder when you talk about all of this."

"Well, he . . ."

Naomi cut her off, "There is no blame here, John is an uncommonly good vampire. All he wanted to do is make sure you knew, so he told you because he can't hold back from you. Girl, you have no idea the power you have, one day I may even tell you. What I saw today when you stepped in between Johnny and John spoke volumes. No one in this house could have ever caused John to do what he did. Mary has some control in that area also, but no where close to what you have."

She came expressly close as she met forehead to forehead, "With great power comes great responsibility, you have that so I say use it wisely. Do we have an understanding?"

Even I had to look at her questioning, as Liz appealed to her. "I'm not sure I truly understand?"

"Liz he may be the most powerful vampire in North America. Now I can't literally be sure of that, I can say a lot of people fear him. He never uses his power to kill good people, which I had heard. I didn't believe what they said though until I heard that story. He could tell you so many stories about the vampires he's destroyed. Don't ask him that, ask him how many humans he had killed? Now, do you understand the power you have control over Liz?"

She had to giggle as she also added, "No, I meant what do we have an understanding over Naomi?"

She had an aggravated look on her face, "He loves you girl, you love him. Is it perfect, no? Stop this fighting and get on with it, discuss what needs to happen. Then you two can live together because I can also attest that neither of you even fathomed leaving this room. Now do you get why I said, do we have an agreement to talk about it? Unlike John though, I prefer getting more to the point."

Now she got up, and she made her way to the door. She stopped there as she also added, "I can feel you staring at my ass John."

I had to say with that joke, "I couldn't help it, it's a great butt."

She turned her head as she placed her finger on it, and she made a sizzling sound. "I know, always have."

Then she opened the door and Kitty came rushing in, she wrapped herself around Liz. Then she spoke, "Now Bright Princess know, you beehive, no? You be the catalyst be in him, you hab musscalles, hehehe."

Then she ran out again, I had to place one eyebrow up with the significance. Naomi had to confess, "I have no idea what was up with that."

I was about ready to say something when Liz spoke, "I think that was her way of confirming what you just said, I could be wrong though."

I had to say, "No Liz, I think you hit the nail on the head."

Naomi now said just before she closed the door, "Now you two lovebirds get at it, we have nasties to destroy and can't have this again."

Liz had to ask, "Again?"

I knew I could have lied, then again I also felt I couldn't truly ever do that to her. "Yeah. I may have been somewhat distracted this morning, but I fought through it so no one would die."

"John?"

"Yes, Liz?"

"Never ever do that again, we could have stopped

and talked about it. Was there any possibility that anyone could have gotten hurt?"

"Well not as to what I was doing, no. I can't categorically tell you that there wasn't the possibility we could be fewer a few also. In truth I do believe we were lucky too, I have seen far too much to say anything other than that. I will also add just the little bit I have taught all of you, may have indeed made the difference. We can't stop though either, as the more primed we get, the lower the chances are we lose anyone."

"What if we do?"

"I have lost a few . . ."

She cut me off with, "No not you or Naomi, I know the two of you can handle it. What I mean have you thought of what will happen if like let's say Cheryl goes down, or worse Pepper? You know Mary and Cibilia would throw everything to the wind to save those two. Then you have the way Andy and Bert feel about one another, I do believe Bert would like that with him. Have you thought about that?"

I leaned my chair on the wall again, "Everyday. Then you have quintessentially those six would fight to the end if any other went down in front of them. I know we have to do this, but I undoubtedly have no idea how to solve that tragedy if it happens." I had to look at the ceiling as I went on, "I guess all we can do is comfort them, hope they don't leave and try our best for them." I had to sigh as I had to add one more thing, "I don't see many of the six surviving if that happens either."

She moved over to the closet as she had to add,

"Me either, but we have to do our best. Now I have to ask you a decidedly important question?"

I leaned down just slightly as I had to ascertain, "What could that be Honey?"

She smiled at me as she disappeared into the closet, "Do you want any of this tonight if so you might want to get undressed."

Okay, even though we did have a fight, and yeah I'm a guy. You also have to know Liz is smoking hot too, so I had no problem moving like the wind. I was also the first into bed, and yeah guys, it was so I could see her walk to the bed. Because even as she walked, she was smoke personified. You that are human, you would have followed her every step. Yeah, as those of the legendary Dryad, all would walk into their own demise.

Now I also won't allow you to think all was alright, we did things that day I won't talk about until the time is right. I will talk about how much we talked, and you will get the gist of it next chapter. With a mistake as well, that may have been a good thing as well. It set us on a truly different road, one that a lot may also love to see and hear. I undoubtedly do love the next chapter, intrigued yet? Good.

Chapter Thirteen

Just another day, or is that a new day?

<u>Day Ten</u>

Now you know how the day went this time, though I also have to say we had a new sense of vigor. We talked a lot also as she shared so much with me, I also had to shut her down on a few things. Some I also said that was a most definite maybe, even with fundamentals that we would have to wait till our problem was solved. She assured me that it was a definite thing, as she perfectly understood what I meant.

I had to admire her as she had this mindset on everything, then you have how intelligent she is. Well, she would be the first to tell you she wasn't that smart, I mean the lady absolutely sold herself short. Now we were in the new day and as usual, there she was sprawled out, which was weird. I mean we did enough to be like this, but she absolutely made sure things were right with us before we dozed off to rest.

I had been doing this since the first night we slept together, I mean she was perfectly nude. I can also see how she jumped into that with such a dogged attitude, so I think I kind of understood why most joined the faith. Okay, maybe there is a substance of faith also when I was a religious man I was more a Lutheran. I guess you could say I lost my faith as I became this, well maybe more in that of people than God.

I undoubtedly can't talk about that, what I can talk about is what I commonly recognized. When a priest of like Liz said a worthy sister, as to the way they generally dress, are targets. Perchance that is why the Catholics went the way they did, they do resemble a regular army set against us. There are certain names we universally don't use, it is more for the others than for us literally.

Just in case I did something I practically never did, and I placed on a pair of underwear. Then I moved to the window to watch the beauty. As the sun was now setting, and the pleasure of his delight had been present with the afterglow of his sunset. I then remembered something that I heard in my youth, and I had to look in admiration.

Which brought it to me, so I whispered it low, "How great is he when you can look at what he created, and not be in bewilderment at his accomplishment."

From behind me came, "John, are you now quoting scriptures?"

I had to look back as I had to admit, "Even Satan can quote scriptures. Good morning beautiful."

"You think of us as Satan's children then? Isn't it technically evening?"

I came close and sat on the bed, "I can't say that I do know that a demon took me over though in the end. I also have a sense of good and evil, I prefer the prior over the later. To our ability of what we are, I'm sure if we were, he would be turning around in the pit as it were. Oh, that is if I'm right, I'm not a wonderfully religious man. As to the time of day, you're right. Just it is more common to say good morning when one wakes up for that time of day, though good evening would be more accurate."

She gave me a sort of smile as she affirmed, "Yeah, that is what the Bible says. In our world it is his minions that have control, we gave them the name demon." Then she appeared to get uncomfortable, "They're absolutely called fallen angels, I'm sure I'm boring you half to death."

I had to chuckle as I came close and tickled her, and told her a truth about me. "Babe you could never bore me, I may appear like I'm not listening. I might not even be able to quote what you say, but I can assure you I'm everything you're saying."

"John!" She screamed as she added, "Stop that."

"What you don't like to be tickled? I could have done what I thought, though that may have been somewhat intrusive." I came even closer as I whispered, "You did give the impression that you like it enough for us to it several times last night . . . I mean today."

"Are you getting philosophical with theology now?"

I had to admit if we did I would doubtlessly be wrong more then right. I did have to wonder how it would relate to us, so I spoke about it in neutral terms. "I do think maybe we should, even as I'm not that versed on the subject. Then again as I have learned last night, maybe all at once is too much at first. I think that many of us have a lot to learn, though I also have to give you a warning babe." I had to sigh as I told her this, "Your faith has come after us the most, and when it comes to your time. You may never have heard this term, but it could be one of the Black Popes own that cut you down with a religious intent of your own purity."

She looked at me curiously as she inquired, "The Black Pope?"

I came close as I had to assure her on this one, "I don't think he is an actual Pope, just that is what his followers call him. We do think he is more like a Cardinal of the church, but in truth, we also think he is more like a general. He is the actual guy that leads the Pope's army, though I'm not sure they have any affiliation with the Swiss Guard. The only thing we can say for sure is that they're an army set on hunting all that they perceive to being evil."

She had to ask, "Do you believe that, or is it just another one of those stories?"

I shook my head as I came back, "No, I experienced that first hand. In fact, I barely survived a few times, as I ended up having to wade through their own cannon fodder. I think in certain ways they're like those Shovelhead's. You see they have all these young guys trying to make the next class. They're usually moderately good, so I have no idea why they have to waste so many lives."

"I don't like this John, are you comparing these men of God, to these evil Shovelhead's?"

"Well no. Just I think if you have so many recruits, why place them in harm's way just to get to us. In a sense they don't exactly place them out there with nothing, I mean pistols, rifles, and swords. Shovelhead's don't do that, though whoever came into this world may have their own arms. I guess where the problem is, that they just conveying the impression that they undoubtedly don't care. Well, either that or the life itself absolutely has no meaning to them save for the chance to get at us."

She had to shake her head as she said a basic truth, "That creates the impression of being highly unlikely, as one of the prime attitudes is to do unto others as you would have them do unto you. I mean why would they stray so far from their basic consignments?"

I had to disclose what I knew, even if it may have fallen on deaf ears. "Babe they wore looser clothes than most priests, but I can assure you that the white collar was always there. Then you have the fact they always had some kind of religious artifact. Considering how well they can do a thing, I mean no real priest can move like any of them. What can be said is for all the world they look the part, though knowing this I can also say they're no real priests. That is my opinion."

"Then why did you say they were?"

"What would you say if there were no real term for them, and all of them went around calling each other brother and father. You have to have some term for them, and all those terms that would be outside the box genuinely don't apply. Then you have the fact of their bosses name, kind of lends to something out of the church. Also, let's say they get to know you, and they come to do their work. You have now chosen to be called Elizabeth, but they will only call you by your old title."

"I don't get it, why would they call me Sister Mary Elizabeth?"

"It would be more like: You have strayed from the fold, Sister Mary Elizabeth. We chastise you in the name of the Father. Sister Mary Elizabeth."

"Well that insinuates a presumptuous to me, why would they just assume that?"

Okay, I was sure at this point she wasn't getting it, "I honestly don't know beyond that, all I do know is how they act. In fact, they do also tend to go overboard, I watched one firebomb a building to get one of our like in the end. Now if he was the only one in there, I may have been able to understand that. Just who he thought he had wasn't even there, and he killed thirty innocents. When the news came out they said there was an electrical short, there was no electrical short. I was there, I'm the one that eventually caught him and ended his life. That guy was one of many monsters I had to go after that the church sent out after just another form of evil."

I knew this would be particularly hard to hear next, "Naomi told you to ask of all the humans I killed, that may be a bad thing as for every normal human, two were men of the cloth. To be honest I legitimately don't think any of them started out that way. What I can say that something changed them to be those monsters, and I would love to tell you it was other than the church. I can also say that as I know God, he is a loving God, so these guys certainly can't be of God. All I can say is that they're exceedingly dogged in their ways, as I have seen many religious people, though not all."

She had this despairing look on her face, "I must resemble the most God awful sort of evil to you?"

I had to smile at her as I had to ask, "Why would I see that? As to that ask yourself, how many vampires have I gone after and destroyed? Then you'll see how evil I see you, I think in the light of things, I may be truly far eviler then you are babe."

"But you . . ."

I had to cut her off with, "Listen, babe. Many good people have started the chain of events, but none of them knew what they were unleashing. I can't blame one man, woman, Priest, or honorable sister for doing what they think is right. It is like the good Samaritan of the modern era, they want to do right. But as the man at the side of the road sticking out his thumb. It would be better to pick him up, but you have to assess your own condition. If that is bad like maybe you have kids in the car, God will understand if you ask for forgiveness."

She then smiled at me as she said, "You know you indirectly quoted scripture again."

I had to say since to me I was just talking, "Oh, did I?"

She had to say, "That does make me think though,

and I do believe this goes with what you were saying earlier. Like you said when we became this thing did change, but as for us as a whole, nothing truly changed. Can I say where the condition of my soul is, the fact is we just don't know. Then you have the fact like our human counterparts, it is suggested that we do have a free will. I can't say that we are more or less for what we are, so it is as much a truth of those facts when we were alive."

I had to add, "Does that mean just like a normal human there is a chance our soul can go to Heaven?"

"Well, the possibilities are there, though to say that is a fact isn't an easy task. I can say that all does suggest this fact, which would be completely counter to what all have taught us. I can go back and forth all day, if I had a Bible with me I may even be able to find scripture. I think for now it is safer to say it is a definite maybe."

"That does remind me." Though right then I had to make sure if anyone was listening, not because they couldn't hear it, but I wanted to give myself some time. "I told you they tend to lie to us in this world as well, I mean we are of the Devil than we aren't. There was one original, then there has to be thirteen, finally, there are as many as there are families. I do believe a lot of it comes in with old beliefs, and the essence that they have to explain exactly what we are."

"Yeah, I can see that. I do have to ask why you looked out the door like that?"

I had to smile at her as I had to admit, "It isn't that I don't want them to know, it is just a fact that it would be much better than having to explain that. I do think with your knowledge you can easily take this for what it's worth, and weigh the pros and cons. I think someone like Pepper may have a hundred questions, and for now, we have to have them focusing on training."

She nodded her head as she agreed on a negligible account, "Yeah, I mean she has a lot of questions, though most are genuinely about her own sexuality. From what you told me that is normal for our kind, the two that I think would truly be questioning are Paul and Andy."

"Sexuality a? You wouldn't have any questions about that yourself?"

She then giggled as she replied, "Why are you going to show me something new again? Like that move I had you show me several times the other night?"

I came close as I kissed her and said, "We could just keep doing that, I know how much you like that."

"Ooo, Mister Williamson, are you going to molest me?"

"I could molest you for the entire night, you do realize save for tissue loss, we absolutely don't get tired."

"I wish we literally could, and I may just take you up on that in each and every way. As soon as we have to do something about Johnny, I mean you saw they just bought him a happy meal with extra fries. I know we aren't human anymore, and we have no need for actual food. He in his own right has become our responsibility, and we have to show these kids how to take care of a ghoul."

Okay, that made me an infinitesimal dark as I had

to remind her, "They made their minds up about all of this, not my choice. Pepper was chosen for this job, it is all her problem now. I also know he's . . ."

She cut me off with, "John! Do you honestly think that eighteen-year-old girl knows what she has to do? I don't think so. You're well over three hundred years old, and from what I understand what they call an archon, whatever that is. Even when you don't like it, you have to show them because they look up to you. John, you have no idea how important to these kids you are, in fact, I think you're rather important to every member of this house. Just like you tell the others, you have to at least show you're walking the walk."

How could I argue with that, I mean I tried, but when I opened my mouth, I realized there would be nothing to be said. So I caved in with, "Yeah, I guess I haven't been acting the part."

"No you haven't," she said. Then added, "You have been acting like a spoiled rotten child instead, then again look why you were acting out in the first place."

With that she giggled again, I'm not that fastest guy when it comes to the romantic stuff. That, on the other hand, was extremely easy to read, and yeah I then lost the shorts. I will tell you we did a few things, and yeah again I'm not going to tell you what we did. There is a point that you can go and you won't go beyond, until this date Liz and I haven't found that position. Yes, I added that specific word for a reason, if you find it funny that is why I placed it there.

Now we did start to move as we heard the kids moving around, and we were still playing even as we dressed. Sometimes what you do can be misunderstood, this was one of those times it literally happened terribly. What I mean you will see, as it happened this day, as we were about done.

Liz had decided to try one of those corsets, I mean it looked so uncomfortable. I also saw her have to draw in breath to get it tied, I had to wonder how easy it would be to untie. So I reached over and gave it barely a pull, I was surprised at how easily it did come undone. Though that got a scream and a slap from Liz, then came a giggle, with her redoing it up in the end. With her comment, "Stop that. If you keep doing that I'll go naked."

I had to say, "That wouldn't bother me."

"Oh really. Me walking around so all the boys can see my naked body, are you sure you're okay with that?"

I had to think for a second, then admitted, "Nope."

"Nope, what?"

I then came close and start helping do up her corset, as I completed what I meant. "Nope, I'm not okay with that. Even if we aren't technically a couple as of yet, I do think what I see is all mine." Then I said in a louder voice, "You can't see what I see boys!"

She giggled, then asked, "What if they got a peek by accident. What would you do?"

"Hmm. Poke out their eyes, bash their heads in, then for good measure pull it off so they can see their own pleasure."

"Their heads?"

"Yep. If I'm mad enough maybe the other one as well."

"Other what?"

"Liz you don't know men's anatomy, as in we have to heads. One is for thinking and the other is for fun."

Okay, that took her by surprise as she breathlessly spoke, "John! You're so bad!"

I had to chuckle as I also admitted, "I think they're too scared of me for that to ever happen, but maybe I should make sure they all know. Maybe I can call a meeting as tell them how I would destroy them slowly if they took one glimpse of you nude. What do you think?"

She gave me one of those looks, "I think you're right that they are scared of you, but we don't need to send them into shock too."

I was reasonably done as I had to tell her, "I know you don't want to hear this, but I do think that my love for you is beyond just the bond. Yes, I know it is way to fast also, but you do have to know that one day I may ask you that serious question."

"John, stop being silly. Naomi already told us all the reason why our race doesn't get married."

"Yeah, I know all about that as well. Though that is like what I had been telling you earlier, they say that but in reality, no one knows why. Then they use the quintessence that we can't enter any consecrated churches.

I have entered a few in my life, to this day I can't figure out where anyone came up with that one. Just to show you what I mean, you know that cross you had to yourself when we turned you?"

She nodded her head as she replied, "Yeah, my rosary."

"Well in accordance with their understanding, as soon as you started the change it should have started to burn your skin. In my fights against those that called themselves of the church were dumbfounded when I grabbed theirs away from them. Don't get me wrong I have had a few hurt, I do believe that it has to have the true faith behind it. So if the person sees it as more of an object, or has no real faith in the Lord, it doesn't burn."

With that she went right to her top drawer and took it out, then she placed it against her cheek. She lifted it away as she had to ask, "So does that mean we could wear anything, I mean I heard the pureness of the metal may also cause damage."

I had to also pull out something eminently old as I said, "As old as this is, it has the purest gold you can get." I gave it to her as I also added, "Try it on, but I definitely want it back."

She had to look at it as she ascertained, "John, do you know what this is?"

I had to reply, "What is there something wrong with it, I mean only one woman wore it. She no longer has any use for it."

"John! Is this your ex-wives wedding ring?"

I had to smile at her as I asked as I got down on one knee, "Oh because of what it is, do you want me to do this right?"

Okay, now is when it happened. As a squeal came from our door, you see Pepper had the same idea that Liz had. She had come to our room to ask us if we should go to the store. So when she cracked the door I was on one knee, and Liz was about ready to give it back to me. Her mind was to tell me that even as it was, that even that could be wrong. I, in my way, had been only joking with her, and I had made all the plans to stick to our agreement.

In Pepper's mind, all she saw was me on one knee, with a ring in my hand. I do believe it looked as if Liz's hand was in mine as well, and she heard me talk, but she hadn't comprehended. So after an absolutely loud squeal that intimated us to deaf, she went running through the house. Yelling, "John is proposing to Liz!"

Chapter Fourteen

The Explanation, and we start a new adventure.

To say we had to scramble now would be an understatement, though there is also more to handle. I can say that I had never seen any lady handle something like which was in Liz's hand with such disdain. The fullness of how much she unquestionably didn't want what I had just jokingly suggested came to the full front. I would have to ask all here if I also knew you could answer me, is it so terrible to be wed if you loved the individual? Then again am I such a repulsive figure that she honestly didn't want anything to do with me.

I had to place my hand out so she could drop the item in my hand as I had to explain. "That is my now long gone dead wives, I carry it as a relic of protection, and I guess as a reminder of her also."

She suggested having to ask me, "Does that absolutely work?"

To be truthful I had thought it hadn't at all, but in more ways than one. "I guess as I had thought, no. As a reminder of why I do what I do, yes. I can tell you she was a redhead like you, even though all the faces have managed to meld together over time. So even as in that manner, I have to also say no. In the time of the Lady's peace, I think we had many Irish gentlemen come over, I think her father was of that ilk. I can also tell you my children had a mixture of our hair, as she would tell you, they all had strawberry hair."

She gave the impression to warm to this statement, as she said, "Oh. I bet they all had beautiful freckles."

I had to reply, "Yes. Yes, I do believe they did. Though their freckles aren't what is important right now. I do believe we have to go around dispelling what Pepper is starting without full knowledge."

She smiled at me as she said, "Two things John, one day I might want to get married. Just right now I have to find out about myself, so don't take my disdain for your wives ring as meaning I don't want to get married. Just in our own time, then you have the fact of my own. When and if I say yes, I genuinely want my own ring, not what your wife wore."

I had to ask her though, "Did you feel any power from how pure the gold had been in that ring though?"

"Oh, that is why you gave it to me?"

"Yes," I had commented. Then I realized that she had thought like Pepper, "Oh! Liz, I'm not that much of a dolt, like you said, when and if we get married we'll go out searching for our own ring. After yesterday I would have never done such a thing, as you made it decidedly clear you wanted to learn this life first. I had just . . ."

I got cut off with Naomi at the door half dressed, "Is it true John? Did you propose to Liz?"

I had to shake my head as I also saw the disconcerted look on her face as I replied. "No. I know what she said last night, just I gave her an old ring to show her pure metals don't affect us. Liz made some strange remarks so I had been joking around with her. I think she heard me say let me to this right as I got down on one knee. She just squealed real loud, that she deafened us, and we haven't had time to stop her."

She then said something that in its own right concerned me as well. "Good. You know how they talk about us and the way churches are on our senses. I would hate to absolutely head for a church."

I had to ask, "Naomi after you became what we are, have you never ventured into a church?"

"No. I never wanted to take the risk."

"Well you know how they imply to lie about everything, well I can also assure you they lied about churches as well. I have been forced to carry a fight many a time into a church, part of a sanctuary, or the inner courtyard of churches. We have also talked about getting married, not that we are going to do it tomorrow, but we haven't ruled it out in the end. So now knowing this, why can't we get married?"

She had one of those looks like she was half

concerned, and at the same time surprised. As she had to admit, "To be honest after hearing all that, I have no idea."

Liz then had to ask with acknowledgment first, "I had been fasting for a fair while before I made my decision. So you could say that as I gave up the faith I would be away from the faithful, but in the state, I had been in I was the closest to God as I could get. If there had been something overall this then I don't think that a Shovelhead would have ever been able to cut my throat. Now because I would have been dying what Tony had to do had been moderately out there, but it could also be said that he shouldn't have been able to give me his blood."

I had to admit she did have a point there, so I had to add. "I have also battled many that would take my life, as they presented a cross to save themselves. Not that a cross doesn't have power, but I do believe if they had more faith it would have worked far better. I mean I saw many of those surprised looks after taking it away from them."

Tony then came to the edge of the door as he now asked, "Are you two going to tie the knot?"

I had to say loudly, "No! It was just all a joke!" I then said quickly as I looked at Naomi, "Naomi explain it to him, Liz we have to beat feet and get this stopped before it goes wild." With this, we ran out of the room, as Naomi pulled Tony aside to converse. I also had to add, "Tell them also we're doing a road trip, and to be out at the cars in let's say thirty minutes."

With this Liz stopped at Pepper and Paul's room to explain, I showed her I had been heading upstairs. I had to stop at everyone's room, I mean it had gone wild as you can imagine. Most were noticeably happy for us as I explained, in fact, Sammy and Johnny listened the most intently. When I got to Kitty's room you won't believe this one, she lifted her spiked boot up high enough to kick me in the butt. I guess it had caught her by so much surprise she had no time to check the visions.

Finally, we made it to the cars where Kitty told me she was sorry. I told her it didn't matter, and that I had no idea she could lift her foot so high. Now as they all calmed down with all the talk about what had happened. I also had to take Pepper aside to tell her a few thing. Like always make sure you have your facts straight first. Finally right after I had Tony and Naomi pull out the micro-bus and jeep. I placed my hands up as I called them all around, even Johnny for this venture.

My first statement was a short one, "Anyone feel the need to suck a few pints of blood from Johnny, go get something to drink right now." I waited for a few to see if anyone took me up on that, then I continued, "Good. We're going to have a human in the house until he dies, so if you ever feel the need go to . . ." I had to ask, "Cheryl and Paul have either of you decided who is in charge of all that yet?"

Cheryl replied, "Since I'm better at finances we decided he would be in charge of that."

"Good, that means you go to Paul. Cibilia and Joe he is the boss, you two will have to sick Bert on anyone that breaks that rule. I then turned and had to add, if you're in an undoubtedly bad state though you can just go and get some, always allow Paul to know. That will always be a given, now to you Cheryl, as you're taking care of the finances what are they like right now?"

She turned to Pepper as she placed out her hand and said, "Can I use your phone so I can show John."

I had to say, "Just tell me, and never worry I'll believe you always. After all, we have to depend on you for this."

She smiled as she replied, "Well Giaus place three hundred at first, then another two hundred. That Veronica literally outdid him in one fell swoop, she rewarded us with twelve hundred dollars. You take out the gas for the cars, and what William said he needed to get the electricity straightened out for us in the end. I think well over fourteen hundred dollars, so not much, but for now good."

I had to ask, "Veronica rewarded us twelve hundred dollars?"

"She phoned Pepper this morning, I certainly haven't had a chance to truly look though. I had been going to do that with Pepper's phone right now, I mean with all the ruckus, I haven't had much of a chance."

I nodded my head as I also had to add, "Treat six hundred of that as if it isn't ours, we may have to pay her a tribute when she takes over the city. Also do that now, we assuredly need to know where we are with what we need to do next with this venture. Pepper give her your phone for now, and now to you, as this is all new to you. Oh, shoot."

I had to look around as Liz asked, "What John?"

I told her, "Everyone needs to have a hat except

for you, Pepper, Tony, Paul, and Cheryl."

I think she was about ready to move, but like usual she asked, "Why exactly?"

Again I had to explain to all, "Where we are going has fluorescent light bulbs, they tend to show us as being as dead as we are. Only those I mentioned can get away with entering a store without a hat, though Cheryl and Paul are somewhat iffy. Let's just say that they legitimately show how dead we are, I mean that is why I had the gas the other night pumped the way it was."

Liz nodded her head as she just guests my measure that night. "Oh I see, then why are we all going?"

"Well Pepper has to do it every time, but as long as there are Shovelhead's in the city, I will send two for the car, and two for the store. This is our first time, and as all training, I want all to see how to do this. Johnny, you're just going this time so you can inform us what you like since time isn't warranted. We have to listen to him, everyone, we can't have him dying because he's allergic to let's say strawberries. Got me?!"

I waited for everyone to acknowledge what I had said, as Pepper just had to speak. "Why does it always have to be me?"

I had to give her a look as I ascertained, "Really? You fought so hard to be his controller, and to who he was ghouled to? Now you're having second thoughts about what it all entails?"

"Sorry John. I knew there was more to all this, I just thought it was cool to have the houses first ghoul."

I had to shoot at her, "What?! You don't want the job now?!!!"

Liz came back as she had to ask, "Why is John yelling again?"

Paul replied, "Pepper found out what being the minder of Johnny entails, now she's trying to back out of it."

"Her are the darn hats!" She walked straight over to Pepper and backhanded her as she said, "I told you! You said you could handle it! What are you?! Some kind of little Daddy's girl?! Look around everywhere! No Daddy would allow you to be what you are, your daddy isn't here to save you now! Get a backbone girl and grow up! You think being what we are would be just for fun! You think we look charming then, we drink blood, and there are no repercussions?!"

She then turned to Cibilia, "I know she's your sister, and you're presumably pissed I just slapped her, but somebody has to knock some sense into her."

I had to step in between them as I added, "Cibilia Liz is done, just get over there and handle your sister. Maybe knock some sense into yourself, do something before I do something. You know me well enough, Liz did that so I wouldn't have slapped her myself."

Cibilia then said, "I know John. Liz just beat me to the punch as well, though next time Liz allow me to handle my sister please."

Kitty came in with, "Yeah Demon Lord be first if

Bright One not see, Harlequin sees all. Little Kitty was thin can, my like see is lower smiley. No good sister need hitting hard, though ya no likely my smiley."

Cibilia had to come close, "What does she mean I no like her smiley?"

I came close so only she and Cibilia could hear, "You know Mister Sharpie?" They both nodded, "She uses that on someone's neck to create an extra smile, they tend to call it smiley."

I could see the both of them grabbing for their throats as she moved to Pepper. I had to wonder what was said as I could see her doing all kinds of things. It was unquestionably easy to also see that Pepper wasn't liking what she heard. She may be like Liz, but I can also say she would be nothing like her, as her repose was apparent. Cibilia then helped her up as she came walking over, the entire time looking at the ground.

Finally, she said, "I'm sorry John and Liz. Oh, and for the record, I thought it was cool the two of you were getting married."

I had to smile at her as Liz let her know the truth of it. "It was just a joke this morning Hun, but we haven't ruled it out though, just saying. For me it just isn't the right time, I have so much to learn." She then looked at Tony, "Yeah, you may have to walk me down the aisle one day. Just it'll be significant while longer."

They had been passing out hats as all this went along, and there wasn't enough. So I had to say, "Okay, we have to do this, but as we also need vehicle guards I think Naomi and Bert are best." I then placed on my white cowboy hat and had to ask, "How do I look?"

Liz had to laugh as she replied, "The hottest cowboy I ever saw, what ya think girls?"

Okay, they embarrassed me. I had never heard so many catcalls before in my life, so I just had to say. "Okay guys lets mount up!"

Before you ask, I had not intended for that to be funny, though everyone laughing assured me it was. We ended up at a Wal-Mart, and though they're local, this one wasn't close. It had been the closest store with groceries around though, and the twenty-minute drive did give me time to blow everything off my shoulders. As we pulled into our parking spots, and we all bailed out of the vehicle. Naomi, Bert and I discussed how they would watch, not that there would be anything important about what happened.

You could say for once we had a night of normal vampire activity. We did what needed to be done as we filled up the cart, then I also allowed them to get two movies. Well indeed after Pepper and Paul had told me the computer could play movies. They also decided to make it a night of movie watching. In fact, I even got a slightly more teased, as I had no idea about this vampire movie. There was of course more to this night, I just wouldn't find out for like two weeks.

To be truthful I had found most movies about us as so crass that I avoided them. Which got all of them talking about the best of them, again I have no idea what they were. I mean I would discover those as we would go on, though why vampires would make an academy is beyond me. I have seen a few of our kind that were self-loathing, but none like that movie daybreak. Oops, Liz told me that movie was called Twilight.

Now when it came to great movies there was one beyond the mark. I mean they took an older movie, made it new, with an entirely new story. Not that any of it was real, but from my time as I have learned, the time of the Mongol invasion had been a lot like that. The time period told me it had been the Golden Horde they were fighting against in the end. Even as it was retold I have heard a similar story of the time period. I without a doubt don't think Vlad Tepes was unquestionably involved, but it did suggest they got their story noticeably close.

There was this one that was beyond, and everyone had to genuinely tear up when they watched it. It was again another self-loathing creature, that was tortured by another of our kind. How he tried to maintain even a shred of his humanity, and in the end, they seemed to just suck it all out of him. The scene that truly got to me was right after he had made the mother, for his daughter.

He said; Bear me no ill will, my love, we are now even. She then asked, What do you mean? He then answered, What died in that room was not that woman. What has died is the last breath for me that was human. Which she then said to, Yes, Father. At last, we are even.

Now for the next chapter, I have to go into a narrative from one of the kids. Bert to be exact, and with Naomi's help, I hope I straightened out all the event. Though there could be those parts that could be questionable, which is normal for someone so young.

Chapter Fifteen

First true contact.

<u>Bert</u>

We had done what we were told, Naomi had made around to keep busy. I had told her I would do the same when she got back, as I saw her coming back I did my best. She had also told me when I get out of sight to go on full transformation. I truly can't tell you that I'm as good as she is, mine is more like the ape-man version of a wolf. I remember talking to her about us being worse than real werewolves, she assured me that we weren't.

Now I also remember early on when John had talked to us about things, he had something about being able to match them. I mean it wasn't a full statement, and I think he was referring to himself, but I took it to heart. I have to be content with being as we are, though I can also say that Naomi assured me that out of everyone. Only

John and maybe even Kitty may be able to do what we do, though it can be done by anyone doubtlessly.

What Naomi literally said was this, 'All of our kind can do what we do, just most don't take the time to actually learn. John, on the other hand, has had to do things outside the norm, so it is a good bet he has the skills as well. So yes it can be seen as a skill only we can use, save the very few, like John.'

Though in truth we don't like to use any sort of weapon, generally because to us it is a very basic thing. That came out wrong, I think the right way is to say we are considerably basic and prefer the most primitive of our nature. I like to think of it as our own cave man mentality, as we look a lot like cavemen. Well, cavemen with really long claws that can slice like razor blades.

Anyway, I had gone off which was wrong, I know that now, as I had not set anything up if I got into trouble. Not that I would get into any real trouble, just I had been gone so long that no one actually knew what happened to me. Late as I explained this Pepper told me what had happened was just short of out of some movie. I have no idea as I had not really seen it at all, so you can take her word on that if you like.

I got to the edge of the parking lot, there was a lot of grass there, so as John would say I vamped out. Now we do get a little bigger as it is, but we're talking maybe an inch or two. I tell you this as to what I would see because it was really an awakening for me. You see I heard this noise and carefully moved to investigate it. I think I was just mere feet away when I heard a low growl, but not of a wolf.

The extremely sleek cat came out of the undergrowth, as black as night. I have to tell you this cat was big, like the size of a lion big, well in a sense it was a lion. I know my ancestors call it a puma, but I had never seen one this close, or this big. In fact, its growl that just kept coming out seemed to be also like a purr, if big cats actually purred.

I had to move to a tree and see if I could hide a smig if I could I mean. Then I saw two wolves join her, one looked like a wolf, though it was smaller. I described this to John in detail, he told me that it was actually a coyote. What came to me full from is that I expected a fight, not the three of them to act almost like best friends. Then it seemed as if the very large puma lead them off, though the actual wolf was just a hair bigger.

Because of how strange this was, I felt like I had to follow them at a distance. They then came upon a clearing that had two cars in it, once that was cleared they transformed. Now I have to describe this to you, though in reality it only took like seconds. The Puma was the first to do it, as it went to two legs and seemed to grow right in front of me. I mean I do believe it got close to eight feet tall, though the wolf was closer to nine feet at mid-turn.

I was five foot ten, when I was in the state I was right then I may get over six feet tall. I could never truly get as tall as these three did, and the coyote was as tall as the puma. What I then saw kind of did me in, as it took me a few to actually recover from this sight. Because all three of them were the most gorgeous Native Americans I had ever seen. I can also tell you it didn't help much that they didn't have on a stitch of clothing.

Not that they would remain nude as they all

grabbed stuff out of the rear of a truck. I can also tell you they were also talking in perfect Cherokee, which made me wish I had paid more attention to my gramps. I had to watch, well it wasn't that I had to watch, it really was I couldn't help but watch. As they all stepped into bikini bottoms, now the one that was the puma also had the darkest skin.

She also dressed the fastest, as then there came three more wolves. I thought I would get another show as they transformed into gorgeous women also. When one of them made a sound that I had to figure as disgust, I had to think maybe I was wrong. Then one of them turned into a very large man-wolf, and I couldn't believe how they spoke in that form. I could easily see any normal human running when they heard that, and because of how tall he was, I moved back a bit.

The one that was the coyote said something derogatory to him in Cherokee, I could barely catch it. Then the big guy sniffed the air as he said something, this made all of them sniff the air. The one that was a puma had to say which I understood, that's nothing but a dead animal. Well, at least I think like I said my Cherokee wasn't really that good. They all seem to go back to work, all the girls then left in one of the trucks.

I can tell you the guys didn't have as much to change into, but one kept going back and forth. I have no idea what he was smelling, but it really seemed to bother him. At this point I had to figure I had to watch as this had to be important, so I stayed. Now that one that honestly wasn't turning actually came at me, so I had to back off further. I think he was about ready to just come running straight at me.

Then without warning, this small area of wood just lite up so bright. That is when I heard John's voice, 'Bert if you're in there please howl so we can find you.' The Wolves said the word I knew for leeches and then ran off to their own truck. I felt safe enough to move to where John was at, and I saw him just out of the Jeep. Naomi looked like she was about ready to come in looking, so I moved it up to a trout.

As I came close she actually hit me in the back of the head, as she growled like those other's, "Get into the damn Jeep." John then jumped in as I got into the back, Naomi got into the driver-seat. She then growled at me, "Do you know how worried I was, what in Gods green earth kept you? I had thought we had lost you, boy!"

I had to admit to them, "Good thing you came, when you yelled they ran off."

Now I had talked to John and the reason why he had not asked further, was he just assumed I was talking about some Shovelhead's. Naomi, I also think had assumed that too, later on, that night as we were doing our thing she finally asked. "Boy, do you know my heart was in my throat. I was sure those Shovelhead's had gotten you, so it was just John calling to you?"

I then replied a tight confused, "Yeah, I mean first they called you and John leeches in Cherokee."

"Leaches?" She asked, and added to that, "You can speak Cherokee?"

I had to admit, "Barely, I missed more than I actually caught. I swear I should have listened to my gram pa far better, I caught a word here and another there. I can say I had never seen the likes of these guys before, I mean John did tell us how terrible werewolves can be."

"What?!" She said with complete surprise on her face. Then had to ascertain, "You weren't trapped by Shovelhead's, but by a pack of wolves?"

I nodded my head as I also had to add, "Six of them, though to be truthful only four of them werewolves. The one I knew to be a puma, the other I know as a wolf, though for a wolf she was really small. Oh, I should even add that there were three girls and three guys, it was also easy to see they were of American descent."

"Wait? They were of American descent, and yet all of them could speak Cherokee?"

I had to correct myself as I admitted, "I'm sorry, as a Native American we tend to refer others of our kind as of American decent. They were all Native Americans, and they spoke two languages actually. I could pick up on the Cherokee, the other seemed to be very guttural with wolf-like sounds. All of them could understand it, I had no clue when they spoke that one. I did see something that kind of scared me a bit, as they transformed they seem to grow like to nine feet tall. What is up with that?"

"Oh my God, You actually did see werewolves, some rare ones can maintain that as their battle form. If you ever see that again it is best to run as fast as you can. In that form, you can fill them with bullets, slash them all you like. All their wounds just heal as fast as you give them out, I have heard John's kind fighting them for hours. You also have to know this as well, John's kind are the only ones that can hope to win."

She just shook her head as she went on, "You see John's kind can bring on the pain at will, as they can hit so hard there is almost no coming back from that. Bert." I had to look close to her as she added with emphasized so I could fully understand. "If they don't collapse from their form, they'll be like new in like seconds. We have no way of coming back from that, except getting some fresh blood real fast. I know a few of our kind that have fought John's kind to a stand still."

Again she looked down as she added, "All of them are far older than John, and none of them had ever taken on John. I do believe only his own kind could absolutely fight John, though many have claimed to be him. We're lucky to literally have him, as there aren't many that have reached his status." She had to giggle, "Do you know they use him like a kids ghost story for young vampires. Remember when your momma told you to eat your veggies or the something or other will get you."

I looked at her as I had to ask, "You mean he is like the Nalusa Falaya to us vampires?"

She giggled as she conveyed, "Now I said they use him like that, but he really isn't that Nalusa Falaya thing. But as they're used like the Boogeyman is used for kids to do the right thing, so is John for young vampires. In fact, as I heard it, he may have taken down a few werewolves himself. Just like what happens with all things though, I can't tell you what is true, or what is fiction."

I had to ask after that, "Has anyone thought to ask? I mean he has been honest about everything else, I bet he would tell us about everything."

She smiled at me as she said, "You're right there,

though I'm also afraid of pissing him off. Bert, I have never told you this, but there was this one Lord that wanted to get away from John. So he locked himself in a bank vault, again I have no idea how true this is. It is said that he just ripped it off its hinges, I have to also admit from what I have seen, which I do believe you can back me on this one. That tale may actually be a true one."

So we sat there for a few minutes, then I had to ask another question. "I had no idea John was known so well?"

To which got a full laugh, then she had to apologize. "I'm sorry I laughed, but you misunderstood me. No one actually knows of John, but they know of his title. There are a lot of wanna be enforcers out there, but there is only one we call The Enforcer. He is the rock star of his race, kind of like that rock star Sia. I will also say that every race has their rock stars, though most are far better known than John."

She then looked away as I asked, "Do we have our rock star?"

She looked at me as she replied, "Ravenheart, not her real name, there was a rumor she was destroyed a few years ago." To which received her patented giggle, "Then she showed up for the ones that were passing that rumor, none are yet alive today. I was in that city at the time, I actually met the raven haired beauty. I mean truly raven, where it is so black that at angles it seemed to shined with green hues."

She pulled me close as she whispered to me, "She is never afraid, made friends with all kind of wilderness beasts. All men want to be with her, all women to be her. I heard that even the head of Tony's family had an altercation with her. What happened after all of that is what made her legend, as they took off their clothes to see who could attract the most men. Tony's whore of a mother won out barely by two men and five women. It is said though they set out to attract just men, they couldn't help attract all that saw them."

I had to say to her, "Wow, now that is beautiful. You know we have one like that here."

She had to shake her head, "As beautiful as Pepper is I don't see her holding a candle to either of them."

"Pepper is gorgeous I'm sure, plus her blonde hair seems so wavy, but I'm not talking about her. But babe even John's daughter is prettier than her, I mean Mary has curves that won't stop. The worse thing is I'm not even talking about her either, except for you babe no lady in this house can hold a candle to Elizabeth. I will also say that you have what I like, so if it wasn't for that, I could see myself trying to get with her."

"I'm pretty to you babe?" She giggled out, I did have to wonder why I got to hear her giggle more than anyone else. I had to be truthful with her, "Babe you're just plain hot. I mean your double D's are fun to play with, and they're so perfect in form. Then you keep everything else so slim, and yeah I know it's the whole vampire thing. Now that would be all I needed, then you have your smoking hot round butt. I mean most guys would be whoa I have perfection, then with your bronze skin. That is one thing Liz will never have, and she can gloat at you for that."

Now at first, I wrote the next part, then I thought I

would never get into our sex life. Now I will tell you that Bert and Naomi are a lot freer at describing it than we are. What I mean is I wrote it all out, Elizabeth read it, and she said it was like reading a pornographic novel or something. I did discuss this with Naomi after I made my mind up, I also showed her what I had wrote about our sex life.

Once she saw what I was doing, and how as it wasn't that clean, I mean our lives. It was refreshing that we wanted to keep something clean with all this disaster. In fact of the whole story, she actually referred it to as a beautiful tragedy, which I thought was closer to the mark in the end.

I will also add that as for Liz and me, we had done some unusual experiments. I tell you this to add a little spice to the end of the chapter, use your imagination. I can also tell you some other things, as Kitty decided to share a few things with the girls. I can also say that her and Andy's love life would be best to describe as very colorful. I'm sure like Liz, all the other girls shared the same with their other halves.

What I decided to also tell you this, is because of this it caused Liz to try a few new things. If the other ladies are half as inquisitive as Liz, I have to think all the guys had to have interesting nights also. Though there was one other thing to why she like all this, you see none of the ladies are virgins when they became what we are. Except for one, which you may have already figured that to be Kitty.

I'll just leave it right here, as all repairs after we drink blood. You can imagine the pain of being a perpetual virgin, or at least virgin like.

Chapter Sixteen

Reservations in spades.

<u>In a Native American tribal house on a reservation.</u>

He had waited all night for this, now it was morningtime and it unquestionably hadn't seemed any better. The four of them sat up front as usual, but if he had heard right this could be the worst case scenario. They had been a proud people all their lives, was this genuinely the first thing that could absolutely cause it? He had to supplement this with the time that was needed, he had to absorb everything that was said.

Finally, his old friend asked for clarity on all this, "Running Wolf tell me what you saw again?"

A tall thin man stood up in his eminently proud manner, "We had been there preparing to come home when we were hit by the head lights of a car. We weren't many as it was, plus Danial had been the only one that knew something was amiss. We had never seen what he said he saw, though we were able to see the outline of something."

He had to gesture over to another smaller man and asked, "You're sure what you saw was a wolf in battle form?"

He stood up now next to his friend, "Running Wolf knows the strength of my nose, I swear I only smelt death. The only way I can explain it is that one of the leeches can or at least could turn into a wolf also. I will add that he had no smell like the Gifs, though it was bad, I have to figure they were of the other tribe of leeches."

Wise Owl then corrected, "We don't think they call themselves tribes, we have heard a few sayings, but none of them referred to themselves as a tribe."

Shadow Raven then said as he sat most of the time with his eyes closed. Even as he spoke he still didn't release their countenance, he had been still doing what he had started. "He didn't follow you, how strange that a puma, a wolf, and a coyote would be traveling together. Oh, my."

He had to ask, "What do you see Raven?"

He had to chuckle as he admitted, "He saw Penelope change first, as we all know she could be a particularly striking woman. He got rather excited when he saw her, though the other two alluded to have the same effect upon him. He was in a set motion to just protect their cars, even he knows not to turn in front of the Caucasians. Ah, they don't use their uncommonly own rage like we do, they simply transform using their own blood."

A noticeably young woman jumped up saying, "There is no way he followed us!"

He had to say to her, "I have only known Shadow Raven to be wrong on the rarest occasions. You may not think you weren't followed, but obviously, their abilities outshine the others. We do know and understand there are those that have entered the city that can even track us. Why can't we believe they may have their own scouts in this small group?"

Shadow Raven then went on, "My, my. They may have one that is better than most, though because it comes from other sources it is mostly conjecture. I see these rumors are correct he has destroyed many of his own kind, and it implies as if he won't stop because of what they did to him. He had no mind to stay here, it was the kids that drew him into all this. I see now. Even as they see him, no one truly knows what he is, and I have no name for him."

Another boy said out of turn, "How bad could it honestly be, all they are, are leeches, why worry?"

Finally, he had to stand up as he confirmed, "Have you ever faced any that are experts at killing, if what Raven has said is true, he may be one! What do you literally know of anything! Have you ever fought one that could do all things, then if that wasn't bad enough! They can hit like you just got hit by a train! I have seen those that were hit, young man! They rarely ever get back on their feet."

Wise Owl then said, "Allow me my chief." He now looked at the young boy, "This is what we kindling is unrepresented in all things, we have never discerned anything like this. We could tell you what has been said, then you may want to just leave them alone. This can't be done as if we do, it is far worse then even we can place any understanding of our own minds. So I want to ask you this, what would you have us do? Just the same as usual, and allow our tribe to suffer?"

Shadow Raven's eyes now popped open with a small gasp as he looked up at the chief. He had to ask him, "What have you seen?"

"Disaster if we don't help, though if we do we maybe have known by the worst of them. Not him that is within the city, but he that can just walk through darkness. I tried hard to see a face, he realized I had been looking. I'm a seer my chief, I have never seen anyone that could force me out of a vision. I can tell you he sees this world spinning, and all he wants to do is save a few of his children. I have also grasped this my chief, though I can't tell whom, one of their members is his child."

Now he stood straight as he had to ask, "Can you truly be telling me the sheer evil has come upon us, and we're trying to be friends with him?"

He had to look at him as he admitted, "Not sheer evil my Chief, but what I think I'm seeing is the O-yo-hu-sa Di-ga-ne-li."

This now seemed to get everyone's attention, as he had to ascertain if what he had said was correct. "Are you absolutely sure that is what you saw?"

He had to shake his head as he spoke, "No my chief, all I can go off is what I felt when he pushed me out in that despair. I think I would feel at least the fact of evil, I have never felt such emptiness before in my life."

He stopped for an instant with a precipitous look around the area. With that he started one of his ancient chants, those of knowledge quickly joined in with him. Then a young lady that looked like the first one, but she was noticeably obviously younger. He moved forward to stop her, and she looked at him as she placed her hands up as a sign. He said, "No Rose, allow them to do their work."

She smiled at me as she spoke, "Daddy he called me, we're under attack and he needs all the help we can muster. All the followers of even Wise Owl would be joining in, they all sense how powerful this entity is."

He then turned to see his old friend now joining them, he had to ask, "Is this true my old friend?"

He replied, "The power is beyond the strain, he is at the forefront of all of it. He doesn't have the strength by himself, whatever he saw he may should not have attempted to see him. I fear that just this infinitesimal site may have caused us to be seen. Now if you please Chief Bear Killer, we have terribly stressful work to do. We'll need all the help we can get, I will tell you that she is far better than the whole."

With that the chief knew not to interfere, so he motioned to his warriors to move off for just a moment. He could easily see they were all ready for a fight, he made motions for those in charge to do their best. As three of them started to yell, two of them you know as Penelope and Running Wolf. The other was obviously bigger than all of them, well except for the of Chief Bear Killer.

He was unusually tall even for a normal man, though he has had generations to get this way. No one now of his tribe had ever seen the worst, as even, he would now have to be threatening. The last of the Chiefs moved up next to him as he had to ask, "My chief, why haven't none but one Ghost Warrior been activated?"

Chief Bear Killer never certainly liked the Shadow Warriors, well except they called themselves Ghost Warriors. He had to wonder that as well, as Udinalihe absolutely well knew. That has to be why he had to bring it up, as he was the only manifested of his kind. Though when he just got this close he had to question why he felt so ill at ease. There was this fact that they may be a kind to those they preferred to call leeches.

There was much that he could ponder this day, but he had to get home also. He knew that Charlotte would not be happy when he told her Rose wouldn't be home for breakfast. Well not for missing breakfast that much, but he could never hold the truth from her. So just the knowledge that she had been helping save the tribe from a spiritual attack. Yeah, that doubtlessly wouldn't sit extremely well with her, though she is the most gorgeous of all his wives.

Now don't believe he has more than one wife, for one thing, she would kill him if he had another. It is a fact that he has been like this a profoundly long time, and he has children that look older than he does. No one would ever guess he was well over one hundred fifty years old. Charlotte is his third wife in his life, and she gave him six of the most beautiful daughters.

She always beats herself up for never giving him a son, but he has had far too many as it was. He couldn't help but love his daughters even more, though Ben stepped into his role surprisingly well. Benjamin was the head of all the Spirit Warriors, and he kept them in line. Even as Penelope became one of us, he was as surprised as anyone was. Though you have to acknowledge that she has made for a great scout.

They all seemed to go their own way, so he had to move over to her. He then asked, "You going to help me with your mother?"

She had to giggle as she spoke, "Someone has to save your sorry butt Dad, but I'm worried more about Rose. You heard Shadow Raven tell you she wasn't ready, and that remark about her suckling at mom's breast still or awhile. Momma isn't going to be happy at all."

I had to smile at her as I had to admit, "She genuinely doesn't like his level of honesty."

It was never a far walk to the house, as soon as we turned the corner there was my beauty. Yep, someone had gotten to her, I knew those folded arms anyplace. Then she spoke to me strongly, "Benjamin David Bear Killer!"

Oh no, my full name. I knew I was in trouble.

Marshal Hershel came into his office to see two men.

He saw it but he literally couldn't believe it, he had to think these guy had to have watched too many Men in Black movies. Though one of them wasn't as dashing as those members, the other one lived up to the movie. As he walked their way why had they picked his desk, he had nothing to tell him. Then if they were who he thought he could tell them nothing. Well not nothing honestly, it was just he couldn't admit he would be doing his own investigation.

Well, he had to get this over with as he made his way over to his desk. Then he had to ask as he pulled out his chair, "Honestly guys, sunglasses in a perfectly well lite office?"

The one that wasn't that well kept asked, "Are you, Detective Hershel?"

He had to say as it was far too obvious, "No, I always sit at his desk till he gets in, like ten minutes ago."

He literally turned to his partner, as I had to think he wasn't the brightest character. His partner said to him, "That's him you idiot, when he said like ten minutes ago didn't clue you in the least."

I then had to add, "Not making the brightest light bulbs at the academy anymore are they."

The one came forward and said, "We're not the FBI, and I can assure you he has nothing to do with the N.S.A. Like me. He was just given me as a hanger-on, I could have done all this by myself. Excuse the suit as we had to talk to them also, they directed us to you. I mean I never wear a suit except when we have to go visiting our friends. Now we need for you to tell me about what you have recently seen. I mean as to dead bodies that don't appear to be decaying correctly."

I had to laugh as I said, "Those gooks sent you on a snipe hunt, as they took all of our material. I have my own opinions, though without any of our materials. I have no way to check up on them, though some of what I think is way out there even for local police."

He then asked, "How so?"

I had to get close so no one else could hear me, "I can't explain any of the rapid decay stuff, I have heard from movies that there are certain people that do that. If I were to set that out forward they would surely place me in the funny house. I do have a question for you also, and tell me I'm right or wrong here. In the movie's vampire rapidly age when killed, do you think they got it right? Just they made the decay happen way too fast?"

The guy that was well kept chuckled as he realized I had been trying to make a joke out of what I suspected. The other guy was the one that answered my question, as he replied, "Well as you know..."

The first guy hit him to shut him up, and I instantly knew it had worked. He then turned away and had an argument as they walked out the place. I just gave them a look as they left, then my chief had to ask me. "Why were those gooks here?"

I had to correct him, "They aren't gooks, believe this or not, those two are from the N.S.A."

"Jeesh Marshal, what does the National Security Agency want with you?"

"Not me chief, they want that case we were forced to give to the FBI. In fact, I'm wondering that exact same thing, though I do have to say one more thing."

He then asked, "What is that?"

"If that fat guy is any sign of N.S.A., members, we have a lot to be worried about in the end."

Father Michael had been waking later this morning.

With the late night the priest would be just getting up, he had to wonder why the other father came in so late. Well not that he had been a real man of the cloth, as he had been told that their positions were more of an honorary affiliation. He was an exceedingly strange man as it were, and all this talk about demons that weren't demons. Then he would be going off on how they just took the form of men, they were never real men.

This Father Horscio was surely a significant odd small man. He had always ventured to be a good host, even he had pushed him to his limits. He always loved this hour as he could do anything he likes before the caretaker got here. Then he walked out of his room and he smelt it, the caretaker must have gotten here early. She knew how much he loved eggs, with bacon, and a side of toast.

When he came through the door he was surprised to see the good Father was categorically doing the cooking. He had to ask, "Does Misses Murphy know that you are using her pots and pans?"

Father Horscio had to ask as this answered his question, "Who is Misses Murphy?"

He had to shake his head as he stated, "Well you can deal with her talking sternly to you, I can tell you she will not be eminently happy."

I then sat down as the door opened up behind me, sure enough, it was her in the flesh. I had to say so she didn't look at me that way, "I was asleep, he took this all on himself. I do have to ask you to check if all that is alright."

Now she was half Irish from her Dad's side, half Vietnamese from her Mom's side. So have you ever seen a redhead Vietnamese woman before, with an Irish temper? Then as she also lived with him and her, when she got angry she could truly say things. When her hands went to her hips, and her oriental speech came out, that simply sounded like it had an Irish accent.

Well to be safe here, it was comical all in its own right. As she truly went off on him, what definitely surprised me is how well he could literally speak Vietnamese. With that, he put his hands up in the air, and she came around, and just threw things on two plates. I had to look down as I saw that he surely wasn't that good of a cook. The eggs looked runny, the bacon looked just overcooked, and well the toast was burnt, with peanut butter on them.

Well, it genuinely looked sad, though it was palatable. I had to whisper to her as we left for the Bishops office. "Please make me something far better for lunch Misses Murphy. That could be extremely disgusting."

She promised me as we left, and I still had no idea why I had to go with him.

Chapter Seventeen

The truth about those that are young.

Day Eleven

You know when you have a thought that things have changed, but you can't truly place your finger on why. When you have that feeling that all can be explained, as there are certain things that lend credence to what you're thinking. You could say this day I woke up just an infinitesimal amount of time before Liz did. Though we all looked at the ceiling thinking of certain conditions that have transpired. When you're a man that sees all as in control, even the smallest loss of this can cause much more wonder than needed.

You could say that I was beside myself just trying to get a hold of things. With these thoughts much could be said about them, but as they came out with Liz as she woke up this night. So let me truly start there, as I had been lying for about an hour or so. Not that I couldn't do my usual and go to the window, it was that I had been looking at the thing in such relief. There is what you already know, and that which you can't as we are about to talk about it.

She woke up and had to ask right off the bat, "Why aren't you at the window like you usually are?"

I admitted, "I'm thinking about things that have happened thus far."

She gave a barely perceptible half giggle as she said, "You know that's dangerous?"

I had to look at her as I had to say two things, "Good morning gorgeous. Now, what is dangerous?" She was about ready to correct me when I did the same thing, "I know it's technically evening, but like I already told you. As we woke up, it is far better to acknowledge this then saying good evening like a B-rated vampire."

She nodded her head as she said, "I guess you're right there, though it is still evening. Plus when you think it is what is dangerous. Though I do have to think also if you were to say; Good Evening." She said in her best Lugosi accent, "Since they know this decidedly well, wouldn't that get across what we want if we were trying to control a human situation?"

Now it only took me a few seconds to think on that, though most of what I said was done while I talked. "I guess you could do that, even though to us that already have accents I find it easier to copy an American accent. Well except that it may also infer that you're trying to be evil, and in a sense, I'm not sure that is the way to go. Now I'm not saying that for someone like Tony it wouldn't be perfect in a sense. Then again I'm not genuinely sure it would even be good for him, though I could truly see Paul getting away with it."

She then interjected, "John?"

I had to stop my train of thought as I had to ask, "Yes Liz?"

"A simple no would have worked far better."

I had to smile as I had to also admit, "Well I hadn't thought of that, so I had been reasoning through it like anyone would. Since it was just you and me, I figured you wouldn't mind me reasoning out loud."

"So you see Paul and Cheryl being more like Dracula?"

"Well no, what I meant was that they could use that tactic. In fact, I think Paul might be looked over if he did that..." I had to think for a second, then I admitted to her, "Though if it wasn't for Cheryl's darker skin, I think she could use it with such grace I can't even imagine the potential there."

"What about me?"

"Dracula? Maybe, though I legitimately don't see you going that way."

"No John. What I meant was what can you see me doing, I mean is there any outside knowledge I need to know?"

"Oh" I had to say, then I went on with what I

knew, "Your kind are known for their sensuality and sexuality, so you could say whatever to enhance that would help. Look at Pepper, and I'm not telling you to be her, just she has this way of using her femininity. Now would I call her a girlie girl, I honestly don't look at her that way? Then you have the quintessence that she can keep right up with the boys, in a line up though, she is far from just another boy."

She had to giggle as she ascertained, "I think she would find it funny that you compared her to just one of the boys. I can do what she does also, but you're right when you say I could never act like she does."

"Good. Because no way would I ever compare you to her, plus I think everyone of your species needs to find their own way. I will admit that I have met a few of your race though, and many think it is easier just to take off all their clothes. I even pointed out to one of the strongest of your kind this, I can tell you when she dressed up she was way hotter. It is a shame that so many have gone the simple way, in fact, I see all the rest sincerely trying so much harder than Pepper. You could say that sexy is also in how much work you place into it, I think two good examples we have are Mary and Cheryl."

"I think that maybe the most chauvinistic thing I ever heard you say?"

Okay, I guess I had said something wrong, so I had to correct it. "Okay, let me try and see if I can bring one of them in after we get dressed. I think I'm not explaining it genuinely well, but in reality, it is more of a compliment, then what should be considered wrong."

With that, She cracked the door and in a loud voice

asked, "Mary are you awake?"

Mary instantly replied, "Yeah Liz. What do you need?"

She gave me a smile as she said, "John has been trying to explain something to me, and he thinks you would know better than any of the younger girls. Would you come here so he can also tell you what he just said?"

"Sure Liz, just let me throw something on first."

With this Liz threw me a robe, as she also placed on her own. Now, these had to be presented from Pepper, as you can imagine they barely did their jobs. With this Mary finally showed up and I also related to her what I had said to Liz as best as I could. She seemed to have a stern look on her face as she had to ask. "John are you forgetting something, or maybe you need to explain more."

Okay, this wasn't going well, but she had brought Sammy with her. Sammy then added, "Hun. I don't think he meant it that way, remember what he had said to you on that first day."

She then said to him, "I know Sam, that is why I haven't jumped all over him yet."

He then said what I think I had been trying to say, "Babe, remember when you said that Pepper found it so easy. Think of why you said that?"

"Well she has, I mean when you get older you have to workout like a mad woman just to maintain your girlish looks."

I then added, "That goes with everything, I think she could have maimed herself and still looked gorgeous. Kind of like Kitty, I mean she has tattoos and piercings all over, but even as it takes nothing away from her. I mean I bet she would never have to wear anything but basic makeup. But wouldn't it be much easier to just go around with considerably blush and maybe lipstick?"

She gave me a look as she stated, "Yeah. I'm not sure I like where this had been going."

"That is it though, not that you look any worse, in fact in a sense you look way better. You see you learn your own style and make it your own when a man sees this they see perfection. So what I mean is as you do certain things, the reason why you look better than someone like Pepper. You've had the years to work on it, so like I said baby, it legitimately isn't the nudity that makes a lady sexy. It, in the end, is the work you precisely put into your own look."

I couldn't believe the relief I felt as they both now smiled at me. Mary then had to ask, "You think I'm sexy?"

I had to tell her the truth, "Mary you're the second sexiest woman in the house. Sorry about this, though I'm sure you know why Liz passes you up so greatly."

Liz then added, "Though he thinks it would be better to get makeup tips from you or Cheryl, then Pepper or Cibilia."

I had to say to her, "Babe I never said Cibilia, She is young, but I do believe she has come into her own. Now would she be as good to go for makeup tips, apparently not, but she has a much better look than Pepper."

Mary had to ask, "What about Kitty?"

I had to smile as I said, "She has a more Pepper look about her, but she has had like a hundred fifty years to perfect it. My question is though, what do you think?"

Liz had to laugh as she admitted, "I guess not, though it may be a good disguise when you need one. Now I'm sure Naomi is within her group as well, though I'm willing to bet it is more of a rustic look."

I shook my head, "She does that because she has to, but just like Mary and Cheryl, I'm sure she knows a lot of tricks. I do have to ask you when she put on that dress, would you say she would be beautiful, or just plain?"

Mary had to laugh as she spoke, "Well he has you there Liz, I mean when she dresses up she can be smoking hot in the looks department."

Sammy then had to add, "Babe plus think on this too. When a lady can walk into a room and is so hot that all eyes turn to her, even though she just got out of the mud. Guys can genuinely be intimidated by this, so even though they get all the looks like Pepper. Their actual sex life is exceedingly dull because most guys are scared to categorically ask them out on a date."

I had to chuckle at that as I had to add, "Well except for those guys that think their self-worth is far higher than what it is. The narcissistic can truly be dull in the mind when it comes to that."

"Yeah." He seemed to say sincerely thinking, as he

had to add. "We had one that had been our next-door neighbor, and he seemed to always be trying to ask out my wife. One day he authentically got on my nerves, so I let him have it with my entire mind."

Liz cut him off with, "Sammy don't, I know how much that hurts you."

He then said, "Listen I have to share it with Mary, even if she only is slated to be my mom. Like I said I hope we go beyond that, but I also understand. Then we have to have John's perspective on this also, I mean he is my true elder. Shouldn't he know?"

I had to tell him the truth, "Sammy if I wanted to know all I would do is ask, you see I made Mary, then she made you."

I was about ready to say more when Liz cut me off, "John, what are you saying?"

I had to tell her the truth, "You see we have power over the blood, I made Mary so I can tell her anything and she would do it. Mary has the same power over Sammy, and I have this power because of my power over Mary. There is more if you want to know, but I have to ask first."

I had to wait till they all nodded their heads, "As Joe has a certain power over the blood, so do I, though as he is, mine isn't that strong. The first time I met Pepper I could have ordered her to do what I wanted. I also have to explain that over time you learn to resist this impulse. When I was just new my master ordered me to do things I would never do to another. Now if he came around I could resist what he had to say to me, as I'm different now. This can't be taught as much as it is learned, so there is no way for me to hurry up your training here."

Mary then asked, "Can you tell me that what I felt that first night could have been you ordering me to feel that way?"

I had to shake my head as I had to tell her, "No, it is more like an uncontrolled response. Think if I had told you with the blood to disrobe, your mind would be telling you no. Here is where the creepy part is, as I have control of the blood it would be doing what you didn't want to in the end. In a sense I aquavit, it to being mentally and physically raped. That is why I said the night after that I would never ever do that to you. I have been for years a champion of a person's free will, and I will not take that away."

Liz had to say, "I could never see anyone having that kind of control over me." I was about ready to use it to show her, then she added, "I don't need a demonstration though John."

Mary then had to ask, "Wait? That statement about Giaus was truly meant for all of us. What would you have done if he had ordered one of us?"

I had to smile as I had to admit, "Either I would not be here, or we would be one less ancient."

Liz then came in with, "John our freedom means that much that you would sacrifice your life for all of us?"

I looked at her as I had to admit, "Giaus has a preference for the unusual, I think most of them were safer than you were Liz. So yes I would have done that, as his most likely target was truly you if he had thought so. I also think he would have had more control over you, as I do believe he is of the same lineage as Tony. My first move without thought would have been to take his head off, I have no idea if he would have been able to react to my moves."

Now from the crack in the door came, "Our kind has a way of moving, we can avoid damage better than most. I have seen where John has learned this also, but he can barely keep up with our ability. So yeah Giaus may have been able to avoid his attack, though it wasn't Giaus that John had to worry about in the end. It had been his entire guard, they tend to just shoot, then ask questions why."

With that Mary opened the door to reveal Tony on the other side, then Liz had to ask, "Tony is there a reason why you're ease dropping?"

He then replied, "Got a message that Pepper told Cibilia, and she told me to go tell you, John. Apparently, William is coming over, they found something strange. I haven't had time to precisely look, and I think during the day Paul and Pepper have been keeping the laptop in their room. I tell you this because I had to think they didn't have your permission."

I had to say, "Appears as we have to get dressed now, tell Paul we need to talk. I did give control over it to Andy and Paul, maybe they came up with this."

Liz then corrected me, "John I think it was Andy and Cheryl."

"Whatever Babe, Tony just found out as you heard. If it was their decision then we have to let it go, otherwise, come to me with the information." I then turned to Liz and said, "I do believe our eighth session maybe for not today babe, now I guess we have to move."

With this Tony, Mary, and Sammy left, as soon as the door was closed Liz had to question. "What did you mean our session?"

I had to smile at her as I admitted, "I know as soon as we got done with Mary and Sammy we were presumably going for another round in our bed. I do love those, though I suspect you may look forward to them more than I do." I had to chuckle as I added, "Then again maybe not."

She looked at me as if I had just spoken a foreign language, then she looked at the bed. In seconds it came to her what I meant, "OH! OH! SEX!" She then giggled as she also admitted, "Yeah, I do look forward to that. If we can just say we both look forward to it the same, I do have to ask you something."

I then replied, "Speak away babe?"

"We don't get tired, we can keep things going through the blood. I'm not sure doing those seven-time accounts absolutely for seven, especially when they happen right after one another. How will we ever get our fill of that as it is, I mean I can say I truly enjoy our time."

"Babe, with you I see no way of ever losing interest, so my answer is. I honestly don't know."

Chapter Eighteen

This enhanced problem leads to a meeting.

We had one of the boys keep a lookout, so we had an idea when they appear. Of course, because of the lack of information, I had thought they're been more coming than there has been in the end. I had everyone of importance come into the kitchen. Naomi, Kitty, Cibilia, Bert, and Joe, oops Liz told me I forgot myself. When they finally showed up, which took longer then I had speculated. It was easy to figure this wasn't as dramatic as they made it sound. With this I now went to Tony to make plans for training, since we hadn't touched on defense that much, that was inferred as we assessed.

Now I would be still standing as they came in, and Naomi who was with us as we discussed this, spoke. "Alex you old dog, does Giaus have you on his leash now?"

A decidedly tall thin man with even darker skin

than Naomi's now replied. "No, but he pays far better, so I'm doing this for the money sweet thing. That is it, he can have his own if danger should show it's ugly head."

I then said to William, "We're straightening out a few details as I figured you don't need us all. We'll be with you in a seconds, just have a seat at the table."

One man was most definitely packing so William explained, "Dave has a high powered rifle, I don't suspect anything though, just being safe. I hope you don't mind as there without a doubt is no place in the car for the weapon."

I had to point to him as I said, "You can keep that, but in this house bolt to the rear and most definitely no magazine. Got that?"

As soon as I declared that, he followed my instructions to the letter. Kitty came over and decided to say something, "Pretty Man need to sway with the bling, ting a ling, Kitty see got the best."

I saw that all looked at her so I went on with what that meant, I think. "I think Kitty means like a music box, so I have to surmise shes talking about dancing. Now, do you know how to use dance so you can show defense moves, Tony?"

Tony nodded his head as he admitted also, "Yeah, I'm not the best at it, but I had to take long hard classes in ballet. Is that what you mean Kitty?"

She smiled at him with a quick nod, so I had to be glad this was decided. I then added, "Lose clothes, give them like twenty minutes to get ready. Also if anyone at the meeting isn't needed I will send them to you. If an elder, you can use them to help you, so are we set?"

With that everyone nodded, so the three of us returned to the table. It was easy to see that William thought more of this then he showed to everyone. So I determined to carry on with, "I'm sorry, you caught us while we were in our own time. You understand I'm sure, as we have to be set for the worse."

With that he pulled out a folder he had in a satchel as he did this he spoke. "I'm afraid we may have even worse then we had thought. Alex here found the place, I would have been sooner, but I had to figure you would need proof to go out there. So we went in and took Polaroids of the main features, now I have to tell you what I think I saw. I hate to give this to all of you, but these symbols remind me of some kind of magic. Though I truly haven't a clue, even with all I know on the subject"

I had to interject, "Darn! I hate Mages."

William then said, "They have their needs, but I have never seen vampires use symbols like these before. I have to bring these to you to see if you have seen anything like this previously." He spread out six pictures as he also had to point, "A couple I had to take other views, as they were difficult to see."

Then he placed what I had to figure were secondary pictures. I pulled them close as I had Kitty and Naomi come close, we had to search as they weren't the best. Naomi then pointed at one and asked, "Is that a sign of all thing natural."

I had to take a closer look, but I couldn't honestly

tell, and I thought we were entirely lost on all this. Then came a word of acknowledgment from Joe, "It is the ancient symbol for earth, that there I believe is the one for water. This one here is what we call the infinite sign, suggests as if someone had been using all the elements for some reason." I had to look at him as he had to admit, "What? I'm just doing what you told me, but this one I saw, but have no idea what it is. The ancient language is uncommonly confusing there, it could mean several things. Don't get me wrong though John, I'm learning what they are, I think I'm at least a year from casting."

I then had to say, "Joe go get the book you saw all this in, Cibilia and Bert I want the two of you in class. Naomi, I think we may be able to do without Kitty, what do you think?"

Naomi then looked at her as she ascertained, "I'm willing she already knew that, and that is why she started Tony in his direction. Kitty any advise?"

She then nodded her head as she talked, "Me know, dow me sees. Yeah, yessie. Take Maggie with the fire, he knows more then even me sees. Now me do the wigglie wiggle with Pretty Man."

After that she left, I had to say something absolutely quietly. "I do believe the term Maggie was meant for Joe, we may need to not tell him that."

We had a small chuckle with that, but just as quickly we had to suck it all in, as he came into the room carrying a profoundly large tome. Then he placed it down on the table as he pointed, "See how that symbol follows the lines, though why yellow chalk instead of silver nitrate I haven't a clue." Then he pointed at the other two pictures, "These insinuate that one as it matches, but there is no way to be sure as they had to try and rubbed them out of existence."

Finally, he pointed at the word in question as Liz came in asking, "John are you, as a matter of fact, going to be having us do ballet?"

He then said, "I think it means Assuroc, but I can't be sure with the way this text reads."

I answered Liz, "Hey it wasn't my idea, but it sure seemed like a good one from Kitty. Don't worry she will be there to help all of you, the way she moves I have to think she knows ballet rather well."

William then asked, "But this isn't right, the lines follow no vampire text I have ever seen."

Joe then corrected, "It isn't an ancient vampire, I have found a lot of it, and have had to use several texts to translate it."

Liz then said, "With my time at school we had to learn ancient languages, you do realize that isn't ancient anything. I recognize it as either late Sumerian or maybe a corrupted form on Babylonian."

With that William had to look closer as he said, "Oh that is Isatum, now I can see it clearly. Thank you greatly, Liz, maybe one night we can discuss ancient languages?"

She smiled at him as I had to say, "Liz you may want to get ready for class." She ran off as I also had to ask, "So what does isomany mean?

He replied, "It's Isatum with a capital I as they thought it was the name of a god also. You see they thought all the elements were one of their many gods. I do believe that in a sense it means fire."

Naomi then came in with, "So they're using the elements for something, Joe can there be any reason for this at all?"

He came back with, "So many I can't even count, though it would be agreeable to see the way they placed them. Now I have heard of a few using eminently old text, none though in a real format here. I mean all those that use magic here in the States are just way too young. I would also like to tell you this means nothing, but as William can attest any ancient language usually means they're up to no good."

William came in with, "Your young scholar is extremely correct, I do hate that we may have to also bring him with us. I have learned a lot, but his fresh mind has a good insert of information. His youth is what may help us here, so what do you think about it, John."

I had to nod my head as I admitted, "Can't say I like it at all, but it is the only answer I can come up with as well." Then I turned to Naomi, "I know it would be better to stay at the house, but just for our own assurance. I want you there to keep an eye out with Alex, though Bert would be favorable too. What do you think?"

Naomi then had to admit, "Bert is good, but I fear his defensive capabilities aren't up to par. So yeah, all we have is us three. I also fear taking Joe with us, I will add to you, Joe. William is defended by a guard, anything starts to happen. You stick to William like he owns you, you got that?"

He nodded his head, so I turned to William with, "Okay, we'll take Naomi's Jeep. You lead the way, now I'll drive so both Naomi and Alex can be out first. Then your guard and me, once we are sure the coast is clear you two will be released. Alex, you lead the way, then break off to investigate. Naomi, you take the rear, once we're in you do the same as Alex. Now we won't have much room, so that means you two stay close."

William came in with, "Dave you have the entrance, like John, thinks, it may be for nothing. We have to be safe with all this, and even though he isn't here. You know as well as I do that Giaus wants a report. Oh Veronica isn't doing well, he thinks this is important, but shes just moderately more important right now."

I then said, "Oh Joe backseat, Naomi in the passenger seat, I drive. I know this means the backseat for you William, but what has to be done has to be done. Now, let's move out!"

With that, we all did as what had been said, and we moved to the sight. They had not told me that it would be out in the middle of no where. I mean there were large oil tanks all around, but the small building could not easily be defended. Joe had a small notebook with him, he had jotted down a few things from the book. I was glad, that book looked way too old to just be replaced.

Now we pulled up and there wasn't any real parking, as we had to park away from the building. Alex went off as planned, then we got inside as Naomi did the same thing. This is where I had made a mistake, as I had not thought to bring a flashlight. We can see a certain amount at night, but this building was set up so we couldn't use any other light source.

I have to be glad that the two of them were there, as they created the impression to have thought of everything. Joe had one of those small pocket flashlights, while William had one of those way to many candle power flashlights. So I stood off as the two conversed between them, though Joe had to use his flashlight to read what he wrote. Finally, they came back to where I was standing, and they were both shaking their heads.

I had to ask, "What's wrong? What did they try to do?"

Joe replied, "We weren't absolutely sure as only half of the stuff was present, but it looks as if they tried to create an eternal flame."

I had to add, "How bad is that?"

William came back with, "They call the eternal flame like the finger of God. It is one of those things that no one is sure can work, but from what we saw they royally disconcerted. We also think they did get close, as to break what had been happening they tried to erase the symbols. Since one has clearly been taken away, I think they ventured into the wrong realm. We can't say which realm as there were several marks that tell it had been bad, undoubtedly bad."

I had to look at Joe as he continued, "John, we have vampire signs all around, but no vampire threw this. They had to get at least a few humans that knew something of magic."

William then subverted in an additive, "We don't even think vampires can do such a thing, as it takes an unquestionably strong spirit. When we were humans we may have had a spirit that strong, but as vampires, we surely don't."

I was about ready to ask something when I saw Dave running toward us. I had to yell, "Dave! What's the matter?!"

He replied immediately, "Alex told me to come and get all of you, Naomi has been trying to lead them off away from us in the end. He told me she doubtlessly will need to come running to her Jeep. We need to move out of here like we were never here, he says there is a lot of them."

I then yelled, "MOVE TO THE CARS! NOW!"

With that we got to the door as Alex came in, I was certainly worried right then about Naomi. Then she came crashing in the entrance, and Joe with William helped her up to her feet. I had to ask in a loud voice, "ALEX! WHAT THE HELL!"

He came back with, "They corralled us in here, we had no chance to break their line."

I had to look at William to see if he knew a way out, his reply was not what I wanted to hear. "Alex is the only one that knows the building, I have no idea."

Naomi then yelled, "John they aren't Shovelhead's, plus there has to be like twenty or thirty of them. In fact, if I were going to give them any knowledge whatsoever. I would call them a well-organized unit of the military, which also means this could be worse then the Shovelhead's."

Alex came in with, "Plus they have several forms because I saw humans and wolves. I have never seen werewolves so well coordinated, so they may look like them, I will swear that they aren't them."

Joe then said, "John?"

I had to ask, "What Joe?"

He pointed out the door as I saw a black sleek figure pass, I had to get closer to see. I had never seen such a large panther, so I had to ask, "I have never seen such a large cat. Wait? This can't be right, as far as I know, America has no panthers."

Alex came close as he corrected me, "John that isn't a panther, but you are right. That is the largest mountain lion I have ever seen, has to be nearly the size of a bear."

Dave pointed then too as he asked, "Is that a werewolf?"

I saw what he had been pointing at, then I had to ascertain what I knew. This would take a few seconds as everyone started to worry. Then it came to me, "No. No, they aren't. I do believe we maybe surround by even worse then werewolves, we may have to fight harder then we have ever fought previously."

Naomi came close as she had to say, "Has anyone else noticed that they aren't charging. I mean they could be in here and it would be resolved."

I had to look as I could see every avenue of movement was covered. When I squinted my eyes I could literally count a few more. They have everything covered, so I had to figure even windows and other doors were covered. I came back inside as I had to tell them all what I saw, "They appeared to be keeping us here for some reason, but also have covered every outlet. We could look for other ways out, but as good as they're here, I would think they have them covered as well. I fear our only option is to just stay here and see what they want."

Dave then said, "We can make our best defense of the door, may get a few if they change their minds."

I had to agree with that, so we embedded to laying our best defense we could have. Then as we worked we could hear a rumble off in the distance. Now I'm not saying like a thunderstorm, kind of like my car. Just I had to think this car had no mufflers at all, as it just seemed to get closer. With straight pipes, you would have thought it was a race car, not the unquestionably old truck that came to a halt. With that, they also had their protectors, as three more got out and placed themselves between the trunk and where we were.

Then an incredibly tall, unusually large Native American got out of the truck cab. Now he had to be like well over six feet tall and could be of equal girth. Not a once of fat as it were, so I had to reason there was a different reason for this. Now he had been also talking in a foreign language, that I would find out later was Cherokee. Now once it could be done with all that, which I had no idea what had to occur. So he would be coming closer now and I had to tell everyone to be ready for anything.

He finally stopped like just ten feet away, he now spoke which you could tell wasn't his native language. "My name is Chief Bear Killer, I do believe we need to talk."

Chapter Nineteen

The aforementioned meeting.

You could say in short that I was taken by surprise, in fact, I think the lot of us were, well maybe not everyone. The thing is most of the time the youngest give the impression of the most resilient, especially when it comes to new information. When confronted with something that is impossible, we tend to go to where our minds take us. These do tend to be the worst of places that can be imagined, like the first time you venture into a vampire bar. All insinuates normalcy, even as you can feel that something was wrong. Doubtless, even a better example is a teen horror movie. You hear a loud bang upstairs, then get out of the house with the kids, don't go upstairs to find out what it is.

Then again Jamie didn't have twenty or thirty Michael Meyers surrounding them either. Listen to me refer to them as the worst horror I could imagine, when in truth they aren't that bad. Like I said though, this was a situational event as it was, and all we undoubtedly knew was that we were in a decidedly bad state of affairs. I had to place one finger up as I saw him, even as he stood he was eminently intimidating.

Just to be safe I had to ask this, "Can we have a small amount of time to discuss this?"

He replied to me, "Take all the time you need, but you're not getting out of here till you talk to me."

Naomi immediately ascertained, "John they came from everywhere, when I went one way they cut me off, then I would try another and there they were."

Joe asked, "John?"

I had to say and ask her, "They appeared to do everything to cut you off, this is a real predicament then. Did you get an idea of how many they absolutely were?"

William then asked, "Do you think they mean to destroy all of us?"

Naomi then replied to me and William, "I can't be sure about numbers, they were every place I looked. I don't know William, though you don't ask the worst among us just for a chat. Alex, you saw them as much as I did, do you have any idea of numbers?"

Alex came back with, "No, they weren't there one moment, the next they were everywhere like you said. Then you have that one that is like a mountain lion, I mean I never had a chance against her. She's quick John, like Giaus fast. Never saw someone that could move as fast as he can, well except you. I swear she could keep any of us at bay, while all the rest did their work. Then you had those damn birds, they came right into your face if you found a seam. All I can say is we need a categorically good plan."

I had to look at William, then Naomi, and Alex, in turn, to see if they had any ideas at all. With each of them shrugging I had to think this was worse, this gave me just one option. So I spoke to the fact of it, "Maybe if I force the issue, then at least some of you can get away."

Naomi had been shaking her head as Alex suggested, "Maybe one, possibly two, but most likely they would be hurt. If we want to get out of here we'll have to all push this situation. That means we fight a withdrawing fight to our cars, this'll ensure at least more than two to evacuate. To be truthful it is the one at the door I'm most worried about, he's a big guy."

Finally, Joe asked again with more emphasis, "JOHN?!"

I turned to him and had to say just as loudly, "WHAT?!"

"You unquestionably didn't listen to what he said dang it!!"

I had to think as I repeated it, "You're not going anywhere till you talk to me."

"No! Jeesh! He said, 'Take all the time you need, but you're not getting out of here till you talk to me.'"

I had to ask him, "Yeah. Something like that."

William then had to affirm what he was saying, "No John, that is exactly what he said, and it hadn't dawned on me till this young one spoke it. You're a credit to your species, my friend, I do believe that is why they name all of you judges." He now turned to me as he gave substance to what he was thinking, "He gave us our out for us John, other words we can leave right after you talk to him. Do you understand why Joe had been trying so desperately to get your attention?"

I had to look at him and ask, "Is that what he said, word for word?" He nodded his head as I now turned to Alex and Naomi and made a plan. "Okay as they may have an idea what I am, they also know that I have a guard also. You two be ready to jump if this doesn't work out, but it gets us out the door at least. Joe, you are a particularly smart young man, but you stick close to them no matter what. If you brought your pistol you can add it to the argument if we do have to fight our way to escape. William does whatever you do to stay safe, but you also know this may be a running fight."

"John?" William had to ask, so I acknowledged him with a look as he proceeded. "Normal elders are given a minimum of three guards if he knows even the smallest information. Knowing this about your enemy would be prudent, so you need a third."

The guy that was his guard then said, "I'll do it."

"No, that would be stupid on two facts. One is your weapon of choice, he isn't going to like it at all. So you would be forced to leave it behind, or beg starting a fight just with its presence. Then you have the second fact that it is much easier to defend me from behind than the front. I do know you'll be hindered with Joe, but the best solution is, in reality, me going out there."

Joe then said, "Well I could do it as I have no real meaning to them."

I had to state the obvious, "Joe as I have already told you, you reek of your own humanity. I can smell it from across a room, they have wolves out there, how strongly do you think it is to them? No. I do believe that William came up with the best plan."

William came to his side with a slight smile, "Noble effort young man. I knew it had to be me from the start, and I can tell you I'm not as noble as you are. I swear if I could think of any way out of it I would, but it is the most logical event. Now, John, I will stay back just in case it does turn into a fight. As you know my kind has certain things we can do, but not before being out of the sight of those we tend to fool."

I nodded my head, "I would expect no less, plus if you can start talking to your animal friends if you can. We may have need of them like they used them against us, I do believe we need to do something." I then looked out the door as to see if anything had changed, it was as I feared, so I had to shrug my shoulders. "Let's get this over with, and as their ancient ancestors once said to the white soldiers. Today is a good day to die."

So we gathered up as we walked out, Alex and Naomi moved off within reason to each side. We waited till they were in place, then I moved off toward this Chief Bear Killer. Now for him as he was an older man about in his late forties or early fifties. It was uncommonly easy to see even through his clothes he was unnaturally big. I had to think his own ability had made him nearly seven foot tall. His clothes did pretend to hold his size in, as even the simplest buttons strained to do so. He had his salt and pepper hair, with that profoundly noble warrior look I had seen a lot.

I came close as I had to start this off, "Well you said we needed to talk, and I have to agree with that. I'm curious as we aren't know as the best of friends, why you would leave yourself so open. It is also clear that if I took you down that you have enough warriors to uncommonly throttle our company. You have a captive audience, so now I ask. What's on your mind?"

"Listen! Leech! We aren't particularly happy about this either. Our medicine man has spoken to the Great Spirit, he has informed us that we don't come out of this exceedingly well. I'm not speaking of this meeting as you can see, though these others of your kind have the qualities of destruction we can't allow to happen. Shadow Raven sees a lot, and he has seen where we are left with only a few warriors. In all that happens, we can't stop what occurs, and they receive the city. We can't have this, so we are forced into this just like you are."

"Wolf!" I blurted out at volume. "I would have us do nothing together, but I know the way of the seer. I also know I have been told none of this, as we have a seer ourselves."

He abruptly put his hand up as he interjected, "My seer as you call him has seen this too. It has been our lack of understanding of something she has said, so yes you have been told, you just didn't understand. I can also tell you we aren't seeking a peace treaty, all we want has to be kind of an understanding. I will also demonstrate this with a sign of weakness, as we'll also let you go, though we could just as easily just destroy you here."

I had to take a step back as I had to say, "You'll find us a far menacing opponent than just a few Shovelhead's. Then you have quintessence that I'm our best, you would have to have far superior warriors than these few. Then you have in essence that we would be nothing like those Shovelhead's. They're religious Zealot's from way back, well at least their masters are. The world would be a far better place if all of them were just no more. They have never had a liking for my kind, as we're all of separate races here. I can also assure you that I have no love for them either, as you heard through my comment."

He had to give me a certain knowing look as he added, "That is why I'm here, as you said, I'm the best of our kind. Though I have to admit I had no idea there were races within your kind. When I call them your kind, I'm talking about fundamentally that they're vampires also. All suck blood as the leech, hence my insult to you. When I referred that you were like them, there was no insult meant with that. I have been told that this may be the most important thing I do, so I do what I can. You will also note that once this is done, I will give you a window to leave. I have assurances that their leaders will hold them at bay, this isn't a given as it would have been, so I would leave right away."

I then had to say as if this man did turn into something, it or at least I would be extremely hard-pressed to fight him. So I had to ask, "What are your terms then?"

"Assured protection as we may help one another, it is only aligned when we fight these Shovelhead's as you call them. This does not mean we would be doing nothing but protecting our own lineage, so this doesn't mean a peace treaty. Just a mutual understanding."

I had no idea this would be as bad as what they had said now projected, so I saw no way around it. Well, there was, just the equal and mutual destruction of all of us. So I had to say out loud as I also had to figure they needed all to hear it. "I can see no way but to agree with this, and if you keep your promise that will appear to be the deal."

So I placed my hand out as it was our way, and he did exactly what I had expected as he grasped my arm also. I can also say that they have been known to use the old way of confirmation for generations. With this, he backed off after we allowed our grips to leave. I can tell you that his grip was far stronger than I had imagined, a fight with him would be long and extremely hard pressed. Now he started to issue orders to all around us, to which I would find out to be Cherokee again as I communicated.

He got into the old truck with a decidedly young girl, she had to be no older than sixteen. With that, I also had to figure he had his problems with young ones also, as we stood there waiting for the all clear. Once we heard nothing I made a signal for all to move, and everyone conveyed themselves as best as possible. Which like I said would cement our decision with them, in truth I could never genuinely tell William this. As we drove off Naomi and I made sure Joe knew why, as it would not be advised for any of to discuss these events while he was with us.

He did have to request why I told him all of this. I explained that he still had to consult with us about what we had discovered. I guess it had never crossed his mind that William would even be at our abode. I did have to speculate as we drove that Veronica being more important didn't bode well for us communally. He also had to ascertain why they entertain this also, again we confirmed the facts as they were. Giaus convey the impression with a special interest in her, that could only mean she would be intended for positioning. Joe understood what that meant, this could only be for this city.

We also added that it without a doubt didn't matter that much as long as Kitty and I were part of the house. This is why he and William catered to our whims because it was sure he saw the lineage of our claim here. I had to also place this down to Joe's inquisitive mind, as he knew we also had a mind to leave. Naomi then spoke for the two of us, as she assured him we would never leave until we received certain guarantees.

Now as you may have also figured out as we drove up the driveway. We barely had the time to shut up as the car slowed to a stop. Then you have the reality that Naomi's Jeep had little between us and the outside world. So we had to figure they heard that last part, not that we would ever hide that last part from anyone. The thing was that we hadn't truly met them when we stopped. I had to think that maybe something would be even more pressing to them. There had been a moment as we got out to search around, then we saw them also drive up onto the scene.

Then we made our way in, I had to call to Tony to release one to me for something quickly. He did as I had petitioned as we moved to the living-room, and of course, it was Liz. I had to wonder what he had been thinking when I noticed the time. Half of the early evening had already got past, they had to have had roughly three hours worth of training. I had informed her to show William and Alex in, but to tell the other guy it may be wiser to keep a wary eye around the surroundings. Naomi remembered his name was Dave, and Liz did a great job.

I also told Liz to have Tony place someone in charge and had him and Kitty join us. Once they did I then started as I had to ascertain one thing. "William, what took you so long?"

He replied, "Giaus wanted to be kept informed, so as soon as I thought we were safe we pulled over to find a signal. Once I did that I discussed what we found with him, and he is exceedingly interested in it all."

I had to lift my eyebrow, I had no doubt that he was interested in what we were encountering. From the insignificance I had already gleaned, I had to think it was more about what I had said to that Chief Bear Killer that concerned him. I'm sure that he couldn't wait to tell his master about all the wrong I had been doing. This had been far more important than all that, so I had to force myself not to say what I thought.

So I then turned toward all that were present, allowed the information we had concerned toward this affair. So I started out with, "What we have to explain is profoundly grave if there is any validity to what we found. I also called you all here because we may need everyone's input for all this intelligence we gathered. First I will allow Joe to lay things out, and explain what he understands. Joe please?"

Joe then took out that mammoth tome for a reference point when talking. With that he also placed out a few pages he had used also, it was easy to see he was also prepared to write more. Then he pointed at the five symbols as he explained, "These are the old symbols of the five elements, we had a close resemblance of two of these. That wouldn't undoubtedly concern us, except the outline of another we could see a third. Then you have the important matter that two were rubbed out, one you couldn't see anything. That makes what I'm about ready to say just a supplication then, as we did find the other was truly a reference to the fourth."

He then opened the big book, as he now pointed again, "I have tried to see or at least figure out what they were attempting. You have to first realize that everything was installed in a ritual manner, even I know that can be bad as young as I am. When you look at the positioning they were trying either of these three rituals. I think the worst problem is when I looked for a sacrifice, all I found were cat remains. You have to comprehend that they nearly never use cats in ritual ceremonies. They think their souls are tied to felines in a way, so you could say that would be sacrilegious to them."

He then pointed at another thing as he went on, "Now this gives the impression to closest to what they were doing, I do fear that this could be the worst they could do."

We all leaned forward so we could read it, though like me I had to added. "Joe, what does it read?"

He then said, "If I'm right this reads everlastingness, and that there reads perpetuity. I do believe in a nutshell it all means, a spell that brings on those that aren't supposed to be."

William then interjected, "John most rituals take a long time to cast because they're supposed to last a remarkably long time. If I have all this right, in the end, it is sort of like a gateway to bring things into existence. I have heard that some real hard magic using humans tried such, but I had never thought they had succeeded. Joe can you explain with better words than my own what we're debating."

He nodded his head as he went on, "This would open those plains of existence that separate spirit from reality. Think of this as things started to happen, all the angels and demons that existed were unexpectedly real. I mean we all know they exist, with their power no one would stand a chance. Now as we can also see as there are none around us, they must not have succeeded. Then you have this one part that is without a doubt unusual."

He now pointed at another part, "This reads like this; 'Vestal Virgin must be in the term of three scores, with their continence instance. Where this forbearance in moderation cast, though the sanguine fluid leaves them in their own delight. As this, they weather the abuse till their virtue is received, then as adumbration prorogues to that point of bereavement. In their hollowness of disposition of substance. With individual toward this enthusiasm without as eyes, all in one blacken as slaves to their worthlessness. As they join a new union of one, as in consciousness, essential, and of temperament.'"

We all looked at each other after that, I had to look at William and ask, "You got any idea what all that means?"

He had to look at me as he had to confess, "Well I do believe the part about the Vestal Virgins means virgins, and the threescore means sixty of them. That next part also means their virginity has to be intact, I have no idea how you would do that in this modern world."

From the hallway came, "I think I may know."

I immediately recognized the voice of Liz, so I had to ask, "Liz share if you have any idea, please."

She came in and then started to talk, "Nuns are known to also be Vestal Virgins, and when they found me they were attacking my house as you all know." I thought she had been going to let the cat out of the bag, but she also knew William so I would be proud when she proceeded. "As you also know the reason why you found me was because they were attacking around the church. I don't know if you know this, but there are a lot of nuns there also." That was my girl, "It would be surprisingly easy to get them all into one place, though that next part is hard to imagine."

I had to ask, "What do you mean Liz?"

"Well, I understood it because you always use it when you talk about blood. So I think it says without them being touched their blood must flow, and they have to be alive and more than willing partners." She hinted to nod her head as she also added, "The next part is also easy for a nun, as many can withstand this test of death. Then you have that next part which absolutely concerns me, their eyes or possibly their souls now darken to a point of blackness. Once this has occurred they become as one person in all ways, how can anyone do that?"

William came back with a fact, "I think that isn't what it means technically Liz, I mean as a slave of old their will was to their master. I do believe that they lose their minds and well everything, and become soulless creatures directed by something else. If we have to place this in religious terms then let's call it Satan."

Joe then added, "Most of a spell has to be done and directed by the individual, so I think that means the caster. If he happens to be casting this spell he can't be eminently amiable either, so again you could use the same term. This may have been a trial run, I did also see many piles of dust. Then you have the basics that those guys seemed to know every part of that place. This may be just speculation, but I do believe whoever was the caster received a rude awakening. I could easily see them having their way with them, though there was no evidence of human bodies."

I had to look at William as I had to say, "Even you said the obvious here, as we feel no residual effects from all of this. Do you think those wolves may have interrupted their little party?"

He then said what I wanted to hear, "I can't even see why we don't have anything here already, so it is also the best explanation I can produce. Though if they were interrupted because of what they are may also explain why nobodies."

I had to shake my head as I said, "Sorry about this Joe, and this doesn't apply to you. But I honestly hate magic users, they can be so despicable."

This got a laugh out of all the others, though for Joe and Liz it was just like a deer looking into the head lights of a car.

Chapter Twenty

This conclave within an assemblage.

This wasn't what I would have called the usual, well unless you live in New Orleans. I had to turn to William and ask one thing, "We may need extra help in this city, I'm not saying that Joe wasn't much help. Even you can see this is far deeper than even you can handle, though a magic using vamp could also help Joe."

He nodded his head, "I'll talk to him about this, but other than New Orleans, I have no idea where we'll get one. You know as well as I do with their queen, there is no way they'll release one right now. They are convoluted with all their concern about the humans there. Giaus has for many years has just wanted to wipe them out, but even he has too many ties to go that far. So here we are in the same place as since the beginning."

I had to give him a serious look as I had to

confront him with what I had to say subsequently. "You know I could always call in my friend Manukul Adaire. I mean all he has to hear is that Giaus is here, and I'm sure he would be on the next train."

I knew just the mention of that name would get a reaction out of him. I hadn't expected one out of Alex also, "That old coot has to be nothing but a fool, he can't do shit."

Then you had Kitty, "Neecow, ooo me likei me Neecow. Demon Lord know af me friendly, Neecow is so cooly, me likes him."

William then said in a stern tone, "No! I'm sure Giaus won't allow Manny into any of his cities without his knowledge first! End of discussion!"

Now you may have guessed two things with those statements, one from Kitty meant he had been her kind. The other is he would be an expert as acting the clown, and most perceive him as completely mad. I met the guy and did exactly what he needed doing, this allowed him to survive. As the clown he plays, he is often on the edge of being destroyed. I had thought many a time that his antics would be his undoing, and I have come to his aid as well. Well not that he ever needed it, by his own interpretations of his own situation.

William wasn't done with his own interpretation of the situation. "Instead we could just place out more patrols."

I had to ask, "Where could they be going to come from in the end? We have one of those that would patrol, and she has to remain close to keep an eye on Bert. All I have seen from your side is Alex here, you would need at least three to four more just as good as Alex. I don't see that many being available on this side of the country. We could place the kids in harm's way, except none of us would be willing to do that. Now from this line up that leaves Kitty, you, and me, and we need to be available for a good fight. So I ask you a second time, exactly from where?"

He had to add on to the pile, "We could stretch ourselves thin until we can get backups. Many of us have had to do that before, and I'm sure that you have as well."

It had appeared I had to shoot back as I also laid down some facts, "Yeah we could do that like they did some fifteen hundred years ago. You remember that don't you? They went out to get rid of this scourge, but they didn't have enough people for the job. Look at the great job they did, I mean these are technically the same guys from back then. Maybe we're good enough, and they move out of the city. Where will they pop up next Wichita, Kansas? Why are your kind always ready to seek the worst possible way to handle a situation. Alex are you ready to place your existence on the line for the likes of Giaus and William?"

Looking at him as he talked, though I also knew I had placed him in somewhat of a spot. "I wouldn't shed a tear for them with remorse when I just got up and left. I explained to him before I came that all I would be doing would be tracking. I had been euphoric when you were there today because what happened was not in my game plan. I'm also sure he isn't extremely happy with me right now, as I had to invoke the terms of self-protection clause after our little stint. So I'm sure he wouldn't have any trouble drawing my blood to protect his neck."

I chuckled after I heard that, then a question came that I hadn't even thought would come. "Protection clause? Little stint? John, what happened when you were away?"

I'm sure he thought he had been doing the right thing, as Joe spoke up for me. "Oh Liz, we had to face off with a few werewolves. John was the cool one of the group as he came up with the plan. It did end up that we didn't need it though."

Looking down as she came back with, "But if they hadn't let you go, I take it the situation was a dire one?"

Shaking my head as I confessed, "We were prepared to give our lives to save William and Joe, so even though I did want to tell it to the group in a meeting format. The facts are that we would have been hard-pressed to get out of there with our lives. Then you have the fundamentals that we have no idea where their powers lie. Even as I had the best chance of getting out of there, we had no idea of what kind of condition. I . . ."

I was about ready to say I don't think I had any troubles with them, but Liz cut me off amidst speaking. "MEETING! WE'RE GOING TO HAVE A MEETING! EVERYONE TO THE BALLROOM NOW! MEETING TIME!"

William leaned across as he said, "I think she legitimately wants to grill you on this, though we have much more to talk about, I dare say. I do think the better part of valor is to retreat, so we'll make our leave right now."

I had to say in all as it did fit my means, "Coward!"

Joe had to ask, "John are we in trouble?"

Naomi then replied, "Yes, with a degree. Bert may get angry with me, Cheryl may be cross with you. You have a release because John and I took you with us. I do believe though John is in some serious trouble as it may be."

I had looked up as they had already left the room, I mean William and Alex. Then I had to agree, "Thanks for pointing out the blatantly obvious Naomi."

Well, we had to get this over with, the first thing I did was to get Bert to move down the street. I told him to look after William and ascertain what he truly does. Once he was sure he was out of sight he was to return. I did this as Naomi also knew, so we would have a surprise if he showed back up for some reason. You could ask me if I was afraid, and the answer would be for myself no. Plausibly not even for the other two elders, now for all the others I sure was. I'm sure that even though I undoubtedly didn't like to be told on, Giaus had some idea of how I acted around anyone of importance.

Now we kept a lid on everything until we were sure, and only when we saw Bert return did we start. I started it out with, "As you all know we went out today to see what something strange had been in the end. I also want to add that even though Naomi, William, and I didn't want to bring Joe. We genuinely didn't see any way around bringing him with us. Though as you can see he is well taken care of, a situation developed where a few of us may not have returned."

Immediately everyone started to talk, it ended surprisingly quickly when Liz spoke, "Shut up NOW! There's more!"

I had never seen anyone that could usurp such control over a crowd. So I had to go on, which was my plan anyway, "I will also tell you we had no way to assess just who was at the disadvantage there. You may have heard me use the term werewolves, well we were facing down with what is even worse than those beasts. I can assure all of you I can take down a few of them, though you never truly want to fight more than one at a time. We all had our ways out of this conflict save one of us, and this is why I didn't legitimately want to bring Joe."

Cheryl immediately asked, "You can't be telling us that most of you would have made it out, but there was no assurance of how Joe would have escaped?"

I had to admit, "Well no. Naomi and I can tell you he was going to make it out of there one way or another."

Liz immediately cut me off, "I knew it. You and Naomi were prepared to give your lives to save Joe! Am I right?!"

I was able to say, "Well it was . . ."

"No!" She placed her finger up, "You don't get to speak till I tell you what I see because this is far bigger than anyone can imagine." She then stood up and came to the front as she continued, "John thinks they were doing the noble thing, but in turn, they would have been sacrificing all of us. Joe, I'm sorry to sound callous in all this, but let's say you didn't survive. Where would the next person to teach you, we have Kitty, but she can do only so much."

She then did a dramatic flourish with her arms, "Cibilia knows just like I do, Andy and Bert went after you. Where would their efforts have gone if this hadn't turned out for the best? Then you have the so young Pepper, Paul, Cheryl, and your daughter. Can you have foreseen what happens to them if you die, no! Yet here we are with a barely escape plan, that you had no assurance would even work. Had you thought of one of us, or is it just how noble you think you're being."

I was at a loss as she was absolutely right, then Naomi tried to talk. "But Liz we got . . ."

Again she cut her off, "No! You're as guilty as he is, where would Bert be? I have said many a time how much I hate your training, but I also know I need it terribly. You have told me that the two of you think of yourselves as the defunct leaders of this household. Would leaders of so many truly place so much on the line for something that may or may not comes to pass. Real leaders would have told Mary for you John, and Bert for Naomi."

She then gave an aggravated shake of her head, "I know there is a lot that has to be thought of, yet you keep going beyond what has to be demanded. I mean when they all left after everyone else that fateful day, and because of that Cibilia got hurt. I heard you warned them on never doing that ever again, but what about all of you elders? Shouldn't all of you have to follow the same example?"

I finally got up and said, "Liz sit down, I want to address all of this in turn." I think she knew I was a fair man so she sat down, I then had to be careful what I spoke. "Liz is right. In a sense, we have to because of your inexperience too. If we get hurt or destroyed I have no idea how this will emerge. I can tell you that most likely Giaus and William won't lift a finger, now Veronica is an unknown quantity. Just like what we faced off against today, and even in that we were at fault."

I then turned to Naomi as I had to ask, "I have to ask as this has to be a legitimately simple thing, why hadn't William ask for more information? Now I'm thinking of it, with what he said the other day, he had no idea. Us as his seniors should have done the right thing, I do think we assumed he had already done it. Yet we all know that flunkies of a lord are that well versed, so we made our own trouble here."

Right then I had a thought, "Wait. Giaus had a more important thing to do, now that even makes me think. Like to keep Veronica out of it, I do think this was a test for us all. In a technical sense, we all failed it."

Naomi did a second take as she had to ask, "Do you without a doubt think he would place his second in jeopardy like that?"

Kitty then spoke, "Naughty poor boy, he know jade of those he sent. Demon Lord predictable with Shiny One, he also knows you take Huntress in da Wild. No sense to that which isn't as seen, though what be lost iffy Demon Lord and Huntress do what they unknown. Shiny One learn the valuable lesson, then he no longer have to be punished with others. Blue Fake King be safe in all he show and do, knowing no sign of the trickster be seen though. Me say because Greater Harlequin show little dreamer, some scene as you can ascertain. Howie you prove as they see mean as just so much drivel."

I had to say, "I see now. So he knew in the course of the event. He is worse than what they say about him then."

Liz had to ask, "If you see what she means, can you share it with us all?"

I was about ready to tell her, but I was surprised that Tony would beat me to the bunch. "Liz you're best at this, as it is also apparent that you're allowing this incident to cloud your eyes. He wanted to test William yes, but he had to see before and he saw what John would do. He also made a good call that he would bring Naomi with him, this gave him a certain freedom in all of this though. You see if there were trouble he also knew that both of them would place their lives on the line. Now with this that would save William, that is if I'm right and her reference to the shiny one is him."

He looked at me and I immediately nodded my head so he went on, "So I think she also meant that Alex would have to also come through for us in the end. Now if one went down John would have been right there to try and help them. Naomi is a reflection of everything John does, so that would have meant her too. Naomi and Alex are of the same kind, so he would have moved to her aid to ascertain her destruction. The only one I think that didn't have a safety net here was John, and he, as we know, is distinguished at what he does. So there would have been a god awful fight, which would have been good for Giaus."

She came back with what could only be pure anger, "He wants this city clear of the Shovelhead's! How can that be good for Giaus?"

I had to speak plainly, "There is a good chance that some of us would have decreased. The higher up they were the better for him in the end, because he has his means. Then you have the essence that I honestly don't think he wants Veronica here. I can't tell you why he has to be having to do this, maybe she has something on him. You can never know. Everyone of these higher up guys have their appliances so to speak. Though as you heard he tried to include Naomi, Kitty, and me in that, we are far from his lackeys."

Naomi then came in, "You see Liz all three of us are like a thorn in his side, so the sooner he can get this house to tote the line the better. In truth, he has no clue what John has done, where the true cement here is Tony. I understood why he did that at first, but now I can even see a deeper cause behind all of this. John has placed Tony as head of training because Giaus has that old way of thinking. He can't imagine why any elder would give up control of what he has."

Then she looked at Liz, "We precisely and truly didn't want to be martyrs. This was an untenable problem we had no idea about, all speculation was out the window with all of this situation. When it comes to looking at insight as you may have already ascertained. We as a whole would prefer to look at someone like Kitty or Andy, as in time we can all do this. Giaus, as he has been into all of this, had no idea the true outcome. I mean if he had he would have sent Alex more as a spy than in the position he did. Now can you see what we meant."

Kitty smiled as she added, "Play Toy had no idea of the matter, though he saw the shaky of the hooves. Me also see much as to what was down, then to bubbles fly around. Looky here and there, nope Boy Toys words fit right here. Me understand note ins be dar, da be no damage to Demon Lord or da Huntress. Kitty never not warn of a dreamy state, so they perfect to be there. Now you can know what was isn't what could have been."

Now Liz nodded her head, then she came close as she had to ask, "Honestly? You would warn us if we were going to take the big nap?" Kitty nodded her head, so Liz then said, "You can go on now John."

Wait? Has been all of this more concern for my welfare, then what she let it on to be in connection with us or them in the end?

I had to stare at her as she now moved to sit down, I had no idea what to think. Naomi then whispered to me, "Woman can get positively strange when they think they're going to lose someone. You might want to place this off to the craziness of a woman's mind."

Okay, now if that was true I now knew I was unquestionably in for it. Then you have the fact of how I felt about her, and all I could think of was, for her anything.

Now I started, "Okay they have people like Kitty, and they knew we were going to be there. It did give the impression of being completely adhoc in the way it was put together. So even as we sometimes have to wait on Kitty, they gave the impression to have the same problem. I could tell you all about what we saw and what it leads us to believe. Instead I think we'll just cover the basics, and first, they didn't come out there to fight. This is strange to all of us elders as for years we have been at war with them."

Tony had to ask, "John, is it an actual war, or one of the perceived ones?"

I turned and replied, "Good point to bring up Tony, with all I have seen I would say it was a perceived one. You see way back when we started a fight with the werewolves in Europe. It literally had to do with fact that our kind wanted to control them, like slaves. Most of you haven't met werewolves yet, but as they are most certainly part of this city we have to tell you about them. They were created with a vigor or pure rage never had a confrontation. Think of it like someone having rabies, and you can get an idea how it hits."

Liz then asked, "John I thought you said they weren't werewolves?"

I had to nod to her also, "Another good point, they most certainly aren't. From what I understand there is a long ceremony they do to find their animal spirit. In a sense, I guess you could call them shapeshifter's, except most shapeshifter's, can use many forms. I guess the best way of thinking of them is as a hybrid, like something betwixt us and them in the end. Now I have fought werewolves and they're easily beaten, but not by someone inexperienced. I also fought a shapeshifter, they're reasonably harder to experience. They can change at will, and if need be use this to get away."

Sammy then asked, "Then have you ever absolutely destroyed either of these?"

I had to make this point exceedingly clear, "Let me straighten this part out, when we destroy vampires we use that because of the belief that he died. We're only coming up with the quintessence that we may be alive also. When you do away with a werewolf or shapeshifter you aren't destroying them, you're killing them. In their full of a set rage state it is either you or them, so just think of those claws ripping through your flesh. Now for the worst part about fighting them, and that is there in-between state."

I allowed this to sink in, "Think of this if you might. You hit them with all the might you have, and right before your eyes they heal." I now turned to Mary, "We can hit them so hard we can send them flying." Now I made sure Cibilia had been looking as I turned to her, "They get up as if we never hit them, and just charge back into the fight." Now I included Sammy, "You can even slice them in two, and if they can pull themselves together, they're healing again. This means you're back at it again in seconds."

I now move my hand to Naomi, "Naomi give them what you know about fighting them."

So she did, "They have mistaken us for their smaller cousin because we do look like them. Our smell has always given us away, as long as we have blood we can trade blow for blow. Don't get me wrong all I can fight is the weaker versions of their kind. I can also tell you when I see them in the wilderness I have avoided them like the plague. They find it a sport when they find our trail, and I have been chased back into a few cities. The one you met tonight is known to have killed a few of them, but even he says it is best to avoid them."

Tony now added, "It is best to avoid any of them unless your job is expressly to kill them. They have one breed that is huge if you ever see any of them run for the hills. In fact, I think they are a race of a bygone era, like the dire wolf they so resemble. The only one that I do believe that is equipped for that kind of fight is John. The rest of you would just be a time it had to clean its teeth."

I had to pat him on the back as I added, "Now for the good news as it was instead of all this doom and gloom. We came to an agreement so we don't fight one another, and place all our forces against the Shovelhead's. I would have like to have the entire house leadership there, but without a doubt, we were flying by the seat of our pants."

This of course started a new round of discussion, which this time Liz did nothing to stop.

Chapter Twenty One

This discussion of our resolve.

You can just imagine where the conversation went after that, in truth this event wasn't finished. What I mean by this is that there was more to be said by the group. Then you have the quintessence that there was still a lot to be known about in the end. Tony tried to get up and leave, I grabbed his arm and as he looked back, he realized all the elders were still there. That was the obvious person to try and depart, as he had never been in this type of entanglement previously. Well to be truthful neither had any of us, we just had more experience to know there would be more questions.

Cibilia was the first to broach a subject, "John when you said you would have rather had the house leadership there. Were you stating that we would have done better?"

I had to acquaint her with another thing about

being part of the influential body. "Not literally. What I meant is that whenever there is a decision to be made, it is those that we call the head of a venture. In truth, we have been including you, Bert, and Joe, the only one that should be present are you, Kitty, and me. Also, possibly Tony, but for me, because I'm the oldest among us, you because you are the head of the house. Kitty gets to come because as she is the next in line, she is my obvious replacement whenever I have to go someplace."

She then added, "But if I heard William right, I won't be there because Veronica will be functioning as the head of the city."

I had to correct her on that part, "When it involves the city, you're right, though technically there are only two here of importance. That would be you and me, in this case, both Tony and Kitty become secondary. So if some decision has to be made, she'll have to call you and me."

Cheryl interrupted me here, "John, that can't be correct if her decision is final."

Tony came in here, "Good point Cheryl, but you see the leadership of the houses kind of play a game here. You see when they want to do one thing, they try to pull out what could be the worst for the city. I'm not talking about what they're doing, but obviously, others that claim to have authority. You see they would oh so love to drag all of you down. I'm willing to say John has had to play this game in far too many instances."

I had to confirm this, "Yeah, I hate that part of our society, though that is who has all the money for our means. It is also why I even agreed to deal with Giaus, I have to think he is truly what we call a cape. Though as I explained to Liz, that term doesn't mean what it used to necessarily."

Pepper then asked, "John this alliance with these dogs, does this mean that we aren't at war with them as you said earlier?"

I had to be truthful with her, "Let's not call it an alliance, but more of a treaty because of a mutual enemy. We all understand what all this can mean in the end, which isn't good for any of us. But it is like real warfare with all of this, as that hill that needs to be taken and can't. You throw more and more troops up there, and yet the same outcome occurs to always be the end result. Most people would say if you want the hill, then change your tactics. Where the problem lies is that they're at the base, it is hard to see around it unless you're removed from all that can happen. So in the end it is far easier to say what the right tactic should have been, but in truth you only know when all your cards have been played."

Liz then asked, "Is that reference to us, or is it a reference to the Shovelhead's?"

I had to smile at her as I stated, "I hope it is them at the bottom of the hill, as it is that has made in a sense of our new friends. In truth, I'm doing a lot of new things here, so I'm hoping this applies to Giaus and all his friends too. Not truly understanding what is going on I mean, and we can be more of a thorn then even he knows. You can also ask how can so few do so much, and the only thing I can say is it is a start is all."

Naomi then came in, "I was brought here by my mother because she wanted us to have a better life. This is what many back then wanted for their children, it just truly wasn't a given, unless you did for yourself. I also know from what I have gleaned that Kitty was already here. Tony is far too young for him to know this, and in fact, I'm willing to bet John knows better then I can explain. Even this world was made to old standards, but a few of the new independents learned about their own freedom."

She had to almost giggle as if she thought of something very pleasant. "Now there is no way that they would have ever given us our freedom, so there had to be a war. Most of you doubtlessly learned about it in high school, but in a sense, we learnt it first hand. Though I'm willing all you would know it as the revolutionary war, but there is far more."

I had to interject, "Particularly good point Naomi, and that is how it is now with those old worlders as I will call them. Even as we deal with them it is a new story, as we have to break away on our own accord. Back then we weren't allowed to join the colonists, even as many of us wanted to give them a hand. We were kept out because of our own fear, in these modern times their ways are at best Machiavellian. I'm willing to bet many of those in that old vulcanized time would have been better to allow us to sink. Though I also have to say that probably wasn't a given."

With that I pulled out my pistol and laid it down, "It is like this, as I have told you it can't kill you. I do have to correct that, as one bullet can't kill you. There are degrees of this, as you have heard Joe's and my pistols. These devices can do far more damage than most pistols, then you have the machine pistols like Andy and Kitty. Again varying degrees of damage, if you keep firing at the same target, the blood loss will achieve the same degree we want. I have had to learn how to use these for the better, though most of our kind have stuck with the blade. Though any weapon of mass destruction has an element of usage that can't be maintained."

Sammy then asked, "John? But you said the sword is the best?"

I nodded my head in recognition, "Nothing is as good as a well-placed blade, but can you get a kill with just a pistol or in Kitty's behalf a machine pistol? The answer is an obvious yes. Most of those older vampires know they can try to trump this, you can defeat them with using both literally. Always be ready with your blade though, always use the pistol as a supplementary device. You could say their true weakness is doggedness in the belief of their old ways."

Paul then had to ask, "But how does all this help us with our new friends John?"

Paul seemed to always have a direct mind, so I confirmed what he must have thought. "It doesn't honestly. I will have to teach you how to fight Chief Bear Killer's people. Right now we don't have to as long as we're fighting with a mutual understanding. Now to another obvious question, can they become our allies? I dearly hope so, though my training may still have to occur. If we can absolutely strike an alliance is yet to be seen, like I always say, stranger things have happened."

Even I could see the millions of questions, even as they are it was also as easy to see each had far reaching answers. So this became a slight time for the room to go silent. Once I was sure that everyone had no idea what to ask next, I stood up and said. "Like I said when we started all this, it is far newer than any of us can tell you. There are many things to be accomplished here, can we know the journey any of us may have to take? Nope. Can we then help you out on that journey? I dearly hope so, and we'll be there every step of the way. Knowledge is the definite helper to our livelihood, ignorance, where we truly stand now, could be our death null."

The elders started for the door, then I remembered how this all got started. "Can we place you in harm's way? Yes, but it is far better if we do it, as we have tools that could save us. Is it stupid if it ends up us getting destroyed? Perhaps, but to make this yours, we have to do what we know, or else it would truly end. Are we always right in what we do? I would love to say yes, but the honest truth is we genuinely don't know. Now is this all we have to say about this? I would love to say yes here as well, but as we're bonded I'm sure the subject we'll come up many more instances. Know that I look at all of you as my sisters and brothers, and in many ways, we're more like family. Yes, you may also hear us call you kids or youths, but there is a sense that we're also equals. I think that is all that has to be said, Tony what do you have?"

Tony replied, "I wasn't sure what we would have to do, so I trained them hard. That means all of you have free time, remedial training get with your teachers. Those appointed teachers get with your students, train for at least an hour. Mary, Cibilia has Liz and Sammy first, then you get to do your worst. Tomorrow it will be the other way around, it's only fair Cibilia. Now I know it is still like four hours till sunrise, so this doesn't mean to go and tear the house apart. Bert, I think Naomi wanted to do something special for you, so get with her. Now you all get to have fun, so get out of here."

Because of what I said that commotion came from everywhere, so Tony's voice had to raise just to be heard. I think they literally started as I said my last line, though there were the usual groans. I did what I had been doing everyday, as I made my way to that same said library. I also found that same nondescript vampire book I had been reading. As you also know I had only made it to like page three because how hard it was to read. So as Joe entered the room I made my way back to the shelves of periodicals along with him.

I placed that book back where I found it, though I did also leave the bookmark for a later day. When I looked at all the books they did have, I had never read the modern classic; Of mice and men. I then pulled it off the shelf and went back to reading, but beforehand, I wanted to add one thing before Joe left.

I recalled, "Joe you have been doing such a great job reading and learning, you were a huge asset out there today. I do worry that you may be trying to do too much, so please when you can take some time for yourself. I mean we do need the best blood mage we can get out there, but if reading the same thing dulls you. Well, we without a doubt don't need that, what we need is the best Joe we can get."

He then replied, "I know, I have been doing my best, though I had no idea how important this could be. When I started before all this stuff he tried to instill in me, my master I mean, but it was way too much for a newbie to know the truth. I would like to say it was you that did this, but I think essentially facing my own death that has truly caused this. I think what I'm doing is in a way playing catch up as it were, though unlike then I had a teacher. I should have done way more and just listened to him, well I guess what has been provoking me on now has to be my own ignorance."

Then a voice came from the door that caused me to turn my head. It was Cheryl and she had just said, "Are you sure I haven't got anything to do with it?"

Okay, I know we can't blush, Joe conveyed his best imitation of a young boy blushing at that moment. I allowed just a slight of acknowledgment as to the event, "Joe?"

He replied, "Yes John?"

I had to chuckle as I now understood he had no clue about these implications. So I also added, "I do believe that look means I want you now big boy."

She came in with all kinds of sultry moves as she grabbed his shirt. Then she smiled at me as she informed me, "He knows John. Just as he is a kid I have to be a snippet more forward than I'm used to, Pepper is an excellent teacher though."

I had to chuckle again, then a thought came to me, and I found myself asking her. "You're still wearing underwear, right?"

"Wouldn't you like to know."

She said that as she left the room with him, and I had to realize that wasn't truly an answer. What may be worse is that it caused me to think of how she would look without . . . well, anything on at all. Though right then I had to be careful as I saw another lady coming down the hall. Liz looked as if she had the worst of it today, though to be honest there existed something different. Okay, now my eyes moved from Cheryl directly to her, as she seemed to be walking differently. Now I had to ask myself what was she doing, as she seemed to place one leg in front of the other. With the movement of her shoulders, and what is that look she came about to be presenting toward me?

Oh, my. Can she be trying to be sultry, and this brought another thought as it did give the impression to be working. 'Pepper is an excellent teacher?' Were they supposed to be instructed by her? Was this what was she suppose to be demonstrating to them? Plus exactly where did Tony get this idea, surely not me?

Then Liz woke me from my thoughts, "John?!"

I had to ask, "What babe?"

"You genuinely weren't paying attention were you?"

I lifted my book as I said, "I have been thinking of getting into a new book, but you have my attention right now."

She then turned and pointed down the hall as she asked, "Was it more important to pay attention to Cheryl?"

I swear I can unquestionably be clueless at times, "Oh no, but she had been certainly acting weirdly." Then my face brightened up as I had to ask, "Did Tony set you up to this to use your special abilities?"

"NO!" I could see that she was upset for some reason, then she told me why they were acting this way, and I felt the fool. "We had our woman's time with Naomi, and we talked about how to bring a man to you. Pepper and Mary had some honestly good ideas, Cheryl even shared a few tidbits. In my application of them on you create the impression that I couldn't get a rise out of you, but apparently, I'm also terrible at this."

Okay, this has to be something that I had absolutely set myself up, and the first results are truly a fail for me. I had to frown when I realized this, I had to kick myself when it came to all of this. Not because of what I had seen and had come to the results, though I had to allow her a release to the obvious.

So the truth seemed like the best avenue, "I'm sorry Liz, I have a terrible way of doing all the wrong things because I'm a thinker. I would think that if I had told you what I had seen, and how it had affected me would have seemed out of place for me. I can tell you that what you had done did get a rise out of me. Instead of going with what you were looking for though, I looked for what could be more in what you had said. Then again you have gotten a rise out of me from profoundly the first day we met. In fact with how I reacted after you rejected me should have told you how terribly hot I find you, babe."

What should have been an easy call was not my best thing, as I was wonderfully the dolt when it comes to these things. I will say that being completely honest did insinuate that gave a change to her spirits, as this appeared to supplant a smile on her face. This did also tell me that I had to do something else which she might not approve. So I grabbed her hand as I spoke softly to her, as to try and not make this too hard, or at least lessen my thought process.

"I have to get Pepper, well more likely to happen with Paul, as my mistake has pointed out a problem I have to correct this finally. I will tell you as soon as we can get this done we'll go to our room for some fun."

She said with a high degree of happiness in her voice, "Okay, but we have to be fast."

"As fast as we can be babe, but I have never used a computer before, that has to be why I'm thinking Paul."

But with that, we were moving to her room since it wasn't considerably far from our room. Liz had to ask as I tapped on the door, "What is so important John?"

I had to confess, "Tony is a good lead in all you need to know when it comes to normal stuff. There is a side of both you and Pepper that has to get better, I'm afraid Tony can never approach that level. In fact, the person I'm thinking of maybe even able to help him out in all this. Then add to that what she can instill into Paul and Cheryl, and this may be nearly the most important phone call I have ever made."

Pepper then opened the door as she said, "John we could hear all your babbling as we were getting up to answer the door. What can be that important to stop us in mid-flow, and I'm telling you this because it can be legitimately important in the end!"

I had to ask, "Paul are you acquitted with the workings of the computer? I need to get hold of someone extremely important for Liz and Pepper. If she can be found she may also be important to you and Cheryl also."

His reply was simple, "I can use it, but the real

computer nerd is Andy. Though. I'm not sure I would disturb him if Kitty and he have gotten started. He's okay with disturbances, she's the one that gets somewhat possessive. Okay, babe, this shouldn't take long. We have to get into the neco whatever web, oh man. Yeah, we without a doubt need Andy for this, but maybe Joe can help with this."

To which I had to say, "Kind of appearing like Cheryl had been undoubtedly possessive with Joe just a few minutes ago. What about, dang I'm sure we can't interrupt them either."

Liz asked, "Whom John?"

Paul answered for me, "I'm willing he meant Bert, and I have to agree with you there. Andy has to be the ticket here."

With that, we turned to go to their room, but Kitty came off the steps. She then said, "Demon Lord better make it fast with Boy Toy, or me be very cross. He now be doing flip, whire, and bleep blip boop, I told him you be there in two and no few. Pretty straight Boy going back to Princess Blue and be wit her, me fix things."

With that she then turned and even as I knew what she had done was normal for them, her kind still had a way to even surprise me. So I did the same as I had also told Liz she could go back to the room. She would have nothing to do with it at all, as she wanted to see why this could be so important. I then came into the place where the laptop was being stored, and there had been Andy doing exactly what we needed.

I then came close as I said, "Her name used to be

Ermete Pariso, though she has been here formerly. That was her name in Italy, I'm sure she may have changed it to something more American comparable."

With that he started to tap on the thing, within just a moment he had a name. I can tell you even I was surprised when I saw it; Wild Cherry. She now lived somewhere in Tucson Arizona, and if I read it correctly she would be a madam. I knew she likes to do that, but after her first gig, I had thought she had relinquished the profession. So even as surprised as I had been I also tempered in my reaction. Then he spoke to me as I had been searching for her telephone number.

"What do you want to say to her?"

I had to lift one eyebrow as I had to ask, "What? You can talk to her through the computer?"

"No," was his reply, then he adjusted it with, "Well yeah you can, but I figure she would be getting close to sleep, so it may be better to send a message."

"Oh, yes." I had to think, "Dear Cherry of course, though that is a weird name, to say the least. Ah I mean just dear Cherry."

"I know that John."

"Oh okay, let me continue. This is John, but spell it jay oh en, she wouldn't know me how I spell it today. I have a couple of your kind, and even as good as I am I have no way to train them in their special abilities. If you could send me a teacher so they can be trained, I need your help. Now I have no other means, and you know I never ask for help. Then just sign it from me again. Let me also know when we get a reply."

Andy typed positively quickly and then hit a button. Liz and I just stood there until he told us it had been received by her. We were about ready to walk away when Andy said, "John just how soon do you want me to tell you when we get a reply?" I had to look at him dumbfounded as he added, "She wrote back right away, though it reads just a sec."

We all now had to look at the screen, then it came to life again. It read; Dear Jony; I have to put a few things in order, but I will be there asap. So let's say 2 or 3 days, though I will require my own bedroom. Signed just Cherry.

I allowed Andy to leave as Liz and I walked into our room, I was completely dumbfounded now. I mean I had expected her to send one of her representatives, not come herself. I then had to look at Liz and tell her what I knew, though how do you start with something like this.

I then turned to her as I had to say, "Liz I have to tell you about Ermy, I mean Cherry. To say that she's different is an understatement, though for your kind she is all the sayings roll up into one. I'm warning you because she can be abrasive at times, but she literally has nothing she won't do. I'm not saying as a vampire as much, but as the hedonist she truly is."

She had to look at me and ask, "Then why was this call so important?"

"I had figured she would send a representative, not come herself. You and Pepper desperately need her help, she will most likely take you places you absolutely don't want to go. Maybe it would be best to say do what she wants you to do, then temper it with your own resolve. I'm right in all this, though I also know that she will presumably start things where you may not want to go. Do you understand what I'm saying here, babe?"

"I think so, you just got us a trainer that will take us eminently near to living in Sodom and Gomorrah. Once we're done we could in our own respects be just short of that."

I had to give it to her, she had a way to say what I would be trying to say in too many words, with a simpler meaning. So all I could do was nod my head.

Chapter Twenty Two

A meeting between the good, the evil, and the gorgeous.

Now I would like to tell you the discussion we got into also, that would also reveal way too much of our sex life. Know this that I have nothing to hide, it is just that I would like to protect something of our own virtue. Elizabeth has told me that it may insinuate that our intimate life may sound far worse than it is. Then again after she usually thinks upon this, she also expresses that it may be better that you use your imagination. I had to ask what she truly meant, and she just smiled as she spoke to the effect.

"Never mind that, as I will stick to what I said."

This always perplexed me, as I have no idea what she had been talking as to respects. I did ask Pepper once, and Cibilia was nearby, and all they could answer with were uncontrollable giggles. I do have to wonder if they're hiding something from me also, then again we do have a wonderfully good time. With this, that is Liz and me, I also have to confess that no where in this story does she ever concede her mind to the way she feels about me. I have heard this in the past, the worst and best kind of love is that of the unrequited variety. Though the real effect is to deepen my despair with every day she never returned my favors. Even as this may be better explained by some wonderful poet or bard.

What I will share with you, is a fact with every argued point it did suggest our closeness. Then you have the fact what I did had just the effect upon her I thought, as I can't be truthful to myself. So instead I will say our love did make the depths elevated to new heights. The bard may make a poem of this in the line of an earlier comedy, with the knowledge that no comedy was truly bizarre. Most were that, of to a point of tragedy, so the title is as much an oxymoron. Now I have given all I care too, as to what transpired after she made her enlightened connotation.

Day Twelve

Now I had my delight with the day that had proceeded, with my eyes after our short slumber were fixed on the canopy. It was a greatly inspired old bed, that was wonderfully comfortable. In truth as I lay there, I had to also wonder if we would ever use the covers or sheets. I mean we did pull them back as if we were going to, then we were usually on top of them sprawled in whatever position we had desired slumber concluded.

What I guess always tickled me is that she was so much a nun-intrusive lady. Even as small as she was, without being the smallest by far, could take up so much of the bed. Then you have that which is odd, as I rarely move as I sleep, to me which is normal. Yet every morning she is in another unusual position that I'm in a bind to describe. As her beautiful curves are so well defined, with a beauty that can't be truly expressed. This was just an impression of the truth, as her head turned with that magic smile. With a magnificent alluring effect that no mortal could resist, even as I am had a hard time doing the same here.

With this I had to figure I could press reasonably more, as I whispered to her after I lightly kissed her lips. "Do you think I'm still wrong, or can you see what I meant that it is better than you find out from an expert?"

She got up and cradled her knees as she replied, "I guess not, though it would have been nicer to be told beforehand. I also understand that there is a lot of knowledge she can impart. What I'm worried about is that if I like this as much as you think I will. What will keep me from doing the same line that she has gone?"

Okay, that was an exceedingly good question, though for some reason I think I was given the answer. "I won't lie to you and tell you that won't happen. Then again you do have me as an example, as I'm far from what my kind is preferred." I had to chuckle with my next thought as I expressed it, "She's the one that pointed that out to me, in fact, she also told me I was more like your kind."

She had a surprised look on her face as she had to ask, "What do you like of my kind."

That is when I realized that I had not expressed the other side of her kind. "Oh, not the hedonistic side, and I have been remorseful in explaining this too. So I guess I should have covered the good with the bad about your species. You see we also call your race the most human kind of this vampire existence. Now, generally, that comes to the nitty-gritty that you can appear more human than any of us. There is also a fact that you can appreciate things better, and have a better grasp on your own emotions. This is where she tells me I'm more like her kind, or as this guy called Beckett said, 'A truly feeling vampire. How strange.'"

She nodded her head, as she also asked, "But what about the thing you said about our thoughts on humans?"

I had to confess this one, "Well that is strange, as right now you're close to what you were, so you have feelings for humans. As we age we tend to get more jaded with everything, so most vampires just look at humans as cattle. Your kind tends to even try to distance themselves, which is weird because their traits usually involve humans. Whereas those farther from the human race insinuate to not be as unfeeling. Of course, as it is right now everyone in here has more feelings for the human species. Naomi and Kitty who are like one step away from not dealing with humans, tend to never talk about them."

I knew even this little bit was a lot to take in, so I thought to temper this with a finishing statement. "You could say that all of you still see yourselves as the mostly human. I won't lie to you as even they could now see the differences in your bodies. Like all of your elders though, we have in a sense have seen the differences and can never resolve that. When it comes to our own resolve I can say that Tony is yet too young. Naomi has her tendencies within preserving our food source, I may be in that club. But even as we are we see why we have to treat them like the men and women they are. So in a sense, we all still feel for our human kin."

She then asked, "What about Kitty?"

I had to be real here, "Liz you know why I didn't mention her, even as I can see she would never intentionally hurt a human. Like when I'm always wary of her spending time with Andy. We, and or even her own mind has no idea about that, as with her mind she can do the worst without truly knowing."

"I guess I did know that." She replied to that, then she seemed to get an epiphany out of no where. "What about the church all of you pulled me out of that horrible day?"

I had to ask as I had no clue, "What about it?"

"Well you did the right thing, but since they started all they had when I was found. Can you say that somewhere along the line they won't try that again?"

I had not thought about any of that, and I had to jump to my feet as I moved to the window. I registered where the sun was at, then I had to look back at her, as she stared curiously at me. I then had to tell her the truth, "I had figured that Kitty would tell us, then again there are ways around her insight. How could I have been so stupid."

She then blinked as she asked, "Does this mean that we're going back to Our Lady of Perpetual Help?"

"Yes!" Then I also added, "Battledress as soon as possible, even though this will be more of a fact-finding mission. We need to be prepared for anything, also I have to get with Paul and Cheryl to get things straight here."

With that, I pulled out my old battle leathers, which were sound, yet worn. I could hear a truly physical moan come out of Liz, so I figured that would venture a good question. "Did you think you reminding me about wouldn't bring on this response?"

She shook her head as she had to confess, "I'm getting used to the lighter frilly things, now I have to put on those heavy leathers. I wish I hadn't said a thing."

Okay, what I said next, was just to the point, "You could do like Mary and wear leather underthings, they have the same effect. In fact, I do believe all save those that are up front could get away with that. I'm not sure I would go with your usual dress, maybe something that is easy to clean just in case," I was about ready to leave it at that, then I myself had to ask a question. "What did you mean, I wish I hadn't said a thing?"

After hearing what I had said she started digging through her underwear drawer as she replied. "I'm honestly beginning to hate those hot heavy leather outfits, I mean I sweat just standing there."

"You sweat?"

"Well no, it was just an expression. But why did you ask me that?"

"Oh. I had to wonder if you had already gotten as jaded as most of your kind?"

"Well, I will never get that jaded as my life has to do with helping everyone. To be truthful it may be my curse in the end, even as I hope it never comes if I can help it."

That caused her to look out as if she started thinking real hard, so I had to ask, "What were you thinking so hard concerning what you could Help?"

She then replied, "I fear I'm wrong, but if all this is, is an intelligence mission, do we all have to go?"

This line we had been following did concern and confuse me, I had to absolutely think about what she asked. With this, I also came to a realization that we could use the kids as a backup. Her inquiry did have a valid point, so in reality, I had to give a small part of this argument. I gave her my answer, "Well I guess not, though all of you will have to be ready at a moments notice. The truth of it the elders would have to do the survey and all of you would be our backup. Let me get with Tony and we'll discuss it, though battle dress will still be of the day."

Once I had said this her usual fancy came back to her, and with some pep, she dressed. I had to wonder why she gave the impression of being fine as I looked at her. There would be a definite lull in our conversation, as my mind needed to catch up with what had been said. Then as I had finished an insinuation came to me, as it had not dawned on how her life had changed here. How would it have been if I had led a life of peace and helping, then I came to this existence. I then had to think that I was truly not the person to talk to her about this. With that, I had made my mind up, so I told her not to leave as I was.

I knew she would be after me asking me why, so I added as I left, "I just have an idea is all, I'll be right back."

With this, I went to Tony's room and told him to meet me in the kitchen as soon as possible. Then after I had done all of this I made my way to Cheryl's room. Joe answered the door, so I asked, "Can I talk to Cheryl if she's presentable?"

She was in a considerably revealing nightgown, but she immediately placed on a robe. Then asked, "What's up John?"

Well, this was eminently simple, "Liz suggests to be somewhat withdrawn, and I had to wonder why. As I had thought about it, the notion dawned on me that coming from into this life may have been moderately hard on her. Mary had told me that you're a considerably good listener and that you have this way of knowing what to say. We had not been to that church since last time, you remember where Tony made her. I have realized that we need to send a team to investigate the area. With these thoughts she had gone into a profoundly deep zone, that is when it dawned on me. Now we will have to use all of you as back up just in case, so that also means, battle dress. I fear this may also have something to do with it, my knowledge about you caused me to think of you."

She smiled at me as she replied, "I understand, though I may need all the girls for this. We'll make it a short bull session, just leave it up to me and Joe. You can send all the girls Liz's way, then I'll meet them all there."

I had to ask, "What should I tell Liz?"

"Oh, nothing. Just tell her that I need to talk to her, and once we get there we'll broach the subject."

"Will you need time for this so I can tell Tony?"

"Yeah, tell him to give us about an hour after we start. Maybe have like Cibilia tell him when we're ready, I don't know. Whatever John, figure it out for everyone."

With this, I went back to our room, and once in there, I told her that Cheryl wanted to talk to her. Then she asked me what I had gone after, and I told her that it was Cheryl. I had to add that this was her idea, but my intention was to get her to talk to her also. Then as this was done I went to everyone else's room and told them all to go to our room. The only two exceptions were Naomi and Kitty, whom I told to meet me in the kitchen. Now you would think that I had done the right thing, boy am I glad we have Kitty in our crew. I told Tony my plan as we waited on the ladies, and he thought it was a good idea.

Then Naomi came into the room in her tightest battle dress, and this was normal. What wasn't was when Kitty came in, as she had Liz on one arm pulling her into the room. I had to look at her in confusion as she did this, then she spoke to the reasoning of her digression.

She communicated, "Dream Lord confused by manner, he sees those that aren't as though. You be wit my place when we go, know ya have a real place. Me mind be what will be, Huntress is in her element, though outside even her norm. Demon Lord know nothing but bang boom, he sees eyes can't see right. You be in place with Harlequin as she venture, know me take care of her as bestie she be."

I saw Cheryl at the door, so I put my hand up as I spoke. "Kitty knows something we don't, even though I'm not truly sure. I do believe Liz has to come with us, remember her way can be mysterious. Just go tell all of them to get ready for Tony's training, and that Liz will be coming with us." I could see that even Liz had been confused as Cheryl left, so I added so she would understand. "Kitty sees that there is an important reason why you have to come. Because of the lack of information, I dare say that there is a reason she also can't tell us completely."

Liz then had to say, "I do understand that, in fact, I do believe she said all that to take away your fear. I also think there can be something that could be confusing you, she sees that it has to be her, or at least them to help with it. I'm not sure why her mind and Naomi's being different, yet I'm guessing normal is important. The part about the Harlequin I may also have, as something about her told her that I unquestionably had to go on this adventure. Then I do believe that ending was a reassurance to you that she would take care of me."

Tony then had to ask, "Could she be telling us that you will run into trouble?"

I had to surmise, "No, I do believe if that were the case she would give us some sign. Though she also didn't tell you to stand down, so I do believe the troops will be needed tonight."

Because I was so good at this, I had to look at Liz. I also had to add a pride as she suggested going beyond my understanding of Kitty. Liz nodded her head as she added, "Yeah. I do believe that is the validity of the situation."

That was enough for me as we also made sure that

Tony had a training scheduled that would leaned to a sudden movement. With this, we made our way out to the garage then decided to use Naomi's Jeep for this excursion. The truth of it wasn't the easy exit though, as this could be a plus and a hindrance. Where we had seen the plus was the ease of escape more than anything else. Before we left Naomi and I had to set the thing up for a completed plan. Kitty would cover the area just off the beaten path, I could handle more so she was set to relieve me.

It was easy to see that Liz wasn't happy when I told her to stay close to the Jeep. I had secured my Glock before leaving, so I also gave her this for her job. I explained that we had no idea what would be there, so if she saw anything that looked like a vampire to squeeze the trigger. I also told her that Naomi would be on the outskirts looking for any new smells so to be careful. Of course, none had to be explained what their jobs were, and Naomi made sure she knew when to turn off her safety. Not that I don't think Liz didn't know, I do believe Naomi had been just being safe.

For me, I had to check my blade and Desert Eagle, though I only had like ten rounds left. Kitty set forth a cell phone she had gotten off Pepper, I did suspect it wasn't with her permission. Tony had come out to make sure we were ready since it could text I told him to have someone watching the computer. On the other hand, all Naomi had to do was stretch her hands, Kitty felt mister sharpie. She wouldn't be bringing her machine pistol, that was more normal for her, and I knew enough never to question her. I had also gotten my old aluminum baseball bat for Liz, I'm sure you can surmise what that was for in the end.

With all of this Naomi now turned over her Jeep,

and we finally set off to what we didn't know. You also have to understand that we were sure we wouldn't run into anyone. Why we did all this is the fact it is always better to be over prepared than under prepared. You have already been told about the ten or fifteen minutes it takes to get there. I told Liz to look after Naomi as we set a time of an hour to be back. You can surmise that I said this because Kitty needs not to be seen with what she had been going to do. Well, she can do this in plain sight, it is just easier for her when no one could see her in the end.

Now when I finally left I had to figure my times were off, so I had to keep a better eye than the other two ladies. When I also said the inner area, there were many different walkways to ascertain this information. Then you have the fact we suspected nothing, and we were correct in our suspicions. I was about ready to leave for our meeting when it happened, though it wasn't those terrible Shovelhead's.

You can see that I was just off where Liz had been found, near a noticeably small house. I was just a few feet to the approach when I heard a slight noise. I had to go on the defensive so no one could attack me, then I heard a voice which I had no idea of with its deep volume.

"Hello?! Who are you?!" Since it was behind me I had to turn around to see who it was, when it spoke again. "You're the evil that has been plaguing this neighborhood aren't you?"

Now I would have never suspected a human out of all these problems. So I had to say, "It would be far better if you just thought of me as a dream."

He stepped from the chair as he spoke up to my

request, "The Devil you say, and allow Jesus to cast you into the bowels of Hell!"

The little priest had his cross in my face, this took me fairly aback when I heard another voice. This time I knew it all too well, the voice to be Liz's running up the walkway. She had been saying far too loud, "John don't kill him!"

I couldn't believe the look on his face, as it was now him that was taken aback. I had to ask, "Liz do you know this fool?"

She came close as she added, "Naomi sent me after you as we have a problem, her exact words; go get John fast, while I go after Kitty. I wish I could talk Father Michael so I could explain all of this. To use words that John has told me, 'No we aren't evil, though I am not sure I wouldn't call us good either.' Just know that we took care of that evil, and there are stranger things on earth than just God and heaven."

I had to blink as I took him in, as he then spoke to her. "Sister are you well? I mean have you been taking good care of you, and are you healthy?"

Okay, I have no idea why I laughed at that, Liz admonished me with a stern. "John! He just wants to know how I am, and I'm as well as can be expected. This evil that was here has taken hold of the entire city, and to how well I may be may change in the future. Now that we're using every asset we have to fight it, and we're having to pull from all over the country. This could be a fascine that this entire city could be in if we aren't successful. We do have to leave but know that even the church in this can be an enemy. Now John we literally have to go."

I told her as I wanted to say one last thing to him as he seemed to care deeply for her. "Run to Naomi and I'll be there in just a second." Once she ran off I had to tell him a truth, "She is a fantastic woman, but she has this hold on me, so know that I will never allow her to die. I can also add that I have seen stranger things happen, so this would be a fleeting promise. You know your God better than I do, so even as I have never asked anyone to pray for me precendently. I now ask for this in our endeavor, though for me I only ask that I would be there for her."

He then asked, "You love her don't you?"

I had to reply, "I have no idea what love is, but I can tell you in my three hundred forty-seven years I have never felt this way toward anyone. If this can be called love, then my actual answer would have to be yes. I'm not sure we have the right to love, so I will leave it at that."

He then said, "Well all things that have life has a right to love, even if they don't understand it, love, that is."

I had to shake my head as I had to lay one more truth, "What if we aren't alive though?"

Then I ran off to meet up with Naomi, Liz, and Kitty.

Chapter Twenty Three

The beginning of cementing a relationship.

There are many things that you could say about what just happened. Like it is easy to say that leaving this kind of knowledge may not have been a good thing. Not that either of us let anything out of the bag, but just the basic comments could be put together. Then you have the fundamentals that just leaving him alive after just such a meeting, may course the wrong way with the others we know about as most we presume to be capes. I can also tell you that in truth I don't know William or Veronica. Even not knowing Giaus wouldn't be hard to figure out, as even they don't care. I have to think he would prefer dealing with this in the old way, which would mean Father Michael's death.

Right then as I saw the Native American boy there, this had to be terribly unhealthy. So I made my way to them in haste, though it did startle him somewhat. As I had to ask the obvious question, he shrugged it off nearly with as much spurn. "What's up?"

He immediately started to talk, "Rose left for some reason, Sleek Puma went after her sister and now we can't find either one. Our Chief sent me after you for help, though I also saw you leave, so I came after you. He told me that we, I think he means us wolves, may need your seer's special talents. He did also tell me that we're using ours also, but he also knows yours has a more reactive effect. Whatever that means?"

I then turned to Liz and told her, "Liz text Tony to meet us downtown at the usual spot, full combat load."

She asked, "Should I add be ready for anything?"

I nodded my head as I turned to Kitty, "I know this is bad for you, but can you help us out with this?"

She nodded her head as she stretched out her arms, with hands raised high. Now I'm willing to bet you would doubtlessly expect something weird to happen. I can tell you that it is weird, the actual effect can be rather disappointing though, as it virtually looks as if they sniff the wind. Then she spoke, "Demon Lord is on the right track, go meet the others as it were to the will of the Great Harlequin."

I turned to the young boy as I had to ask, "We're on our way, tell your chief we are. Though I would offer you a ride, then again it might be weird riding with bloodsuckers for you. So in a sense, this will be up to you."

He then told us, "I came on my bike, so I'm good

to go. I mean I won't be nearly as fast as you, I did do well keeping up with you while you drove at normal speed. Then you have the essential detail that you are bloodsuckers, that concerns the elders more than it does their children. We have seen what you have done with our enemy, those that are an enemy of ours is a friend. Running Wolf loves to go with that saying, it makes far more sense to us then I think he believes it does. I have no problem riding with you, I do have to get with others to see if they're moving to the downtown area. So even as my heart says yes to me, I would have to resign to my fate riding my bike first."

I had to nod to the kid as he now ran to where he had laid his ten-speed bike. I knew he would have quite the effort before him, and to be truthful I had to say I liked this kid. I turned to Kitty as she got into the rear of the Jeep, and ask generally. "Did the text go through Liz?"

Liz who was already in the passenger seat replied, "Yeah, and it even read that it had been received, but we have no relay signal to see if he's read it."

I started to get into my seat waiting on the nails from Kitty, as she had never been sure of riding in a car. I then pulled out my pistol to make sure it was still fresh, this was an act of dogged ability. Not that it isn't a good thing to do, but could anything have changed in the last hour. Liz then asked as I place my pistol back and Naomi wheeled off with steadfast resolve.

"John do they have to be our enemy because I find myself liking that kid."

I had to give her a big smile as Kitty's nail just started to draw blood, with a simple comment. "Liz I find myself liking that kid also, but we can discuss this later."

You can imagine that little talk transpired after this because I had to set myself for the pain Kitty would be inflicting. Naomi being busy with all that arose on the road, and with the movement of the Jeep Liz had been holding on for dear life. Now Kitty and I could use each other to help hold on, but the rear of a Jeep had occurred to even be more harrowing. Given the state of our predicament, the reasoning is easily seen why.

Now as we had to do what we were doing, it gave me time to think about what had been said. Though in truth it was what Liz had said: No we aren't evil, though I'm not sure I wouldn't call us good either. Just know that we took care of that evil, and there are stranger things on earth than just God and Heaven. I had to look at this in the full content, as it did imply to an important connotation to me.

She listened to me far better than even I had thought, not that she hadn't been a good listener, it was just I had imparted so much to her. Most of those that I had taught things like this I may have had to repeat like five to eight times in turn. That statement was doubtlessly the truest I ever said to anyone, and that is why most usually miss it. I had also told some that second part, but as of late I had avoided it because so many didn't like it.

There is a complete truth about the essence that there were stranger things on earth than God and Heaven. I had always agreed with that, where my problem came with the explaining of such a statement. What I mean is if he created everything, then that would mean me, Liz, and to add to the strange Chief Bear Killer. When you realize these basic facts you then have to ask for what purpose, though as we are now there did insinuate to be some aspiration.

What in this world would be considered evil we fight against, yet as I have lived this existence there is this interminable battle. So you can see where this would be what could be a damnation, even as you can see this, could it be that easy? To be truthful I had to think at one time it was just that simple. The older I get with all that has filled my existence, this point has become convoluted in a sense.

I have fought my own wars in my own time, I have also seen a lot in the human world. It gave me the impression that these things weren't as they appear. I know that I have been lied to why we fight, the world outside has been lied to also. There are men that will tell the common law we fight for this, then when it is all over they say it was for that. When it comes to these lies it would appear that we are best at it.

Then you have to look at the world as others see it, and you realize those humans are better at it than we are. There are these avenues that are taken, like a hurricane that directly hits one place. Well, that is an obvious truth, but where the deaths are can't be reported because this other city has more people. This is one way though also public opinion has a lot to do with it. Nothing can cover up the truth the best then what we would call public opinion.

It is the reality that we and those of the feral nature exist. Yes, I'm placing a note toward my own kind, that you're told that we're a figment of your imagination. Not that we don't benefit from these same said lies, plus I also think it is far easier to believe that there isn't some monster that loves your blood. Yet when you find out we do exist can all the rest you were told all be lies? Have you ever had that thought?

If you are of warm flesh I would consider it, because what I'm telling you here is just the edge of the truth. What I could tell you and these children would raise all their fears, which I have learned isn't the best of ideas. Not that the truth isn't the best weapon, and in truth, if the question did come up I would answer truthfully. I just don't want to be that person that brings such a subject up before it has to be told.

I do have to tell you a thing though, as to the result to this has a question to it. As to what has to happen, can this be the resolve of our Lord? Can these be placed to such evil, and yet it turned out for so much the better? Finally, can so much death, in reality, because for good, or as death is it just so much more the evil?

This will we have been given is such a fickle thing, yet it was his will to give it to us.

Now we happened onto this site where we were to meet, and I knew there was a good chance we may beat them here. As we all bailed out of the Jeep I had to wonder if I could take another ride with Kitty. Evan as we had moved I also knew it was the degree of our speed that caused her such distress. What concerned me was the quintessential point that Liz moved right to the other end of the movie theater.

We had to run after her to try and keep these things straight, I could barely make out what she had been looking at with my vision. There were three faint figures in the darkness, I was glad Naomi came up because she pointed out the obvious.

"Look John! They look like those guys were going to surround those kids, can they be the Chief's kids?"

I was about ready to ask Liz because I knew she could see them far better than we could. It transpired that I had been too late as she had already started running that way, and I immediately said to Naomi.

"Aw Hell! Apparently, they are, Naomi go after her. I'll be behind you with Kitty, now hurry up and get to Liz."

With this she ran after her on all fours, she could be as fast as Liz could this way. Kitty could run at a better rate than any human, but she had no chance of keeping up with Liz. I bent down so she could climb on my back, as soon as I knew she had a good grip, tightly enough, I moved. Now it had to be a good thing this wasn't the car, but I had never truly done this before with her. So I had to worry her grip would be the same, and apparently, she had been completely used to this kind of movement.

Once we got on the other side of the river, I could see that Liz had placed herself in between the threat and the three girls. In the interim two of them had changed into wolves, whereas a dark-skinned Native American stood over a fourth girl. Her hair had been extremely long and flowing, with a set demeanor that spoke no one would be going to touch the lying girl. Then it hit me. BLOOD!

I came close to her and had to ask, "Are you Sleek Puma?"

She then replied, "Yeah . . . I mean no! What's it to

you!"

By this time I had made out that there were seven without heartbeats, "Your Father sent us to help."

"My Dad has no idea of what's going on, I mean he yelled at my sister for doing what she could do. It is no wonder that she ran away, then who does he send. Leeches!"

I had to smile at her as I had to affirm something here, but also find a way to set things straight. "You may not like us much, and we aren't here to fight them. This is your tribe, your sister, and his responsibility, but we are committed to helping in all endeavors when it comes to Shovelhead's." I then had to look at the seven that were wanting their meal back. "Guys you truly messed up, do you know who's daughter this is?"

The one that I had to figure was their leader spoke, "They're nothing but blood bags to us. We treat them like the cattle they are."

I had to look at the closest wolf to me and spoke, "Howl as loud as you can, they need to be able to find us and soon. LIZ! I need you to look at Rose and see if she has any chance at all." I then turned to Sleek Puma and told her, "Liz used to be a sort of nurse before she became like us."

Yes, I lied because I had no idea how she would act at the word nun. It was for a good cause, and to me, that justified the means. Liz came close as she checked her out, she looked at me and had to confirm. "John that is way too much blood for a young girl to lose."

I had to add, "Liz she comes from a strong family, we have to do all we can to help them."

Then that guy just had to speak, "Good, while you're doing that we can tear these little girls apart."

I had to turn to him and state the obvious, "Hey Stupid! It is bad enough that only have you signed your own death warrant, but do you understand that you killed all your friends too?"

With this comment, the two wolf forms let out the loudest howls I had ever heard. Then we could hear some hooting off in the distance, I had to shake my head as more created the impression to enter the carnage. I do believe all their noise had spoiled what I had hoped would happen. None of them could have possibly heard the howls coming from the distance. They all believed that this would be a short war here, what they didn't realize that they were right. Just there was no way they were going to be the victors.

With this, I could hear driving up a VW microbus, so I spoke in a normal volume as I knew Tony would hear me. "Tony we need you and Pepper right away, tell Mary and Cibilia to set up a defense just past the river. Once we get things straight here I can tell you what has happened. Also tell them that this isn't our fight, we're just here to make sure no one gets away."

Sleek Puma then looked at me and said, "Maybe some of your kind are okay, but I can't leave my sister's side."

I perfectly understood, so I had to say, "Okay, then allow me to take your crew over, and we'll protect you and

Liz." She nodded her head, so I spoke to them, "Hey you, this is Naomi and for right now you stay close to her if there is a fight." Then I turned to the other one, "You're next to me, be careful though." I then pulled out my blade, "When I get to swing this I can drop like twenty of them."

The guy then spoke, "Oh, like I'm scared of just another vampire."

Talking to Kitty to stand right in front of Liz and Sleek Puma when Liz did a bad thing. She screamed out, "Oh yeah! Well he's the Enforcer, and that isn't an enforcer, he is the Enforcer."

Yeah. They likely happen to have no idea what that was. There was also the reality that there could have been anyone listening. His response absolutely confirmed that, as he said, "Hey Red?! Is that supposed to scare me?"

I'm glad I had learned restraint, though it had taken years to come to this point. I had to tell him the simple fact of being a man, "You speak to my wife that way one more time and your head will be the first I take. Like I have always told her, it's a terrible thing to boast because stranger things have happened."

"Well . . ." He said while his head started to turn to and fro, as now the howls were becoming apparent. Then he had to say in a slightly scared tone, "What the hell?!"

With this I heard the unmistakable sound of an old truck, that was my sign to give them hardly ever any information, as Tony came running up with that expeditious nature. "Tony show Pepper and Liz what to do, we have to know that young ladies condition." Then I turned my attention to this idiot, "You see we have become allies in our fight against your kind. As you're a common enemy, so yes we're here to help these people. You have no answerable means toward me, but you do them for what you have done."

With that, I saw that old man driving as the chief was in the back. As soon as it came to a squeaking halt, he had jumped out and run right to Rose. I then said, "We held them at bay, but you may want to ask Tony and his about her condition."

Then his other daughter said, "Daddy she was pissed so she ran off, I got my crew and came right after her. We were too late." Then she signed the guy's death warrant that had been doing all the talking. This also gave me a realization why he had been talking, he wasn't the strong figure he wanted to be when I first heard his bravado. He what could be seen just as a scared kid, "I pulled him off her neck if she's dead he's the one that did this."

I had to laugh as I could see the anger forming in the chief's eyes. With this I just had to say, "Well I had thought you had unquestionably screwed up, to tell you the magnitude of this mess up is beyond me. If I were you I would try to run away, because I'm not sure he'll allow you to get two steps."

The old man stepped in between them all, and he placed his hands on his chest. "No my chief, let your warriors handle this. You know what I told you, this is a time of decision, not war for you."

With that, he started to bark orders, and though I didn't understand what was spoken, I did understand it to be Cherokee. Then I could see two others starting to bark orders also, I told the one next to me. "We protect your chief!"

With this, the older man went and talked to Tony as the chief had to rain in his anger. Once he had done all the talking he could do he came back, with this he had now spoken to the old man. "Is it as bad as Dark Raven told us Wise Owl?"

He now replied, "It is my chief, just like he said this is the point that has to be made, your choice." Now before I tell you more, I have to tell you how efficient fighters these Native Americans are. You see they had trapped them all, and one at a time they tore them apart with no mercy. Even a few tried to jump into the river, but they had them even out there. There had to be at least three different kinds of fish, and they feasted like piranha.

Back to the point, he was making, as the chief now turned to me. "My seer told me that I had three choices, one was to allow her to be gone. I could never do that to my wife, which makes the next even worse, which was to hasten her trek. The third was to allow you to have her, which to us is just the same as her dying. So I have to ask you if my lovely bride could visit her favorite daughter?"

Okay, this surprised me and again I was glad Tony was there, as he spoke. "I'm sorry for your loss Chief Bear Killer, but he could never guarantee you that. We have the quintessence that her newness would make her want for blood to great. Now over time, she may be able to resist that human taste, but even my girls have a time holding their breath while they worked on your daughter."

He then had to ask, "But I'm not blind, I can see you have no taste for our blood. Is there a reason for this?"

Naomi then said from where she stood, "Supers don't have the same smell of human blood to us, we resist because our senses tell us we would die if we drank from you. You could say that as your instincts protect you, so does ours when it comes to certain things."

I added because I knew he had been looking for an out, "This also means you and your daughter could visit her for your wife. I will tell you that it can and seemingly have to be on neutral ground. Not for your sake though, as it would be more for her sake."

He looked at his other daughter and asked, "Do you think your mother could live with this?"

She then replied as she looked at me, "Like she always says, Dad, she'll have to learn to live with it. But are you sure your turning her won't just kill her?"

I had to shake my head no as I also replied, "No. I'm sorry but even then turn isn't a guarantee, though as of late we have been having great luck. I have to be honest and tell you our luck may run out any moment." I had to look at the chief and tell him, "It isn't much of a chance that your daughter has, but at least it has to be something."

Then the chief made the choice, "Any choice is better than nothing. Do it!"

I then commanded, "Liz feed a moderate amount of blood, but not enough for the change. We have to get her to the house before the change, there is a purpose for this. You see when the final act comes it is better where she will live. Now you're welcome to come along, plus if she wakes you can say your goodbyes. If she doesn't we'll need one of you to make a choice, as we never just say who will do the deed. So even as this is, we can't say till it is about ready to happen."

Running Wolf and the older wolf came up, and I had to say, "This is up to him, and I know you look at this as a trap. We have to do this fast, so make up your mind as we take Rose to our house. Know that I'm a lot like your chief, once I make a promise I keep it. We came here to protect these girls, in all that happened we couldn't accomplish what needed to be done. Now we pay the greatest honor and allow one of you to join our ranks."

Now I turned to Tony and told him, "She's in yours and Pepper's care if she gets hurt you'll have to face the wrath of the chief. We'll all meet up at the house, Sleek Puma I now give you back you kind. Naomi and I will meet with you out of the house before we go in, I swear this with my own honor."

With this Naomi started to bark orders, I watched as Tony and Pepper took Rose into their arms. Now the rest of us made sure we moved to the vehicle well, with even Liz's help, though there was no doubt there. When we were finally able to move, she asked me a basic question.

"I don't understand. Why did it have to be you and Naomi?"

I replied, "I'm the oldest among all of you, so it is expected of me."

Naomi added, "Then you have the essence that they already know I'm the closest to them we have. That was a safety measure on John's part, I understood it had been forthcoming anyway. Heck, I would have done the same thing, but he only promised his honor. Which I thank you for that John."

Liz had to ask one more question with a sobering feeling after it was answered, "Why was John's honor so important?"

Naomi replied though I would have thought it would have been better for me. "John's honor is in his trust toward Tony, if something should happen it falls upon his shoulders, not Tony's."

She looked at me as we piled into the Jeep, as to what had happened earlier, I had to fear I would get some kind of reprisal. So all I did was nod my head, with that her head went down as Naomi now drove to the house.

Chapter Twenty Four

All in a timely manner.

You have to know something I had said earlier is also the truth of our existence. In a light, I will say it different then I would normally portray this remark.

When you look at the world with eyes of an elder you can see what isn't a truth. With this shroud that gives the impression as to cover all that has darkness. Out in this fabric of the truth, there is a fact that this world would be coming apart at the seams. I won't tell you this will be your end when the sun is no more, or the moon becomes a distant memory. I'm what has and will become, I'm like that of a god, though I can't claim to be God. Though our evil was set a long time ago, and even as I can't take that requisition. I have always confirmed that I'm not evil, but in this same statement, I also can't have any virtue.

This being known we enter a different kind of

meaning, like that of a drunk. I have a certain level of this passion, with every shadow that crowds into my conscience. I can't ever be a perfect creation like his son, though as we read this source I have learned that he wasn't perfect either. Not that his perfection wasn't there as he existed, but on his own, he had to reach a point. Because he had a mission that had started so long ago, and even the completeness is where he strived to be in the end. Even as I'm this relatively unfeeling creature, his sacrifice allows a tear to run down my cheek.

I won't lie to you and not tell you I had to recognize this point, and to that, I have to say my lady had helped greatly. This journey was approached with a mutual demeanor, as we both had much to learn. You could say this was the second or third step in our journey, though it will always be an ongoing measure. I do believe as we are we have to live that note when the disciples tried to keep those children away from him. Do not forsake the children, allow us to do what we may, or at least be what we maybe in the end.

Though as I have said there has to be one last comment, as I have seen how this story may create us as heroes. We can easily be a champion to anyone that needs it, but to use these terms would be far beyond what we are. So, at last, we aren't what this world would call us to be, save the monsters we are, or would be seen.

Now just as I had suspected Tony kept on his job, as Pepper sat next to him cradling Rose. I knew his driving technique was with a par to Mary, even as his reaction time was far greater. Naomi and I were on par with each other, and I was sure she could easily keep up with him. To my delight, he didn't hit the back of the garage when he came to a stop. I was worse for the wear as you already know why this factor had occurred in my knowledge. For her own size, you would never think such a creature as Kitty could inflict such damage on me.

I knew I would need blood before they showed up, so I ran into the house and left the matter to Naomi, though not long. Liz would be extremely concerned about my wound, I then directed Tony as she pondered the injury. Kitty had been already on moving the rest of the kids to another room. When I made for the door after drinking Liz scolded me with, "John?!"

This caused me to turn to discern why she had acted in such a manner. So I comforted her with a simple truth, "Liz my darling, we live by the blood. Yes, it looks terrible, but it will heal. I have a far pressing engagement right now, and I can't be late less they think the worse. I will allow you to treat it once all has been done, for now, I have to be off doing need to be accomplished."

"John?" She repeated, then added, "They think you and I are married?"

Ok, that may have been a mistake, but I had to speak to that fact fast as I could hear the truck now. "I'm sorry Liz, but I thought it would hold a greater impact if they understood a few things. I had no way to give this though unless they thought you were more to me than just another lady. I do have to go as Naomi is the only one to greet them, and the worse we can never know. I'm sure we have a lot to talk about, right now isn't the time, but later after this is all over we can speak at length."

She nodded her head as I barely had time to entertain the thought. Then I turned and move to where Naomi had placed herself. I had gotten there as the truck they were settling in, and three girls jumped out of the rear. I had to place my hand up as they did this, "Hold there, I can only allow so many in for your sisters' safety. Right now my kids would be suffering from having to hold their breath, just the sight of too many could cause them to release their air."

Chief Bear Killer was out of the cab asking, "Can my daughter attend with Wise Owl and me?"

Wise Owl then spoke, "My Chief we have talked about this at length, I do believe your daughter can take my place."

I had to wonder why he would do this, though I also knew with me there that might be enough. So I added to my statement, "Wise Owl I could never take away from the sister relationship, I would never band her. My statement would have literally meant for her crew, then I would never be myself without my council. So I beg you also enjoy this time in a forsaken place to all of you. With this, I present our hospitality, though we will have to wait as we enter as Cibilia must do her best in this."

He nodded his head as he said, "I knew you to be a gracious man, and we thank you. Now can we progress, as the demeanor of my daughter worries me the most."

With that, I had to wonder if he understood what had been about ready to happen. I had no thought of stopping his direction in all this, so I placed my hand out so he would go ahead. As we walked I told Naomi, "Tell Cibilia to come to the kitchen so she can invite Chief Bear Killer in once he is ready. We have no idea how the low threshold will react upon his type, so just being safe. Then tell Joe we'll need the full change ceremony so all things can be understood."

She then ran off as I turned to him to speak, "Chief there is a lot that must be done, but I'm having this so you can hear the means of how we are created. I will also tell you that this could take as much as three hours to progress. I can't tell you anything as it may have been toward your kind. So if there are similarities you can keep it to yourself if you deem. I am sure that if you need it we're glad I invited Wise Owl now. We'll visit your daughter's body first to see if there is any change."

Now we entered the kitchen and Cibilia had been standing there, the words she spoke were elegant, though directly to the point. "Chief Bear Killer, Daughter Sleek Puma, and welcome guest Wise Owl, I greet you for what we call our family. I invite you as I had to with all our elders, and greet you in the vampire way of friendship. I place my forearm on you for our shake, and say enter to our house."

With this, she placed out her hand, and I had to add, "Yes we all had to go through this too, all you have to do is grab her forearm, then you can enter freely."

With this I moved to where Naomi was now standing, they all in turn and shook Cibilia's arm. Then we moved on as Kitty hurried her back to the room, as we entered the room where Tony and his daughter now sit. Tony then said in a normal tone, "We kept your daughter safe and she has awoken to a low-level state. You may try to talk to her if you would like, but please try to keep it brief."

Sleek Puma went first, "Hey you stupid little girl, why did you have to do that, we were essentially too late.

Dummy, you could have gotten killed."

Tony was right there, so as we could barely hear anything. He was able to say, "I have no idea what this means, but she said; Who's the dumbest here, the one that led, or the one that followed."

Sleek Puma kind of half laughed and half giggled, as she turned to her dad. "That's your smart ass daughter for sure Papa."

Now it was his turn, and he even came closer, as he had to look at her. It had been an incredible thing to see such a large man get down that low. He took her noticeably small hand into his, as he spoke to her. "You know I worry about just as much as your sister, there would be no stopping her, I should have known better. That argument had been just an old man trying to protect his little girl. I do the same with Haley, but she was for sure to become a warrior."

He placed his hand up to stop Sleek Puma's objection, "But babygirl you had no thought of ever becoming a warrior, I mean Haley could absolutely fight with me. I have no idea what you were thinking when you went out in front with all those enemy in front of us. We had no way to protect you! I still love you even as this has happened to you, but you know your journey will be different now. I have no way to protect you."

I placed my hand up as I added, "The elders of this house will place their lives to keep you alive. We just need you to pass the final event, then you can join our family."

With this, another voice came from behind all of us, which I knew to be Liz's. "We are as a family, and as all families do, we will all place our lives to save each other." Then she looked at me and said, "John Kitty told me I was the only one that could resist her smell, so I have to tell you something. I am not sure how to do this, though she did tell me you would understand."

It would be a simple thing at this time to state, "Since these, our the friends we have, we have to be open and honest with them. Especially if it involves his daughter Rose."

She smiled as she spoke, "Well she tells me that her journey can be completed, that if it is what you want. There are two that can complete this, one is Boy Toy, and the other is the Great Harlequin. John if you forgot that means Andy and Kitty, though I do think she also wanted you to tell them about all of their traits. Ah, though she did say stick to the girls, I have no idea why she would say that."

I had to smile at her as I had to add, "No father would ever what to think their sweet sixteen-year-old daughter had to sleep with a guy willingly. Which is if you remember an effect of our ability when we turn."

Chief Bear Killer had to also smile as he spoke, "You know fathers thought extremely well my friend, she is correct in their assumption."

I had to add, "You have to also know this Chief, as the maker is that of the creator of the beings. So whoever does the turn they will be her profoundly own mother. Now they can never replace a real mother, but we always suggest they do get close. Not because it is better to be away from their mother, but that one day their mother and father will die, There can be nothing better if they have a shoulder to cry on in the end."

With that I placed my hand out as I started, "Liz and Pepper are the most human of our kind, their abilities are also said in a simple statement. When one becomes a vampire their looks go up or down by one step, though when they join their family they skip a number or four."

I pointed to Mary and Cibilia as I spoke, "My daughter Mary, and her better the house Princess Cibilia are of my species. They say you can't move an immovable object without an unstoppable object, we're that unstoppable object." Now I turned to Cheryl, "Cheryl as what we are maybe of the most refined, though they are most of our better, we enjoy telling them they aren't. Naomi behind us are known for their abilities with the beast and animalistic nature. Her kind is plausibly the closest to your."

I saw Joe there so I had to add, "We have none of the womanly variety of Joe's kind if any were even close to a human magic-using creature it would be his kind." I did this because I realized I had no real idea what her journey would be. You could say it was just a safety measure, now I pointed to Kitty. "Here is Kitty, and as you say her kind are like your seer, though she is far more. Never allow her small stature fool you, she can to dastardly damage to the enemy. Though Rose would have to learn this over time, and she shares the duty as an elder in this house."

He had to ask, "Her? But she looks no older than my daughter."

I had to state a basic fact, "I will never tell my age in public, and with this, I can never reveal her age. I will tell you as I do know your kind, as I'm sure you heard the tale of those ghost warriors. Though your race has coined many names for me, I heard when one of our kind forced their will on a few tribes. I have always been a friend as I had to end all their lives for this transgression. Now that you understand this know I was far older then they were back then. This will date me to a certain point it will also give you a date to how old I know Kitty to be."

Wise Owl then said, "My Chief that is far older than you are, though not by much."

"She was made in the time around the Civil War than?" Did he ask?

I replied, "That would be me telling you how old she is, but I am sure she may have a reply."

She did just that, though it was far from what even I would call normal. As everyone could hear battle cries, gunfire, cannon fire. Then she looked down and said, "Missy, oh my sister Missy you dead, please dear God Noo! Ooh, what be that, it burns like fire. I need help. I crawl to those in blue, blue boy looky but no help. Gray-man find me, why gray man bite Dreamia. No, no me be Debbie, not Dreamia."

That last part was in an entirely different voice, then we heard the cannon and gunfire again. With all the added screams of the dead and dying, it had been virtually like being there. Then she spoke again, "Where be me, why it so dark, is it nighty night? Why he just sit there, seem to watch Dreamia." That voice came back, "You were not Dreamia, you as a cat to be a kitten, tasty as it can be. No, You be higher than just a Dreamia." Then her voice came to her own, "Why you tell me all dis, who be you?"

Then in a thunderous voice came, "I be swirly, I be the first, I be more than all be scene, I be our kinds master! You are a party girl for the Great Harlequin, now go forth wit da gray one. Now he not know me, so shush between you's, okay?"

She smiled at the two of us, "What is so Civil about a War anyway?"

Okay, this made both of our eyebrows go up as we realized what this meant. So I then turned and spoke, "Unconventional, but does it answer your questions?"

He replied, "It certainly does, I choose her to change my daughter."

With that, we all now moved, though I also had to add something. "We can allow you and your daughter to meet you after the change if you like to discuss things more with her in the end. Now Wise Owl will have to wait outside because he smells far too human." I then turned to him, "She may be able to resist your human smell, but not usually right after they have been made. Though to be truthful Kitty's kind is kind of known for enjoying their human blood. So it is far better to be safe than sorry, though we will have her drink even before meeting the good chief and his daughter."

He replied, "I have no will to die just yet, so I'm comfortable waiting in the chief's truck."

With this he and the rest of us came into the room, I then said so all could hear. "The decision has been made, I now revolve your stead Tony to that of Kitty."

Now I knew that Kitty knew what this meant, but I did have a concern that Tony may not. I would be happy when he lifted her up, then waited for Kitty to sit. With a care you would rarely see with other vampires he placed her on Kitty's lap. I also have to confess it could be weird to see this, as Rose was approximately as dark as her sister. Kitty was so appeared to have literally no pigment, that it look as if you had darkness with the light as a token. Though as Kitty had been already a vampire the light would be the darkness, and Rose would be the darkness though without knowledge would be the light. To me, it would be the opposite of what ying and yang stood for, and that is why it was odd.

Joe then started with, "I would like to say welcome to a private event that we usually never share with anyone else. John has shown us why we have to learn the reason why not to turn anyone. So we understand why the entire house has to be privy to our change, though we call it our awakening. I now invite you to take a seat, though these three over here are for you three."

Then he pointed at three separate chairs, I added so they knew. "They did this so none of the kids would be tempted to take a nibble. Not because of anything about you in general."

Now Joe started in earnest, "We are that which can't be, so we need what can't be to go on with everything. The children of the age are how we go in through the blood thins. We preach to that God in the sky to end this, we're told we must go on to exist. So we take a small sip of flavor our system, is this their terror? Yes, it is, in truth it is also out terror as to whom we must do this too, witness that first sip."

I had always done it this way, but to be truthful I had only heard the complete ceremony a few times in my existence. Kitty picked up her wrist and her teeth barely dug into the flesh. Rose's moan wasn't that of pain as I could see the blood on her lips before Kitty bit her. This would be a way we had to change the pain from discomfort to ecstasy. I do believe she did this to comfort the good chief, I just added a simple comment.

"To show the common man we can be better then what we are, we give them the delight as if they're having a sexual encounter."

Sleek Puma giggled, I'm not sure the chief was so happy at this event. Joe went on with, "This can be drawn from the oldest of places, though they have to take the first step. It is now time to share our own sanguine fluid in that respect, with the dawn of this her first turn. We allow our vital fluid to flow, though it is still up to her to take it all of her body."

Now Kitty cut into her forearm, though it barely displayed the redness within her sanguine fluid. We as our time if we could hold our breath as this had been something we could desire. Not as much as the fluid of the one being changed, then again Kitty had been an elder. I would be happy when Rose found the blood flow coming from Kitty's arm. I will also add that not everyone can be as willing as Rose now seemed. As to what Chief Bear Killer had told me, I had to wonder if this had been spiteful toward her father.

Now as Joe called out to Rose there had been a visible sight that it could be working that I had never seen before in my existence. "To her, that has now taken the first step, as this has come to pass, we call your name to be released." Like I had said she would be nearly as dark as her sister, now her skin visibly turned one shade lighter, "Rose see what can be in all, feel the first prong of this rebirth!"

Her entire body now up-heaved from the ground, as I had to place my hand on the chief's arm. I knew this would catch his heart, as for the first time he had never heard his daughter scream like that. I spoke under my breath, "This happens to everyone, though it will be some of the last pain she'll ever have."

He whispered back, "Does it get any worse?"

I had to allow him to see my whole face when I spoke, "I'm afraid so, and most will remember this as far better then it appears. This is just the first step into what we are, the problem is we have to drag you down before she can release it all."

Joe continued, "See as all she knows is ripped from her, though she has no ponderous to the real difference of her new body. It is ashamed that we were human before we take our first step because this knowledge is what holds us in the past of all that exists." With that, he came close to the floor for effect, "Look as even all can see then life come forth, and this death would be taking hold. They say that our Lord has to be he that would be the greatest damned, even as our master has to be more of an equal. This is the recognition that this existence would be draining away, and the omnipresence would be slipping into an imperishability factor."

The only thing Joe had been missing would be the ancient long robes, though they had certainly gone the way of the Dodo bird. "Now she has to leave her mark in the most precious of locations."

Oh my, I had completely forgotten about this part. With this Joe lifted her skirt to turn both legs out, now he didn't reveal anything. But you can imagine this would be truly uncomfortable to see happen to his daughter. I had been also sure that I had told Joe to do this, I had forgotten to also tell him the G rated version. I could already see that Kitty would be drinking lightly from one arm. Though the position she now moved to show the true location. As her own vital fluid slightly ran down the inside of her upper arm. To anyone that hadn't known this, you might figure it would be just the arm, not so close to the armpit.

Joe went on and I was happy I heard this part, "This has no risk to her virtue, as to what we are we never release these panoramas. All that is damned have the cause to be equals, so no true being can take what is given to them." I had to hope he understood this, though I have to say it did imply to translate well. "Now as her parentage, it could be a virtue feeling given, as she also is allowed to assist her."

Kitty now did just a slight slice in each upper arm, but only after Rose had fed from one wound did she create another. Now she also hit all the location just like Kitty had done to her. Her reaction was virtually as fast as she stopped with the drinking of the last wound. I have to give credit for Kitty moving genuinely fast and Rose relatively knowing by some instinct. I had to lean close as I told them, "Right now she feels as if every hair on her body has been ripped out of her body. Her muscles would be twisting up so tightly that you may even have a problem getting through to her. As you can see Kitty has been struggling to hold onto her, but she has to as the time is essentially here."

Wise Owl now asked, "Do all of you go through this part?"

I nodded my head as I replied, "Most see our kind are so truly exotic in a sexual nature, I do think if they saw this they would change their minds. In truth, she is lucky as most of our kind don't have her choice. Though in truth this is to save her as much as it is to also kill her. I would also tell you her crying will be soon over, as to the next act to come. We never think of this as anything but what it is, the tragedy of a new life to our existence."

By this time she had changed enough to tell she was dying, though this effect still allowed her Native American color to come out in the end. Joe spoke the last few lines, "Now Kitty will you allow Rose to know you as her first mother into this life?"

With that, she lifted her mister sharpie up to her neck, with a slight smile she allowed it to travel into her neck. Even the elders had to gasp at the blood that came forth, which she now placed Rose's face. She had no reason to help her, and she again knew what to do as she lapped it up into her mouth. "Now the violence of this existence take her into this life, as this her point of ending." Kitty drew back with her fangs fully extended, her teeth grabbed hold as the flesh came away. The Blood flowed so freely that even I knew she would be dead in a moment. Kitty took it all in, no one had ever seen this side of her before to be truthful.

I jumped in front of the Chief because even I knew what he thought, as I said, "It is better this way, now we wait."

Naomi stepped in as she told him, "We can see if it would be working in about ten to twenty minutes."

Tony then added, "We can't promise you anything, but there are clear signs that it appears to be working."

I then allowed him to now see Kitty, as she was on the floor with Rose cradling her like her own child. As I also added, "No one can get close to her till this has come to pass, or she has crossed over to the other side."

Tony came in with, "As the light has gone out of her, allow this spirit to enter her, be the child she is meant to be. We see this as a good application, though it is as random as your will our Lord."

Naomi then added, "This journey has been led into, open those inner eyes and allow her to see. Walk the trail of our existence with us, as we are so we can be again."

I then said, "As we are, so we shall be. Take this into our lives, stand with us as the brave children we are. Fighting the good fight till these days are ended, though our struggle may be as hard as the wind blows." I lifted my head as we had never done this in front of the kids. Then I spoke the loudest with my voice, "Father we stand here to make you the proudest, we walk this to honor you. Though all our deaths are as random as the running waters!"

Joe then said something in the ancient tongue, which I do believe I could relatively understand. Then all the Elder spoke a single word loudly, "SEE-LOME!" It would be easy to understand that all repeated as they now understood, finishing with our three newcomers. Not that they had to say anything.

Chapter Twenty Five

A transition of a new Unlife.

After we were sure things were ready, I called Sammy to me. I explained to the three that we were moving Kitty to a more comfortable spot. We then picked both her and Rose up, I told Liz to help out with our guests. Mary and Cibilia now helped so we kept Kitty level. Tony instructed Pepper to keep a close eye on Rose. Naomi now told Bert to also help Liz out, and that she would be out to run a circuit for a moment or two. I also told them that they could follow us till we got Kitty in her room. I also had to tell Liz to make sure Wise Owl got to the truck safely.

The kids were absolutely doing great, to be honest, it was all for their protection.

Even as I was sure that they would give us a heck

of a fight, and I was sure I was the only one to match the good chief.

With this as things were now set, I had to ask Kitty if she wanted the door closed? She said yes.

With this I had invited Cheryl to come with us, then we came out to everyone else standing there. I had to stop Naomi for just a moment, as I had to show him why I had done this. I placed one arm around Liz as I also place one on Cheryl's shoulders.

Then I spoke, "Chief I never asked you what nation you belong to, but we honor our Native brethren. Like I said all of us are equals here. I ask Cheryl out because my daughter told me she was of the Choctaw Nation." I then pointed toward Bert as I confessed, "Bert here is of a nation, though I can't tell you which, I never asked."

He then spoke to the fact, "My Grandpa is of the Kiowa Nation, my Grandma is of the Osage. They met at the Great Powwow and as Grams said, the old magic happened."

Naomi then added, "I know I look mostly black, and my mother comes from Jamaica. Even I have some Indian as I have Muskhogen also with a Creole side. Though I do believe my Nation is only seen in Louisiana, sorry I can't genuinely say exactly where or why."

I then spoke to the obvious as I was sure he wanted to know exactly all that I could swear to as was known by me. "Now for your daughter, like I said we legitimately won't know truly for about three hours. You see it has to do with a lot of things that would confuse everyone except for the best of scientists. Though it is easy to say that every system is different, so it is truly up to Rose as to how long she takes. We can tell you we generally give her more than three hours if she doesn't wake up anywhere before this period. Now there also has to be things done, we all try to help in this."

Liz then chimed in with, "Our bodies go through this terrible change, and to place this among other things. When I had been around as a human those that have died this closely mirrors it. Now, true death you never come back from, but because it is so drastic and for the lack of a better word we call it the first death. This is also why when we're destroyed we tend to call it being destroyed and not killing. Once she does take that final step we use my first analogy as the true death. It isn't a given to that time or place, and there has never been given a promise to us, but there is a chance we can live an extremely long time."

Naomi came in with, "There are rumors of those that have lived up to two millennia, though I would never tell you this will happen to your daughter now. There is also a rumor that there is an original vampire, no one has truly met him or her. There has been also a second and third generation, again it has been an extreme rarity that anyone has seen or talked to anyone like that."

I had to jump in to say, "I'm sure you don't want the history lessons your daughter will now receive. I can say that over time a lot of Christian zealots have called these two Cain and Lilith. Though when I looked up the later I had to go to the Torah to precisely find the two names together. In reality, it had to be a warning story to the young, and even though they did marry, nothing truly about them becoming vampires. So even as this has been done I feel it may have been done to them as things have been to us by the church. I'll leave it right there, this was just to show you what kind of a family Rose has now joined."

With this Naomi started to bark orders to Bert, I decided to explain this part also. "Now this has nothing with you, as I just wanted Bert and Naomi to go out and make sure the area is clear of Shovelhead's."

He nodded his head as he also looked at his daughter, with that I think she also realized what he meant. She then asked as her warriors joined her, "Can we join you just for our own security, not that we don't trust you guys at all."

Naomi turned toward me to which I spoke, "I asked for this Hun, but in truth, this is all your show. I'm just to back up her just in case she gets into trouble."

I also had no problem with this at all, but I did have to trust the others with things. So she turned to her as she replied, "They usually say the more the merrier, I'm not sure that applies to a scouting recon mission. I'm also sure there is most likely no one watching us, so I can't see the problem in it. We do have a strong reaction group, so if we're forced to call them, you'll have to move to avoid them."

Sleek Puma then replied, "I have no problem with that, as I'm also sure there is no one out there as well."

With this all five of them ran off, it was extremely easy to see the three wolves, one Puma, and profoundly large half human half wolf. If you remember Bert wasn't that good at the change yet, heck some never master it. I had to feel that he had an exceedingly good teacher, I'm also sure his awfully young libido had to be up then. What I mean is the chief's daughter was decidedly good-looking, her girls were extraordinary close seconds. Naomi could also easily be a runway model, which he now got to observe as they stripped before running off to their mission. In truth, I had to hope no one was about to see this, not that it wasn't a fine sight. Just not absolutely sure it alluded to acceptable attire.

Liz had to whisper after they had left, "Do they have to get naked every time they change?"

I had to whisper back, "No, they could hurt themselves in the transformation as it tears their clothes with the excessive metamorphosis."

"John!" She said with considerable disdain in her voice, as she also added, "You don't have to make fun of me!"

I put my hand up as I shrugged my shoulders, "What? You asked a simple question, and I gave a simple answer. If you don't like my answer you could have asked Chief Bear Killer, as one of those ladies is his child."

He looked at us strangely as Liz told him what was said, "I asked if there was a way for them to change without getting so naked in plain sight like they had just done. John told me they could, though the destruction of their clothes could hurt them."

He replied, "Yeah, though her mother has also asked me the same question. On the other hand, any boy that has tried to take advantage of their condition has had a surprise. She was the one that petitioned me for those three to run together. We had gone back and forth because we never thought they wouldn't be strong enough. That group has always proven us wrong if he should do anything I'm sure he would be fairly embarrassed. Let's just say I also think that is why they did that, so no woman would have to strip in front of the boys."

Liz had to smile as she had to say, "Like a rude awakening after a bad dream, that is terribly good. I can see it right now."

Okay both of us looked at Liz, as we had to wonder what she meant. Though because Cibilia had not left yet, I could hear her giggling. So I had to think it was one of those girl things we men just didn't understand. Now it was Pepper's time to show up rapidly, as she now spoke to the chief. "Tony told me that John will be needed in the house and that when she would be close to the change I will come out to relay stuff to Liz. Liz has to stay because she can resist the smell of a human better than the other young kids. He also told me that you will not be able to bring in Wise Owl until we can surely be sure about Rose."

I put my hand up as I knew all this, but more because I was also about ready to relate all this as well. "Tony individuality being his efficient self, I was about ready to tell you all that. I want to also add like I said before, you can visit your child one last time this night. Then if you have reason to visit her, which I'm sure you will with your wife. Allow Liz to give you our cell phone number, with also Pepper's. It isn't that the first isn't right, but it is new to us, so it may be easier to get hold of Pepper."

I was about ready to walk off when I heard Liz add

relatively, "Tell your wife that we're all sisters here and that Naomi and Kitty are like our mothers. John is more like a father figure to us also, and to be truthful you witnessed tonight why we tend to call him Demon Lord."

I knew what had to be coming next as he replied, "I have never heard so much anger in a voice, I do believe I understand young lady."

I had to place out my hand as I had to say, "I would never use my ability on an ally."

He took my arm as he said back to me, "Just a, I would never do the same, once we are enemies we can do whatever. I would pray to the Great Spirit that never happens."

I had to reply as we ended the handshake, "I would do the exact same thing, but as I have always said to the chaos of our existence. Stranger things have happen."

"That is a true sentiment, I agree with it also."

Then we released and I was on my way to the house behind Pepper. As we moved I had to ask, "Has anything happened with Rose?"

She replied, "Yeah. Tony told me to make sure you got into the house, then relay it to Liz. Oh, shoot! I was supposed to tell her to meet me halfway. Oh well, I guess I'll have to go out there one more time. I guess I should tell you too, that wound was huge, but he had me measure it. What he believes is it is half its size, and to him, that is a good sign."

I had to tell her, "That is a noticeably good sign,

just go and tell Liz. OH! Remember to hold your breath, then bring Liz away so you can talk. Tell her about meeting you halfway, and if you feel anything come running into the house."

Now we were at the back door by now, so she had to turn and trot off to confer with Liz. I came through the door and had been met by Tony, as I also had to say, "Sorry, that chief can be a remarkably interesting guy."

He then ascertained, "I saw those wolves run off with Naomi, what's that about anyway? Is there anyone out there that we have to be worried about and deliver reinforcements?"

That was a simple and honest question, "Well I had to have Naomi make the decision whether they could go with her. I saw no harm in it as their leader stayed behind, and in truth, they're just seeing what is around us. I do believe with all the newbies, and especially adding a new one. We have to be extra careful, then you have the essence that I truly wanted to refuse this call. They are our allies in this, and I truly couldn't see a way to refuse what he had asked. In another way, I can see how this could cement our friendship."

He added before I could say another word, "It also places us in the wake of destruction in two ways if she is destroyed."

I nodded my head as I replied, though I was moderately confused because of the remark two. "We can't be sure of that, as I know they'll be set even harder if she should die at the hands of the Shovelhead's. Though to be truthful I can't see any other problem here."

"That is because when you look at things all you see are the Shovelhead's, and my remark wasn't toward them. Where I see the problem is Giaus, as he won't be happy about this at all. So you can imagine when he hears about it he may want her in so many ways. I mean I agreed that the wolves would be great allies, but as you know the elders and wolves have been at war for years. Can you think of anything that he wouldn't love more than to have one of their kind at his disposal? This means we'll have to stand against him, which also means our goods would come to an end."

He had to shake his head as he went on, "I will have to agree that I also saw this as a great benefit for us. Later as I thought about the consequences of this he came to mind. This could have caused any of us to do the same thing, so I'm not saying that you could have avoided this. Though I would have never thought of them as allies, after the fact I can see why things would turn this way. In truth, if I hadn't thought of this either I'm sure if not you, then someone would have advised you of this."

Pepper then came in the door as he finished, he told her to stand right outside Kitty's door. I waited till she had left, then I went on, "I can see what you mean. We have to keep her hidden somehow from him, yet she needs to be approachable for her parents."

He interjected, "Even her mother?"

I had to admit, "I would say no, but he did this all for her, as most of his kind would prefer her to be dead. With that kind of love, I fear we have to be ready for her to visit her, which will present a problem to us all. Right now I just suspect it, with a high expectation of it being a reality. Then you have the reality what will he do if she digs in her teeth. As you can easily ascertain this would be profoundly bad, which also means all of the elders would have to be there to help out Kitty."

He shook his head as he had to admit, "We without a doubt didn't think this through, which there is also another variable with Kitty. What I mean is what if we have to lay into Rose, and she thinks we're too harsh. Do any of you truly know what her reaction will be?"

"Do you have the kids training?" I asked him. Then after he nodded his head I then added, "We need to go up to Kitty's room any way you look at it, though as she is all we have to do is to assure Rose should make it." Then I had an idea, so I had to say, "Tony meet me across from her room. Go talk to Mary, Sammy, and Cibilia, I want Mary and Sammy at the back door. Cibilia will be on the landing one floor down with Bert when he gets back. Naomi and I will escort her to her sister and Dad, to which we can't be sure nothing will happen. The two at the back door will stay, as we move Cibilia and Bert will be our backups, just in case. We have to discuss this with the good chief, but maybe we can clue him in enough so he can help us."

He agreed with me as I moved, I had not given him instructions for what Mary and Sammy had to inform Naomi and Bert. I'm eminently happy when he came back he had thought of it and had told me exactly what I would have said.

Then I had to look at Pepper as I had to ask her, "Pepper her clothes were truly torn up, can you get a washcloth and something for her to wear?"

After she left Tony had to ask, "John I just thought

of this, as we're having to deal with Shovelhead's and an ancient. What are you thinking of telling all the kids the legends real soon, I do believe they need to be told. I would have placed them myself, but I never had the teaching on that as much as I would have preferred before saying a word."

I had to shake my head as I knew I literally had to do this, though I was surprisingly unwilling to also do or explain all this dribble. I had to say, "I know they need to know, but I can't absolutely see it helping them fight at all. You were the first to point out that my species are far more into combat than any other race. Where can we go where they keep their humanity and don't take that step over to the religious zealot side?"

Tony then added, "Excuse me if I'm ignorant, but on a technical side aren't the Shovelhead's the extreme side of zealous behavior?"

Of course, he was right, so I had to relent as it was the only way. So shaking my head I affirmed, "Yeah. I guess that does give us no choice. Get together after we talk to Kitty, with Joe, see if he can help with the stuff we need. Naomi, Kitty, you, and I can present it to them, hopefully, we can spin it well enough that we don't have converts."

With this Pepper came up with a dress, something I had to figure had been underclothes. Behind her came Paul with a water basin and pitcher, and about four towels, though I can't be sure on the latter. Pepper lifted up the dress as she said, "With the flower print she already has on, I have to figure she's kind of like me and loves flowers. In truth, she is the first one I have had a problem figuring out her size. I do believe it is somewhere in between Cibilia and Kitty, so I think I'm extremely close."

I had to smile at her as Tony said, "You do remarkably well Pepper, Paul go in place your things, then leave. Got me?! Now, do you have any of the other ladies coming up to help you, Pepper?"

He never said why he stated that to Paul, but I'm sure Pepper did the best job she could do also. "Yeah. Cheryl will be coming up right after she can get a certain move Tony showed her right. You know that everyone else is on duty, I mean even I'm technically on duty."

Tony was right on it, "I'll get Cheryl, this is fairly more important than the move I showed her. She can train after the two are done with Rose, but you can get a start."

With this everything was set, and one thing was for sure the thought was a good one. I was able to get close to Kitty even with her growls, I knew if she bit me I could take it. The wound on her neck is what I wanted to see, I knew exactly how big Kitty's mouth was, which isn't that large. So I had to figure it two or three inches in diameter, not the half inch I had been seeing. I moved back to Tony as he was virtually right next to me, though timider with her growls. I then told him, "It has gone to about half an inch."

He replied, "That is decidedly good news. Pepper go out and tell Liz we think she'll make the full turn. We're still not out of the woods because anything can happen. We can essentially say she has survived, though to them she will be dead. They'll be able to tell her mother she yet still lives."

I then added, "Them, not her mother. I'm sure he'll

know what Tony means, but it is better to be completely clear."

"John I did use the word tell, as in tell her, not that she can go out to see her mother."

"I'm sorry Tony. I think our conversation has gotten to me, though you're absolutely right. Go, Pepper."

With that, she ran off, but I have to say it may have been too early. As once she was away Rose moaned, I now came close again. Then I had to ask her, "Kitty is she honestly close to the full change?"

I think she was about ready to answer as a new voice did its best to clear her throat. I looked over at Tony as I said, "Get some of our move juice right now!"

I can tell you I was really happy he had also found his speed, as he virtually disappeared. Her eyes now fluttered open as I placed my hand out to silence her. As I added, "Not yet. I sent Tony after something that will clear the cobwebs, just be quiet until he gets back."

With this, he just appeared into the room, and as he handed me the cup I saw Naomi enter the room as he confirmed it. "Naomi came in as I got the cup, so I told her to run behind me."

Now I had to speak, "Good, Naomi help out Kitty." Then I leaned down to give Kitty the cup, as I smiled at her so she had an idea about what she was now. "I'm the senior elder in the house, your mother is my second. We're exceedingly happy for you to enter our family, vampire family, not human. All thoughts of your human family have to be placed in the back of your mind.

You're far too young to see them until about a century from now. If you ever have the temptation remember this, though it may not happen. Think what it would do to you if you drank all the human members dry. We do this to serve your own conscience."

Naomi then came in with, "How do you feel deary?"

She barely whispered, "My throat is so dr . . ."

Tony then said, "Drink so the liquid has the time to do its work, though Naomi who is the third elder. I'm the fourth elder of our little family, you can come to any of us if you have questions. Oh, they call me Tony."

She then placed her hand upon her teeth, so Naomi added to this. "Yes, you have canines now, though not all species have this same effect. I will explain once you're ready to meet the others, as Kitty has to present you to our house. This certainly is your first meeting is conducted by the elders though, as there are certain things you must know. We do not live off the blood of humans, and now we can absolutely truly drink other than from the vein. I will add one of John's favorite comments, we try as hard as we can to nearly be human-like, after all, we are civilized."

I had to chuckle at that as Kitty now said, "Me be ya dead mommy now, me be first in front of all dees. We be da team of helpers, you never be alone as with you be guys and gals. Me knows dat ya hab lots of dealings, though you knowy not, I do so just ask. They say that we can be what we aren't, so even as our minds are as they are in truth." I couldn't believe how her language cleared up, "You're my sweet child and as all within this house, we will defend you with our lives." She smiled at me as she finally ended, "Demon Lord be the greatest fighters of allie, not jue worry eber. Allist be yus parentage."

I had to figure she said it best, though we may have to explain it to Rose later. I had to smile at her as now I told her the best part. "We have a certain repulse to your Dad's kind, so I have to tell you this also. Once we're sure you have had enough of that blood, we're going to take you out to your dad and sister."

She seemed to just look at me, then she said in the sweetest voice. "I'm not honestly sure how I feel about that, I mean my sister is fine, my dad on the other hand."

I had to smile as I understood that, and I had to confirm this as well. "I did understand you had a fight with him, but this is also sort of a goodbye to them. You know the traditions of your own tribe, you can give your old man the benefit of the double in all this."

Naomi came in with, "You have to understand why John had been also implying it that way, as he could just command you to do this. He wants all of us to be equals, though to be truthful no one can equal him. Only he equals your mother, your mother is one of two that equals me. Tony even as young as he only has John, your mother, and me as equals. So know how important it is to him that you do the right thing because he even mentioned it to you."

With this, we all stood there as we waited for her, and her final nod conveyed the impression to thaw the cold within us. Now we all rushed around to make sure she was ready for this, with Tony telling her how to avoid the smell. Well if it was too much for her, I have to say that Pepper had done particularly well on the dress she had picked for her. Now came the time to introduce the new improved Rose to her Father.

Chapter Twenty-Six

This torrent of pain we create.

Sitting alone in the dark corner. Knees against my chest, head in my hands. Watching the tears run from eye to floor. Happiness left my soul, now so dark and cold. Life in my eye is no longer shown.

If only I could escape these chains and cuffs and once again run from my thoughts. I'm a prisoner of life. Contaminated by this strife. With Death hanging by my side black tears were all I cried.

Anger was built up in my blood, all the revenge has been creating a flood. These chains will one day break. You are all I will seek. Like a snake, I will slither. Once you sleep I will smother.

Look at me now, try to read my heart, all my love and joy is forever departed. You shouldn't have locked me away. To think I was once your little girl.

This is what you made me, sick and angry. I'm a prisoner of life. Contaminated by this strife. With death hanging by my side black tears were all I cried. Anger was built in my blood, this is what you made me.

You're fast asleep in your bed. Your words echoing in my head. This can be my soul is unleashed. In my pocket, I reached, grabbed the knife you once tried, but unlike you. I will not fail.

A sharp pain opened your eyes. You have a look of surprise. Look at me now daddy. Aren't you happy? During your last breath, I grabbed the key. I'm all alone, yet still free, as you don't see me.

Now ask why I told all this?

This is how things could be as even she was the same as the splendid Gazelle. In this evisceration of my view, I did make clear to my love that this didn't include her, as she absolutely had my heart. With this pain that could scorn even the most stoic, as if the gates of exasperation had been opened to her. Without the full perception of the reality of her existence before this. Even as the ascertained truth of our phenomenon had yet to come to bare. This particular night she would get a lesson with this earnest value. You may also ask why I do this exhortation in my former manor?

With mad disquietude on the dull sky, the pall of a past world; and then again with curses cast them down upon the dust, and gnashed their teeth and howled: the wild birds shrieked yet, terrified, did flutter on the ground, where flap their useless wings; the wildest brutes came tame and tremulous; and vipers crawled plus twined themselves among the multitude, hissing, but stinglessly - they were slain for food.

Now if you understand this excerpt from Lord Byron's poem the Darkness, you can perceive why I started this way. Then add to that the poem I have given you from another great author. You can now see the consummate authority to which will have to be advertised to the formation of this decidedly horrendous complication. To my own exhortation, I had aspiration this would be the only instance. You can also divine that was misguided.

Now as we walked out things implied that all was copacetic, even as our own selves perceived things were amiss. I had to make sure that Cibilia and Bert were far enough away, though close enough to react. It was easy to see that Sleek Puma's ladies were secure in the rear of the truck. Wise Owl, doing his best as he secured the cab, so the only ones that were ready to receive Rose were her father and sister. Liz was particularly close as we now got closer, and it was right now she caught something.

Liz's total fleetness did serve her and us well, with a blinding speed she now moved to stop Rose. I had never even thought that Kitty had given her a thing, even as it was their way. Now even as fast as she was, there is still the fact of resolve can be even more nibble. As even all of us could ascertain how deeply the pair of scissor dug into Liz's chest. I had Rose by the neck as her feet now dangled in the air, and Tony was right there as if he had a premonition. Cibilia and Bert placed themselves in between the Chief and us as he was sure to react.

With all this action I felt a tug on my arm as I had to look down at her. Kitty looked up at me with a smile, then she turned her head to look at Liz. Without a word, I knew what I had to do, so I gave her to her mother as I now joined Tony. Liz had always been so pale, never had I ever seen how deathly pale she was right then. I now saw Pepper right there so I had to yell, "GET LIZ SOME BLOOD RIGHT NOW!"

I now turned to the chief as I had to say, "I never knew her intent to stab you, I can assure you she will be punished in the vampire way. I'm also sorry that my only thought was to save my beloved by ripping off your daughters head. You can be assured that Kitty saved your child in all this, though now we must attend to my wonderfully same beloved. Know that no one could have saved you save my beloved, and to this, she may have lost her existence this eminently profound night. Though only time will tell us."

Sleek Puma came forward as she had to ask then tell us something. Well though whom she asked was her father, "Daddy I never knew she hated you so much, may I do the expulsion from our tribe?"

I think he was as dumbfounded as all he could do was nod his head. So she turned as in her intent of disdain she now spits out, "You have done the worst that anyone could have, you have attacked the leader of the spirit warriors. You know the rules that this would also call for the walk from our tribe. Even as this can be done and if you survived it, I can never look upon you ever again. To this you have repulsed your entire family, I can never say how mom will react. I do what is of our tribe and turn my back on the dead."

I could hear her starting to cry, as now Sleek Puma with her warriors turned their backs on her. With that, I also saw Wise Owl look down as it would be decidedly difficult to turn his back. Now I had to look at the devastated father, as even his hardness had been spent. Then I saw that slight glisten roll down his cheek, as he now did the same as all the others.

Kitty had her daughter by her throat as she now laid curses on her fathers back. I then moved to Tony and instructed him, Cheryl, Pepper, with Paul to do their best. Then I sent Bert and Cibilia into also guard Rose, and that Kitty knew where all of them had to go. Finally, as I was sure she was out of sight, I had to tell the chief the truth of the situation. But not so much as to comfort him, it was more like to get a word from him on this disposition.

I now said, "I had no idea she would ever do such a thing Chief Bear Killer, though she is now in the house."

He turned with his reply, "I hope her punishment won't be to serve, even as she hates me, I still love her."

I had to confirm those basics as I was also worried about Liz. "She attacked an ally, that this would be paramount to attacking a family member. The punishment isn't final death, but it can be as severe as to the point of deprivation. I'm sure she had no idea that as she is she'll now be tried as the vampire she has become. I have no idea why this evilness has prevailed, in truth we are what we were before we became this. I will also admit that this life can change you, though her young age I doubt she has had the time to become jaded."

He then asked, "When you said beloved, did you mean roughly as a wife would be?"

I had to admit as I knew he had an understanding of this, "I do love her, and she, me I hope. Though this existence has caused her not to want to admit her feelings. I could tell you why, but I fear that would be far too much information, and I do believe just the admittance of this is enough."

He nodded his head as he now said, "I know you stayed out here to make sure I was calm with this. We all knew this had to happen in the end, it has been only my brides feeling that led me. I will have to say that what Sleek Puma has said has created a dilemma for me. What I mean as all her sisters are far too young to make the switch yet, and her mother being mostly human. I'm at a loss."

I had to add one more that could possibly help, "We use what is called complete restraint, that is where she has to be pinned so she can't move. With the help of both Naomi and I, we can assure you she would never place the bite on your wife. Then as it does give the impression that my beloved can resist human smell, she can be there to greet your wife in this endeavor. Does this give you any coalition of thought."

"That would help I do believe, now I know you will want to get to your future wife as well. I will have my beloved get hold of your Pepper, so your beloved can speak with mine."

I now placed out my hand as to our agreement, then he took it in the old way. I do have to say I'm so glad his way was the same, as he now added, "Till this scourge is exterminated that has caused this night."

I said back, "And to a friendship, I hope will last longer than any other that has been set."

With this, he and his other daughter trotted to the truck, and I waited till I was sure they were on their way. Now know I didn't do this for the house, but because of the type of vampire Kitty was, and how easily it would be for her to escape. Now as I didn't see some little figure following them I had to turn. To be honest, I had no knowledge of what was said to her, but it is particularly easy to ascertain what may have been told to Rose.

My first priority was to see how Liz was doing, and with my speed, I was in our room that fast. I could now see that Pepper and Cheryl were doing most of the work. I already knew this would be the case, as those pair of scissors had dug deeply. I looked at Tony as he and Paul were handing way too much blood to the two girls.

I had to ask him, "How is she, Tony?"

He replied, "She took a gasp a moment or two ago, as we all know if she can control her body that is an exceedingly good sign. John, I have to also ask you as you know her target was truly her father?"

I had to state the truth, "Yes, my anger has been quelled. I would do what I will, but what may be worse is she attempted to attack an ally. Even you have to know the punishment for that, so in light of this I can't go easy on her my friend."

Then came the gasping voice of Liz, "John?! Please don't! I know you love me, but we also have to be an example."

She was right, and she has just tied my hands. I had to reply, "I will my love. I can quell my anger if it means that much to you."

"It does . . ." as she now clasped onto our bed.

I looked at Tony as he spoke, "She did far too much, but I'm sure she'll survive, just give Pepper and Cheryl the time they need. Now go meet with Joe and Kitty, I know she is as worried as all get out about her new child."

I nodded my head as left, though in my long steady trek to the room where we passed judgment, I had to think. I will also tell you that my footsteps had to be telling, as within the room the worry did mount as I approached. I had to think back when we had tried Paul, and now how unjust it truly set. I wish I had thought of this so long ago, then as I came close the tragedy that had occurred at my genuine own hand came to me full force. What I mean is her cold dead eyes always have this way of going through me. It had been like being judged for all I have done, though she has been dead so many years.

I had suspected for many years these thoughts had been finally getting to me. As I know had to whisper, "I know my love, I meant none of it. If I had known what I do today, would that disaster have happened? This can never happen again, I have promised you that I would protect those that can't."

Then came that whisper that always seemed to follow, 'But can you truly say you have done all you can?'

With this, I always had to shake my head no as I replied, "No my love."

Naomi then came out of the room as she had ascertained incorrectly, "John she'll be okay, we now have work to do here."

I smiled at her as I had to say, "Yes we do, though I do believe Liz wants to be here as well." I had to look in the room as I had to ask, "Sammy go ask Tony what I forgot if he thinks Liz wants to be here as well."

He was out of the room that fast, but Mary had to ask, "John are you okay?"

I had to reply to her truthfully, "No. If I had my way I would give her the final death one inch at a time. We have a lot more to think about here, so I have to rain in my distaste for all of this." I now turned to Rose and had to say, "You have to know you're getting off lightly, as you have no idea what I could do to you. Kitty is a friend of mine so I may allow you to live, but I can assure you it would never be a good death." I then saw all that had been in the room, which brought a smile to my face. As I had to inform her, "All the terrible things I'm sure my daughters have related, think of this, I have never shown them my worse side. Now ponder this even as I'm sure Kitty can even tell you worse."

With this Sammy came back in a flash, he then spoke to the lack of volume in the room. "Why all the doom and gloom, Liz is honestly looking better. Oh, Tony told me it may take like thirty minutes, though he also added, though the time may not be accurate."

Mary then answered, "John just told how bad Rose's torture would be if we didn't have more to think upon in our general situation. You could say that once all our mental juices got to flowing, he even scared the piss out of us."

I had to smile at her as Sammy had to ask, "What did he say?"

I then spoke, "I said . . ."

Cibilia then cut me off with, "It doesn't matter, let's just say we never want to get on his bad side."

But I had to put my hand up as I also told them a truth, "You'll never suffer this, as I see you as my daughter, and Mary is my daughter. Sammy, you're her son so that could also exempt you because I can never try or be part of these decisions. Just like Kitty cannot be part of this decision, and to her own credit, she has stayed to see what happens." Even as I knew this wasn't her way of thinking, so I had to turn to Rose and say to her. "Consider yourself lucky as I'm sure your life won't be ended this particular day."

Cibilia had to ask, "John how do you know . . ." Then she looked at what me and now Sammy were looking at, then she had to say, "Oh, I had never thought of that."

Mary and Naomi came in with, "What the . . ." As they also did as Cibilia to now see Kitty petting Rose like a doll. Naomi then had to ask, "Does this have that much importance?"

Cibilia had to ask, "Do you think we could destroy all the Shovelhead's without their help?"

She just spoke the obvious words as I added, "But we can't treat her any different than any other true vampire."

Naomi came in with, "I agree John, Joe do you know what that means?"

He nodded his head as now Cheryl and Paul showed up, and she said, "John, Tony said all Liz needs now is blood, so he sent us on our way."

I had to smile at them as this was good news, but I had to speak to a fact. "Paul even as this still isn't my final decision, I think I'm understanding better why you did what you had done to Cheryl. It is unforgivable to do what you had done, as I now know her better it would have been a miss if you hadn't done it. So in this, I can never cast a judgment of reprieve, but also know I can never cast a judgment of guilt. So now you know if you are ever found guilty it can never came from me."

Paul then had to say, "John I have been having so much, ah, I guess you would call it precisely is easy for us. Will it be so easy for Liz till she heals?"

I had not thought of that as I had to look to Cibilia, and she spoke. "On it John. We can move that recliner in here for her, then she'll be here but in a healing position."

"Good idea Hun." I looked at Sammy as I had to ask, "Will you help me in this?"

To which he replied, "You have far too much to worry about, allow Bert and me to do this man. Bert, you ready?"

With his nod they trotted out of the room, I knew there were three in the front room. They came back with the best out there, I had to be happy they did this for her. Once they had it set Pepper came into the room, and she practically sat there.

Cibilia's fast, "Sissy if you don't want to face the wrath of John I would move."

I guess I was amazed at the level I had placed with my kids, even as I had to suspect this wasn't a good thing. I would have to correct this eventually, for the time being, it had been doing an effect that I do think needed to be applied. With this thought, I had to move closer to Mary, as I wasn't sure she would understand, but she would be the only one I could think of right then. In truth, this would be something I would have bounced off Liz, for right now her health mattered far more. I had no idea she would draw in Sammy as well, as she had to ask the first question.

She asked, "John what do you need?"

I had to say what I thought in the plainest of examples applied to a whisper, "I truly don't want this kind of fear, but I could also see that this had an effect on Rose. Right now we need that, but I have to ask if this may be taking it way too far?"

Sammy chimed in with, "I know the rule of law is important, in a sense though you passed it onto Cibilia. Shouldn't you place it right back into her hands?"

Mary and I had to shake my head, as I had to turn toward Pepper as I laughed. "You know I could hurt you undoubtedly terribly, but I take it you also know I will never use my strength that way. Cibilia you should have explained it to her so she knew, as she wasn't here when we decided. You see Pepper we all decided this was best for Liz, so that was set up for her." I had to turn toward Rose, "Cibilia is correct that I can be your worst nightmare, though her authority far outweighs mine. Even in all this because of my feelings for my beloved, I will have to allow this punishment to be transferred to another in the house. You see you're far too new to receive one punch from me, as I could cave in all your organs."

With a small amount of added effect, I now bowed toward Kitty as I had to allow her to know some truth. "As we all are. You, my dear Kitty, Naomi even as young as she is, and I can't be seen taking sides in any of this. As you understand my dear, the formal is that we're civilized, there are many things we have to pretend to not be concerned with these formal affairs. Though in many ways you could say we're just playing our parts in this scene of outward logic. So know," I had to give the effect of a real elder as my gaze caught Rose, "You have the welcome reprieve of the houses authority, and disaster won't be coming to your door."

Cibilia was right next to me as she asked, "What the heck is that all supposed to mean?"

Tony came into the room carrying Liz as she spoke, "It means that I asked John to be kind to Rose, and he had to search for a way he could honor my request. Cibilia as you know what he can do, think of it as a way for cooler heads to prevail here. Then if you also think about it as Joe is the judge, he has literally laid this in his hands."

I think no one had thought of that, and I will admit not even me. My intent was absolute to place it in her hands, but what Liz had to say was far better. So I had to add as a sign toward this, "What? Oh, yes. Did you think this was an attempt to place this on your hands, no it was just a way to place it in the houses authority? Though that does mean you in the end, but primarily into the hands of the houses judge."

I had never played this many tricks on any of my kids before, the one light is I could also see Liz realized this too. I came next to the chair where she was sitting, as I had to whisper to her, "Thanks for the save, I owe you."

She replied in a whisper, "No you don't, who you owe is Cibilia. She needs to know why you said all those things because she has to learn as the house princess."

What may be true the phenomenon that Liz started to understand these things far too well? That didn't concern me as much though as the pain she openly showed as Joe started the show. I can't tell you more, though as you may also understand this was one of existence or true death.

Chapter Twenty-Seven

The truth is that the passion can be nothing.

When most think of what we are, they contemplate the horrors that we truly can even exist. Then of course as we have become the avenues of such love as of late. You have those that speculate that our beauty is what can easily be had by anyone. Wear most lose the factual aspect is toward the obvious observation to our truest state. To this fact it is wonderfully easy to recognize that this facet can be definitely given due consideration. Though in the circumstantial evidence, this site can be recognized to this basic truth. That which has already been experienced all this death, can't be hurt as they should be after their renewal.

This is where the truth now brings us to the facts of the wrong done to the entire house. Most even in this existence see things as they were, not as they are with all this recreation. Yes, as I have spoken many a time, we must be alive, therefore how couldn't we in this continuation. In that facsimile of what we were, I can't find blame, as we have all been there at one time or another. When you have been on earth as long as I have been, you can see how my vision could have changed so much because of those horrors and terrors that can be perceived.

I guess this may have been better acquainted it I had just done all this myself. With the foreknowledge that doing for them would accomplish nothing. You also have to realize we had been told about this for many years. To be truthful even his word talks about this fact, as once they get old enough we're to release them into the world. Though I can also tell you none of these were truly ready for the real world of the bogeymen of reality.

Now, this couldn't be accomplished with Kitty at her station, so I lifted her up to sit next to me. You could have done anything with the power of our house, as with her came Liz and Andy. Even as things were getting ready to start, I had to voice to Andy to keep Kitty's other hand. You also have to realize that what we create does become nearly our real children. Mary with Bert now set to either side of Rose, this gave Cibilia the ability to sit right behind us. With Joseph running the proceedings, there was a decidedly narrow space of distance. Not that I hadn't understood we needed more spaciousness, though I dare not move her farther away.

I have explained what we are to all, even as to the passion that we can hold for all that is ours. Moments into this a thing would have to be the effect to change our world. Now when I say this I'm not just talking about the children, but even as we are the elders.

Joe now started things off, "It is a high crime that

has proceeded this particular day, and because she had no idea we serve it up as to being ignorance. With the also to the essence that this intent was to her real father, so we have to look aah . . . what?"

I had to ask him, "Joe is something wrong?"

His reply did confuse me for a moment, "May I be of help to you?"

Now all heads had to turn to see what he had been staring at, as all now observed the shadows become a mass, then a human being. With that, the man it had formed into now walked forward with a grace unseen before by any truly living. You could never give it the favor of a feminine stroll, even as close as it may have been toward this mannerism. Later I would ask Liz on what we saw, and she had an even harder time explaining this phantom phenomenon. In truth, I have to truly consider this was meant just for that, but learn as he presented himself to us truly for the first time.

Now he did speak perfect English, though his accent was also eminently strong. I do have to think the best of linguists would have been hard-pressed to tell where it came from in the world. You can also tell that it was the first time I saw with my own eyes a truth beyond this world. Even as many truths would have to be set this remarkable day, as my head did now turn as he walked to the front. You see there was one I saw that also seemed to recognize this being, as to her practically bulging eyes as she saw him. I had to figure the mystery had been solved to the creator of Cibilia.

Now he spoke to all of us, though I'm sure you can see a problem that could also present another dilemma.

"Thank you, young man. I can assure you I never need help. In truth to what I am as it were, doing right now lying a screen to confuse other that would infiltrate these proceedings."

Joe had to ask, "Then why . . ."

I had to place my hand up as I had to correct him, "Joe step to the side, I think this may even be far too much for me to handle."

The man to whom, I do believe we had a pale example of before this time period. You have to understand the elders had felt this from before, though no real understanding what it had been. He then spoke, "I dare say you would be, even as this truly isn't I." He said a few things in an extremely strange language, to which would be his only mistake this extraordinary night. "I implore you with my mistake, the word isn't I, but the word me. They say that this language is one of the hardest to learn, I fear that maybe the truth."

He leaned down close to Rose and whispered something, though he was so efficient with this, none could surmise what was said. He now bent low as he voiced his opinion, "This one is far beyond what you need to be concerned about right now. In all my years I have never seen such a bride, yet all have to be tested with the strife of our own. Not that I would ever give such claim to anything that vulgar. All have a purpose in the grand scheme of things I dare say, though even myself have ways to separate from situations."

He then had to chuckle, "What would you call it if you knew this scheme, and to all the endings you couldn't tell the outcome?"

He looked at me, "I told this daughter that if she ever did anything like that she would become my handmaiden. Now you also understand we live precariously through our children, so you may need to explain that better. Now I have seen all that is correct would show up here, though there are three more puppets to come to this theater. I also have to explain that not all the characters can be controlled by me, so there are those that shouldn't be here. As to what I am you also have to understand as he created us, so we have to leave you also."

He now turned to Kitty, "You know the will of your mother well, she has seen you and it has given her a great smile. With her smile as she knew where I was going, she told me, 'Youngest of all that have pleased her. Not all who started out that way have joined her, you are the mine of this age. Be what you can be, and know that his Demon Lord has been sent to you. The red earth is going to become red as the crimson tide, with our Lord shaking his head in disgust. Many must fall, but also know not all that fall can't get upright. Dust yourself off with pride of your mother, know the love she has just for you and your kind is the purest.'"

Even I knew what that meant, she just told Kitty someone didn't have long for this life. I also understood that last reference it would hurt Kitty terribly. It was easy to literally see her pale with the thought, so I took Andy's arm and placed it to comfort her. He now turned toward Naomi, "I had a time finding your lord, he had nothing to say to you, though to me that spoke volumes. You see he always talks to those that have no worth, but he said nothing about or to you. Naomi, you have to be something undoubtedly special for him to do that."

He now looked at Bert to explain, "I have never seen him do that before young man, this tells me she has to even be greater." He spread out his arms, "You have to understand this though, I have asked for and received the best of my sisters and brothers. To try to explain this I can be quite good at making long speeches, though I feel a recent comedy may have had a better quote to explain this."

Now he cleared his throat before he said the next line, as he quoted something. Though for those of you understand, I can tell you I did not when I heard this. "'It's an extraordinary thing to meet someone who you can bare your soul feeling about truths. And who will accept you for what you are? I've been waiting, what is assumed to be an absolutely long time, to get beyond what I am. And with her whom I speak, I feel like I can finally begin. So I'd like to propose a toast to my beautiful lady. No measure of time with you will be long enough. But let's start with forever.'"

Now most of you that know this quote to which I had to find again, can understand why only one lady didn't do the aw thing. Yet again that one lady that hadn't used that vernacular showed what I suspected about her beforehand. He now turned to her, Rose that is, "Understand that what they would have had to do to you would have driven you away. Not that this is of any concern of mine, it is to who found you that I had to step in this particular time. I do want to think upon this as I also do what needs to be done."

Okay, all he did was point and you could hear cracking of bone, which followed her screams. "When you are what we are, only pain speaks to us." He did it again with another bone snapped, "They would have had to literally kill themselves to do this, why? Because they truly don't enjoy hurting anyone." Again the same act came forth as a bones voice could be heard. "Where you were running toward would have gotten one of the elders killed, do you understand how much that can disrupt a house like this?"

She now as she sobbed nodded her head, to which he said as another bone cracked. "I don't think you do, but you aren't Daddy's little girl anymore. You have to become the adult you want to be, learn from those willing to teach you." He now touched her last good appendage and the snap was clearly heard. "I never do any of this lightly, things have to be done, and who better than an outsider?"

He now looked at me as he spoke, "Know if this had been me I would have left her a bloody mess. I have curved my enthusiasm for the houses sake." He turned just significantly as he told Liz, "Allow John to take care of this, his way isn't that wrong, and he knows far better how to set a bone. Though I have also talked to your mother, and she told me that you left the fold. This would normally be a bad thing, but she added to what she said. We may have one that can exceed our own existence, so never look at her as something small. Though I won't lie about how small she is, it is just we can never truly know the outcome."

Now he seemed to address everyone with this last part, "I would love to stay with my children beyond all times, somethings are better left alone. So to this, I must release all those that can't-do a thing, and I leave. Though I will also say this won't be forever. They used to call me the sleeper, but the rest of the world has to quake. For as the mightiest of all my brethren, the sleeper has awoken."

With this he appeared to turn into shadow, then that had been shadow just dissipated within the light. For the first time, I do believe I had an idea of why I had been called here. Now where the problem may lie is to all he stated, because it gave us far too much to worry about than we truly had before, and truly needed.

I had to turn to Naomi as I had to confess, "I knew this would be a far bigger adventure when I came here, though I had no idea why it was that I had been called to . . . this calamity."

I do believe Naomi has been going to answer, but Liz interrupted her. "John could you please, as he told all of us you were better at this."

I walked over as Kitty came with me, "Demon Lord takie goody care ub Rose Pestle Rock."

I smiled at her as I thought this would be good to show Liz. "I'm glad he did this where there was one bone, your forearm and lower leg are hard to get to heal. Now you have to set the leg with one hand, then because of how strong I can be, I can pull it just once into place."

With this, I did exactly what I said I would, even though she couldn't help but scream. Joe asked, "Would I have had to break her arms and legs?"

I had to smile at him as I spoke the truth, "It could have come to that, but in truth, I'm sure it would have fallen to Mary and presumably Bert." As I kept speaking I set her other leg with her wail again, "You see they have the strength to make sure they don't mess it up." I had to

look her in the eye as I asked, "Do you need a breather?"
She shook her head as even Paul could see the blood-soaked tears. I did as she wanted as I went on, "You see when it comes to punishment as little damage as possible is the best way."

Liz then said, "John she passed out with that last one." I reached for her other arm as she tried to stop me with, "John shes out like a light!"

To which I had to speak to just before I set the last one. "She has to drink some blood, so this can't be helped."

This woke her right up as it came out, then as I had done with the other three, I made sure it landed properly. Naomi came close to her as she said, "Know that we would have done this the old way, and that is why John backed out because of his overall strength. Yes, Mary and my Bert would have hated doing what they wanted to, but know what he did was far better than what they would have had to do."

I had to add, "We don't punish lightly, but when we do it can be profoundly gruesome. Learn from the description he gave you, as you wouldn't have been dead. I can assure you would have wished you had been after it, also that the punishment should have been destroyed. I did this for our new friend, though he did that for his wife, your mother. Tony set her up for her training, she'll need the hardest you can give her."

"John!" Liz said exceedingly loud.

I had to look at her as I spoke, "She has to reach at least your level before we can allow her to fight. But I'm not a fool, I also know she'll need healing time." I saw that I was about ready to be admonished so I added that last part. Then I knew I could use what he had said, "Even you heard what he had said to Kitty, if I'm right we're about ready to enter a time where blood covers Oklahoma. I can't say it'll be our blood, but would you rather me not do this, and allow Rose's blood to be one of them that sheds it for us?"

She shook her head as I had to add, "Liz you are right though, Kitty, Liz will help you all she can in this. I know you seemingly know what needs to be done better, but she does have a lot of knowledge in that area. Now I pass it to you, Tony."

Tony then said, "Mary you do her physical activity, Cibilia you go round and round with her. If you hurt her know that we're here if you can't set a bone, Sammy you have the sword matches. Now don't hurt her too badly, but always stay one step up against her. Joe, you cover her history classes, Cheryl you handle the mysteries of a vampire female. Bert, you have the fun of playing tag with her, I suggest a stick instead of your claws. Andy as your mother will be busy with her also, you take care of that obfuscate thing you guys do so well. Now did I forget anyone."

Paul placed his hand up right away as I had to openly laugh. He then asked, "Why is my hand up so funny?"

Naomi replied, "Who do you think has to make sure she has enough blood?"

To which he said, then asked, "Oh. John, we may need some more regular blood soon, now I do think we have enough, but I figured the earlier the better."

I nodded my head as Liz was about ready to speak, but now Johnny chimed in from the doorway with a cough. "I do believe that should be me, though Sammy was the front man for Sister Liz. I can take your car tomorrow while all of you are asleep because it is best when he's at lunch."

I knew he had been there the entire time, but in truth, I had completely forgotten about him. So I had to ask, "Johnny how are you? Do you have enough food? It has been awhile, but had Pepper been keeping you in blood?"

He nodded his head as I could see the embarrassed look on Pepper's face. I knew that I would have to have a talking to her because that told me even she had forgotten. I leaned over to Liz as I spoke, "You go with Pepper so you can make sure Johnny had enough. Get that blood drop setup, then get home because it is getting late." I leaned close to Liz as I had to add, "I don't want to ask her in front of Johnny, but I suspect Pepper may have forgotten about Johnny."

She to ask, "I saw your face, you forgot about him as well. Why would you want to know about that if you also forgot?"

She was right, then again she creates the impression to always be right, that was without a doubt my intention. So I whispered back, "I don't, in fact, because of what you used to be. The quintessence that Johnny is a far better friend to you than me, I figure you could handle it best."

Now I can also tell you nothing truly happened for the rest of the night. Sammy went with Liz and Pepper to help them just in case there were a few of our friends. There wasn't any real need, though it was better to be safe than chance the situation. There were, however, two things that had to be talked about, so next, I took Cibilia aside with Naomi just in case she missed anything. I can assure you that she hadn't, as we asked Cibilia to come and talk to us in the study. Which I have to think she had an understanding why we did this.

As she came in it was Naomi that spoke first, "Dear Child, when you try to hide something, the way isn't that of a deer caught in the headlights. I do believe John and I saw it with recognition before anyone else. Then again we're the elders here and the rest are just like you. I dare say an older one, not of us would have seen it clearly, though he nearly admitted it himself."

I then had to ask what I had already known, "He was your creator wasn't he?" She nodded his head so I added on top of that, "He was also that heavy feeling the other night? When he came to you, though it was correct to hide it from us."

She then said as she had done something wrong, "I'm sorry John and Naomi, he told me it was better to hide this from most. The problem was that he didn't explain who was most, so I was stuck in between a rock and a hard place. Though he did say something that literally had me worried. He told me from this day forward he was my lover, and all else pale in example. Not that I truly knew what this meant, but I was sure I had to hide it from Tony. I do have to ask though, what do I do?"

I had to tell her the truth as I knew it, "I'm sure that even Naomi knows a secret is never good to keep. They tend to cause you to lie, with a single lie comes another one. Not that anyone ever truly wants to lie, but with one always comes more. Where the final problem comes up is when you forget even one little thing, then you're tripped up and found out. You can see how that can feel to the other person, so it is best to start with a clean slate."

Cibilia had to ask, "So you want me to tell him the truth? I mean I have no idea what all of this absolutely does or mean?"

Naomi then added, "John doesn't mean that you can't lie, what he means is you have to fix this as quickly as possible."

I had to lay a truth up in her, "Cibilia I have never seen power like that before, so I do believe he is greater than I even care to mention. Hiding his identity maybe paramount for this house now, but even we can't tell you how. Within the house though has its own importance, which means all have to know something. If he claims you as his own there are also things that come with that. Like as his own that also means that you're a queen, to some eyes even a mother figure. Let's say someone learns this and comes to pay tribute, do you think Tony won't be able to place two and two together?"

Her eyes got big as she had to ask, "What do you mean tribute?"

Naomi came in with, "That may not happen, but it is a thing you have to worry about anyway. You do have to understand that one day he will announce that though. What we undoubtedly are trying here is to instill within you is the possibilities. Then you have the feelings of Tony, what will be his resulting reactions to this information. You saw what happened to John when Liz spoke wrongly toward John. Things can always end terribly when our attention is not on what we're doing in the end."

I then had to add just so she understood the final result also, "Now I'm reasonably good at this, in fact, all my children are, to which I think of you as such. Yes, in truth that other guy is your maker, but he left your training up-to me, which means also to me as parent. Tony is particularly good with firearms, and think of how many times I have told you nothing is better than a blade. So if we make a mistake a lot can happen, but to others, most likely not us as a whole. When he makes a mistake it is usually directed toward him, so learning this the wrong way could be departmental. So just think on this before you have to head toward bed today."

Naomi ended with, "This is all on you Cibilia, all we wanted to do was to give you our thoughts on this subject."

Now the two of us headed toward the door, but I had one more thing to tell her, so she understood something else. "We all have a certain power, and this is greater than what humans receive. The best thing I ever read had been something I hadn't intended to read. With so much great power comes even a greater responsibility. Now we leave it up to you."

I didn't want to just leave it there as I was truthful that I thought of her as my daughter. Yeah. I had to also learn this fact an extremely long time ago, and in the end, I had learned it is best this way, no matter how much you want to jump in and help. The thing I had told you earlier was even truer in this existence, so I had to allow her to fly on her own. No matter how much I wished I hadn't.

Chapter Twenty-eight

This change in the spirits.

You have seen that which I wrote two chapters ago, can you believe it happened twice in one day. To be truthful though I do presuppose you have to comprehend when something has been truly occurring. We were then and still are even now ignorant of so many things. You would think as long as I had been in this world I could to which be this easily surprised. I can't truly get into the particulars of these changes, and to be truthful in a week I would understand more.

There is also that we had no other visitation, though this one had caused certain events to unfold. To a hapless crew, this can't be seen as well as they should have to this degree. As to what went on it was rather informal, as soon after they all went to their training. Liz, Pepper, Johnny, with Sammy as their guard, came back after an uneventful trip. To which I sent the three right to work so Johnny and I could do the work needed. In truth, this can be seen as truly an even time, as the two of us joked as we put things away.

You can be assured that it had been a long time since I had done something so mundane. I had given them our card and told them to be careful with what they spent. Pepper, while they were gone, had found out more money had been placed on the card. With that she found out Johnny loved particularly strong coffee, so she bought him coffee and a maker for that use. I did have to ask as she showed me what had been done, so after all that, I felt there was no harm done.

When we were sure everything had been done I also helped him set up the pot. He did also explain to me that the first use of the pot had to be done with just water and vinegar. Before it had absolutely started he told me it had a terrible smell, but the coffee was truly worth it. When he did this I do have to say none of us liked that smell at all. Once that had been accomplished he set up for what he called Joe worth Army mud. Liz explained that was coffee so thick it would nearly stick to your insides.

Yes, if you think that is a vulgar remark, I have to agree. Once the first drops came out the heavenly aroma literally made me want a cup also. I do believe this had the same effect on everyone else, as they all now gathered once he had poured his first cup. He also told me he loves to roll his own, at first I could see why he couldn't roll his own. Then Liz explained that is what they call roll your own cigarettes, and how she loathed that smell. With that I had to ask the general house because I had no idea upon that, it was voted down in the end.

Though Tony did add that it could be done outside the house, as outside was out of our space. No one disagreed with that. Liz did add to that if he wanted to harm his lungs then it should be done with his own money, not the houses. Even Johnny agreed with that, and to be truthful I was so happy how the kids were handling this new situation. So once we had that settled I had to ask one more question toward Pepper. To which she told me she decided to feed him just before she went to bed.

This perturbed me, but Cibilia handled it right then and there. She told Pepper without any doubt that she would watch her do this. If she didn't she would be assured to be brought up on charges of neglect toward Johnny. I was so happy at this I had to literally smile, then with a slight bit of bravado I released the kids on their own time. Well except any extra training that was required by Tony to be done. Johnny then made a ham sandwich to which Pepper faithfully decided to help him. Not that she wasn't trying to get out of her extra duty, but her excuse was still right to her keep, which was good.

I even spelled Bert as I decided to go out with Naomi this night. Not that we did much in the way of searching since she had done it earlier. So this was just a simple once around, and like I had told you it was basically uneventful. When we came back there was a car in our driveway, and to our relief, there had been nothing done to conceal it. So when we came in Naomi was the first to ask, "Do we have a visitor my sweet children?"

Tony was right there as he said, "Veronica is here, and she looks way better than last time."

When we came into the room it was easy to see she needed to still heal. Just that now she wouldn't need any blood as she talked to us. So I had to ask the obvious, "Hello there Veronica, by the way, did you have anything to do with the extra cash in our bank account?"

She replied immediately, "No, that was from Giaus. He wanted William to secure your help till I got on my feet, though William has been partially busy with my health. Then again you know how well elders think things through, I did add that money I told you about beforehand. Just as it was today, I had to figure it was the money he spoke about the other day."

I had to nod my head with a slight chuckle, "It is as it always is, I guess even as we change, somethings never do that particularly. So how may we help you?"

She smiled at me as she confessed her thoughts, "Giaus told me he would pay you as he could get it, I did think of another way since we have talked about it. He told me that you had two of my species and that you may need my help in that area. I thought this may be of a fairer exchange then just money, not that money wouldn't also help."

I then called out to the five, "Cheryl, Paul, also I think we need Liz, Pepper, and maybe even Tony here." Now you have to know they were right there, so it wasn't as if there was any search. So I went on, "Paul is the father of Cheryl, and to my own degree, I have figured they're glorified office workers. So those are the two Giaus spoke of, though Tony needs help with the finer things with his two ladies. Pepper is the sister to one of mine as a human, Liz is an unusual case, so take real care there also, plus the daughter of Tony."

Now you can imagine the reason why I had not used either case to which made Liz special. I had to add on all of this, "Now we know certain things and I would feel good if anyway you allowed Tony to accompany all of them. Plus for their exceedingly first day, I would also love all the elders to go with them. This will be hard as to the substance of the entire house, though that will be on you."

She nodded her head as she said, "Then tomorrow night, we'll make a party of it. Kids know that what we call a party isn't what you would know as a party. I do believe that even John can assure you to this knowledge, as it can be an affair. I will send where and when I will expect you, via Peppers smartphone. I do hope to be in better spirit as it should be for tomorrow, I will see you then."

With this, she stood up, as I did the same, and we shook hands on it in the old way. Which she did in the exact order of me, Kitty, Naomi, Tony, Bert, Joe, and lastly Cibilia. Which she did all the right things as this would be considered her house. I turned to all the kids after she left, then told them that we follow the same order as she did. I then allowed Joe and Tony to go through the reasons why. So another piece of a puzzle had been laid out for all to see, though again this would be seen later as well.

When everything was over Joe came to me, with Naomi as he called her to us, though he just waved to Kitty and Tony. Once we were there he said as quietly as he could, "I called you all here because of something unusual has happened."

We all had to look at him curiously as Tony asked, "What Joe?"

"I know I checked it two days ago and it was still sealed, but just before Veronica got here I checked it again. Guys, the seal on this unquestionably old book has been unlocked, and I'm sure it was locked beforehand. What may be even more particular the writing I found inside this book."

I waved my hand as I said, "Show us so we can ascertain what we have here."

With that, he took us up the few flights of steps, with a stairwell I knew not of, which was to the few with us as well. Then we entered the library that I had been acquainted with, though the secret room I had no idea until this certain time. Not that any of this surprised me, I just had to figure Andy or Kitty would find it first. Well and of our newest child Rose too, so I had to conclude he already knew of all this. With that, he placed a tome that was even older than the first one he had brought out to show Giaus. Not that this room had any absence of tomes, even as I had always thought the original had come from where I knew of particularly.

Then he showed us the queer lock, as it had been truly unfastened. Finally, he opened it, and the weird writing appeared to be like hieroglyphics. Even as we looked closer there also gave the impression of being of a form. Kitty traced it with her fingers, as Naomi watched with a certain intent. I had to shake my head as I had to ask, "Do you have any idea how to read any of this?"

He had to shake his head as well with the confession, "I can't say that I do, though I did find this as I leafed through it." He then gave me a piece of paper, then he pointed at the old vampire script. "You see this does appear to have some kind of translation, but I haven't had time to go through it undoubtedly. I thought it may be far more important to show all of you first."

I turned my head to Naomi, "You have any idea?"

She shook her head so I turned to Kitty, "What about you?"

She then said what I had not thought, "Demon Lord hate these sguiggleies, but not Fair Gut Liar. He see these sguiggleies as mean to an opening, whereas you see what can be to him. Dees bing to da world worst, though not in hes hands. Great Harlequin know all, as she sees, yet me only sees in passing. So no Dreamia Witch can't help, but Kitty knows the importance."

I had to then say just, "Hmm."

Joe had to ask, "Does she know or not?"

"No, she doesn't. She has though seen the importance of you, and she told me I absolutely don't like these. I can think of many things I don't like but in truth only one thing in written form. Which to me means it has something to do with magic. Listen we need you at your fullest, so I would tell you to go through these, but with extreme care. Stuff that looks this old can never be good, we can't go losing our only magic-using fella. I will also tell you I certainly don't like this because we don't assuredly know. I will confess some of this stuff has far higher costs then even we can imagine."

Tony placed his hand on Joe's shoulders, as he

now spoke. "Kid, what John has been saying is this can be even of more importance than even he knows. All Magic has a purpose, and for it to open like this it took a certain event. Now if you think of any event that has taken place, that may also mean it is older than any man can remember. These things were all new back then, and they just placed them in a book without reason. So one spell can be about growing flowers, but the next could be on how to end the world."

Naomi then added, "Joe, we love you as a son also, those high prices can be as much as like a piece of your soul. It may not literally be the piece as a fact, but as to who you have to sacrifice it too. In all that is done, we would never want to lose Joseph in the process. Then you have the fundamentals that if it's wrong, we can't know to force you to take a step back, till it's too late."

I then came close, "I told you that you can be the most powerful of all of us, but these things can also take you away from us. So like I said, just be careful." Then I had a thought, so I said, "Just a moment I want to ask Cheryl something." Then I stuck my head out the small door and called to her, "Cheryl can you come here please?!"

She came in with just a second or two, "Yes John?"

"Come here please."

She now joined us in this extremely cramped room, so I pointed at the book and gave my idea. "Could you help Joe categorize all of this to help him simplify the translation of all this?"

She looked at it as she had to say, "I think so, though I can see this taking a lot of time. What I mean is that this and this look the same, but with that little symbol it could mean another completely different word. Then you have the essence that this scarab is blue and that one is green, so we would have to see that as well. I guess you have already discussed how difficult this could be. Once we can divide it into an essential syllable way, that could help us out in the long run."

I had to chuckle as I had to confess, "I can see I picked the perfect person to help Joe."

She smiled at me as she also added, "Plus we can ponder these means when we go to bed, I do believe I'm a perfect choice as well."

With that, I had to nod my head, though I would have to ask Liz on that last part. As we all went our separate ways right then, to be truthful we had nothing that could be added. Now we got together to discuss this extraordinarily long day, and this is when Liz clued me into that last part. I swear I can't tell you who had been bonded to another, as that was a reference that they shared a bed. I knew that I had to be the luckiest of the bonded ones, to which if she hadn't been bonded to me. Well, I have to confess I would presumably forget that as well.

She did have to give me a reason why I forgot, as I had far too much to think upon in the end. So this was the end of day twelve, you can also see why I have to thank all days weren't like this one. It is a shame that there are still far too many days left to tell.

Chapter Twenty-Nine

The first sign of a crack in the marble.

<u>Somewhere in an unforgotten place in the city.</u>

He couldn't believe his terrible luck, not only had he met an unforsaken few of Baali, he had no means prepared to meet their type. Now he was a shattered shell of what he had been, even with a full bloodbath he knew what it would take to be whole again. In his lifetime no one had ever bested him, had he gotten too sloppy in what he thinks of others. He had been a man of virtue when he had been so young, it had been profoundly easy to slip the bounds of reality to the existence. Though in a recent years this had left him a shallow being, it was this power that had taken him over in the end. There had been no doubt when he had made his Faustian bargain, in all her beauty she had made him.

Not that any human would have ever called her beautiful, even with all the twists and turns of her body, she was truly a horror. Then you have the nitty-gritty that he had spent so much time instilling this in all those others, that night he had not suspected anything with those cloves he understood. Though she also knew this should have never been placed within at such a rate, he had to wonder what he impatience truly meant. Then you have the fundamentals that he wasn't truly ready to be embroiled in a fight, there just wasn't any time for that, so what of that?

In fact, there was no assurance that he would ever survive this in the end. How could he go on with such maiming, no beast living or dead had suffered such and came out of that inferno, as if he had entered Dante's flames themselves. Yet, it had to be such an upstart as he to do this to me, he had sent her to make that dreaded call he so loathed. When she had been sent to him he realized that she was truly a wonderful find. Nothing compared to those dogged few that thought they were tough, only the fear he had instilled had caused them not to rise up against him. To be truthful he could have never shown himself to them, as his vantage may have been lost.

As to what happened after that is far beyond him, all he can be sure of is what she saw, and it surely was a pleasant outcome if she is proved correct. He had no way to communicate well right now, though the replenishment of those hemoglobin's has done wonders. Her vacuousness femininity has proved her to be worth much more, even in her own plain spectacle pictured youth. With a wish to validate her use as his second, she has gone beyond his imaginations of earned duty. Though she could never have perceived the bonds required of her, within this diminished shell she compulsory applied the vital fluid.

There has been many that have tried to usurp the powers of those perceived, even as precarious this may truly be in the end as we have proven. Not that the powers that maybe have been complete in getting rid of any of us, it is this Claudia that creates the appearance to have the wear for all to do what needs to be done. None could ever understand her true nature, as it has been implied that she could be the first Methuselah. Well not first in the world, just the first in this new world, though she also told us don't believe all we are told, they lie, they lie to all, they lie even to themselves.

It is hard to believe that she would be the first to come up with such a plan, though some say that she may have been sent by a higher authority. I doubt that. Why would a Methuselah serve anyone else?

So when she came up with all this, there were so many that wouldn't follow her, the fools. This may be the most he had ever gone outside the comfort of his religious bounds, but it truly wasn't a place he hadn't been unfamiliar with in the end. You have to understand in the old world all they thought of had been how to confront those of so many years. Even the young had to ask if that had been prudent, yet only she came up with such a wondrous scenario, with a complete end scheme. Only he appeared to understand this justification of this frugality.

All those fools had made their way in this new world, though they were right that this was the place to start our domination. How could any have believed that the old ways would work, and not perceive they wouldn't fight back?

Yes, I understand that myself has to get out of those old ways, though I yet fear I wallow in my own self-doubt. Where the problem lies, in the end, is how painfully slow this would take in a time that could prove fruitless, though extremely warranted. Only she truly understood this power vacuum here, so it has been her plan to disrupt the authority that exists in this land. Who could ever perceive this lay not at the ends, but truly within the exterior, well center. This forsaken land is so dismal, why couldn't New York City lie in the center of this land?

It was a stroke of genius to get for these areas, as most of them think this is barren lands, with no worth for anyone. Though it is easy to see why as these haven't the number needed for us, as this city also strains at the existence of just a few of our kind. Their great strength was essential idea no one truly appreciated, as most wouldn't allow these acknowledgments to be known. He had come up with his own center of captainhood, as even this appears to have dissolved into discord. His attention had now been drawn as this was no surprise as he heard their loud engines come into the city last night.

He understood she never loved those truly high heels, but she did have this way to place one in front of another to allow herself to be heard. He would never truly ever show his fear, though what use had this been in the end. The only thing that it had ever given him, as he knew this was done to instill a fear only her lessors would acknowledge. He had thought to ask her for her help many a time, in those few it does promote weakness, and this is always what prevented him. Then you have the fact of how childlike she acted, he had never truly enjoyed this demeanor she nurtured.

Even in all that black taffeta she so loved, that doll-like look set her apart from all the others. As she now cleared the door with a smile that nearly sparkled, and those Ragity Anne cheeks she loved to paint. Though most would have gone with ruby red lips, hers were this sheer black like ash. She needed no makeup to cause her flesh to gleaned so white, just tattoos so the diamond under her right eye and the tear inside her left looked proper. I'm willing to bet the extremely short dress would cause any human male to want her. With a bobble like an effect which caused her black Mary Jane slippers so dainty a conclusion.

In his recollection, he could never remember seeing her wear anything except black, but in truth, it was easy to perceive what this would look like on her. Maybe to the determent to the one that proposed such a thing, especially with the mechanical rocking walk she so favored. The honest truth about her grin was a diabolical state of her mind. This wasn't a large room as to hide him from public view, though the closeness of her now unsettled him, as her unconcern toward anyone else but herself. He knew she would look at him up and down to take the course of his overall condition.

He also knew how important he had been to Claudia, she would never do her worst to one of her lieutenants. You see she had been well known for taking advantage of any particular being, human or vampire, to the point of discussing what had been happening to them in the end. Oh, I'm not talking about when she creates another, but when she would be feasting on the totality of a person continuance. He did hate that small voice she used as she now spoke, "Nikki! Did you fowl down and go boom?"

Oh, he had forgotten her nickname for him, it had to be the worst, and there was no way for him to stop her from calling him that awful name. Then you have the essence that I tried to scream for her to act her real age, which she would hate if I told anyone. My beloved soon to be second now spoke on my behalf, "Lord Nicholas was involved in a fight with a powerful man, though he had barely challenged him when he played a trick on him. He came to me this way, and I have been doing my best to resupply his blood."

Valeria had always had my back as in response to what she said, Lidia now could only uncontrollably laugh for a few minutes. To which now Nicholas scratched on a pad of paper close to him, as he did his best to write what he felt. To which Valeria knew to lift it up so she could understand, which was written, She's just plain MAD! With this, he had to recoil with the pain of just how hurt he truly was, as he could see the empty tub he had been lying in just moments ago. Now he also added on the pad as she came close with his discomfort, BLOOD NOW!

He knew why his body was so light to her as it still lacked the victual it desperately needed. Not that any vampire would truly do any of that, as it was the wholesome flavor of plasma he needed. She looked at the seven bottles that had been so recently been full, and it was easy to understand her concern. Not that they hadn't done there jobs, it would be just so much tissue had to be regrown. It was now that she was shoved out of the way by Lidia, as she said, "Get what we need, you've been doing this wrong all along, let me do this for now honey."

With this, these vital needles and tubes appeared so she could start, and she used what she knew as if she had been a nurse in her former existence. Instead of just poking the skin as a nurse would do, she used a scalpel to crest better holes. She instructed Valeria how to place the bottles up, and this allowed the blood to flow better. Lidia then appeared as a ballerina in the French style of the Great Harlequin. Though I knew Valeria to be slightly dense in her movements, soon she also caught the tempo. I had never seen the Harlequin Mistresses, but if I had it had to be as I had been now witnessing. Before long the two of them had seven IV lines going to Nicholas, and it was true he could feel the blood far better now.

As she now withdrew from him, he had to grab her arm in a sign of recognition. This caused her to smile as she knew what he was asking, so she gave him a slight nod as an answer. Valeria had the idea to ask a stupid question, "How long have you and Lord Nicholas been friends?"

This caused her to give a wanting smile, not that of a friend that wants to kiss you for the favor, but one that spoke I would love to let him bleed out right now. Which of course cause her to have one of her uncontrollable laughing fits, to which Valeria was dumbfounded. This caused Nicholas to try and scribble something out, to which caused Lidia to stop his hand from moving. To which I did have an answer, though I do believe hers was far better, "Nikki and I aren't friends, you could say that we tolerate each other. Friendship, in this case, would be a far stretch, to be truthful I would call it closer to loathing each other."

Valeria had to keep her stupidity going, "Then why did you do what you did for him?"

Her evil in her smile was so obvious as she replied, "Ask yourself a better question, why would she do this other than kindness? Now that you know that we aren't exactly friends, there is an easy implication. She has to fear the person that ordered this even more, and as I am, as it were, where would that leave me? Do you understand?"

You could nearly see the wheels rolling in Valeria's mind, and once this brought recognition, Lidia would be off laughing again. Though this wasn't the end of their discussion by far, I could also see the irritation on her face. I scribbled out just for her, I know she can be irritating, but just resist your urges. She's only here till I can get healthy, and what she has done for me is greater then you could have done. Not because you don't have the capabilities, but because I haven't had the time to show you yet.

Afterwards, as I exhausted these few bottles, Lidia came close to see how well they had worked. To which she know said, "We'll need a lot more blood, and from what she has shown me, you truly don't have enough. Where is all your help?"

To which Valeria had to sadly admit, "My Lord had me send them out to get some a few days ago, to our knowledge we have no idea why they haven't returned. Nicholas thought they may have just ran off, because as he has been he isn't now, so this is a complication. When they left he had no ability to put the fear of God in them like usual. . ."

She had said the end as if she wasn't so certain about what I had surmised, and I had to wonder about that, as Lidia now came close to her with something I had never seen in her before this time. I mean Lidia, not Valeria, essentially as if she saw something more, as the plain blank spoke volumes. "You know more, I can see it in your face, though you have no remembrance of who I may be."

She then admitted, "I know who you are, though I'm not sure I can call you what you told me."

I was about ready to speak, though more in thought then in reality, as Lidia's hand came up to silence me. "I told you I gave you to Nicholas, he is your Lord now. Just do what I told you to do when you had a waking dream. Now tell us what you saw!"

This only perplexed me for a moment as she spoke, "It doesn't make sense, all I can tell you is I saw teeth and many claws. They appeared to be cutting into them without mercy, though none of them feasted upon their blood. In fact, if I were to call them anything, it would have to be a pure rage I had never seen in my lifetime. Once it was all over is when Lord Nicholas showed up, and I took him into this room. They were all worried how he looked, and if something like that could do that to him, what could they do to them. I knew that we had a fridge full of blood, but Lord Nicholas ordered me to tell them to go and get more. That is also when he told me to call you."

She appeared to be searching for something in her mind, then asked, "You didn't get a vision of anything except teeth and claws?"

She now added the one thing that even clued me into what this might be, "Glowing Yellow eyes, and they gave the impression of penetrating the essence of the soul."

Okay, even I knew the eyes of a werewolf but never had I ever seen a pack attack a group of vampires. To which Lidia now spoke, "I came with our latest installment just in time Nikki, we were barely able to get the twelve Claudia wanted. Don't worry I can handle things until you get better, and I'll strive to take a few youths from this terrible place. Now You!"

She corrected her with, "Valeria."

"Okay then, Valeria get me maps of the area, and if you have a place to move, we may need to put that into action. We don't know for sure, but this place may not be safe anymore."

With this, she placed her hand near her mouth and appeared to make a whistling noise. Twelve young men and women entered the room, though it was clear the men were in dominance. They had that wannabe biker quality to them, though you would truly see this more with werewolves. Then she ran to the largest of all of them, and she jumped on him with her legs wrapped around his waist.

Then she appeared to apparently coo to him, "Babycakes! Those little Aces ran out on Nikki, we have to correct this as we will, but for now by him some time. See if you can knock-over a few juice factory's, plus bring us a few young fatties, please. I don't know, maybe three. It would be better if we had four, but don't go stretching out too far."

He heard her orders as he now turned to all the others barking in a deep voice, "Get to your bikes idiots, you heard the lady! We have to hit a place before we can nab the blood bags, once we get all into place when we sleep! This means all of you peons, so let's get the hell out of here before dawn comes! NOW!"

With this, they all appeared to leave the room in confusion, with a great amount of commotion, as they hooted and howled. To which you could see Lidia's self-satisfied stance, with a twist she was back with such a scowl. As she now spit out, "You have to play up to those that would be a leader, they haven't a clue about what true leadership is Valeria. Oh, and I know you know my real name, in anyone else's presence you have to call me Lidia."

That kind of intrigued me as I pondered this, then she took me in as she asked me. "Mind if I take Valerie with me for some fun." I had to search her face as I knew her kind of fun, and she allowed me a moderate amount of peace. "Oh God no! As you have figured out, she's my child. I don't do that with my kids, all I want to do is have sex with her."

I had to look at her as she now responded, "No my Lord, like I said I'm bi, I just don't like to be touched. I can do this for you though, so please don't worry about me, my Lord."

To which all I could do was nod my head, what I didn't expect was for her to start striping Valeria right in front of me. You have to also understand, Lidia wasn't a fully developed woman, as her chest size had to be noticeably small for a lady. I think the reason she so loved large breasted women, is she loved to play with what she didn't have in the end.

I added this because it was also among those papers we found, plus I also know this happened on day fourteen. Though I still had no idea that Nicholas had survived, even though he would never truly be a bother. You can see he thought he had been dealing with common vampires and werewolves. Then you have the quintessence that this Lidia would become another pain in our sides, but truly it is now you heard of our common enemy Claudia. The Next Day will start with a new book, even as things start running into one another.

~ Fine ~

Yet more to come.

Made in the USA
Middletown, DE
05 February 2022

60512414R00219